THE GLASS LINING

By Natalie England

The Glass Lining

First Edition August 2025

Published by Natalie England Publishing LLC

Print Cover by Damonza.

To my loving parents who taught me
the most important thing I could ever know.
That Heavenly Father lives!
And He loves me!

To my readers,

While I've tried to make this series fun and full of adventure, the root message behind these books is based on depression and the struggles that go with it.

Which means there will be dark moments.

My hope is that you will finish the series to the end when you can.

That is where happiness is discovered.

Chapter 1

I stare at the Mixed Blood girl in front of me. She's lying on her bed against the cold prison wall, covered in heavy gray blankets. The firelight flickers across her short-freckled nose, and her brown tangled braid hangs off the side of the mattress.

She's Jax's daughter, Iris.

Every time I've visited her, she's been peacefully asleep.

I wish I had an abundance of sleep like her. She never seems to run out.

"You could heal her."

Jax's accusing voice is heavily muffled through the glass overlying the prison cell bars, but I hear him just the same. His words make me shift uncomfortably in my wooden chair. He's in the prison cell across the hall, sitting in his own wooden chair, staring at me, while I stare at Iris. He doesn't know it, but his words only echo the voices bouncing around in my own head.

I *could* heal her.

And yet I can't.

I don't have any more black power. I used it all on Aitin, the only other Mixed Blood I've met.

I close my eyes, picturing the generators I found in Aitin's blood vessels. I recall the heads of his generators, the sound of the Doler they make. More importantly, I recall the odd sacs attached. There were *two* sacs, unlike the generators found in the Pepps that only have one sac.

Our theory is that one of those sacs is a power sac, which harnesses *black power* for the Mixed Bloods if they were ever to morph.

They've never had access to that black power, though, because of the second sac, which is actually a Peppate generator. The Peppate produced in that generator somehow eats away at the power in the other sac, like acid, deactivating their ability to produce power. Black power.

Unfortunately, eating away at their potential power is not all the Peppate does in the Mixed Bloods.

I open my eyes and sigh.

It makes them sick. It took years of research for the Pepps to figure out why the Mixed Bloods were so sick, only to come to the realization that they're *allergic* to Peppate, and they produce Peppate within their own bodies.

They're allergic to themselves.

This girl in front of me, Iris, the Mixed Blood daughter of Jax, is living proof of the pain endured by those like her—those children born of both a Pepp and a non-Pepp parent. I come to visit her every day hoping to find answers, only to leave feeling more and more discouraged. I need more black power, for multiple reasons.

A small table to my left is filled with ointments, medical wraps, and medicines a Pepp found in some non-Pepp stores outside of Petrichor. While Iris sleeps, I use those medicines to relieve some of her discomforts.

They heal the blisters and sores, and ease the stomach pains, but she's still far from being okay.

I reach into my black snowpants pocket and pull out a vial of Dilo's dinosaur serum. This is what I distributed through Aitin, the Mixed Blood, at Jeter's command. Its paralyzing properties disabled the Peppate generators in Aitin, stopped them from producing the Peppate that was making him so sick on the inside.

It worked. I saw him a day later, witnessed the incredible recovery within just a short amount of time. He was feeling better.

Without the Peppate there to eat away at that extra sac, though, the serum *also* gave Aitin access to his natural Mixed Blood power. The same black power that flowed through the totems Mark and I both host after we morphed at SilverDen. I created another one of us, including the ability to create lightning.

At least that's what we think.

My father had been researching the Mixed Bloods at the request of the chief and had a theory that the manipulated vine attached to Mark and me was created using the generators from a Mixed Blood's vessels. Before the generators were put into our totem, though, a unique sac had to be removed from them. The Peppate generator.

If Aitin has power like Mark and me, the Pepps are in danger. Lightning is the Pepps' one weakness. All it would take is one morph from Aitin and he could destroy all the Pepps—forever.

That's exactly what Aitin wants to do, too. He told me so in Dakdete.

I can't say that I blame him, especially since the Pepps experimented on him for so many years, trying to figure out why he was so sick. Then, after all the experiments, he was ultimately told that he's allergic to Peppate, and Peppate is produced inside him.

Now he wants to eradicate Peppate forever.

And we have to stop him.

Unfortunately, that won't be easy. For two reasons. The Pepps can't fight him at all. Which means that everything regarding Aitin is up to Mark and me and potentially other Mixed Bloods. It seems logical that with Mark's ability to control nature and my ability to control the body we'd easily defeat a weak inexperienced man with power. But, we don't have black power to fight him with, and Aitin isn't alone. He has Jeter, which is the second reason things are complicated.

I recall the night two weeks ago, when Jeter shot Sef and me out of the sky, the night Jeter forced me to heal Aitin. I tried to attack Jeter's heart to get away, but Jeter knew what I was doing. It was like he could feel the power nipping at him, and because he could feel it, he could fight it. He did the same thing with the chief and council members at Dakdete. He deflected their attacks just before crippling the chief.

I want to know how he did it, and I want to master it for when I see him again, but I don't even know where to start.

I rub the center of my chest, where a fresh vial of yellow Pepp power sits. In order for me to learn how to resist Jeter's attacks with Pepp power, I need to know what Pepp power sounds like, but that's been difficult. Every time I put the power in to listen, all I hear is the other elements surrounding me, like millions of bees flying around in my head. I don't hear the sound of the yellowish power. It's as if the Pepp power doesn't even have a sound.

I guess, if anything, Mark and I could morph together. Produce lightning. That would kill Jeter, get him out of the way. Though, the thought of that makes me sick. I really don't want to kill anyone.

I stand and walk to the fire crackling in the corner tucked behind more safety glass. There's so much I need to learn before I can face Jeter and Aitin, and yet there are so many conflicts in my way.

I've come here every day since we got back, hoping to gain insight. Hoping to figure out how to stop Aitin.

I've come to the conclusion that I need to undo what I've done with the serum. I need to take it out of Aitin. By doing that, the Peppate generators will eat away at the power sac again, essentially making him powerless. It'll be easier to stop him, even kill him, if he doesn't have power and can't create lightning.

I've held this serum in my hands every day thinking that if I could just control it with Pepp power, I could inject it into Iris, distribute it, then practice removing it, like I need to do when I see Aitin.

The problem is, I can't control the serum with Pepp power. Jeter himself couldn't get the serum out of Mark's neck after I so stupidly injected it into him at SilverDen. The fact that even Jeter couldn't do it makes the whole thing seem more hopeless.

Plus, experimenting on Iris with Pepp power will make her sick. Jax would probably kill me if he ever got out of that cell.

The serum just can't be controlled with Pepp power. I need Black Power.

I sigh deeply, then remove the cell key from my coat pocket. The new warden of the prison was nice enough to give me my own personal key. All I had to tell him is that I need access to Iris in order to figure out how to defeat Aitin. He handed it right over.

After inserting the key into the hole, I open the door to leave.

"All you have to do is morph with Mark!" Jax is standing now, shouting at my back from his cell as I relock the door behind me. "Create more black power, and then you can heal her!"

I turn and walk down the hall leaving him behind.

Jax is right. All it would take is a morph, but he seems to forget one very important thing: a Pepp has to die during that morph in order for the black power to fill.

That's just not a sacrifice I'm willing to make.

***

I walk through a large pile of freshly dug dirt, one of the many now littering Petrichor's borders. Small pebbles spill into my shoes with each sinking step, but I've long since given up trying to keep them out. Instead, I bend down on one knee and run my fingers through the cool soil.

It's sad how much things have changed in the last two weeks.

Because of everything that happened with Jeter and Aitin, all drop-downs and runs have been stopped. We're simply living off the massive supply of power the chief had before Jeter immobilized him. There's still a lot left, but it's being used very carefully, and apparently controlling the weather is very low on our list of priorities. I pull my sweater tight. The natural climate of this northern snowy land is slowly taking over. It's getting cold.

Rusty, our new chief, is focusing all his efforts, using the power to protect the Pepps.

My eyes scan the massive piles of dirt. Every free Pepp has been assigned the task of digging a huge, deep, widespread hole that's overtaking most of Petrichor. Mountains of loose dirt now lie on the outskirts of the excavation site, the same dirt I've been walking through for the past three days. Mark is directly below me in the hole, making it bigger, deeper.

Protection. That's why we're doing this. To protect the Pepps from Aitin and his lightning.

I lean over the edge to sneak a peek at Mark. He's hacking away at the dirt with a large shovel, putting it in a decent pile beside him. I quietly admire the way his muscles pull and tighten. If I could, I'd just sit on the edge here and watch him all day.

When Mark's pile is large enough, he uses his power to send it up and over the edge in my direction. I step sideways now to avoid getting hit by the dirt he's throwing out.

Then I get down on my knees again, more pebbles spilling into my shoes, and search the dirt Mark just added to the pile for large rocks. Since I can't command the dirt like Mark, he asked me to collect rocks. He'll be able to use them when creating the walls and tunnels below.

Feeling a large rock just beneath my fingertips, I brush away the dirt and pick it up.

As I work, my mind slowly drifts to Petrichor's leader, the chief.

He's still not doing well.

I've gone to see him every night since the incident at Dakdete. Each time I feel his steady pulse and see his wavy gray hair spilling over the pillow, my hopes rise. There's still so much life in him.

But then I hold his hand, speak his name, encourage him to wake, and all I get is nothing.

Nothing.

He's gone. Unmoving, with his perfectly trimmed beard still streaked in silver.

Every medic has examined him and come to the same conclusion. His brain is no longer functioning.

The dirt in my shoes works its way into the small spaces between my toes, but I just keep walking, searching the piles.

I didn't always like the chief. In fact, most of the time I hated him. The little antics he used to get things done never resonated with me. Like the time he searched my memories with a memory bug to learn if I was a spy or not. Or the time he sent me out to the prison with a blank note for his brother, just to teach me a lesson about the dangers of anger.

He sure had an *interesting* way of teaching.

But each time I visit him, I realize more and more how important he is to me, how valuable those lessons are. And now a painful hole has burrowed its way into my chest. I miss him.

Scance tried to explain her theory to me. She thinks Jeter disassembled the chief's brain into hundreds of little pieces and scattered them throughout his body when they were fighting at Dakdete.

The medics have been able to reassemble the pieces, but the chief is still unresponsive. Scance believes it's because the memories and neurological connections the chief has made throughout his life are gone. Forever. It's like putting a blank puzzle back together. The pieces are all there, but they don't mean anything without the bigger picture. And there's no way to restore what's lost. The chief would simply have to relive his entire life in order to become who he was, but now his aged body is taking over. He's too tired. Too old.

He simply won't recover.

I shiver and look out at Petrichor. The chief seemed to extend life to Petrichor itself. And now with him on the brink of death, everything seems grayer. Even the wind has picked up.

We still haven't heard or seen anything from Jeter or Aitin. A small part of me hopes Aitin died, but then another part of me is sure that he's still out there. The way Rusty is preparing everyone tells me he's confident they're both alive too.

Rusty and the council have considered separating the Pepps and sending them away to live in mountains where they'll be protected. But Aitin will just destroy everything until he gets them all. Which would put the entire human race in danger.

So, Rusty has decided to keep the Pepps here in Petrichor but protect them underground. Aitin's lightning won't be able to reach them if they're below. We hope.

Then the dinosaurs will be set free to protect the Pepps above the hidden bunker. In fact, they're free from their shrunken state now, roaming the borders of the pit. Bud, my little baby dinosaur friend, is out there somewhere now with his mother. This is what they were brought here for. To be protectors, and now they're being put to the test. Trainers assigned to each dinosaur have been working tirelessly to instill our protective needs into each of their vicious minds.

A large cluster of cold dirt and rocks comes flying out of the hole and slams into my right shoulder before landing at my feet. I curse and move back a bit.

I used to wonder why the Pepps kept the dinosaurs. They don't absorb Peppate, which makes them ornery all the time. It's funny how things work out sometimes. The simple fact that dinosaurs don't absorb Peppate is what might keep the Pepps alive. The lightning can't destroy the dinosaurs, just like it can't destroy Mark or me.

Mark helps the dino trainers when he can. Although, I think he's still grieving the loss of Dilo, who was taken by Jeter. So he mostly digs now.

My eyes scan the giant dirt hole before me. It spans for miles, reaching from the hospital, past MossyHollow—where I stand—all the way to GreenGrotto and the school. Once all the dirt is dug out, they'll create wooden tunnels, concrete rooms, and special sleeping quarters with disguised air tubes that reach the surface so they can breathe. The dirt will be placed back over to cover it up once it's done. The tunnels will connect to the Post for easy entrance. Then the Post will be blocked off.

The Post. It's mostly empty now, with the chief in the hospital—and the communicators gone.

The communicators were brought to Petrichor last month, when Jax started seeking them out and killing them to get to my black power. But after what happened with Jeter and Aitin, all the communicators decided to leave. They know as well as anyone that Aitin will be coming here to destroy all the Pepps, and now that Jax is in prison, well, they had no reason to stay. There's only one threat now. Aitin. So they're gone. They even turned in their Magbabies, which means that communication on what's going on in the world outside of Petrichor has been cut off. The Pepps in Petrichor are completely isolated and uninformed. It's a little scary.

Rubbing my dirty hands on the front of my filthy pants, I bend down, grab another large rock sitting in the dirt, and heave it over to my growing pile next to MossyHollow.

This underground bunker, though, it's only the first part of Rusty's plan.

The second part of Rusty's plan is up to Eli and me.

According to Mark, Eli, the chief's brother and previous prison warden, knows a woman named Mia, who lives with a large group of Mixed Bloods somewhere in the southern lands.

I recall my terrifying visit with Eli at the prison, the night the chief had me deliver that stupid blank letter. His cabin was bare and undecorated except for one personal picture above the fireplace. A picture of a woman.

Eli hasn't said it, but based on how nervous he is to go, I'm guessing Mia is the woman he used to love, the woman in that picture.

Apparently, she used to be a Pepp but left to help take care of the Mixed Blood people who live in the community.

Rusty believes that we need help fighting Aitin. He doesn't want everything to be left up to Mark and me, which is why he wants Mark, Eli, and me to make a visit to the Mixed Bloods. Rusty's goal is for me to do the same thing I did to Aitin to the other Mixed Bloods, give them access to their power, as long as they agree to fight for *us*. If we have more people like Aitin, then we could possibly defeat Aitin and Jeter.

Hence another reason I need to control the serum with Pepp power.

Unfortunately, like with Iris, if I figure out a way, the Pepp power will make them terribly sick, since they're all allergic to Peppate.

Another problem I'm worried about is the Mixed Bloods letting us reverse the process. If they ever do agree to let me experiment on them, and if I'm miraculously successful, they would have to allow me to remove the serum if we defeat Aitin. We can't have so many Peppate destroyers running around.

But would they really agree to let us take their power away when we're done? To me, it sounds like a stupid, hopeless plan.

We were supposed to leave a week ago, to visit Mia and the Mixed Bloods, but after Rusty told Eli what he had to do, Eli went and got himself very drunk—for an entire week. According to Rusty, he's stopped now, but he's having some nasty withdrawals. It's scary knowing that the warden of the jail was allowed to drink so much. Perhaps the cold weather does most of the work in keeping the inmates in line and Eli was only there as an ornament. But his withdrawals have made him very hard to be around. Fortunately, another medic has been assigned the job of assisting him with the detoxifying process.

Now the prison is under the watch of a new warden.

I shudder in the cold air.

Suddenly, Mark sends out a bunch of heavy dirt, burying me up to my knees. A rock hits me in my leg and I cringe. I should really back away.

I'm heaving myself out of the trap, when my body stills. There, at the edge of the pit a little way away is Danny, with his fingers resting against Kapri's back as she shows him something in her hand. Her golden curly hair is falling out of her loose ponytail, and she's covered in dirt from head to toe, but she looks absolutely beautiful. A small seed of jealousy creeps up inside me, catching me off guard. It's the same stupid feeling I get every time I see them together, and I don't understand it. Anyone could see that they're perfect for each other. Kapri adores him in a way I never could. She even shares Danny's same obsession with music.

I might have led Danny on in the beginning to appease him, but I always had feelings for Mark. *So why on earth would I feel jealous?*

Another pile of dirt lands on top of me, but this time something heavy, cold, and hard bangs against my skull. I gasp as pain explodes through my head.

I double over, waiting for the pain to subside, but then cough from the dirt I accidentally breathed in. The stupid dirt. It's everywhere! I swipe it out of my face, then blink rapidly, trying to get it out of my eyes. As I shake it out of my hair, my fingers graze over an angry bump taking form on my head.

Ugh. *Please tell me Danny didn't see that.* I turn my body and blindly walk to my measly pile of rocks, when I hear heavy footsteps and Gabbro's voice behind me. "Alena."

I curse. *He saw.*

My feet slow, but I bury my face in my arm, hiding the tears that spring to my eyes from the pain. *It's just a stupid bump on the head. Why am I crying?* Two strong arms wrap around me, pulling me in for a comforting hug. I resist at first, but when Danny doesn't let go, I melt into his chest and let my tears flow. All from a silly bump.

He guides me over to a pile of dirt and sits me down. Taking in a deep breath, I bite my lip to choke back my tears and then wipe my face, probably smearing the thick layer of dirt even more. Danny sits next to me, leaving a space between us, something he's never done before.

I'm immediately reminded of how much I've missed being around him. I miss being able to talk to him freely. I even miss the subtle touches and silent jokes.

I wipe my nose. In this moment, I'm simultaneously struck that things will never be the same. I need to make things right between us.

"I'm not sure I'm helping much," I whisper.

Danny chuckles before lifting his fingers to the large bump on my forehead.

I look in the direction of Kapri. She's there but distracted by controlling little amounts of dirt out of the hole. Nothing like the mountains Mark keeps throwing out, but more than I can control.

Danny still can't speak for himself. With him having a full Pepp totem *and* a defective totem crammed into his brain, his communication channels are still blocked. Gabbro, his black Magbaby, still has to speak for him.

Gabbro opens up now on his shoulder, changing from his rock form into a little man, much like a potato bug would open up before crawling around. Gabbro's tendrils on his head are still purple and swollen from stretching too far in Jax's prison. One is piled high on his head, and the other is woven into Danny's ear, relaying Danny's words. "You okay?"

I laugh and wipe my nose. "Yes, I'm okay." Then I point at Kapri. "She must know what she's doing. I don't see a single bruise on her."

Danny follows my gaze to the girl. I watch his face, the way it brightens at the sight of Kapri.

"Yeah. But she's not working with Mark." That's all Danny communicates through Gabbro before his cheeks flush.

I scoff. True.

I need to continue. I need him to know that I completely approve of them.

"Well, I've learned that Kapri is not only *good at this*, she's also really smart, she's disgustingly beautiful, she's a great dancer ... and ..." I glance at Danny's face, observe his strong jaw and dark hair. "And she's really good at making you happy."

I don't know what I expected. For him to smile. Blush even more. But instead, out of the corner of my vision, I see his eyes fill up with tears, and he leans his elbows on his knees.

Oh boy. I bite my cheek to keep my own emotions in check. I watch his profile for a moment. *Should I say something else?*

Finally, Gabbro speaks for him. "Thank you, Alena."

I blink rapidly. *Don't cry.*

"Thank you for everything. For being my friend. And for coming to get me from Jax."

I want to wrap him in my arms, reassure myself again that he's okay. But I refrain. I'll never forget the way I found him in Dakdete. Starved, burned by the sun, being eaten alive by bugs. Jax kidnapped and tortured him, all to get to me and my black power so that I could heal Iris. Fortunately, we found Danny. Barely alive, but alive.

"No, thank *you,* Danny, for being *my* friend. I'm so sorry you were taken. I wish it hadn't happened. But you need to know it was Kapri that found you. She worked tirelessly and pushed us all hard. She never gave up."

Which is true. I was pretty worthless after what happened at SilverDen. Kapri had her head on straight, her sight only set on one thing—finding Danny.

Danny smiles, and his eyes glance toward the girl again. They're light at first, but then they darken. It's in this moment that I catch it: a hollowness in his gaze I hadn't noticed before. A haunting just like in Mark.

"How are you, Danny?"

Danny sighs deeply. "I'm scared, Alena," Gabbro mutters for him. "I know I'm safe now, but sometimes I feel like I'm still trapped back there with Jax, hungry, hurting, wondering what kind of pain will come next. I can't tell you how happy I was when I saw your face. Unfortunately, it's not over. And that's what scares me the most. Jax might be in prison, but Aitin is not. Who knows what kind of pain he's capable of causing." His back rises as he fights to take another deep breath even though Gabbro is the one talking.

"I also have my own guilt to push through. If I hadn't attempted to find you myself when you left the dino dance, Jax never would have captured me, and things would be very different now." Danny taps his head. "Unfortunately, there's a lot going on in here."

I know how that goes.

"I've been going to see my mom," Gabbro continues for him. "Sepharine. You met her, right?"

"Yes." I still have the note she gave me from Pam, Tom's wife. It's a note I'll hold on to forever.

"I wish Mark would go see her too," Gabbro says, lowering his voice so Mark won't hear. "I think he needs a little extra support right now."

I nod and let my gaze drop to my hands, noting the dirt lodged beneath my fingernails. Mark is struggling. I've known it from the moment I got him out of that Dakdete cave Aitin was torturing him in. Sadly, I don't know exactly why he's struggling. He won't talk about what happened. All I know is that he's kept a frustrating distance from me. He doesn't touch me like he used to. It's been weeks, and I don't think he's even hugged me. He needs his space, and I'm trying to give it to him, but I think he would feel better if he talked.

Sepharine. Would Mark talk to her? As quickly as my hopes rise, though, they fall.

"Somehow, I don't think he'll go to her. He seems too ..." I don't know how to finish. Too scared? Too proud? Too embarrassed? Maybe all of the above. I scuff the dirt with my toe. "I don't know. But maybe I could talk to her. Maybe she could give me some ideas on how to help him."

Danny nods. "I bet she could."

I roll my shoulders back. "Also, I've decided that once this is all over with Aitin, I'm going to take a closer look at your totem, Danny. I'm going to figure out a way to get the defected one out, so you can talk for yourself again."

This makes Danny almost fully smile, showing off his attractive crooked front tooth. "Wouldn't that be great. To not have to use this *little* rock to communicate anymore."

Gabbro rolls his black eyes through his own words.

I laugh, then things fall quiet.

I'll never forget this boy who taught me about Peppate. I'll never be able to repay the one who chose to be my friend. Out of all the unlucky things that have happened to me lately, he's the one lucky thing I'll always remember.

"Hey, Danny," I whisper, changing the subject, asking a lingering question I still have about happiness.

"Yes?"

"The wiggems. I think I learned what one of the G's means. Grace. But what does the other one stand for?"

The corner of his lip lifts.

"Gratitude," Gabbro says.

Hmmm. Of course. "Gratitude. Being grateful." That seems fitting for Danny's made-up acronym. Doing the things in his acronym chases away the Doler, which tends to make people feel sad. I make a lot of Doler inside me, thanks to my totem, so I need all the help I can get.

Danny's face grows serious. "It's more than being grateful, Alena." He rubs his jaw thoughtfully. "It's allowing yourself to see more."

I narrow my eyes, not sure I understand.

"Exercising gratitude is like putting on special spectacles that allow us to see everything that matters, including the small miracles." Danny chuckles a little, through Gabbro's talking. "There's this little four-year-old girl Sepharine is taking care of right now. Whenever I'm around her she's always talking about the things she loves. Like, 'I love my shoes' or 'I love this food' or 'I love that tree.' They're always simple things she mentions, things I don't normally notice, and sometimes she mentions them repeatedly."

Danny laughs again. "It's funny how, being around her, I find my eyes being opened. I'm more grateful for the small things.

"I think true gratitude is a deep, warm feeling of appreciation, and when it's used correctly it makes you feel almost instantly happy."

I nod. I understand what he's saying. I've felt that before. Sometimes during the sunsets in the courtyard above GreenGrotto. The beauty, the colors, the magnificence, can fill a person to the brim with an invisible yet powerful light.

Danny takes my hand in his and turns his body so he's fully facing me.

"There. I've taught you everything I know about happiness. Now all you need to do is go out and practice."

The warmth I always remember feeling from Danny seeps through my skin and warms my heart. I'm going to miss being his number one. That's why I feel jealous. I *want* to be his number one, but I can't be anymore. I squeeze his hand and smile.

"I'll always be your friend, Alena," Gabbro says. Then Danny's gaze slides to Kapri, who is still picking up rocks within our view. He's officially saying good-bye to the relationship we once had. I touch his face one last time.

"And I'll always be yours," I whisper.

Danny nods soberly. But then his eyebrows lift, and a teasing smile spreads across his expression.

"Maybe tell Mark to be more careful." He points to my forehead before moving to stand.

I reach my hand to my temple, feeling the new bump that pounds in response. I smile. "I should."

Then Danny turns and walks to Kapri. I watch his back silently, happy to have finally talked to him.

Once he's safely back within Kapri's reach, I carefully walk forward and peer over the edge of the hole. I spot Mark immediately. He's deeper than he was before, and dirt clings attractively to his sweaty skin, along with his blue shirt. I want to ask him to teach me how to control the dirt so I can be down there with him, not up here, but when his eyes meet mine, he doesn't smile. Just nods and keeps working.

So I wave and step back, hoping more than anything that he'll talk to me soon.

Chapter 2

I work with Mark for another four hours, but when my body tires from lifting heavy rocks and my spirits plummet from Mark's indifference, I tell him I'm going to the hospital and say good-bye.

I shake the dirt off my body as well as I can when I reach the hospital, then climb the stairs to the top level. The chief is being held in Jeter's old spacious office, where all the medics can keep a close eye on him. I like that the room is bright with all the windows. Better than the dark, cold Post office room where he used to sleep.

I go see the chief first, ease my worries by feeling his pulse. Then I move on to the honeycomb rooms. Without any Pepps going on runs, there hasn't been much need for Toboggans or honeycomb medics. But, from up here, I can see the progress of Petrichor's bunker. It's massive. And scary. *Would this be happening if I had never come here?* Maybe. I have a feeling Aitin would have found a way to get what he wants, no matter what.

Turning away from the evening setting sun, I shake the heaviness from my shoulders and grab a small power sphere from the cabinet in Jeter's old office where all the medics get their power now. Then I walk to the clinic. Even though nobody has left Petrichor lately, there are still minor injuries resulting from our bunker digging and dinosaur training. Over the next few hours I work through minor cases. The work takes my mind off Mark—and Aitin—and Jeter. Before I know it, it's late, and everyone has left.

Rolling the kinks out of my tense neck, I walk down the stairs and out into the dark night. With how quiet it is, I gather it's later than I thought. Man, I probably missed dinner. Hopefully, there's something left in GreenGrotto's courtyard.

My tummy growls angrily on the walk back to GreenGrotto. I reach the girls' dorm stairs and walk all the way to the top of the mountain. You'd think that after all this time my body would be used to the climb, but occasionally I still get winded and my legs get stiff. Tonight is one of those nights. It takes me a long time to get to the top. Only a few Pepps linger in the cold torch-lit night. I grab some food, eat quietly by myself, then head down to my room to grab some clean clothes and take a shower.

Cody has moved back in with me. After I saved her from Silver-Den, she stayed at the hospital to be watched. But going on the run to the GreenLands with Rusty was good for her, allowed her to see her homeland and come to some sort of peace within. Now Sepharine has discharged her, allowing her to stay at GreenGrotto with me.

She's asleep when I get to our room, so I quietly gather my clean clothes from my closet, shut the door, and make my way to the showers.

I don't get there though.

"Danny?" I whisper when he appears down the hall.

He sees me immediately, Gabbro still talking for him.

"Oh good, you're awake."

"Is everything okay?"

Danny nods, but his expression darkens with worry. "Mark's just having another nightmare. I was wondering if you could help him calm down."

I bite my lip. *Not again.* The nightmares have become a regular occurrence lately—for all of us. My nightmares involve a lot of fire and screaming. Lots of screaming. And even though I wake up panting and sweaty, I still wake up.

Mark doesn't seem to be able to do that. Danny says he suffers in the claws of his nightmares for hours, leaving Mark physically and emotionally exhausted the next day. Mark doesn't know it, but Danny has been quietly getting me when the episodes last longer than an hour. I perform the Ataractic on him—the shortcut phrase that calms the mind. The same thing I used on Cody after experiencing the bombing in the GreenLands.

The Ataractic seems to put Mark in a more restful sleep, but I don't know if it changes the dreams he's having. For all I know, he's still trapped in the nightmares while only appearing to suffer less on the outside.

"Yes, I'll come," I tell Danny.

I follow him through the halls in silence, down the stairs, then up to the boys' side. I silently remember the way Mark's skin was sloughing off when I found him in Aitin's cave. Relive the horror I felt when I learned it extended far deeper than his skin. Aitin had made Mark swallow acid, completely eroding his esophagus. I don't know how he survived.

I swallow. Flint burned me with acid once. It hurt. But it was nothing compared to Mark's torture. I don't even want to imagine the kind of pain that caused him. I keep wondering if that's the reason for the hollowness in Mark's eyes, the pain, but I feel like there's something more, something deeper that's bothering him.

I miss him. I miss my friend.

When we reach the room, Danny opens the door and walks in. I slowly follow behind.

A single candle lights the area, and I bite back a smile.

The tiny room is crammed with Trevor, the bear, in here now. No bed could hold the large animal, so he sleeps sprawled out on the floor, swallowing up any spare space, and snoring through some obviously very obstructed nasals. His fur, soft and clean, glistens a dark brown in the candlelight.

I'm still getting to know Trevor. Like Danny, he can't really talk, and like Danny he left Petrichor that night years ago to stop Case from creating the defective totem. As a Pepp he was a special morpher, and to attack Case, he morphed into a bear. Then both he and Danny grabbed a portion of the totem to destroy, but in the process the extra totems attached themselves to their bodies, crippling them in different ways. Danny came back unable to talk, and Trevor was unable to morph back into his human form without suffering extreme pain. So now he remains a bear.

My eyes move from the bear over to Mark.

Mark is in his bed, sleeping, but very restlessly. He must have stopped digging soon after I left him and came straight to bed, not even bothering to change out of his dirty clothes.

I step further into the room and close the door behind me. Inching my way to him, past Danny's bed, carefully avoiding Trevor's hairy arms, I see that Mark's body is trembling, and he's mumbling something to himself.

Gabbro hums to my shoulder. "It's been over an hour and a half."

Nightmares. The never-ending nightmares that have a person crying before they even fall asleep. It's so unfair to be haunted when the body so desperately needs to rest.

I kneel next to Mark. Letting my hand graze his arm, I try to calm his body by listening to his elements like I've done several times before.

My hand has barely touched his skin, though, when Mark whips his other arm around fast, catching me by the throat. Before I can blink, I'm hovering in the air, over his bed, unable to breathe.

Danny is suddenly there, pulling on Mark, trying to get him to put me down. Gabbro is shouting in his ears. Trevor immediately jumps out of his sleep, tipping over Mark's collection of guns propped against the wall as he tries to stand.

But I just stare into Mark's eyes. They're empty, glazed, as if Mark is somewhere I am not.

I know the moment he finally recognizes me, because his eyes clear, and he drops me to the ground.

Bringing my hand to my neck, I stare at him in shock. When he meets my gaze, his face is surprisingly hard.

"What are *you* doing here?"

His coldness slams into me like a physical punch to the gut. He's never treated me like this.

A deep chasm splits between us. A part of me wants to leave the room and get as far away from him as I can. But the other part of me wants to take him into my arms and force him to tell me what's going on.

Fortunately, Danny is there and interrupts both of my reactions.

"Mark." It's one word from Gabbro, but it's etched with a heavy warning.

Mark raises a trembling hand to his forehead and drops down onto the edge of his bed.

"I'm sorry, Alena," he says after a while. "I don't ... I don't know what's wrong with me."

Those words.

How many times have I thought those words to myself? *What's wrong with me.* It takes me a few seconds to calm my hurt and simmering anger enough to see it again. Mark is suffering. I should know better than to take his reaction personally. And considering how patient he's been with me all along, how could I be anything but understanding?

With a clearer head, seeing what's really going on, I kneel in front of Mark and gently rub his neck.

He flinches at my touch.

I swallow and drop my hand. "Nothing's *wrong* with you, Mark."

He grunts.

"Do you want to talk about it?" I ask as kindly as I can. Not that I need to know what happened to him, but it might help him work through things.

Unfortunately, Mark immediately shakes his head. I try not to feel frustrated. I know that talking will help him, but I've been just as resistant to talk in the past. Forcing it, or getting angry, won't help.

"Okay." I think through my scrambled thoughts. I could ask him what I can do to help, but chances are he won't know. I wish I could just stay here with him tonight, be with him, but that wouldn't be very appropriate. Instead, I pull his hand away from his face, bring it to my lips, and kiss it.

"I'll go. Good night, Mark."

He mumbles something inaudible, obviously not wanting me here. I rise to my feet.

It's difficult. Walking through that door, leaving Mark behind when he so clearly needs someone to stay. I guess it's good that Danny and Trevor are there.

Closing the door behind me, I take in a deep breath and lean my back against it.

How in the world do I help him?

I slide to the floor and close my eyes.

I should go shower, but I've lost all my energy. Maybe I'll just stay here with Mark in the only way I can. I should be able to hear if he has another nightmare, right? If he does, I can try to help him.

This time without touching him.

***

Boots scuff the floor loudly.

I lift my head only a few inches, then groan. My neck is kinked. I must have fallen asleep at a bad angle.

Sitting up, I try to remember where I am, when the door opens behind me, making me fall back.

"Alena?"

Blast it. I'm still outside Mark's room. I should've left hours ago.

I find my balance and sit up.

"Did you sleep here last night?"

I grunt and move to stand, but Mark bends down and catches my arm. His touch hurts. I must be more bruised from the rocks yesterday than I thought.

"Alena? Are you okay?" His eyes scan my body, no doubt seeing the bump on my forehead I never healed and the dirt caking every pore. Man, I'm a mess.

"I'm fine," I say, then raise my face to his that's only inches away. I groan again. *Why does he always have to be so frustratingly handsome? Even with dirt smeared across his cheeks.*

"I'm sorry about last night," he says, letting my arm go.

The events of the night before creep back into my mind. The nightmares. Him choking me.

I can't stop my hand from touching the dark stubble on his face.

"Don't be sorry, Mark. Did you eventually fall asleep?"

The muscle in his jaw twitches. "I can't believe I tried to hurt you, Alena. How could I hurt you?" Mark hangs his head, not bothering to answer my question.

I've never seen Mark look scared. That's the only way I can describe the look in his dark eyes now.

Fear. Fear of himself.

I want to reassure him, tell him that it wasn't his fault and that he'll be okay, but the truth is, he scared *me*. That Mark from last night was totally foreign.

Instead, I gently rub his face and tell him one thing that I know for certain. "I'm here for you. Okay?" I attempt a smile.

Mark just shakes his head, his irritation palpable. "I'm going for a run," he murmurs.

"Okay." I drop my hand.

Standing, Mark shuts the door behind me and walks down the hall. "I'll see you later."

As soon as he's gone, I lean my head back against the door and groan.

Oh my.

I don't know how anyone has *ever* dealt with *me and my* moodiness. This is exhausting.

I roll onto my knees, cringing at the pain in my body.

Mark and Danny have both been so patient with me when I needed it. *I can do the same with Mark, can't I?*

But frustration bubbles up in my throat, and I stand.

I wish I could do the same thing with Mark, but I'm just barely surviving myself. Sorting through my own mistakes and fighting off my constant guilt is exhausting. I don't know that I can take care of Mark as well.

I walk down the hall.

I feel like a blind person, wanting to lead another blind person.

I don't know that we'll get very far together.

Chapter 3

I can't believe I've never been to the Burrows before. I've lived in Petrichor for half a year and still haven't seen where the Pepp families reside. Where Mark and Danny lived when they first came here. I walk slowly past MossyHollow and then veer to the left, trying to form my thoughts for Sepharine.

I felt so sure, talking to Danny yesterday, but now, actually walking toward the Burrows, my palms are sweating. *What exactly do I tell her? What will she tell me? Will she be able to help me help Mark?*

The trees get thicker as I go, until they open up into a large clearing. The grass extends up and over the hilly terrain, met by fingers of sunlight reaching through the trees. Tamed flowers grow neatly in well-kept gardens, and a perfectly groomed stone path leads the way to the first door buried into the side of a large hill. I'm not far away from that first hill, when I hear the high-pitched squeals of children.

Children.

How long has it been since I've seen a child? The sounds of play draw me forward, making me homesick for my own childhood, the time when everything seemed easier. I climb to the top of the first hill to get a better view. That's when I see it. The burrowed hill I stand on links with more to its sides, which extends to more and more burrows, eventually meeting again at the far side of the clearing.

It's a circle of burrows.

And in the middle of the Burrows sits three large trees with the most extensive treehouse and jungle gym I've ever seen. Dozens of swings hang from their branches, bridges and ropes reach from limb to limb, and a large wooden house with windows and a slide sits right in the middle.

Then I see the culprit for the squeals. Children, dozens and dozens of them swarming the treehouse like ants in an anthill, running from place to place, lost in their own little games of pretend. Mixed in with the children is an occasional adult, most of them women. I look closer at their totems and find the same twinkling jewels woven with the white mark of a mother, much like the one I saw on Sepharine.

I smile. This. This is how life should be, for all of us. Not just children.

A loud roar breaks through the air, and I search the group for the culprit. I easily find it—not because the roar is instantly followed by dozens of squealing children but because the source of it is an actual bear.

Trevor.

He's playing with the little children, stomping around the much-too-small-for-him playhouse. My smile widens. I recall the first time I saw Trevor, hidden in the bushes during initiation. I was terrified of him then. I thought he was a normal bear. But then he intervened when Case tried to lure me away from my initiation group and take me to Aitin. He protected me. He also protected Mark from attaching the second totem.

Those little kids have no idea how lucky they are to be in the safe hands of Trevor.

Without realizing it, I've sat on top of the burrow to watch the scene in front of me. This part of Petrichor with the crowded growth of trees reminds me of my home. These aren't pine trees like I'm used to, but they smell good and are a bright, beautiful green. I take in a deep breath.

"It's pretty, isn't it?"

I jump at the voice next to me and look up to find Sepharine observing the same scene I'm so captivated by.

"Yes. It is."

"You know, the pureblood Pepp children?" she says. "Those who don't have to wear the totem but who carry the natural Peppate generators in their vessels? They produce more Peppate than four Pepp adults combined without even morphing." Sepharine smiles, her straight teeth brightening her face. "In other words, just being around those children can make anyone feel happier."

I smile, then Sepharine pauses and cocks her head, looking thoughtful.

"Well, I guess I should say that they make you happier until they get hungry or tired. Then they do the exact opposite. They suck the Peppate right out of you."

I can't help but chuckle. I don't know too much about children, but I can imagine it's tiring taking care of them.

I quietly observe Sepharine. Her wavy brown hair, with golden and red highlights is pulled up into a long ponytail that brushes against her bare shoulders and her sleeveless top attractively exposes her beautiful totem. She finds me watching her when she looks my way.

"May I sit with you?"

"Of course," I respond with a nod of my head.

"It's good to see you." She settles herself easily in the grass.

"Good to see you too," I reply, trying my best to keep my eyes from wandering to the diamonds and jewels hanging on her totem. They've always captivated me. I like how they enhance the colors of her ribbons.

She sees me looking at it.

"It's a promise mark," she says, answering my unspoken question while sitting. "From my husband. He gave it to me when he asked me to marry him. It's much like the wedding rings most non-Pepps use."

Ah. That makes sense.

"It's beautiful," I say, then look back to the kids playing. *What do I say now?* The peaceful feeling from moments ago is quickly dissipating with her by my side. I almost sigh in relief when Sepharine breaks the silence.

"How are you, Alena?"

Jeez. She seems to know exactly what to say. Except, I didn't come here to talk about *me*. I let my eyes wander around, trying to collect my thoughts. "I came to ask for some help, with Mark," I whisper.

She smiles softly but doesn't say anything. Somehow that makes me feel more comfortable to talk. Like she's ready to listen.

"Last night, Mark was stuck in a long nightmare," I say. "Danny asked if I could help calm him down so he could sleep. When I touched Mark's arm to perform the Ataractic on him, he woke up, wrapped his hand around my neck, and choked me." I touch my neck now, my eyebrows furrowing. "When I looked into his eyes, it was like ... he was gone, in a totally different place than me." I sigh. "I know something's going on, but I don't know what to do. I'd recommend he come see you, or talk to *someone*, but I don't think he wants any help right now. I think that'll only make things worse. I just don't know what to do." I look at Sepharine.

Compassion works its way over her soft face. "Alena, you've both been through so much. I think you're right about Mark not wanting help right now. It's difficult for him to admit that he needs it. I actually felt the need to talk to him this morning so I paid him a visit."

My body straightens. I wasn't expecting that.

Sepharine smiles softly. "I just gave him a big hug and asked him how he was doing. When he didn't answer, I reminded him that I'm here for him. That's all I said. But for *you*. I think the best way for you to help him is to help yourself. You're naturally patient and kind. I have no doubt that under different circumstances you would know exactly how to help him. Those traits are just a little difficult for you to access right now because of the things you've been through. Alena?" I look at her green eyes. "How are *you* doing?"

She cares. She genuinely cares. I can feel it. I don't know why but this touches me. My throat catches.

I hadn't planned on talking. Now that she's asked the question, there seems to be so much to say. *Does she really want to hear it? It'll take way too much time.*

But one look at her and I can tell. She's not going to back down. Just like the chief. I can almost picture her sitting here all night until I talk. I might as well start now.

"I'm doing better than I was," I say. "But I still struggle."

Sepharine nods. "Please tell me everything."

I talk about the things occupying my mind most lately. About finding Danny and then healing Aitin. I tell her about the heavy guilt I still feel daily. Guilt over Mitch's death. Tom's death. Creating a weapon through Aitin.

I tell her the things Danny taught me and how hard I'm fighting to see the truth, but how tired—just utterly tired I am of everything.

For the first time, though, I talk without crying. I speak the events as they happened, as if they're simply fact. And Sepharine listens. Occasionally, she asks me questions, and then listens some more.

By the time I've said everything I have to say, I realize we've been sitting here a long time. My legs are stiff, and my back is aching. The sun has dropped, and it's almost dusk. *Golly sakes, how long have we been here?*

I finally look at Sepharine.

Her eyes are kind and sorrowful. "Alena, I'm so sorry for everything you've been through."

Her words are nice to hear, telling me that the heaviness I've been carrying lately is validated.

After a few more moments, she says, "You mentioned that Danny advised you to look for truth. To focus on the things that are most important for you to see. Have you been able to see those things? Is there anything you've found that makes you feel better?"

I remember the day Mark and I got away from Aitin. The day he told me something that felt like the truth I've been trying to deny all along.

I slowly nod. "I think so." Then I pick at a piece of grass. Wow. I've plucked a lot of grass based on the large pile sitting next to me.

"I will never be a Pepp," I whisper, then look at the treehouse in front of me. "That's the truth I've needed to accept. All along I've wished that someday, somehow, I could fit in, be like everyone else here. *Normal.*" Then I look at Sepharine. "But even though I'll never be a normal Pepp, that doesn't mean I'm ... worthless." I whisper the word that's haunted me for so long.

Worthless.

"I still have a place, somewhere. I may not be able to make Peppate, but I'm the key to destroying Aitin. I can feel it. I created him, which means I can uncreate him. I just have to figure out how."

I glance back at the grass and pat down my pile.

"Do you believe it?" Sepharine whispers next to me.

Her question confuses me. "Believe what?"

"That even though you'll never be a Pepp you still have worth? That you still have a purpose? It's one thing to *tell* yourself something, and it's quite another to *believe* it."

I stare, thinking carefully. "Yes. I believe it."

Sepharine is quiet. When she doesn't respond I look at her face. Her eyes are misty.

"Alena, you never have been, nor will you ever be, *worthless*. And you definitely have a purpose." She smiles, but it doesn't reach her eyes. "I wish I could say that things will magically get easier from here. They might, but there will still be moments where you doubt." Turning to me, Sepharine grips my hands in hers. It's an odd gesture coming from her, yet comforting. "Alena, that's when you must be strong. In those moments of doubt, I want you to look back and remember what you just told me. That even though you'll never be a normal Pepp, that doesn't mean you are worthless. Tell yourself that over and over again. It'll take time for you to heal and, unfortunately, the worst is not over. You might continue to get hurt. But please keep fighting."

I can't speak past the lump in my throat, so I nod. The warmth I always remember feeling from Danny seems to seep from Sepharine now and warms my heart.

Sepharine lets go of my hands and turns back to the scene in front of us.

"How long has it been since you've written your family?"

My family. Since Rusty took me to visit them on our dropdown, I've been better at writing to them.

"I try to write a couple times a week."

"Good. Keep that up. Tell them everything that happens. But, more importantly, tell them how you feel. I think it'll help you. Also, I'm going to ask you to write to me while you're gone with Eli. Write to me about everything, all the bad things you experience. You can even write to me about Mark and your interactions with him. I'll try to get back to you as soon as I can, but sometimes just the act of writing things down can help. When you get back, and when things settle down, we can really address what's going on inside you and get you feeling better. Does that sound okay?"

I actually smile and take in a deep breath. I feel lighter. "Yes." But then I remember I still don't have Breccia, my Magbaby. Jeter kept her when he captured Mark. I explain this to Sepharine.

"Well, then, you can use Gabbro to send your messages to me. He'll be going with you, and he usually has too much time on his hands anyway. Putting him to work will be good." Sepharine's smile is contagious.

Then her smile fades. "Alena, as far as Mark goes, it might help you to know what's really going on with him. The experiences he's had have altered the way he views the world, and it makes him feel lost and alone. As with what happened the other night, his mind quickly takes him back to the place he was tortured, when triggered in a certain way. Try to be mindful of those triggers. It could be anything, from something he sees, hears, feels, smells, or touches. These moments will come when you least expect them, and they may even be inconvenient for *you*."

She sighs. "There's a fine line when dealing with things like this because you don't want to trigger Mark and send him down that dark path, but at the same time, in order for Mark to really get better, he has to retrain his brain. Ultimately, he has to face some of those triggers and realize that even though he sees or hears something that reminds him of that experience, that doesn't mean *he is in* that experience. That's something that takes time, though, and is really challenging. It's something I can help him with when he's ready. But, for now, with you when he's triggered, he just needs to be reminded, *kindly*, that he's safe. In other words, Alena, just do your best to love him. I have faith that he'll fight hard to overcome these things so that he can keep you. Just take care of yourself first."

I wipe my nose with my hand. It's sad that Mark not only had to go through what he went through once, but he has to relive it over and over again, stuck in something terrible. I appreciate Sepharine's words. I had guessed at all this before. I've even experienced being triggered myself, but it makes things clearer coming from Sepharine.

Sepharine looks back at the children now, and we sit in silence for a couple more moments before she speaks again.

"Alena, as a side note, how are things going with Aitin? Do you all have a plan?"

I sigh. "Yes, Eli has stopped drinking, and now we're waiting for him to feel well enough to go down to Lake Maracai. We'll hopefully be able to convince the Mixed Bloods to join our cause, to let me heal them like I did Aitin so they can help us fight."

Sepharine picks up on my hopeless tone. "But you don't think it'll work?"

I shake my head. "I don't have the black power anymore, so I would have to use our Peppate power, but I can't figure out *how* to control the serum with Pepp power. Even if I did, the Pepp power will make them sick. I don't know why they would agree."

Sepharine is thoughtful for a moment. "Is there a way to get more black power?"

"Not without killing another Pepp." My mind goes back to the night on my dropdown with Cody when she told me why she was tied to that stump outside SilverDen. She thought it was because a Pepp had to die in my morph in order for my totem to create the black power. Which makes sense. "It would be really nice if Case was around. Maybe he would know of a way around it. But I'm not really willing to experiment."

"You know, my husband is on the council." Sepharine lowers her voice as if what she's about to share shouldn't be shared. "He's been assigned the task of getting information from Jax."

Information from Jax? I lean in, anxious to hear what she has to say.

"They've been trying to get Jax to share what he knows about Case's whereabouts. Jax hasn't shared much, but he did say that after Lilly was taken away from Case, Case started disappearing for days at a time when he could. Jax wondered at first if he was looking for Lilly, but over time he felt like that wasn't quite it. He said Case always came home with sand in the tread of his boots."

I furrow my eyebrows. *Sand?*

Sepharine looks at me. "My husband doesn't think he was looking for Lilly. He thinks he was creating something." She looks sideways at me. "A place to hide."

I stare at her. *A place to hide once he got Lilly back*? Gabbro had mentioned Case was creating a hideout. That's why he wanted more time before I went down to free the prisoners from SilverDen.

"But where did he create it?" I ask. "He had sand on his boots? Isn't there sand everywhere?"

Sepharine scoffs, nodding. "Yes, but wasn't the chief searching the deserts not too long ago for Jax? I'm wondering if Case would have done the same thing Jax did. Create a home in the desert where Peppate isn't spread. Wasn't Lilly, his girl, a Mixed Blood?"

My back straightens. Of course. Case is probably living in one of the deserts to keep Lilly away from Peppate. What if I ask Eli for that map in the prison where the chief was keeping track of all the places he'd searched? Could I continue the search myself? I don't have Breccia anymore, but there are plenty of other Magbabies I could adopt, aren't there?

"It sure would make things easier if we could find Case," Sepharine repeats.

I sit in silence. *Yes. Yes, it would.*

With the sun now setting, a group of children heads toward Sepharine and me. When they reach us, a young girl with brown hair and bright-blue eyes melts into the woman's arms dramatically. "I'm soooo hungry." She places the back of her hand against her forehead as if she's about to die.

Sepharine looks at me and mouths the words *help me.*

I laugh.

Her expression lightens with a smile before she turns to the girl. "How about we go eat? Does spaghetti sound good?"

Small squeals answer her question, and Sepharine stands up with the brown-haired girl on her back. "Thanks for visiting with me, Alena. It was good to talk to you."

I stand now too. "Thank *you.*"

"Good luck with everything!" she shouts behind her as she runs away with the children.

I force a smile. *Luck.* We'll need a lot of that.

Chapter 4

I shift the weight of my body to my left foot. I hope Mark gets here soon. I don't know how much longer I can sit hunched behind this bush. If my timing is correct, Mark should have already found the note I left for him in his room, and he should be headed this way. I hope.

I wipe my sweaty palms on the fabric of my jeans. I'm not sure why I'm nervous. Perhaps because I know Mark will kick my butt at this game. Or maybe because I don't know if my plan will work.

After my visit with Sepharine a couple of days ago, I've been trying to figure out a way to reconnect with Mark. I've continued collecting rocks with him at the digging sights, but things are still awkward. He's quiet, and I don't know what to say. So, I've thought up this plan.

I just hope it doesn't backfire. It could easily go south if Mark isn't in the mood.

I hear the crunching of feet down below and duck my head deeper behind the bush.

"Alena?" Mark's confused voice reaches my ears, and my heart beats faster. Good—he got my message to meet me here. And he came.

Mark looks around.

These woods located on the east side of Training Mountain are thick but also quiet. None of the other Pepps have been training lately, so we're alone. Mark calls my name out again, this time more irritated.

My spirits fall. Maybe this was a bad idea.

Slowly, I pick up my paint ball gun loaded with blue paint balls and aim it directly at Mark. He's about to turn around and leave when I shout out his name.

"Mark."

He turns back, his eyes scanning the bushes around me, still unsure of where I am.

Pulling the trigger of my gun now, I let the paint ball fly. It slams into a tree several feet in front of Mark, blue paint splattering noticeably. I try to pretend that that tree was exactly the one I wanted to hit, and then I search Mark's face.

He steps forward to eye the paint curiously. He has to know what game I'm playing at, but he doesn't seem instantly excited like I'd hoped. I take in a deep breath and grab the other gun sitting next to me, throwing it over the bush toward him. It tumbles down the hill, landing only a few feet away from him.

"You better move before I shoot you for real," I say.

I have to strain to see it, but the corner of his lip pulls upward. I take in a deep breath, grateful for the tiny crack in his mood.

He still doesn't move toward the gun, though. Not yet.

"*You're* going to shoot *me*?" he asks. He's looking right at my bush now, and I can already sense that I'm going to get my butt kicked. But that's the whole point. I figure shooting the heck out of me will help him feel better. I let out my breath.

Mark lowers his voice, forcing me to strain to hear him. "I'll only play under one condition. For every time I shoot you, I get something in return."

He's playing along. Now I full-on smile. This is going much better than I'd hoped. But then he starts pacing the ground as he thinks. I quietly watch him walk slowly back and forth, observing him through the bush branches. The circles beneath his eyes have gotten darker, and his facial hair is longer than normal. Not that I mind the facial hair. It makes him even more attractive, if that's possible, but it means he's tired.

My knees start protesting my position, and I'm just beginning to wonder if he's changed his mind, when he raises his head back to me. His smile is gone. "A dance," he says quietly. "I never got a full dance from you the night before SilverDen. For every time I shoot you, I get a free dance."

I swallow past the sudden catch in my throat. He's serious. I pick up on the true meaning behind his words. He's accepting my offering, telling me that he still cares about me.

I clear my voice and blink my eyes. "I accept your condition," I say through the bush, trying to keep the mood light. "But I have one of my own." I frantically try to think of something I could possibly want more than to dance with Mark. I shout out the first thing that comes to my mind. "If I shoot you more times than you shoot me then you have to take me to that hot spring outside of Petrichor. The one you told me about."

Mark's lips lift in amusement. "If you shoot me more than I shoot you, Alena, I'll do anything you ask."

His comment sends a warm current through my body, and I smile, almost wishing I really could beat him.

Mark leans down to pick up his gun, and I start counting out loud to five, giving him a chance to hide. But he doesn't bother hiding, so I pull my gun up to my eyes and take aim. I've been practicing for the past few days after getting this gun from MossyHollow, trying to become somewhat of a competition for him, but when I target his chest and pull the trigger, my paint ball falls short. Way too short.

What?

Now Mark really does smile, looking directly at me through the bushes. He raises his gun, aims, and shoots. There's no way his bullet will reach me if mine couldn't reach him.

I cringe at the sting in my shoulder. Looking down, I see a dark red paint splotch. I gasp. *He shot me!* Right through the bush!

Turning around I search for a thicker tree. I need better shelter to hide behind. I scramble up the slope and slide behind a wide trunk. I cock my gun and peek around to take aim at Mark again, but he immediately pelts me three more times in my leg.

I hiss, hiding behind the tree again. He's getting closer. I can hear him chuckling.

"Sorry, Lena."

Having no idea what I'm doing, I jump out and shoot him right in the chest before sliding back behind the tree. Ha, I got him.

Small twigs crack under his steps, telling me he's getting close. I need to find another tree. I eye another wide one only a few yards away and bolt up the hill. Just before I reach my next hiding spot, though, I feel more shots on my back. I scream at their stings.

Did I choose this game?

"Tuck your arms in and hold the gun snug to your body," Mark says. "I'll close my eyes and give you a five-second chance to get away, as long as you don't shoot me."

I grit my teeth. *He's giving me advice?*

"One, two ..."

Against my pride, I take his advice and hold the gun snug against my shoulder before peeking around the tree, but I don't run away. His eyes aren't even remotely closed. He has no intention of giving me a head start. Taking aim, I shoot him right in the stomach three times before running down the hill into another bush, the branches scratching every inch of my exposed skin.

"Cheater," Mark says, bristling at the balls that just hit his stomach.

"*You* had your eyes open," I mumble under my breath, pushing aside the branches so I can get a better view.

Mark doesn't bother hiding like me. He stands out in the open. With a good view, I shoot at him over and over again, but most of my bullets miss him. Only a couple catch him by surprise.

Finally, Mark plants both feet in the ground, places his gun against his shoulder, and shoots. Over and over again. I curse under my breath. The paint balls fly right through the leaves of the bush and catch me in my legs, knees, and arms. When one hits the fragile skin of my neck, I scream, but the balls keep coming. He's close, making them sting even more. I turn my body away to protect my face, but when the stings still don't stop, I stand and run through the trees, leaving my gun behind.

What was I thinking? Where do I hide?

Mark runs after me, shooting me several more times, until I slip on a slope. Blood floods my mouth from biting my cheek. I flip over onto my stomach and cover my head with my hands.

"Okay, okay, you win!" I shout into the dirt, trying to keep the pain out of my voice.

Mark laughs out loud.

That laugh. It floats gently through the air, making all the stings in the world worth it. How long has it been since I've heard that laugh? I'm almost tempted to tell him he can keep shooting me. Almost.

He walks to me, branches crunching beneath his boots, then rests his hand on my back, sending tingles up my spine.

"Sorry, Lena. I won't shoot you anymore." As if to prove his words, his gun lands on the ground next to me in submission. I slowly peek my head out of my arms and find him kneeling there with his left hand surrendering in the air.

He's smiling. Wow. I've missed that smile.

"I think I won," he says, waving a hand over my body.

I don't need to look down to know what he's talking about. Instead, I let my eyes wander to his chest, and then his muscled stomach, where I got him a few times. I scoff. My shots are too easy to count.

He helps me sit up, then stands and extends his hand to me.

I eye his face carefully, wondering if he really wants me to take it. His eyes are kind, though, so I allow my hand to slide into his. Even though it hasn't been terribly long since I've held his hand, it feels new to me. I take special note of the calluses, lines, and warmth.

Mark's fingers slowly close around mine, and then he gently pulls me up—close. With him towering over me, I want to reach out, touch him, wrap my arms around him, but the moment feels too fragile. So I let him lead, hoping he won't end it too soon.

Mark steps forward, his golden-brown eyes only showing a small amount of guilt for what he's done to me. They look mostly amused. Lessening the gap between us, he raises a hand to my cheek. I close my eyes, leaning in to his touch.

My heart skips when I feel his other hand gently touch my neck. There's a welt there from where he shot me, but his gentle touch silences any pain and only has me wanting to lean in more. I open my eyes and look at him.

His dark brows are furrowed and he's no longer smiling, but I can feel the icky barrier that's been present for the past two weeks slowly melting away.

He's so close.

His eyes break from mine, moving to the welt on my neck. He leans down and gently caresses my skin with his lips. Shivers encompass my whole body at his rare touch. He doesn't pull back right away but lets his lips hover there, his distracting breath teasing my skin. It takes every ounce of restraint to keep myself from stepping into him.

Then I feel his right hand slip around my waist, and I practically melt.

His lips trail up to my jaw line, to my cheek.

"Will you dance with me?" he whispers against my skin.

I clear my throat, surprised that he's already cashing in on one of his *many* owed dances. "Of course."

Then he grips my right hand in his and brings it up. Gentle music starts playing from Dacite, his Magbaby.

I raise my left arm to his shoulder, and Mark sways gently, back and forth, our feet crunching the dead leaves beneath our shoes. I relish every detail of him, noticing the warmth of his hand on my back, his chest pressed against mine. I feel his breath moving the hair at my temples.

"You did this for me?" he whispers, his eyes wandering over my face.

My throat feels too dry to adequately respond, so I just nod.

Mark frowns, and for a brief moment he lets me see his inner turmoil, the struggle that's consumed him for the past two weeks. He lets me in, ever so slightly, and I feel it. His pain.

He tightens his grip around my waist, his nose touching mine now. "Thank you." His whisper sends goose bumps across my skin.

Finally. Finally, his lips close the distance between us. They're soft at first, but then his fingers dig into my back, pulling me closer.

That's it. That's all the restraint I have. I allow myself to touch him. I reach up and tangle my fingers in his hair.

Mark's lips coil with mine. Suddenly I can't breathe. Everywhere he touches burns, aches for more.

For just a moment I feel that we're both free. There're no demons or plaguing memories haunting us. It's just Mark and me. Here.

I grip the shoulder of his shirt and cling to him.

His lips break away from mine to trail kisses down to my ear again before moving on to my neck. I bring my other hand up to his face and finger the stubble I've been aching to touch for so long. Oh, my fingers love touching him, moving across his skin, to his face, back through his hair. I hold his jaw, enjoying the movement it makes as he gently bites my neck just under my ear. Then he brings his lips hungrily back to mine, pushing me back. When I get the chance, I grip his lip between my teeth and slowly release it.

A groan rumbles from the back of his throat, and his whole body goes still.

Then I feel it, the moment the demons are back for Mark.

I brace for his retreat, for him to pull away from my embrace and move back into his sorrowful place. But when he slides his other arm around me, clutching me to his chest, burying his face in my hair, I have to blink back tears.

His sorrow leaks into me, tugging on my heart. He's sharing it with me, allowing me to carry it for just a brief moment. And I embrace it, gently wrapping my hand around his neck, allowing him to burrow more into mine.

His pain, the ache that starts in my heart, spreads throughout my body, consuming me. I wish I could take it all away, remove whatever battle he's fighting. But I know more than anyone that that's not how it works. So, I hold him. Tight.

I don't know how long it takes for his heartbeat to slow, for him to win some internal battle. But I don't care. I just know that when he finally takes in a deep breath and lets it out, the struggle seems to go with it. Without releasing his grip on me, he breaks the silence.

"I'm sorry I've been so mean lately."

So mean? Dozens of things to say flitter through my mind. *How do I assure him that I don't hold anything against him? How do I put him at ease and let him know that I'm here for him, without pushing him further away?* Suddenly I'm taken back to the night after initiation. When Mark came to me. He had seen me throw up against the tree, but with good, kind humor he instantly showed me that he truly cared and that he wasn't leaving. I wonder if I could do that now.

"Mean? You mean like coming out here and shooting me to death?" I lower my voice and whisper the words into his ear. "Yeah, that wasn't very nice."

Mark doesn't move. Still unable to see his face buried in my neck, I begin to doubt my response. *Did I offend him?*

When Mark finally loosens his grip on me, he pulls back. I hold my breath until I see a small twinkle in his eyes peeking through the darkness. Even the corner of his mouth twitches upward.

I sigh in relief and continue, letting my nose rub against his chin. "But I guess that was my fault. Next time I want to show you how much I love you, I'll choose an activity that's less painful."

Mark's smile disappears, and the amusement in his eyes changes, to something deeper, stronger. His arm tightens around my waist until I almost can't breathe.

"I love you too, Lena," he whispers.

My heartbeat quickens, hearing those words from his lips. I can't help but hope he'll kiss me again.

But then the ground beneath us rumbles as if something large is approaching. Reluctantly, I look past Mark's face just in time to hear Gabbro's voice break through the silent air.

I want to groan out loud. *Seriously?*

"Mark, Alena?"

It's Eli with Danny, Kapri, and Trevor, the reason for the heavy footsteps. My eyes narrow when I see someone following behind Trevor.

Flint.

Without letting Mark go, I shift slightly so we can both face them. "Eli?" I say, still staring Flint down. My good mood is slipping away, and I hate it.

"Alena, Mark." Eli greets us, his tired eyes flittering awkwardly over Mark and me. "I guess it's time we leave." He runs a hand through his gray hair nervously. He seems to be doing much better than before, but he's still jittery. I don't know if that's from nerves or not having any alcohol.

"Mia sent an urgent message to the chief saying she needs help," he says.

"The chief?" Mark asks, pulling away from me now to face Eli. *Man, why did they have to come now?*

"Doesn't she know the chief's condition like everyone else?" Mark asks.

A guilty look shadows Eli's face. "I debated whether or not I should tell her in a message or just tell her in person. I was hoping that once we got a large enough team together, we could visit her and catch up on everything. But it sounds like she needs to meet with us sooner rather than later, so we'll just have to make do with the team we have." Eli waves his arm to those standing beside him. I don't miss the fact that Eli blames the delay on finding a bigger team. *He really expected to find others to assist us, considering how much the Pepps despise me?* I eye Eli carefully. There are still dark circles under his eyes, but he's cut his hair, shaved, and showered. The fresh clothes help a lot too. He seems ready enough.

Then my eyes land on Flint, and I can't help but glare at him.

As if reading my mind, Eli speaks up. "I promised Flint that if he came along with us to help protect you, I would free his uncle from Algor. I also may have told him that this will act as his initiation. If I'm pleased with his efforts, he'll get to choose the field he wants to work in."

A small part of me feels bad Flint hasn't matched yet. Because of me. But I instantly squash that empathy and raise my glower. This was the boy who never accepted me in Petrichor, the red-headed boy who burned me with acid.

Eli steps closer to me and lowers his voice. "We need him, Alena. Unlike all the other Pepps here, he's been training since he was born. He's efficient in every job—tracking, navigation, fighting, you name it, he's the best in it. He makes up for all the teammates we're lacking."

Flint returns my glare, making it clear that he doesn't like this any more than I do, but then his look turns smug. He heard what Eli had to say about him, and he knows it's true.

Eli speaks to everyone now. "Grab anything you need, and meet us at the airfield." He doesn't give me a chance to respond before turning and leaving. Danny and Kapri both nod encouragingly at me before following behind Eli and Flint.

When they have almost disappeared, Mark puts his arm around my shoulders.

"You owe me like a *lot* of dances," he whispers into my ear.

His comment lightens the burden weighing on my heart, and I smile. *Does each dance come with a kiss like that?* If getting shot a million times can bring my true Mark back to the surface and earn me some kisses, I'll gladly do it any day.

Chapter 5

By the time Mark and I reach the aircraft, packed and ready to go, the others are all waiting inside. Well, everyone except Trevor.

"Trevor insisted he needed a few more minute to get ready," Eli says, not bothering to hide his agitation. "As soon as he gets here, we'll go."

I look around the aircraft. Danny and Kapri are sitting in the seats on the left side talking softly. Well, I guess it's more like Kapri is talking and Danny is listening. Gabbro is not here.

It's getting easier seeing them together, especially after our last conversation, our official good-bye.

Perhaps everything will feel normal soon enough.

Mark guides me over to the right side of the aircraft, across from our friends, and pulls me into the seat beside him. He changed his clothes after our shootout, into lightweight tan pants and a loose white shirt. Somehow the loose material still manages to flaunt his chest muscles.

I fight hard to ignore them now.

When I changed, I also settled on a loose white V-necked shirt and gray joggers. Supposedly these clothes are supposed to be more comfortable in humidity. And where we're going is supposed to be awfully humid.

Taking a hair tie off my wrist, I pull my hair back into a high ponytail. If I leave it down it'll only get icky and in the way with the heavy air.

When I'm done, I slouch back into my seat.

I'm nervous for what's to come, terrified of leaving Petrichor. Not that Petrichor is any safer than everywhere else.

I'm also scared that we'll somehow run into Aitin.

Preparing for this trip has reminded me a lot of preparing for Silver-Den. The big difference, though, is that this time I'm not going alone, and this time I'm not going in secret. Having Mark here, knowing that he's a part of it all, relieves me greatly. I just wish he'd had more time to heal.

Something touches my neck, making me jump from my thoughts.

"I'm sorry about your welt," Mark says, rubbing the spot that got hit with his paint balls.

I smile. I had forgotten about it—and all the other ones on my body.

"Do you think you could heal it? It would make me feel better."

I silently reach out for my elements with the power Rusty gave me, commanding the bruises to dissipate.

"Is that better?" I ask, expecting Mark to sit back and relax, not having to worry about my welt anymore, but he just continues to stare at my face.

"You were at the prison again today."

I straighten. I was, before our shootout. How does he know about my daily prison visits?

"What do you do there?" he asks.

I break eye contact. I haven't told him. He's been so weighed down lately with his own struggles. I thought telling him about my worries would make things worse for him, but I know better than to keep a secret from Mark. He hates secrets, especially after the secret I kept regarding SilverDen.

"I've been visiting Iris, Jax's daughter."

"Why?" His tone isn't accusing or angry, just curious.

I scratch my head and sigh. "Well, I keep thinking that I'll figure out a way to command Dilo's serum with the Pepp power. If I can command it, then I can practice distributing it on Iris—Which means I can also practice taking it *out* of Iris, like I need to do with Aitin."

Mark continues to stare at me, thinking, giving me the courage to continue.

"I've also been trying to listen for the sound of Pepp power, trying to figure out how Jeter deflected our attacks so easily. I want to know how he did it." I rub my face with my hands. "I guess I go to the prison mainly to be close to Iris, to think. I'm hoping answers will surface there."

"Have you had any luck?" Mark's breath is a whisper against my neck.

"No."

Mark nods in understanding, then rubs a finger against my cheek. "Maybe we could practice together sometime. Practice deflecting the power, that is. It's something I'd like to learn too."

I meet his golden-brown eyes. "I'd like that." I'd like that more than he knows.

With a tiny smile, Mark leans his head back against the wall and closes his eyes. "I'm still sorry about shooting you."

I laugh and then stare at him silently, resisting the urge to touch him. He needs to rest.

Unfortunately, this is the moment Trevor decides to grace us with his presence. When he steps onto the ramp, the whole aircraft leans to the side, forcing Mark to sit back up. I look toward the back. There, perched on the shoulder of the large bear, is Gabbro, ready to go.

There better not be any secrets during this trip. No more hidden quests.

Without hesitation, Trevor moves to the empty seat beside Kapri. Taking up at least three spots, he gently places his large hairy arm around Kapri's small shoulders and pulls her to him, his body practically swallowing her up.

Kapri laughs at his gesture, but Danny doesn't think it's funny. Leaning forward, Danny shoves him away, drawing out a deep guttural sound from Trevor's throat.

It's odd. Trevor's laugh. It makes me laugh.

I recall Cody calling morphers immature. Her words couldn't be more fitting, but I have to admit that just having Trevor here instantly puts me at ease. We're lucky to have him.

Eli clears his throat now, interrupting Danny and Trevor's little quarrel, pulling at our attention. We all look at him, except for Flint. He's getting ready to fly the aircraft.

He knows how to fly this thing?

"As you all know, we're going to Lake Maracai, where the group of Mixed Bloods lives. It sounds like there's a lot of contention down there. The Mixed Bloods have never liked us. They blame us for their suffering, and I have a feeling that dislike has only grown over the past few months. We need to stay together and be careful."

Eli rubs his wrinkly face.

"Also, you need to know that Lake Maracai is very dangerous for Pepps, naturally. Lightning storms plague the sky above it almost every night. The Mixed bloods have chosen to live there because the lightning seems to help their condition, but it is dangerous for them as well, which is why they live below the rock and only come out when the storms subside during the day. Be aware of the skies around you. If you sense a storm, we need to get out."

Lightning seems to help their condition? I guess that makes sense. The lightning would zap any Peppate in the air. But the Mixed Bloods have Peppate generators inside themselves, which is probably why they live below the rock. I wonder if the Mixed Bloods know the truth of all this?

A weariness sets in over Eli's face. We aren't even there yet, and he already seems tired.

"Last, we will never morph around Maracai. The Mixed Bloods are already very sick because of the Peppate we produce. We don't want to make them any sicker by creating Peppate within their space. No morphing. In fact, I've removed my totem altogether, to prove I don't want to hurt them." Eli lifts the sleeve of his shirt to confirm the totem's absence. "If for some reason these people become aggressive, try to fight them off without using power if you can."

If they become aggressive? Wonderful.

"My hope is that while we're there we can convince the Mixed Bloods to help us." He mutters these last words before sitting next to Flint.

I stare at him. *That's it?*

Man, couldn't he at least *try* to sound a little more hopeful? Sit a little taller, pretend like he's not leading us to our death? Instead, I watch him slouch into his seat as we take off into the sky. I guess I can't blame him, especially when I feel the same way.

Hopeless.

Nobody talks for a while. The only sound is the shuddering of the aircraft metal. Mark leans his head back and shuts his eyes. I don't know if he sleeps, but I hope he does. Kapri eventually starts whispering to Danny again. Trevor leans in to listen, and Danny pushes him away.

I sit there, silently, trying to figure out what I could possibly offer the Mixed Bloods that hasn't already been offered, but I come up with absolutely nothing.

Eventually the comfortable silence is broken by Eli, who announces our arrival after what seems like a couple of hours.

"We'll land just outside the lake area in the trees. Mia will meet us there."

Uncovering the small circular window beside me, I look out.

I see it, there below. A large crystal lake, shimmering beautifully in the sunlight, the brightness of the blue water amazingly complemented by the deep-green color of the trees surrounding it.

"Good thing I brought my swimsuit," Mark whispers into my ear, pressing his chest to my back, his fingers brushing against my hips.

My body warms at his touch.

Swimming. That actually sounds fun. And considering how hot it's getting inside the aircraft, I'm guessing the water would feel great. Unfortunately, I didn't think about bringing a swimsuit. Mark is probably joking. We really wouldn't have time to swim. Would we?

As the aircraft circles around the area, I narrow my eyes and look closer. I didn't see it before, probably because it was blocked by the trees, but now it sticks out so much it's difficult to miss.

A brown patch of land butts up next to the lake, with dirt buildings, dirt walls, rock chairs and tables. It's a small town made up of just dirt and rock.

Not a speck of living green is found in that area. At all.

That must be where the Mixed Bloods live. Just the sight of it makes my spirits fall. *What kind of a place is this?*

The aircraft drops and Mark sits back. Soon, we're landing with a thud in a grove of trees just outside the community.

I take in a deep breath. Here we go.

Eli gets up first.

Then the back ramp starts to open.

Man, I thought it was hot in the sky, but the Pepps must have some filtering system in the aircraft, because when that door opens the true elements of the land seep in. The hot, humid air hits me like a wall, leaving me gasping for breath. Bugs immediately swarm our space, and I suddenly feel claustrophobic and icky in my clothes.

Following Mark off the aircraft, I squint in the bright sunlight.

I see the trees, and something churns in my gut. From up high, the trees had seemed like such a deep, vibrant color. Standing here so close to them, though, I realize I was wrong. Their color is deep because they're wilting; the leaves are turning brown.

They're dying.

Is this the same phenomenon I witnessed in the GreenLands? Or do the Pepps purposefully avoid this area because of the Mixed Bloods? It's probably the second explanation, which makes me sad. How would it be to live without the pure beauty of nature? To be hidden from such a magnificent earthly mystery.

My eyes land on a woman standing just at the edge of the trees. Her face is familiar. Not that I've ever seen her in person, but I've seen a picture of her, in Eli's cabin. It's Mia. She *is* the woman he used to love.

Her hair is shorter than it was in the image, but it's still dark and wavy, extending almost to her shoulders even though it's pulled back with a black headband. Her eyes are a deep hazel, and her eyelashes are unfairly long and black for someone her age.

Mia sees Eli right away, and, based on her expression, she wasn't expecting him to be the one coming off the aircraft. Her face pales, shifting from shock to anger, to disgust, and back to shock again. One moment

I expect her to walk up and punch Eli in the face. The next moment I expect her to turn and walk away. Eli was wrong to surprise her like this. I'd be angry if it was me.

"Mia." Eli whispers her name into the heavy air, his voice thick with pain. That's what brings Mia out of her shock. The sound of her name. Her expression melts into something new. I catch a glimpse of it, but just for a moment. Hurt. Then after swallowing hard, she straightens her back and sets her jaw.

"Eli." She nods. It's a formal greeting, one that successfully masks the emotions inside. One that causes Eli's shoulders to slump.

"What are you doing here?"

Eli takes in the deepest breath I've ever seen someone take.

"I got the message you sent to Leo."

Leo? Is that the chief's real name? Mia was apparently close enough to Eli to be on a first-name basis with the chief.

Eli turns to our small team. "There are many things I need to tell you, but, first, this is my team."

Eli introduces everyone by name and then reaches Mark and me.

"I'm sure you've heard of Alena and Mark."

Mia's hazel eyes reach mine, and her lips turn down. "Yes, I have. They're part of the reason things are so bad here." Her tone isn't accusing, but it might as well be.

Mia's comment makes Flint snicker. Thankfully, Mark is standing right next to him and punches him in the arm.

"Where *is* Leo?" Mia asks.

Eli takes in another deep breath. "Mia, he's ... sick."

We all stand there, in the blistering heat, listening to Eli fill the woman in on what happened between Jeter and the chief. When he's done, shock returns to her face.

"Leo is dying?"

"Yes," Eli says, "Rusty is taking his place for now as leader until we can come up with a better option."

Eli doesn't bother explaining that he himself is the better option for leader.

"So, *you* decided to respond to my request for help?" None of us miss her icy tone.

Eli sighs. "We were planning a trip down here anyway for a different reason. Then I got your message and decided we could handle everything at once."

"Why were you planning a trip?"

Eli rubs his temple. Things probably aren't going the way he'd hoped. The fatigue I saw so often on the chief's face now crosses his brow. He might as well get everything out.

"We need the help of your people," he finally says.

Mia's eyes flicker between Eli's face and mine. *Can she already guess what kind of help we're asking for?*

After studying us for a moment, she speaks, "Well, there are some things you need to know now before I take you inside. Eli, Aitin and Jeter were here."

Now Eli's face pales. He wasn't expecting that.

Neither was I. My hands start to tremble.

"They told us the truth about our condition. That we're allergic to Peppate, and that Aitin was healed by Alena. Jeter promised the same healing to anyone who chose to go with him."

"How many left?" Eli quickly asks.

"Twenty."

Eli shakes his head in frustration, but I furrow my brows in confusion.

"How could he promise to heal them?" I ask. "He doesn't possess the same black power I used to heal Aitin, does he?"

"That's why there were only twenty that left," Mia says. "Jeter said there was a chance they would experience pain during the process since he had to use his normal power to distribute some sort of serum. But he felt confident that after the procedure they would be able to heal. If he had been able to promise a pain-free transition, I'm sure all of my people would have gone."

I can't help but notice the way she calls the Mixed Bloods *her people*. The statement hits me hard. How would it be to claim an entire social society as "your people" with such confidence of fitting in?

Then my head wraps around what she just told me.

Was he able to do it? Find a way to control the serum with Pepp power? How?

"Is this your urgent matter?" Eli asks, his face growing wearier. "That some of your people left?"

Mia shakes her head, her fists clenching. "Only part of it. Three of those who left were found dead on the far side of the lake. The procedure apparently didn't work for them." Mia lowers her voice. "Eli, my people are angry. They're blaming everything—their condition, their deaths—on the Pepps. They're angry that others knew the truth of their allergy and didn't tell them before. They're angry that a solution to their condition was found and they were not informed. They're angry that Alena has been hiding up in Petrichor while they suffer. And, to be honest, they're not going to be happy that the chief's condition has been withheld. I'm afraid that if I don't get them under control and give them some reason to keep holding on, they'll start going after the Pepps themselves." Mia steps close to Eli, speaking through gritted teeth. "They're already turning on me, Eli. On me."

Eli places a hand on her arm. "They'll never turn on you, Mia. They're just angry. I'm going to help you."

I suddenly understand in the smallest measure why Eli was so afraid of facing Mia. She might be beautiful, but she's a little intimidating. That's probably Eli's fault, but, still. The way she's referenced me during this one conversation has already left me feeling small and insignificant. I can tell she cares a lot about *one* thing: healing her people. If we don't fall in line with that devotion, well, we might as well be dirt.

I guess that's what makes her a good helper for the Mixed Bloods, though. They need someone who understands their sufferings. Someone who fights for them.

If we can get her to agree with our plan, then I have no doubt the Mixed Bloods will follow.

If we can get her to agree with our plan.

Eli straightens his back, and for the first time I sense a little more confidence.

"I'll let you speak with a couple of our leaders," Mia says, taking a step back. "I'll let you see for yourself their discontent."

Then her hazel eyes glide over our, apparently, displeasing group. When they land on Trevor, she frowns deeply. "You'll have to leave the bear here."

Trevor shakes his head in protest, but Eli sends him a withering look. Trevor grunts loudly, not bothering to hide his frustration, but Eli nods his head in the direction of the aircraft, telling him to stay there.

While this is playing out, my head is spinning. *Aitin was here? He's still alive.*

Mia turns to lead us down the path. I want to stay out of her way, but there's something I need to know. I gently grip her arm, stopping her.

She looks at me in confusion.

"I need to know how Aitin looked," I say. "Was he healthy? Did he mention anything about being able to morph successfully?"

Mia pulls her arm away from me. I expected nothing less, but I still need to know the answer, so I lock my eyes with hers, refusing to back down.

After frowning at me for much too long, she finally responds. "Aitin looked healthier than I've seen any Mixed Blood look. He was still having some troubles with his skin and seemed physically weak, but, overall, he was starting to heal. As far as morphing, he promised us it had worked for him. That was one of his selling points. He of course couldn't show us, otherwise he would have killed us, but whatever you did to him must have worked."

"Did he have power?"

Mia eyes me carefully. "He said he had a little. He was still unable to use it though. Said he needed time to learn."

Without another word, she turns back to the pathway, anxious to move on.

"Maracai is this way."

I follow, watching the pathway slip by while my mind works through Mia's words. It worked on him. The serum must be protecting the Peppate generators from the lightning he produces. He can morph without killing himself. *But he has power?* Does that mean he's killed a Pepp?

Who?

If I can just figure out how to heal these people using the serum and Pepp power, we might stand a chance against Aitin.

I turn around to look at Mark. He's close behind me, lost in his own thoughts, and based on the deep furrow of his brow, his thoughts are not pleasant. I'm just grateful Aitin has come and gone. Now, hopefully, he'll just stay away. Mark doesn't need to run into him here.

We walk through the trees until they open up ahead of us, revealing a tall dry rock wall. The wall blocks our view, but I can only guess a community is behind it.

"This is where we live." Mia guides us to a wooden door. "Please stay with me and don't wander. I don't want any of you to get hurt."

Pff. She sounds like Eli. So not *hopeful.*

The door leads us into an open dirt courtyard where dust immediately flies in my face, sticking to my sweaty skin. I wipe at the dirt on my forehead, but it's no use. More quickly replaces it.

Bordering the courtyard are small brown buildings with no windows, just a single wooden door in each, and a small overhang for protection from the sun. Right now, we're the only ones in the lonely courtyard except for two little boys wrapped in loose cloth all the way up their bodies. They're playing kickball. That is until they see us. Then they freeze.

I wish I could see more of their faces. *Are they afraid of us? Angry with us?* All I can see are little bits of their eyes, and they don't tell me much.

"This is our courtyard," Mia explains, ignoring the two boys. "The doors surrounding the area lead to shops where people work in their certain trade to keep this place going. They try to stay inside most of the time because coming outside always seems to worsen their condition. We always figured they were allergic to something, but it wasn't until Aitin visited us that we learned exactly what. I sure wish we would have learned that sooner." Mia frowns at Eli. "Regardless, they've learned what makes them feel better and worse. I would offer to show you their shops, but any Peppate on your skin will rub off and irritate them."

Mia continues around the corner. "When my people aren't in their shops, they're down below in the rocks, where they're the safest. That's where our council room is, where I'm taking you. The entrance is just past our greenhouse. Before we go down there, though, I'll have you all change into some of our clothing. My people are very sensitive to even outside clothes."

That's when I catch a whiff of a something familiar, a smell that immediately makes my gut roil.

It's the same sour, deathly odor I smelled in the prison Aitin kept Mark and me in. At Dakdete. I glance at Mark. *Does he notice it too?* I can't guess by the stoic look on his face, and there's no way I'm bringing it up.

"This is our greenhouse." Mia leads us through a stone archway toward another structure made entirely of green glass. "All the food plants inside are grown with water that sits in the rocks below, outside the natural elements. We learned pretty quickly years ago that the lake water and any water out in the open air makes our people very sick. We experimented with wells below, let rainwater sit for weeks before drinking it, and found it to be better for them. After hearing what Jeter and Aitin said about Peppate being the source of their pain, it all makes sense now. Peppate has to be absorbed by living plants or animals to continue living on. If it isn't absorbed by life within seven days, it dies."

"So you let the water sit for weeks, and then you water these plants with the *clean* water?" Gabbro asks from Danny's shoulder.

"Yes, we have large wells underground that hold our rainwater for seven days before pumping it up here to the greenhouse to water these plants. The plants themselves are also sealed off from the natural elements. We enter the greenhouse from a tunnel below."

I take a peek inside the glass. The plants are unlike any I've ever seen: small, dull, lacking any color.

"They're all brown," Kapri says, obviously making the same observation I did.

Mia is more patient with Kapri than she was with me. "Apparently Peppate is an important element of life. Plants can be grown without it, but only at a cost. They aren't as lush or bountiful as normal plants. The fruit they produce is smaller and harder too, but it's better than nothing. The vegetation that seems to do the best without Peppate is what grows underground: potatoes, radishes, carrots—that sort of thing."

I shake my head. *What a process just to get some food for these people.*

I'm still shaking my head, when I see a reflection in the glass. A man who steps up next to Mia.

The man looks terrifyingly familiar.

That's when every cell in my body freezes.

Aitin.

Chapter 6

Everything is a blur. One moment I'm slowly turning around to face the man, and the next moment I'm being shoved aside by Eli. When I get to my feet again, I see that Mark has the man pinned against the greenhouse, his hand gripping his throat tightly.

"Mark!" Eli and Danny are there beside Mark, trying to pry him off.

I just stand there frozen.

The man is terrifying. His scarred skin is splotchy and rough, his hair pretty much gone, and his eyes watery, swollen, and gray. If it wasn't for the mole on his right cheek, I would swear this man was Aitin. But it's not.

Seeing someone who so closely resembles that man has me fighting off panic.

And apparently Mark is having the same reaction.

"What is going on?" Mia shouts.

When Eli finally extracts Mark from the man, Mark's eyes clear. It's almost exactly the same thing that happened with me the other night, how Mark was taken back, stuck in a memory. This time, I was taken back too.

"What the hell is going on, Mia?" the man shouts, spittle flying from his mouth. "Did you really allow Pepps in here? To attack us?"

Mia ignores the man's question and shoots an intense look at Eli, demanding an explanation.

Eli doesn't have time to respond before Mark releases his grip and takes off in the direction we came.

I hesitate for only a moment before following him. I wish I was further away when Mia decides to speak.

"You brought an *unstable* man with you?"

I sure hope Mark didn't hear that.

I push myself to a slow jog well behind Mark, running through the wild bushes and growth. If I catch up to him, he'll just insist I leave him alone anyway. He's embarrassed. Heck, I'm embarrassed. And scared. My brain was totally irrational back there.

Finally, when we've almost reached the aircraft, I call out to him.

"Mark?"

Thankfully, he slows and then stops.

Huffing, I reach his side. It's hard to resist the urge to touch him, to pull him to me.

Instead, I just say, "I thought it was Aitin too, Mark." I breathe deeply trying to catch my breath. "I don't think it was a good idea for either of us to come here."

I search his face, wondering what I should do next.

Mark just stares at the ground and swallows. I'm surprised when he does actually speak.

"The smell," he whispers.

So he did smell the same thing I did, and it's affected him more than he let on. It doesn't help that the smell still sits heavily in the humid air, even from this distance.

"I know. It's exactly like Dakdete."

Mark shakes his head and closes his eyes as if attempting to get away from it all.

"Here, let's get back on the aircraft. Maybe if we can figure out how to close the hatch, it won't be as noticeable."

I'm guiding Mark up the ramp when Eli runs up behind us, heaving.

"Alena ... I need you to come with me. I can't do this without your help."

I take in a deep agonizing breath. I don't want to go back. I can't heal the Mixed Bloods anyway. This was all a stupid idea.

When Eli pulls on my arm, I rip it away and grit my teeth.

"I'm staying here with Mark."

"No you're not!" He practically shouts in my face. "You are the link between these people and hope. It's the reason I brought you. You *have* to come with me," Eli's eyes burn with a fire I've never seen on him before.

I hate it. But he's right. Nobody else can do what I've done.

"Fine." I grind out the word before turning to Mark. "I'll be back soon." He's staring into nothingness.

Blast it, he's lost! The last thing he needs right now is to be alone.

Before I leave, I tell Trevor to keep an eye on him. Make sure he stays safe.

Then I stomp back to the sickly community with Eli. Mia is standing there stiffly where we left her, holding out an outfit of gray clothing to me. I don't dare look at the scary-looking man standing at her side.

"Change into these."

Guiding me into a dark side room made of nothing but musky dirt and rock, she lets me pull on the scratchy clothes before taking our little group to the black smelly tunnel entrance.

"Here's what's going to happen," she says, still angry. I resist the urge to cover my nose with my sleeve.

"Eli, you will explain what's going on with the chief, and then you will tell them what you plan to do. Allowing them to see Alena and hear that you're working to find a cure may give them hope, but you have to understand that they've been promised too many things by the chief that have never come to fruition. Many of them knew Aitin personally. They saw his own mother die here and saw Aitin leave with Jose. Most of them don't have any hope left. Be careful down there."

Mia's eyes send us all a silent warning before entering the tunnel after the Mixed Blood man. I follow after Eli, feeling the hard dirt beneath my feet turn soft. I wish Mark was here, but at the same time I'm grateful he's not. The stench of death is getting stronger.

The air grows colder and wetter the lower we get, and the walls turn to rock. These tunnels aren't nearly as smooth as those in Petrichor. They look like they've been carved by hand, not by power. Several small torches try to light the way, but their fire doesn't seem like it could ever burn brightly enough.

Soon the tunnel leads into a large dark cavern ineffectively lit by more torches.

A few other men and women trickle into the room after us, their faces a mixture of physical pain, anger, and confusion when they see Eli.

Mia guides us to the circle of chairs sitting in the middle of the room and indicates that we should all sit.

I count everyone when Eli clears his throat. Ten Mixed Bloods. Six men and four women. At least I think four women. It's hard for me to tell since everyone's hair is missing, and their skin is all scarred. Even their voices have the same low croaky tone. The biggest difference I can see is the bone structure of their faces. The women are slightly slenderer. And their body shapes are different.

Eli introduces himself and begins explaining the events from the past few months. I find myself surprised at his knowledge and ability to demand everyone's attention. He almost seems like a ... leader.

While he explains things, I observe the faces of the Mixed Bloods, measure their responses. Man, are they easy to measure. Their resistance and hate is potent.

The closer Eli gets to asking for their help, the more I find myself gripping my seat.

"Ultimately, from the information we've gathered, we have reason to believe Aitin is planning to destroy the Pepps. To eradicate Peppate altogether," Eli finishes.

I hear several whispers echo off the rocks.

"At least he's doing something about the Peppate."

"It's about time Peppate disappears."

Eli doesn't rebuke their comments but listens to them until a small woman in the group asks, "So, what is it that you want?" The question is a challenge. Aitin has presented his plan, and it's tempting for them. We have to present something better.

Eli looks to me, but his gaze is sad and defeated as if he just now realizes we can't compete with Aitin. If only we could provide pain-free healing.

"You want us to fight him," someone states.

The room silences, and everyone's gaze slides to me.

"Did you come to heal us?" a woman asks. There is too much hope in her voice. Before I can dash it, someone else answers for me.

"Of course not. She can't heal us any more than Jeter can—not without making us sick. Can you? Aitin told us you used all the good power on him."

My shoulders sag. They've been through too much to accept the offer I can give them. I slowly shake my head. "I'm sorry. The power I used on Aitin is gone. If I am to heal you, I would have to do it using Pepp power."

Angry scoffs and mutters weave their way through the group.

"Aitin was right," someone says. I furrow my eyebrows, trying to figure out who said it. Man, I wish it was easier to tell these people apart. "He said you'd end up coming here. He said you'd come looking for a way to redeem yourself. Well, you can't, unless you heal us with black power."

His growl hurts me more than anyone could possibly know. *How dare he say that about me.* That's not why I came here. Is it?

"So, you can't offer us any more than Jeter could," someone else says.

"Oh, she could offer us more." A loud voice speaks above the rest. Everyone turns to a young bald, pale man who's been quiet until now. He leans forward in his chair, resting his scabby arms on his knees. "She and Mark could morph. They could produce the power needed to do the procedure without causing pain. But they *won't.*"

Eli speaks up. "Not at the expense of lives."

A cruel smile spreads across his face. "Not at the expense of *Pepp* lives. In my opinion that's a small price to pay, especially since this is a problem you caused."

I don't like where this is going.

Flint and Danny straighten up beside me in a protective stance. For a split second I notice that Flint is clenching his fists, his red hair dark in the poor lighting. He's not looking at anything in particular but is probably preparing himself for a fight.

"Where is Mark, by the way? He came with you, did he not? I hear you two are inseparable. At least you were until you injected Mark with that serum."

I gawk at the man. *How much did Aitin tell them?* The man's wicked smile grows, showing several missing teeth. Deep down inside I know I shouldn't let him get under my skin.

Shouldn't.

"You know what I say?" he says. "I say we keep Alena and Mark here and *force* them to morph. It won't take long. And think of all the good they could do."

"Sayo." Mia's warning voice rings out loud and clear.

The man's cruel expression melts into a snarl, and he jumps to his feet. "She's right here! The answer to all our problems, and you want to ... what? Just let her go? The solution is simple, and, yes, maybe it'll take some Pepp lives, but think of all the lives that would be saved!"

Several other people mutter in agreement. I grip my hands together, sensing the loss of control this group is about to exhibit.

"What if we could find another way?" Eli shouts.

Sayo's face turns bright red. "Case has tried! He spent years experimenting, and this is what he came up with. There *is* no other way."

Case. If there's anyone who knows the totem and its capabilities, it's Case. The wheels in my head start turning, remembering my conversation with Sepharine.

Now everyone is on their feet, except me. There's so much shouting it's difficult to follow.

"Two weeks," I say, staring at the floor. My voice isn't loud, but somehow I've gotten their attention.

Sayo stops and slowly turns his head. "Two weeks for what?"

"Give me two weeks to look for another solution."

Eli eyes me care carefully, probably wondering why I would say such a thing.

"What makes you think you can find a solution that hasn't already been found? Even if we do give you time, what if you don't find anything? Are you willing to morph? To gain power?" Sayo spits as he speaks. "Perhaps there's a weak Pepp you're willing to sacrifice. Or maybe even an enemy within your own people you're dying to be rid of." Sayo stares at me when he says this, as if he knows I have many enemies within the Pepp community.

"Give us two weeks, and then we'll consider what you've said," Eli says. He's trusting me without even knowing my plan.

Sayo shakes his head, "*Consider?* No, we need a promise. A promise that Alena will come back, and that she and Mark will do what it takes to get this done."

I don't really know what to say to that.

Everyone stares at Eli, including me. Can he satiate the man? Eli's quiet, thinking. Then finally he speaks.

"The chief. The chief is incapacitated." His sad eyes meet mine. "He's likely never going to recover."

My heart sinks when I realize what he's saying. No! *The chief might be dying, but that doesn't mean it's right to kill him! I* won't *kill him for the sake of creating black power!*

Eli ignores my look of horror and turns to the Mixed bloods. "Is that enough of a promise? That Alena and Mark will morph and create your precious power using the chief's life?"

Sayo finally steps back. "Maybe. We don't know how far that power will stretch, but it's a start," he says. "In the meantime, we'll keep Mark here. Give Alena a little incentive to speed things up and come back."

I'm ready to pounce on the man for suggesting anything of the sort, but Eli is already on him.

"No," Eli responds calmly. "Mark needs to help Alena. *I* will stay here."

Sayo is irritated with this offer, but then he seems to come to an agreement in his nasty little head. "Make it one week. If you don't return, Alena, I promise that I will kill Eli myself."

The way he says those words, the way his face reeks of hatred, leaves no doubt in my mind that he will follow through.

"You've got a deal," Eli says. "As long as you promise us that when you're healed, you will help us protect Petrichor. Even if that means killing one of your own. One of those Aitin has recruited, no questions asked."

Sayo looks around the group. Each Mixed Blood nods their head at him.

A woman speaks up softly. "Eli, if Alena heals us, we'll do anything you ask."

With that answer, Eli waves his hand, indicating the meeting is over and leaves the room. I eye Mia, who stands and tips her head, hinting we should follow him.

Eli is standing in the tunnel waiting for us. When we approach him, he speaks to Mia. "Is there a place we can talk together privately?"

Mia confidently leads us through the tunnels again. Murmurs and shouts rise behind us from the group, but I don't look back. The ground begins to slope upward again, and soon we're outside. Mia leads us further, to a door in one of the strange buildings. Opening it up, she guides us in.

The room is covered in stone, brown and dead, like the rest of this place. Even in my frustration and worry, though, I can't help but notice the one thing that isn't brown or dead. A small plant sitting by the window in a glass case. It's the only green life I've seen since we entered the community. For the first time, I realize what Mia has sacrificed to live here and help the Mixed Bloods. She must miss the vibrancy of normal life. Life with Peppate.

The tension in the small crammed room builds, when Eli turns to me. "What's your plan, Alena?"

I open my mouth. "I want to go find Case."

Confusion wars across Eli's face. "What? That's your plan?"

"If there's anyone who knows the abilities of our totem, it's Case. He might know of another way to get around this."

Flint speaks up. "We've searched for Case, Alena. Nobody can find him."

I nod but then add, "I don't think we've been looking in the right places."

Eli shakes his head, still not understanding.

"Eli, don't you remember what you said about Mixed Bloods when we were trying to find Jax and Danny? You said that if you were a Mixed Blood, 'You'd get the hell away from plants.' We know now that it's not plants they're allergic to but Peppate. But the concept is the same. Lilly, Case's girl, was a Mixed Blood. I think that when he found her that day at SilverDen, he took her away to a place where Peppate isn't spread. I think he took her to one of the deserts. Jax said that when Case was creating the totem, while Lilly was being hidden from him, Case left for days at a time and came back with sand in his boots. I think Case was creating a hideout."

"A hideout," Eli says.

"Aren't there many places that would fall into that category?" Flint says in irritation.

Eli shakes his head. "Not necessarily. Dakdete was where Aitin and Jax hid, but I think Case would be stupid to make his hideout there. It would be too close."

Kapri chimes in now, her usually tamed golden curls frizzy in the humidity. "That leaves only two other places."

"The two deserts, Kalahaki and Namib," Gabbro says.

The room is quiet. Does that narrow our search down enough? Based on the falling looks on everyone's faces, it doesn't. I don't know how big one desert is, but it sounds overwhelming to search it completely.

"It's a start at least," Eli says. "Case's first lab was in his old home, which is on the way to the deserts. Why don't you go there? See if you can find some of the sand Jax was talking about. See if you can identify it. Maybe it will lead you to one of the deserts."

At first that seems pointless in my mind. All sand looks the same, doesn't it? But then I remember the sands of Dakdete, the deep-red color. The sands could very well be different enough to give us a good lead.

"And what if they don't find Case?" Mia interjects softly, stepping to Eli's side. "Are you really willing to offer up the life of your brother for this?"

Eli's eyes sadden. I speak up before he can respond. "I'm not."

"Then let's hope you find Case. For all our sakes," Eli murmurs.

"I had a thought," Mia says. We all stare at her.

"What if Alena and Mark were given a totem from the totem tree, one that's *not* attached to a Pepp. What if they took it to a place without people and morphed. Would that work? Produce the power we need?"

I stand, dumbfounded. *Why didn't we think of that before? Surely that would work, right?*

A smile pulls at Eli's lips, and without warning he takes Mia into his arms. "I've missed you," he whispers. I watch as the strong, confident, smart woman melts into Eli's embrace.

"While you're searching the deserts, Alena," Eli says, "I'll send a message to Rusty. See if I can convince him to send down a totem or two. If you guys don't find Case quickly, just come back."

The window in the room darkens, and Mia pulls away from Eli to look outside. "You guys should probably go. It looks like there's a storm coming. I need to get everyone down below. I'll take you to your flyer."

***

Mark is sitting in the aircraft staring at the wall when we get back. One shake of Trevor's head tells me I shouldn't disturb him.

So I sit down a couple seats away.

We all wave good-bye to Eli, then I lean back, gripping my seat.

Danny gives Flint directions before sitting. I realize just now that Case's old home is Danny's old home too.

Oh dear. *How's this going to go?*

Needing a distraction, I take this time to write a letter to Rusty and Cody back in Petrichor. I need to let them know what's going on.

Then I ask Kapri if I can borrow her Magbaby since I don't want to disturb Mark and I'm not ready to bug Gabbro. I hold Kapri's Magbaby in my hands after placing the message inside, ready to flip the switch when we arrive at Case's old home. Seeing the Magbaby causes my worries about Breccia to surface. *Will I ever get her back*? Is she okay?

It's been weeks since I sent her to deliver a message to Mark in Petrichor when I was on the dropdown with Rusty. I thought Danny's memories were being hidden in Lake Wintriness. Mark went to Wintriness and found the memory bugs, but then took those bugs to Jeter, the only one able to command them. Jeter took Mark, the memory bugs ... and Breccia. I never got her back.

Mark, doesn't say anything during the flight, and I hate that the icky barrier between us is back. Trying to break it a little, I scoot closer to him. I want him to at least know I'm here. Then I brace myself for what could happen, trying to hope for some sort of miracle.

Chapter 7

Case's old home is not close enough. After an hour of flying in silence, my mind is heavy with worry.

I bite my lip. We're hoping Case has more answers, but even *if* we do find Case, will he really be able to help, or will he just end up telling us what we already think? That a Pepp, with the totem on them, has to die in order to create the black power.

The more I think about Mia's idea, the more my belief in it wavers. If zapping a detached totem is all it takes to create the black power, then why didn't Case do that at SilverDen instead of tie Cody to a stump? Does a Pepp really have to die?

Why in the world did Eli gamble the chief's life like that?

I look over at Mark. *Will he be willing to do what Eli is asking?* I want to talk to him, tell him what we decided, see what his opinion is, but his expression is still dark.

I close my eyes instead and lean my head back. The words of the angry Mixed Bloods instantly flood my mind. I replay the meeting over and over again, the way everyone in the room had openly displayed their distaste for us.

No, for *me.*

As much as I hate to admit it, that one man was partly right. I *did* hope to find some acceptance there among the Mixed Bloods. I hoped that because of what I did to Aitin I would have somehow earned their respect.

I frown. Based on their reactions, though, that was a stupid thing to hope for. The only way I'll ever earn anything from them is if I do to them what I did to Aitin. Even then, it'll be my totem they appreciate. Not me. *I* mean nothing to them.

I sink further into my seat, keeping my head down, trying to hold back the sudden onslaught of emotions flowing through me.

When Flint announces that we're here, I'm not even remotely ready to face anything. Unfortunately, I don't have a choice.

The aircraft thuds violently, but one look out the window tells me we haven't actually landed yet. I hold on to my seat. Apparently, there's not much area here for the aircraft to land, so Flint sits it on top of the trees. I watch the trees slowly bend and bow, their branches scraping against the metal, until the aircraft has somehow shuffled to the ground.

We finally land, and the back hatch opens. I flip the switch on Kapri's Magbaby and let her go, then look around at our group. Danny, Kapri, Trevor, Flint, Mark, and me. Obviously we're capable on our own. We got here okay, but without Eli here, I feel more nervous, more exposed.

I glance at Mark. He doesn't meet my eyes, but he's ready to get out of the aircraft, so I stand as well and follow Kapri out into more hot, humid air. Flies immediately swarm us, pecking at my mood. I swat at them impatiently while looking at the white mansion in front of us in the bright sunlight.

It's beautiful, at least two stories high with three large pillars in the front, and dark-gray shutters around the many windows. Based on the large yard and bushes out front I would guess that this was once a magnificent home. It could probably be magnificent again with a lot of help, like trimming the weeds in the yard and washing the mold off the walls.

Walking through the tall grass, we follow Danny to the front porch. He seems hesitant, and I don't blame him. He's about to see his childhood home for the first time in years. Trevor too. The last time they were here, things didn't go so well.

When Danny steps onto the creaky wooden porch, he stops, takes in a deep breath, and then opens the front door.

I peek around him to find the inside hot, dark, and moldy. Danny doesn't move.

Thankfully, Kapri takes charge of our sullen group.

"Let's split up," she says. "Look for anything that might lead us to Case."

"Case." I hear Mark whisper the name and find him observing the house. He doesn't ask any questions, which must mean he's probably figured out what we're doing here, right?

Trevor makes his way to Danny and pounds him on the back before practically pushing him through the door. Danny reluctantly walks in, immediately stopping in a room on the right. Trevor continues on to other rooms, his footsteps shaking the wooden floors.

When I enter the house, I see why Danny went to the right. It's the music room, with a large grand piano resting in the middle. It's dusty, but Danny doesn't seem to care. He slowly sits on the black bench and opens the fallboard, exposing smooth ivory keys. He runs his fingers over them, tapping one here and there. Then he slouches somberly. *Is he okay? Should I go sit with him?*

Kapri moves past me into the room, and I back away. She's right. Danny needs *her*.

I turn and slowly move through the rest of the house. *Where did Mark go?*

The large sitting room on the left is empty. I look down the hall to find a staircase leading both upstairs and downstairs. Past the stairs I spot the remains of a kitchen.

I don't really know where to start, so I wander around. The soft notes of a composed melody eventually drift down the halls from the piano, telling their own sad story of what once was and what has now become.

I observe the old pictures on the walls. Most of them are of the three young boys and their father. There is only one picture with a woman in it, and she's holding two boys. I'm guessing they're Case and Trevor. The chief told me once that their mother died while delivering Danny. Danny never knew her.

I pick up pieces of paper here and there, search through old moldy books, and eventually find myself wandering upstairs. There are several bedrooms up here, one that has a large bed with posts, a writing desk, and its own bathing tub. Others are simpler with only a bed for sleeping. But the one that captures my attention has two twin-size beds in it, a soccer ball, several baseball bats, and two closets full of boy clothes.

I run my fingers over the dusty shirts before my eyes wander to the shelves on the wall filled with old photographs of Trevor and Danny. This must have been their room.

I'm staring at the pictures when Gabbro hums his way through the door. He sits on my shoulder to look at the same photos.

"Trevor always took care of Danny," he says. "Danny was young when Aitin came to live here. I don't think he ever really knew what dark things were going on in this home, and that's mainly because of Trevor. Jose was so consumed with his work that he'd lost his ability to father. He almost had to in order to get the research done. Case followed in his footsteps. He was always right there beside Jose. I don't think he worked hard to learn what Jose knew but rather to come up with a way to end the torture. He hated that Aitin was in so much pain. He even intervened when he felt he could." Gabbro shakes his head. "But Trevor knew that this home was not where a young boy should be raised. Especially with all the screaming. Danny sometimes hated being dragged out of the house to go play in the woods, but Trevor knew what was best for the boy. *He* was like a father to him."

Gabbro looks at me. "He's almost like a father to everyone. Constantly watching out for others, especially little ones. Keeping them safe. For a boy who had very little parental guidance growing up, he has a pretty darn good internal compass. We could use a few more people like him in this world."

I recall seeing Trevor play in the Burrows with the children. He seemed so free there. So happy.

"What did Trevor match in?" I ask.

"He's a morpher, obviously," Gabbro says.

I roll my eyes. "Of course. But did he match in anything else? Some Pepps have more than one job."

Gabbro shakes his head. "No, he didn't."

I turn back to the pictures. I wonder if he'll obtain another job one day. Officially become some sort of guardian or protector. Maybe a father.

When I don't find anything else in this room, I head back downstairs, then round the corner to the basement entrance.

"I'm going to stay up here," Gabbro says when he sees where I'm going. "I don't have the greatest memories of that place."

"Wait." I pause, just now internalizing what he'd said upstairs. "You were here when Aitin was being tortured? How is that possible? I thought you were Trevor's Magbaby. He wouldn't have gotten you until after he left this place to live in Petrichor. After Jose died. After the torturing stopped."

Gabbro cringes. "I'm sorry, Alena. That was another lie. I wasn't Trevor's Magbaby. I was Jose's. He used me to communicate things going on here back to the chief."

Hmph. *Gabbro was Jose's Magbaby.* I guess that makes sense.

"Okay." I sigh, not wanting to let this bother me.

"Good luck down there," Gabbro says, backing away.

"Thanks," I mutter.

The stairs squeak when I descend, and chills run up my spine. It's as if my body can sense the disturbing things done down here.

When I reach the concrete floor at the bottom, I find two doors. One on my left and one on my right.

I open the door on the left. The room is dark, no windows, stone walls, and a cot pushed into the corner.

I freeze.

I know this room. I saw it in Aitin's memory that was placed inside my head while he kept me prisoner in Dakdete.

I shiver, hating the thought of memory bugs in my head.

If this is the room where Aitin slept, then ... I turn around to the room on the right. That's the *torture* room. I already know what it looks like. Closing my eyes, I take in a deep breath and push the heavy metal door open.

Mark is in here.

The windowless room smells strongly of mold, rodent droppings, and decay. I bury my nose in the crook of my elbow when I walk in.

Unlike the rest of the rooms in the house, this one is a mess. Papers and broken glass cover the floor as if someone has already been here searching for something. Sharp tools scattered across the counter glitter in the flickering light of the candle Mark has lit. I observe the cot in the corner. Old blood stains the yellowed linens. I turn away and move next to Mark.

My eyes are drawn to two pots sitting on the edge of the counter. Planted in the soil of each is a small dry branch that strongly resembles something in Petrichor—the totem tree.

Is this how Case created our totems? I reach out to touch the tip of one, but Mark's arm blocks me.

"It could attach to you." I stare at his hand touching mine, then bring my eyes to his face, grateful he's talking to me again.

"They look dead," I whisper.

Mark still shakes his head. "We don't know anything about them."

He's right of course, but if these are the totem trees Case worked so hard to create, why didn't he take them with him? Did they die after he extracted the totems? Probably.

I wonder which one created the totem on Mark and me and which one created the totem shared by Danny and Trevor. It was probably a taxing process creating them. Case probably just didn't have enough in him to keep going. Instead, he focused on trying to collect Mark and me, the totem he knew worked.

My eyes move up the wall in front of us. It's crowded with all sorts of pinned papers and pictures mapped together with string. It's the layout of Case's plans, creating the totem, collecting Mark. There's even a detailed diagram of SilverDen's construction.

Then I follow some strings that lead to a picture of me. My skin crawls, seeing my face eerily posted on this wall. Next to my picture are pictures of Danny, Cody, and Mark.

And beneath my photo is a small note.

Weak. Cares too much about what other people think.

Make her believe she's an outcast, then when she decides to leave Petrichor, collect.

My face flushes, and I grit my teeth. I felt hurt before, knowing that Case had played me. But seeing it here on the wall as plain as day cuts me to the core. It's true. Everything they wrote is true. What hurts worse is they didn't make me *believe* I'm an outcast in Petrichor; I *am* and *always will be* an outcast in Petrichor. And they used it to their advantage.

I clench my fists and fight back tears. They took my weaknesses and wove them right into their brilliant plan. It feels as if they've not only stabbed me in the back but continue to twist the blade over and over again.

I rub my nose in irritation. It's not just the Pepps I don't fit in with either. Images of the stupid Mixed Bloods come back to my mind, slamming me with the painful dark truth.

I'll never fit in. Not with the Pepps. Not with the Mixed Bloods. Not with humans. I'll. Never. Fit. In.

Tears spring to my eyes. I don't want to be here anymore, so I turn to leave.

Before I get very far, though, Mark grabs my arm and pulls me into his chest. With one hand, he rips my picture and the label off the wall, crumples them, and throws them across the room.

My chin trembles at his touch, at his concern. Even though he's drowning in his own troubles, he's still aware of me and mine. I shouldn't let him worry himself over me. I should insist that I'm okay for his sake, but I grip his shirt just for a moment.

It's while Mark holds my shaking body that I realize Case's words aren't entirely true. I might not fit in with everyone, but I did find *some* friends in Petrichor. Mark. Danny. Kapri. Cody and Rusty. They've made me feel as if I'm a part of something. I never really wanted to leave because I wanted to be with them. I tighten my arms around Mark.

Case's plan also didn't go as planned, and it was because of my same weaknesses. I do care about others, not just about what they think of me but about *them*. I cared enough about Lilly to help her out of SilverDen. Freeing her led Case to leave Aitin and allowed Mark and me to get away. No, I'm not as worthless as Aitin might think.

I take in a deep breath, feeling my tears slow. The conversation I had with Sepharine pops into my mind. She told me I would have moments of doubt, moments when I would forget the truth. She told me that in these moments I had to fight. To remember that I'm not worthless no matter how forsaken I feel.

I choose to remember the truth.

I breathe in Mark's scent.

"You okay?" His voice rumbles through his chest.

"Yes. Thank you," I say, then add, "Sorry I'm such a baby."

This has the effect I hoped it would. Mark chuckles that very attractive chuckle.

"I'm not sorry. You're a beautiful baby."

I pull away enough to look up at him. *Does he know he can be a baby too?* That it's okay if he cries? I hope so.

"Did you find anything?" I ask.

"Only this," Mark whispers, reaching around me, still holding me tightly in his arm. Grabbing an old leather-bound book from the counter, he brings it to my hand. "It looks like an old journal of Case's."

I release my hold on Mark and turn, taking the book. Mark reads over my shoulder, his chest warm and distracting against my back.

I open the book. He's right. It's a journal dating back several years.

I search through it until I find an entry that intrigues me.

New Patient Case

June 23, 2006

Subject: 17-year-old female found in the trees just outside our home. She says she's from the copper mines. She ran away from her stepfather, Mateo, after she found her mother beaten to death by him. She traveled over a hundred miles on foot through the forests. I found her almost dead. She doesn't know what's wrong with her and says she's never been this sick, although she did get some skin blisters at home and occasionally had severe stomach pain after eating—when she did get to eat. The only place she ever felt well was when she was in the mine. That makes sense. She was away from the element.

Condition: Critical. She's lucky she survived.

Skin: The usual skin blisters have become infected and are now gangrenous. Many on her left leg reach down to the bone. If they don't heal, she might lose the limb.

Respiratory: Lungs are severely inflamed, resulting in wheezing and coughing. She's barely able to talk.

Eyes: The whites of her eyes are red, and her conjunctiva are swollen and tearing constantly.

Nasal: Severe congestion in sinuses, possibly infected from long-term inflammation.

Gastrointestinal: She keeps grabbing at her stomach as if she's in pain internally. She refuses to eat.

Observation: There's no question: she's a mixed child.

Side Note: Aside from the usual symptoms, her nasal septum is slightly deviated. She has several broken ribs. When I asked her about it, she avoided the question. She's also severely malnourished and thin. These are possibly the effects of abuse and neglect, maybe from her stepfather.

Bastard.

I set her nose as best as I could and wrapped her torso.

The safe house in our basement would be the best place for her to heal, but that would mean telling Jose about her, which I can't do. Not even for the sake of research. I don't want him to hurt her. Instead, I've put her in the shed outside. With its wooden walls, it's not an ideal place to keep her from Peppate, but it'll have to do for now.

Follow up: I've cleaned her wounds every day for the past three days with the purified water and given her purified food to eat. I've warned her to stay inside and out of sight. Not that she would be able to leave the shed. She's still too weak. In the meantime I've started building a small place for her to stay, further in the woods. Rock and concrete with a few glass windows should be okay. Keeping it airtight so Peppate can't enter is almost impossible. If I can keep at least most of the inside Peppate-free, then she'll be better off than she is now.

Her name is Lilly.

August 14, 2006

Patient's condition is improving.

Skin: The gangrene on her skin is starting to heal. No new blisters that I can see.

Respiratory: Using gloved hands, I listened to her lungs and heart. They're clearer. Her breathing is not as strained. Even her voice is softer. It's quite beautiful, actually.

Eyes: Her sclera is now white instead of red and no longer watery.

Nasal Sinuses: Clear

Observation: Patient condition improving.

Plan: Continue purified food and water treatment. Continue to keep her contained within the shed, away from Jose and my family. New home for her is almost finished.

Also, need to find her things to do, books maybe, and art supplies. She says she likes to paint. I wish Mom was still alive. She'd be able to help me find some pretty clothes for her.

November 2, 2006

New rock home is finished, and Lilly is living inside. She's better physically, but I think she's lonely. I ate lunch with her today. Or tried to. I tried to take special care not to touch her, as I was not purified. But sitting next to her, my hand accidentally brushed against the skin of her arm.

I asked her if her skin hurt, but she denied anything. I tried to keep track of time.

It took one minute for her skin to turn red and then an additional minute before she had full-on blisters.

Sensitivity: High. This is almost as severe as Aitin's sensitivity, which means repeated physical exposure to an unpurified being for more than thirty minutes means severe skin wounds.

I left immediately. It was irresponsible for me to interact with her so closely.

January 30, 2007

Out of necessity, I've stayed away from Lilly. She's been angry, I think, even though I thoroughly explained why I couldn't come see her.

I don't like her being angry with me. So, I've been purifying myself, and today I finished the process. My reason for staying in the cellar for three days was not easy to justify to Jose, or to Jax, who's been making more frequent visits. But Lilly needs someone to talk to. I put on the safety suit, left the purification cellar when Dad was busy, and took her some lunch. It took her a minute to warm up to me again, but as soon as I took off the suit and sat on the floor with the food, she joined me. When I asked if I could touch her hand again, to test the effectiveness of the purification process, she willingly let me.

Observation: My touch didn't hurt her this time. No skin blisters, not even any redness. I think I was happier than she was to see that. I even kissed her. Probably shouldn't have, but there was no response to that either. Well, no skin response.

When I left she was in better spirits than I've ever seen her.

March, 13, 2007

Lilly was *doing well, but the past few days she's been having internal pain. She's tried hiding it from me, but it's getting terribly worse, which doesn't make sense. I've kept myself purified for the past several weeks. I wear the suit through the woods to keep myself from absorbing any of the Peppate on the way to her little home. She even promises me that she hasn't been outside, but she's still sick.*

Findings: Her sickness is unusual. Her skin and eyes seem to be fine, no blisters or tearing, but her insides are flared up. She can't eat, and when she does eat she throws up. Her breathing has also become harsh again.

It's almost as though Peppate is coming from inside her. This is an idea Jose has entertained a couple of times, but it's been difficult to prove with

Aitin. Perhaps it has something to do with how happy they are? If they truly can produce Peppate inside, does it only happen when circumstances around them make them happy? Lilly lives in much better circumstances than Aitin. Perhaps he doesn't produce it so much because he's being tortured.

Plan: ... I don't know.

April 27, 2007

After my finding with Lilly, I took my ideas to Jose. He experimented on Aitin.

Control: All torture was stopped on Aitin. His body recovered internally and externally. Then we allowed him to go outside in the protective suit and play soccer. Jax is the only one he agreed to play with—thankfully he was here. He played outside every day for one week.

Findings: The first couple of days Aitin seemed to be in a better mood, but by day four, Aitin couldn't go outside because his stomach was in pain. He started throwing up, and then his lungs became distressed. This is the exact same reaction as Lilly. Jose tested Peppate levels within Aitin and found them to be high.

Our hypothesis is true: The Mixed Bloods produce Peppate. They're allergic... to themselves.

The defeat in Jose's face mirrors how I feel, especially now that Lilly is here. There's no cure for the Mixed Bloods. Even if they are kept away from outside elements, they'll never escape what is produced inside them. Jose's attempts at creating an anti-allergen have also fallen short. They aren't strong enough. Jose hasn't told Aitin or Jax the truth about the Mixed Bloods' bodies, nor do I blame him. The only consolation we've ever been able to provide Aitin through the torture all these years is that someday we will find the cure for his disease. I fear what he'll do if he finds out there is no cure.

Jose has notified the chief to let him know the findings. After years of research, this is a low blow.

As a side note: Danny found out about Lilly by following me into the woods. I swore him to secrecy, promising to wreck his beloved piano if he breathed a word to Dad. He promised he wouldn't talk and admitted to only wanting to be her friend from a distance. Perhaps that would be good for her.

June, 12, 2007

Jose is dead.

He was bitten by a snake, of all things, after living in this snake-infested part of the land all his life. I still can't quite wrap my head around it. I didn't get a chance to say good-bye, which I never thought would be a disappointment to me, considering how much we fought and disagreed on about the research of Aitin's condition. His methods of finding out the truth will never resonate with me.

But even though he never did right by Aitin, he's always been an incredible father, especially considering he's been on his own for so long. He was also the most intelligent man I've ever met. Everything I've learned, I've learned from him.

After notifying the chief of his death, the chief came to get Danny and Trevor. They've decided to go back to Petrichor to live with the Pepps like Jose used to. I chose to stay here, convincing the chief that I can further Jose's research best from here, which is true. But I really can't leave Lilly. Or Aitin.

I've brought Lilly inside the house to live with me, now that it's empty. Well, almost empty. Aitin still lives here, and Jax visits occasionally. Aitin wants the chief to believe he's dead. I don't think he liked the man much and hated that the experiments involving him were under the constant watch of the Pepps. On the flip side, Lilly doesn't seem to like Aitin or Jax too much. She even thinks Aitin had a hand in Jose's death. So does Jose's old Magbaby, Gabbro. I've asked Aitin about it, but he denies it. I sure hope he didn't kill my dad.

Unfortunately, Aitin and Jax know about the outcome of our research. I found them in my lab, and to say they were angry is an understatement. But Aitin says he'll forgive me for not telling him as long as I agree to let him help me with the research. So I've explained everything to him: that he has generators just like the Pepps do, that produce Peppate. He also seems to have Doler generators attached to them with a separate mysterious power sac. This sac is unique from my observation, as it is not attached to the Peppate generator, like Pepps, but attached to the Doler generator.

Which has raised some new questions. What if his unique Doler generators produce a different type of power? It's a long shot, but I have to experiment with this. I still have extra totems from the chief, and I wonder if I could purify the totem, extract the Doler generators with power sacs from Aitin's vessels, place them within the totem like they do in Petrichor, and ultimately create a Peppate-free totem that can create a Peppate-free power? If I can do that, perhaps whoever hosts the totem can use the Peppate-free power to somehow disable the Peppate generators within Aitin and Lilly.

January, 19, 2008

The process of purifying the totem and extracting Aitin's generators has been very tedious and painful. Aitin has become quite pushy with the work, and I'm beginning to wonder if Lilly is right about his character. Sometimes he feels a little dangerous, but I can't really blame him. After all, his whole life has been shadowed by pain. I would probably be acting the same way if I was him. But after months of work, I finally finished the totem. Unfortunately, when I triggered it to morph, I found something terribly disturbing.

The totem puffed up, like a normal totem would do when morphing outside a human host, but then it produced a strong electrical current that shocked me. I don't know for sure, but I'd say the current was at least 30 amps. It did produce a small amount of different power within its veins, but I'm worried. The electrical current was very minimal due to the testing size of the totem. But if it was in a human host and the host morphed, the electrical current would most likely be much stronger and could potentially cause a lot of damage.

I'm also worried about the host that wears the totem. Electricity is drawn to Peppate. If this single totem produces an electrical current each time it morphs, there's a good chance the current will kill the host. Even humans have Peppate within them from breathing or ingesting it.

In addition to this, I can't help but wonder where these electrical pulses are coming from. Doler created within normal humans does not create electricity, and neither does Peppate, of course. If the Mixed Bloods possess only the traits of their parents, where is the electricity coming from? If it is from the Doler, then why don't humans create it as well?

For now, I have to keep this information from Aitin and Jax and try to find another way. Creating a totem that can produce electricity is dangerous. Especially for the Pepps.

March 2, 2008

I've further examined Aitin's generators and found the reason for the electrical pulses. Normal human Doler generators produce what is more commonly called the force behind an electrical pulse. But each electrical stroke needs a leader that carves the pathway for the electricity to flow. That is lacking in humans. There is no leader stroke, so the electricity just sits. With Aitin's generators, though, it seems as though this leader is produced in some of the Doler generators during a morph, hence producing shocking electricity in the totem.

I wondered if it was possible to create a totem without those leader strokes, create the power without the shock. So I split the totem in half, removing all the leader generators within it. I found that even though it was able to puff up and activate without hurting me, it did not produce power. It seems as though destruction of Peppate is the one thing that creates Peppate-free power. Both parts of the totem are needed.

March 27, 2008

I knew I should have burned the new two-part totem when I had a chance. Aitin was snooping in my notes again and found out about the electricity created. He was elated. He said it was the answer. If we destroyed all the Peppate in the world he wouldn't be as sick. I was dumbfounded. I tried to explain the consequences that would present for both nature and the human population, not to mention the fact that he has Peppate generators within himself. But he was adamant that if we use it to destroy Peppate and collect power, we would then be able to heal him.

I tried to take the totem then and burn it, but Aitin calmly exclaimed that he would kill Lilly if I did. Jax is, of course, on his side, and openly admitted that Jose was killed because he was slowing the work. They threatened to make me disappear too, or Lilly, if I didn't continue.

Lilly was right about them, and I didn't believe her. Now we're trapped.

April 7, 2008

Lilly found out about the potential weapon I've created. We argued about it for several hours. I couldn't tell her that Aitin was using her life against me, so I made up a bunch of lies, but she's too smart.

I never imagined that she would use Jose's Magbaby, Gabbro, to send a message to my brothers in Petrichor, asking them for help. Danny and Trevor showed up here and found my new totem on display in my lab. Lilly must have informed them of its dangers because they immediately tried to destroy it.

I tried to stop them, but then Trevor morphed into a damn bear and slashed me badly before both he and Danny each grabbed one half of the totem without gloves. Why would they be stupid enough to grab it without gloves?! Before I could reach them, the totems had willingly taken hold on their bare hands. They began to scream in pain, holding their heads. I wondered if they were being electrocuted.

Unfortunately, they ran away before I could help figure out what was wrong. I wanted to follow after them, but had a gut feeling that I needed to check on Lilly. I've searched everywhere for her: the house, her old house, the woods. But I can't find her. Aitin and Jax are nowhere to be found either.

My Lilly is gone.

Chapter 8

That's when the entries stop.

I search the remaining pages of the journal, but they're all blank.

Closing the book, I stare at it in my hand. My brain has snagged on one piece of information.

Case was able to trigger a morph in the totem before it was attached to a human. When he did, it shocked him, but it also ... *created a small amount of power.*

It created power without killing a Pepp in that setting. Does that mean power can be generated without a Pepp death when it's actually in a human?

I need to find Case. I need him to tell me the truth.

My mind spins more, thinking of the girl. Lilly. I slowly lower the journal back to the counter. It was all for her. Everything Case did.

But where is Case now?

I'm running my fingers over the journal leather, when something catches my eye. In the dim light I almost miss it: a word scratched into the material.

RAT

Rat? Mark studies it too, his fingers brushing against mine.

I look at the floor, the smell of the room re-registering. There are rats in here.

That's when I see them for the first time. Several rodents squished on the floor. The image of them forces me to recall my time in Aitin's prison, when he squished the rat in my cell without any remorse. These rats seem to have been extinguished in the same way. Snakes too.

Aitin was here.

But what do the rats have to do with anything?

I'm about to turn away, when I see it. A snake lying dead beneath the cot.

I inch closer and crinkle my nose. There's a white paper sticking out of what can only be the decaying body of a rat *inside* the snake. I gag at what I think I'm supposed to do. Moving myself closer, I carefully grip the tiny piece of paper and pull it from the hardened bones and hair of the rodent.

"What is that?" Mark asks behind me.

I stand and turn, trying not to get my hopes too high. Carefully, I open the paper.

Kalahaki

That's all it says, but my heart leaps. Mark takes it from me and stares at it.

"Kalahaki. That's a desert across the ocean," he says. "It's one of the three deserts in the world the Pepps never distribute Peppate to."

Mark looks at me, a smile lighting his face. "We came to this home looking for Case, didn't we?" he says, figuring out our plan without me needing to explain things.

"Yes," I say. "And this is a clue."

Mark immediately runs upstairs to tell the others, but I stay put, studying the word on the note. I compare it to the words in the journal. They don't look like the same handwriting. If Case didn't write the note, then who did? *Could it have been Aitin?*

***

The aircraft shudders in the wind, jerking me awake. By the time we packed as much fresh water as we could and left Danny's old home, the sun was long gone. According to Mark, the Kalahaki Desert is on the other side of the world, which we must be approaching now, because the sun is high in the sky. Based on how groggy and irritated I feel, it could have only been a couple of hours since we left. If we don't stop and get some real rest somewhere soon, I might just cry.

The heat of the desert seeps in through the metal of the aircraft, and I fan myself with my hand. At least it's not heavy with humidity.

We changed back into our thin desert clothes but have also pulled out our scarves and hats to protect our skin from the sun.

Mine are sitting beside me, because I can't bring myself to put them on. It's so hot! The energy is getting sucked out of me with every passing second. I have to admit, I'm looking forward to getting back to the milder climate of Petrichor.

"We're almost there," Flint shouts back. I look down at Mark, who has sprawled across the seats beside me. The sight of his messy hair softens my discomfort. It's unfair that he could still look so handsome during such dire circumstances. I'm glad he's finally getting some sleep.

Suddenly, the aircraft jumps in the air. I'm able to brace myself with my hands and feet, but Mark isn't so lucky. He rolls off the seats, thumping to the floor. I bite my lip. So much for getting sleep. Mark groans before slowly pulling himself back into the seat next to me. Resting his head on the wall of the aircraft, he closes his eyes.

"So, what's the plan?" Flint shouts from the pilot seat. "Do you want me to land at the edge of the desert? Then we could morph and fly across. We'd cover more ground that way since it runs for hundreds of miles."

Flint's idea is reasonable, but I have one reservation.

"Case brought Lilly here—well, we hope—to keep her away from Peppate. If we morph, we'll spread Peppate, which might make her sick and upset Case. Is there another way to travel across sand quickly?"

I try to ignore the hateful glare Flint sends my way after dashing his idea. The past few days have been mostly bearable with Flint. I'd almost forgotten how much I hate him. His glare now, though, is a healthy reminder.

"We could use sand buggies," Gabbro says. I look at the rock, who's sitting on Trevor's shoulder now. With Danny and Trevor both needing his interpreting services, sometimes it's hard to know which one of them Gabbro is speaking for—or if he's speaking for himself. I narrow my eyes to see who's ear his tiny tendrils are pressed into. Danny. He's speaking for Danny.

"I got these before going on a run to the islands," Gabbro says for Danny, who is searching through his satchel. "I thought it would be fun to use them on the beaches there."

He pulls out tiny gold equipment capsules. "Sand buggies."

"Sand buggies?" Flint looks annoyed. "That would take even longer. Not to mention all the land we'd miss."

I hate to admit it, but he's right. It'll take days that we don't have.

I recall the map Eli showed me in the prison several weeks ago, the one with the deserts circled on it. I remember Harper's comment about water sources. Then I sit up straight. This is the same desert Breccia searched before, when she was trying to help me find Danny.

"The water sources," I almost shout. "If I remember correctly, there are three water sources here in the desert. Case would need water, to live here. Why don't we go check them out? See if there's anything around them."

I'm grateful my mind is finally working. *How did I forget about Breccia's visit?* What had she told me she observed? The water being low. Perhaps Case really is here, using that water.

"Alena's right. Here, let's look at a map," Kapri says, stepping into the middle of the aircraft. She spreads her map out on the floor, and we all kneel around it. "Here, here, here, and here are some water oases. Four water spots throughout the entire desert. Why don't we just fly in the flyer to these water holes? If we see anything in the air, we can use the sand buggies to travel on land for a better look."

I look at the faces of our team, and they all nod in agreement, including Flint, who is still piloting the plane.

Kapri circles the spots we plan to go to. Then, finding the one closest to us now, she picks up the map and shows it to Flint.

All it takes is one look at the map for Flint to make the proper flight adjustments. "We'll be there in about five minutes."

And we are.

When Flint lands, he opens up the back. A blast of hot air sucks the moisture from the aircraft the moment the door opens, making me instantly grateful we spent so much time collecting water before we left. My tongue is already parched, and based on how hot it is, I can tell there will be no using our power to create water here. Combining the rare elements will take too much power we can't afford to lose.

I walk off the aircraft after Kapri and Danny, shielding my eyes from the bright sun.

Flint takes charge of the group. "When the sun goes down, the air will be much cooler, but for now let's look around as much as we can."

We start walking toward the oasis. I step carefully, trying not to get sand in my shoes that reach halfway up my shin. If sand does somehow slip inside, I'm pretty sure my skin will be raw by sunset.

We walk only a few steps further, when I realize why everyone insisted on wearing the scarves and straw hats. The sun is scorching. My skin already feels like it's blistering, and it's only been a few minutes. I pull out my hat and scarf again and reluctantly put them on.

Topping a small dune, we finally reach the oasis. The blue water shimmers in the bright sun, surrounded by tall palm trees drawing up the water at their roots. *How does water even get here?* The sand around the oasis, rippled to perfection, makes for a beautiful sight.

I wonder if I could just go lie down in that water.

"Danny, why don't you pull out those sand buggies," Flint says. "And take Kapri around the area. See if there's anything that would indicate someone is living here. Don't go further than a mile away from the waterhole, though. I doubt Case could carry the water much farther than that on a daily basis. We'll search around here."

Danny gladly accepts Flints instructions and pulls out a sand buggy. It looks like a go-cart with two seats and has no glass windows, only bars for rolling protection.

It looks fun.

Kapri and Danny quickly slip inside, start it up, and spin away from the oasis, kicking up a cloud of sand behind them.

"Look for footprints in the mud around the water." Flint calls out when the sand has settled. "Or anything that would indicate someone has been here."

I carefully walk around. I search the mud and the sand. I look at the tree trunks for scuff marks, but I find nothing out of the ordinary. The place looks completely abandoned except for the tiny fish I spot in the water and the bugs skimming its surface. It takes Flint all but ten minutes to decide nothing is here.

"We should get going when Danny and Kapri get back," he says.

Unfortunately, they're gone for a long time, which makes Flint grumble something about how stupid it was to let *them* take the buggies. When the wind picks up, blowing sand in my face, I pull up my scarf.

We continue to wait.

Finally, they come whizzing back, kicking up another cloudy trail behind them. Right before they reach us, Danny sharply turns the vehicle and spins it around, spewing sand in all our faces.

I cough through the dust and spit out the gritty stuff. Kapri gets out of her seat. Her blonde ponytail is filled with orange sand, and her face is turning red from the heat, but she has a huge smile on her face. "Anybody else want a ride?" she asks.

"No," Flint says impatiently, his red hair glowing in the sun. "We need to get going. There's nothing here."

Danny carefully collapses the vehicle before we all scramble back into the flyer.

***

Flint doesn't allow anyone to use the sand buggies at the next water oasis. He's hoping to save time. Unfortunately, the second oasis looks exactly like the first one, with no signs of life. Or Case.

"The next two oases are only about twenty miles apart from each other," Kapri says while we head out in the flyer. "I suggest we land the flyer and then travel from one to the other on land. These are our last water sources, so let's hope we find something here."

I look out the window of the flyer and see the sun slinking downward in the sky. It's going to be dark soon.

"If we don't find anything here tonight, then we'll make camp and start again in the morning," Kapri adds. "Maybe there are more water holes that aren't on the map. Maybe we just need to spend more time flying over the entire desert like Flint suggested."

Kapri is trying to be optimistic, but her comments pick at my worry.

Reaching into my satchel, I pull out the clue we found at Danny's old home, the note in the rat. I flatten the paper in my hand, then stare at it. *What if it really isn't a clue?* What if it's a distraction, left by Aitin, to send us on a wild goose chase while he does something terrible?

I guess that could be what happened, but it's hard to picture Aitin putting a note in a rat and then smashing it. It seems too chancy a plan for him. *What if I didn't find the note?*

If Aitin didn't leave the note, though, then who did? And why do they want us to come here? I'm pretty sure Case doesn't want us to find him.

Flint lands the aircraft at the third oasis, and we all emerge. Thankfully, the air is starting to get cooler.

When we reach the far shore of the water, I stop.

From above, the water hole looked the same as the others, but the moment I reach the trees, something seems different. We all notice the same thing at the same time.

"The water is low," Mark says next to me, and he's right. You can tell based on where the tree roots are. They're completely exposed, several feet from the surface of the water line. In fact, when I look up at the trees, I notice they're wilting.

"It could be a coincidence. Not enough rain lately," Gabbro says.

"Or not," Kapri says, walking toward the water. "Question is, if it is Case using the water, where is he taking it? There are no buildings in this entire desert. At least none that we've seen. Mark and Alena, why don't you take the sand buggy and travel to the next oasis—see if you find anything there. We'll stay here and look around some more."

Suddenly my sluggish body comes to life. I probably shouldn't get my hopes up, but I can't help it. There's obviously something different about this place. *Could Case be close?*

Popping open the buggy capsule Danny gave him, Mark walks to the passenger door and holds it open for me. My mood lightens even more when a mischievous smile slides across Mark's face.

Stepping into the buggy, I notice the seat low and filled with sand, but I don't bother brushing it off. I'm sure I'll be covered too in only a couple of moments.

After shutting my door, Mark walks around to the driver's side. I quickly wrap my scarf around my face, put my hat back in my satchel, and place my brown hair in a loose bun atop my head. This might be fun.

"Which direction do we go?" Mark shouts to Kapri after starting up the vehicle.

Kapri points to our right. Mark pulls out his compass.

The compass. That's something I still haven't mastered using. Mark shifts the buggy into gear and waves good-bye.

Then he guns the gas, burying me in my seat. I grab the door to brace myself when he turns sharply to the right, then to the left, making us slide on the sand. I brave a look behind us and see large clouds of sand rising into the sky, kicked up with our speed. It's amazing how fast and smoothly the vehicle glides across the rippled ground.

When I look at Mark's face, it's glowing, and not just from the setting sun. This moment, this buggy, this desert, has somehow drawn out a puff of joy that's been tucked away in some small corner of Mark's mind. It changes every feature on his face, making him appear ... free.

And terribly handsome.

I memorize his features, wanting to engrain them into my brain forever. Then I reach my arm out the window. The wind whips against it and through my hair. Sand pelts me on my cheeks. I close my eyes, breathing in the beautiful moment, feeling the dry air, smelling the sand.

When I open my eyes again, I look into the sun, still against the land moving swiftly past us. Its colors are now matching that of the land. Perfectly orange. Perfectly beautiful.

Suddenly, the buggy jolts, bouncing me almost out the window. I scrape my knuckles trying to grasp for something to hold on to while Mark slowly brings the shaking vehicle to a stop. He shoots me an aggravated look. "I think we've popped a tire."

I open my door at the same time Mark does and heave myself out of the buggy. Sure enough, the front tire on my side is blown to bits.

Mark rolls his eyes when he sees it. "These tires are designed to last on sand. It shouldn't have blown apart like this. Not unless we hit something"

I look behind the buggy at the path we created, but all I see is a cloud of dust.

"It should only take me a few minutes to repair it, if you want to go sit."

Mark points to a rising dune next to the buggy and I make my way to it, then lower to the ground, resting my arms on my knees. I'm grateful Mark knows how to repair a blown tire. I sure wouldn't know where to start, even with power.

I quietly watch him, the way his lose shirt hangs when he leans over to pick up the blown rubber pieces. I swallow hard, seeing the muscles in his arms move.

Have I really been held against *that* body?

I bristle under my breath and look away, focusing on anything else but him.

But then I hear a soft musical beat pulsing through the silent air. I'm confused for a moment before I look back at Mark.

He's stopped working, and he's watching me with a look that makes my skin shiver. Dacite, his Magbaby is there on his shoulder playing a gentle song, which can only mean one thing.

He wants to dance. I almost laugh out loud at the idea. Dance here in the middle of the desert?

Mark drops the rubber piece in his hand and slowly walks to me. I watch him carefully, feeling my body already responding to him. When he stops in front of me, he holds out his hand.

"The tire ... can wait. Will you dance with me, Lena?" he asks. His voice is attractively low and raspy from inhaling too much sand.

My body speaks for itself, slipping its way into his grip. "Of course."

He pulls me up and uses one of his hands to unwrap the scarf from around my face.

"Have I ever told you how unfair it is that you look so beautiful covered in Doler."

My lips slip into a smile. I must have expelled some Doler during our short buggy ride, but I'm not the only one.

I reach my hand up to his Doler-covered jaw. "That's funny, because I was just thinking the same thing about you. Not that you're beautiful ... but *terribly* handsome." I gulp.

This makes Mark smile, his white teeth standing out against the dustiness of his skin. Oh, That smile. It makes my heart pound against my rib bones.

"Man, your brown eyes are a deep red in the sun, Lena," he says in awe. "Beautiful."

"And yours are bright gold," I whisper, tucking the color of his eyes into the memories I intend to keep forever.

Mark's smile fades, and his gaze finds my lips while his hand slips around my waist.

Dacite's song still carries through the air, but Mark ignores it.

I drape my left arm around Mark's shoulder, unsure if he still wants to dance, but then swallow, watching his mouth get closer.

His lips brush against mine, achingly light. They're dry and sandy, which makes me want to taste him all the more, every last part of him. I hold back a groan when he finally presses down harder, pushing me back. Wrapping my fingers around his neck, I pull him to me, letting my teeth grip his top lip.

Sweet fire.

One of Mark's hands finds its way up my back and pulls me to his chest, his lips still working through mine. I'm instantly praising the thinness of my shirt. It feels as though his hand is pressed right against my skin, burning me with his heat.

Man, it's hot.

"Mmm," Mark groans. "Why does sand taste so good on you?" His lips hover for a moment before pecking at mine as if he's eating me, which makes me laugh. Then his mouth drifts to my jaw, where he takes an actual bite at my skin that makes me gasp.

"Sorry," he says, "you're just too tempting." He bites my neck one more time before resting his forehead on mine.

Standing on my tiptoes, I wrap my arms around his neck and whisper into his ear, "We should come to the desert more often."

Mark chuckles, wrapping his arms around me tightly. I lean my chin on his shoulder and look out over the landscape.

We stand there, for a long time, the sky orange, the temperature perfect, the air peaceful with the quiet sound of sand blowing over the terrain.

Mark's arms around me.

When Mark starts to pull away, I tighten my arms around his neck, refusing to let him go. This makes him laugh again.

Then I let my lips graze his neck.

"Are we ever going to actually *finish* a dance?" I ask.

Mark's chest moves softly with silent laughter before he asks Dacite to start playing more music. Then he begins to sway, slowly. I release my grip on him just enough to drop to the heels of my feet and lean my forehead against his scruffy chin.

A tender appreciation slips into my heart for this man. For his goodness. His respect. His love. I graze my fingers along the back of his neck, then weave them into his hair.

The beautiful sunset on the horizon, the silent air of the desert, the gentle sound of Dacite's song, somehow all make me more painfully aware of every part of Mark pressed against me, every beat of his heart, every touch of his fingertips. I only have to lift my chin a bit to hover my lips over his again. He meets mine, gently this time, working through them as if they're something precious and unexplored.

I cherish the taste of him, the warmth. The dusty sandiness of him.

When the song is over, I wonder if Mark will let me go, but he doesn't. He only tightens his grip on my waist. "Just so you know," he says against my mouth, "that counts as our *first* dance. Our last one got interrupted. Which means you still owe me many more."

I smile. "Good."

Now, he releases his grip around my waist.

Breathing him in one last time, I reluctantly pull away, very aware of how cold I feel outside the man's arms, even in the heat of the desert.

This time, while Mark repairs the buggy tire, I try to ignore him and instead look back at the trail behind us. Now that the dust has settled again, I wonder if I'll see something that popped the tire.

I walk back, following the general direction we just came from and look around. *Maybe it was just a rock we hit.* But I don't find even a rock.

Mark finishes the tire, we get in the vehicle, and drive away. Hopefully there's something at the next oasis.

Chapter 9

The fourth oasis is exactly the same as the third. The water line is low, but other than that, there are no clues that we see. With the sun now set, the night is dark. The stars and moon in the sky provide some light as we drive back to our group, but it takes us longer than it took to get there, and now I'm tired and discouraged. We still don't know where Case is.

By the time we get back to our team, they've set up a cabin, one from an equipment capsule. I pause. It's identical to the one Jeter made me heal Aitin in: small, made from clean wood, and with only one window. It's hard to believe that I was in Jeter's cabin only a few weeks ago. So much has happened since then.

Mark and I quickly find Kapri and Danny, who are making dinner around a fire.

"Did you find anything else?" I ask Kapri after I tell her what we found, but she shakes her head.

"Flint flew the flyer around some more, searching further into the desert, but he didn't see anything either," she says, then tries to encourage me. "We'll look some more in the morning when it gets light again,"

When dinner is cooked, we all sit around the campfire eating our potatoes and hamburger.

Danny and Kapri eventually leave the fire to "star gaze." Trevor tries to follow them but is immediately sent back by an annoyed Danny.

Just as I put the last bite of dinner into my mouth, I hear a whistling sound in the air.

A Magbaby. Kapri's Magbaby.

She appears out of the dark sky and slowly descends into Kapri's open hands. Kapri opens the letter compartment and exposes a piece of paper.

"Here." She hands it to me. "It's from Cody."

Mark places his hand on my knee. "Can you read it out loud?"

I nod.

Alena,

I'm sad to hear about the troubles with the Mixed Bloods. We've been in communication with Eli throughout the day. I don't know if Eli has informed you yet, but, as of earlier today, six more of the Mixed Bloods who left with Aitin and Jeter have been found dead just outside Maracai. It appears Jeter's experiments aren't going so well. I have a team searching the lake now to see if we can find Jeter.

We aren't sure what approach Aitin is taking at this point, but we can only suspect it won't be good. It's only a matter of time before we find out. Please exercise caution and be safe while looking for Case.

The bunker is going well. We've started building the tunnels, and everyone is moving their stuff in. We're trying to hurry. Rusty decided to give up on maintaining the protective fog since it'll be destroyed anyway if Aitin blasts it with lightning. I can't tell you how vulnerable we feel. With our communicators refusing to interact with us now, we're blind to the events of below. Rusty is starting to send out teams just to collect information on what's going on, but it's dangerous.

I think the dinosaurs are picking up on the urgency because even they seem anxious. The trainers are having a hard time controlling them, but I guess it won't matter once everyone is safely down below. They'll run free. We're just hoping they at least know enough to attack Aitin on sight.

Anyway, we're all hoping you can find a way to recruit the Mixed Bloods. You're our only hope.

Take care, my friend.

Cody.

Cody's worries add to mine. The Pepps are trying to protect themselves, but they can only hide away for so long. I need to recruit Mixed Bloods to fight Aitin and end this. All the energy fizzles out of me at this thought.

"I might go to bed," I tell Mark, rising to my feet.

He's still eating but he nods. "Good luck."

Luck. It's sad that we need luck to help us sleep.

I stop and drop back down into my seat. Mark has seemed better today, at least here in the desert. I reach my hand out to touch his cheek.

"Will you be able to sleep?"

Mark nods, leaning into my touch. "I think so. I'll just think about you."

My cheeks blush, very aware of how the firelight flickers in his brown eyes, bringing out the golden specks.

"Well, I guess you can think about me all you want ... as long as you sleep."

Mark grips my hand in his, kissing the inside of my wrist.

"Good night," he whispers.

"Good night."

***

I sleep well for the first couple of hours. But somewhere in the middle of the night I wake up, restless. Eating dinner and being utterly exhausted last night sent me to sleep, but now that my mind has received a little rest, it's uneasy again. I keep imagining Petrichor, the bunker below, and wild, unpredictable dinosaurs roaming free atop. Without Pepps there to guide them, will they just run away?

And only nine of the twenty Mixed Bloods that left were found dead. What if Jeter's experiments were successful on the other eleven? If Aitin has help, there's no way the Pepps will survive.

No, the real solution for us is the Mixed Bloods. But I have to find Case before that can even be an option, assuming he has an answer to our problem.

Trevor snores loudly, and I put my pillow over my ears.

My thoughts still don't let me rest, bouncing around until they land on another question. Why is the water in the oasis so low? Is it being pumped to another location? Case would have to have some sort of shelter, but Flint didn't see anything even from the vantage point of the aircraft in the sky. If Case is pumping water somewhere, could he take it farther than ten miles? Unfortunately, I don't feel any closer to answers as the night drags on.

I toss and turn in my suddenly uncomfortable bed. Finally, I glance at the bunk assigned to Mark but find it untouched. Did he ever come inside?

Quietly, I sit up and put on my shoes, Trevor's snores rumbling through the cabin. Man, how is anyone getting any sleep?

Tiptoeing, I make my way outside. The fire from last night has died with only a few red embers left. The stark contrast of temperature between day and night surprises me, and I go back into the cabin to grab my sweater. Then, scanning the outside darkness, I search for Mark, finally finding his dark silhouette sitting atop a sand dune.

I climb the hill, slipping a few times on the loose sand before reaching him. I try to gauge whether or not he wants me here, but it's too dark to see his eyes.

"Hey, you okay?" I whisper instead.

He doesn't speak but pats the sand next to him. No, he's not okay, I conclude. At least he's not shunning me. I slowly slide down and wrap my arms around my knees, making sure to leave some space between us, but Mark reaches for my hand and pulls me in, forcing me to scoot closer.

I'm okay with that.

I lean into his warm body, gently rubbing his arm with my free hand.

I wish I knew what was bothering him so much. *Is it the pain he experienced?*

We sit in silence for a while. The black sky eventually fades to gray, and then a sliver of bright orange appears on the horizon. I can see Mark's tired face better now, and it only increases my worry. I really wish he could get some sleep.

My butt is starting to go numb, when Mark begins fidgeting with the sand. Trying to be as sly as possible, I lean my head onto his shoulder to catch a glimpse of what he's doing. When I see it, I can't help but lean forward to get a better look.

He's not just fidgeting with the sand, he changing its form—to glass. It shimmers in the dawn light.

"What is that?" I whisper.

Mark stops and slowly turns his head to me, his nose grazing mine. The sorrow he's been trying to hide immediately finds its way toward me, leaking from his very core. It's like a thick wave of tar that oozes into my body, seeping into my bones. He doesn't cry, but he's sharing his agony with me just the same. I reach up and gently cup his jaw in my hand, thankful he doesn't pull away.

"What did he do to you, Mark?" I whisper.

Witnessing his emotions humbles me greatly. I feel fortunate to be the one here with him, no matter how much it hurts me to see it. I carefully watch his face. His forehead, the way it furrows deeply, as if in pain. His eyes, how they stay closed as if trying to fight off a terrible memory. His jaw, how it clenches tightly, as if it's the only thing holding him together.

I'm just beginning to wonder if he'll be able to talk at all, when he finally opens his mouth.

"He chained me to the wall, Lena." Mark swallows, but it doesn't do much for his suddenly dry mouth. "I couldn't move my arms or legs. Then he ..." His voice catches, and he swallows again. "He poured acid on my skin." Mark's body begins shaking in recollection of the memory. It catches me off guard, but then I wrap my arms around him, pulling him closer.

"It hurt like hell, like I was burning alive," Mark whispers, shaking his head. "And it didn't stop. I couldn't get away from it." Mark squeezes his eyes shut. "It. Didn't. Stop," he repeats, bringing a trembling hand to his hair.

"I've gotten so used to having power," he continues, "and being able to control things around me, but I couldn't do anything there. I was so weak."

He doesn't speak for a long time after that. And neither do I. I just hold him, willing his trembling to stop. When it eventually does, Mark opens his eyes and looks at me. "I wanted to die, Alena. And I—" He pauses, shaking his head, as if contemplating whether or not he should continue, but lowering his voice, he finishes. "I still have that feeling, especially when I sleep. I just want to die."

His words sink in. I know that feeling. Maybe in a different setting, but I still understand it. I rub his neck, trying to tell him silently that I don't blame him. That wanting to die under such immense pain is a perfectly acceptable reaction. That it's nothing to be ashamed of. I try to push as much compassion toward him as I can. Mark sighs, gripping my hand in his.

"And then Aitin told me he'd captured you. That made it worse. I couldn't do anything. I couldn't help you. Being burned was unbearable, but wondering if you were being burned the same way ..." Mark's voice catches again, and he shakes his head.

Part of me wants to tell Mark that Aitin didn't burn me, but he already knows that. Instead, I hold him, waiting for him to continue.

"There's something else," he says, his words scraping dryly against his tongue. "I figured out why Aitin chose me to host the defective totem. It all made sense when I saw his eyes and nose. The shape—they're exactly like my dad's."

I furrow my eyebrows. *Like his dad's?* "You think he's ...?" I don't want to say it.

"He's my father's son," Mark finishes for me. "My half-brother. That's probably what's been bothering me the most. My dad never mentioned having another son, but apparently he did. And Aitin confirmed it, said that my dad visited him and his mother a couple of times before she died, and then Aitin never saw him again." Mark's face hardens slightly. "Why didn't my dad tell me? Did my mother know? If he created a Mixed child, why wasn't he disciplined for it like so many others? Did this happen before the law was made in Petrichor?" Mark shakes his head, clearly tormented. "I'd always looked up to my father; he was always perfect in my eyes. Taught me to respect women and myself, but did he practice what he preached? How did he have another child?"

Mark shakes his head. "When Aitin burned me with that acid, I realized I didn't know much about my father. He'd lied to me, and it was his lies that eventually got him killed. Aitin hated him so much for abandoning him, and he hates me ... for being the one who was loved." Mark pounds the sand angrily. "This is all my dad's fault. If he had taken care of Aitin or, even better, if he hadn't made that mistake with Aitin's mother ..."

Mark takes in a deep breath, but then slowly lets it out, slumping forward.

I remember the photo I found in Mark's old cabin. The one of Mark with his dad. I remember how one side of it was torn as if the part with his mother had been removed.

Aitin probably found that picture when he was searching Mark's cabin. I'm sure he hated Mark's mother. He must have torn her picture up. But why did he leave the rest of the picture, only to tear it up in front of me later in my prison cell?

I don't know the answer, but obviously he was very hurt by Mark's father.

"What's worse is now I'm questioning myself." Mark's pained expression lands on me. "The man I respected turned out to be weak when it came to women. Does that mean I'm weak too? Could I make the same mistake?"

I furrow my eyebrows.

"Alena, every time I look at you ... I ..." He swallows again. "You're incredibly beautiful. I don't want to make the same mistake."

It all makes sense to me now. His hesitancy, his frustration ... around me. He's worried that he'll do the same thing his father did.

I tighten my grip on his arm. "You aren't your father, Mark, and you aren't the only one who doesn't want to make those mistakes either. *I* care about the same things you care about."

I sigh, then look out at the horizon. "Your father was also a good man. I know, because he raised you to be a good man. That has to account for something."

"He's still out there, Alena." Mark's voice shakes, ignoring my comment. "Everything we're doing is moving us closer to him. I can feel it, but I don't ever want to face him again. I ..."

He's talking about Aitin now, and he doesn't need to finish his sentence for me to know what it would be. *What if Aitin captures him again? What if he tortures him?* I tighten my grip around Mark. Unfortunately, Mark's fears are my own. If Aitin did this once to Mark, there's no telling what he'd do if he somehow gets Mark again. *What if something does happen to him?* What if Mark doesn't survive? I close my eyes. I wish I could force him to stay as far away from me as possible, away from this quest to find Aitin, but the truth is, nobody's safe as long as Aitin is alive, and there's no way Mark will let me leave him behind.

How do I comfort Mark without being able to promise him safety? Without being able to fix the problem?

Mark's brown eyes finally meet mine. "I'm sorry," he says.

I lower my eyebrows. "Sorry? Mark, you have no reason to be sorry." I raise my hand to his jaw. "Thank you for telling me." Then my voice catches. "*I'm* sorry for everything that's happened." Those words sound so shallow compared to the depth of heartache I feel for him. "The way I found you ... I don't know how you survived, how you held on."

My words might seem inadequate to me, but to Mark they might be enough. The thick agony oozing from him slowly seems to dissipate. He breathes in deeply now, expanding his lungs fully. It's a refreshing sound, hearing him breathe like that.

"Thank you for listening." His words seem lighter. It's as if he simply needed to know that he wouldn't be abandoned for the things in his heart.

Never would I abandon him.

"I will always listen to you," I say.

His mouth twitches at my words, but then he straightens his body.

"Alena, if something does happen, if I somehow do end up back with Aitin, I want to make you a promise." Mark reaches his hand back over to the glass items he created in the sand and lifts one up. A piece of glass shaped like a drop of water shimmers in the waking sun's light, connected to three more.

I blink. It strongly resembles a totem marker, like the one Sepharine wears.

I look at Mark, confused.

"I know this looks like an engagement marker. I guess that's what you can call it if you want. But it's more of a manifestation of my promise to you." Mark swallows again. "My promise to you, that if I ever *feel* like dying again, I'll do my best to fight." Mark's eyes bore into mine. "I will fight, Alena, so I can come back to you."

I blink my teary, blurred eyes.

I know exactly what a promise like that requires. I bring my gaze back to the glass drops that shimmer through my tears.

It requires faith to fight when you are weak. Faith to stand up when you want to give up. Faith to try when you want to succumb to the darkness.

That's not an easy promise to make. As grateful as I am that he would promise such a thing, I'm suddenly terrified. How can I let him make that promise to me without returning it?

"Can I put it on you?" Mark asks. I blink again, forcing out the tears that have collected there. Then I nod, unzip my jacket, and pull it down to expose my totem. I try to watch as he weaves it painlessly in and out of my skin around the vine. He even creates tiny little metal loops, piercing them through the glass and around the totem so the pieces dangle. When he's done, his eyes find their way back to mine.

He's not expecting it, but I know it's my turn.

I bite my lip and scoot my numb butt so that I'm facing him. I gently take his hand in mine and bring it to my lips. Then I stare at it, tracing the lines in his palm, trying to muster up the courage to say the words.

"Mark." My lip quivers, and I raise my eyes to his. "I promise to fight too."

He pulls me forward, into his lap. I wipe at my nose, wrap my legs around him, then bury my face in his chest. I breathe him in, unable to keep my tears from soaking his loose shirt.

Then I try to imagine what difficulties my promise might require of me in the future.

Fighting probably won't be the same for me as it will be for Mark. Aitin has never tortured me the way he did the man whose warm arms are now wrapped tightly around me. Even if I was captured by Aitin, I don't see him pouring acid over my skin or down my throat.

No, the battle I see myself tempted to succumb to is the battle I've fought all along. The battle to see my worth. To know that I have a place—and that place isn't with Aitin. Even now, just thinking about it, I feel the pull of doubt trying to drown me.

But I promise to fight.

I listen to the beat of Mark's heart, feel the bulge of his totem through his shirt.

If he's giving me a marker, then I want to give him one too.

"I don't know if Pepp men wear markers," I say, pulling away from his body. "But I'd like to give you a promise marker too."

Mark nods, but he doesn't move.

"Can I take your shirt off so I can see your totem?"

That same seductive eyebrow arches over his eye, just like it did the last time I tried to examine his totem.

"*Just* to see my totem?" he taunts.

I try to ignore his teasing, silently grateful he seems a little better.

Then I slip my hands underneath the bottom of his shirt and pull it up, swallowing at the heat beneath my fingertips. Mark willingly raises his arms, letting me pull the shirt over his head.

I suck in a quick breath. I've seen him without his shirt before, felt his skin, but I must have forgotten how dangerous it is to be this close.

How could I have forgotten?

His skin is irresistibly smooth and defined, calling for my fingertips. I gulp loudly, bringing out a soft chuckle from Mark. Replacing his arms securely around me, he pulls me close.

"I'm not good at creating glass," I whisper, trying to get control of myself. "Could you help me?" This draws out a tiny smile from Mark. With one arm still wrapped securely around me, he creates another piece of glass in the sand.

It's a plain, thin glass tube.

I scrunch my nose. "I think you need to make it more pretty like mine."

Mark grins that smelting grin but ignores my advice. "Where do you want me to put it?"

I trace the vine on his chest gently. I wish his vine was more exposed like mine so he could see the glass better on his arm. I follow the totem to its furthest point just under his heart. A place he could potentially see if he looked down.

"Right here," I say.

Bringing the glass tube up to the spot, I watch Mark wrap it around the vine, leaving the ends slightly poking out. I nod in satisfaction, touching it carefully. It looks like a tendril wrapped around a vine, and it's easy to feel.

Now, I suddenly become aware of Mark's breath on my face. We're close, and my heart loves it. I bring my fingers up to his neck and then his jaw. I run them through his hair and gently pull him closer to me. Mark willingly responds by slipping both arms beneath my jacket and drawing me to his chest. I rest my nose against his, breathing steadily until he places his lips softly on mine. They're still dusty, dry, and stupidly satisfying.

Mark moves his mouth fervently with my lips, his fingers sliding up my back.

It's amazing how much comfort I find in his arms.

He's afraid.

I'm afraid.

We both have death looming over our heads, and there's so much uncertainty, but right here, right now, none of that matters. Just Mark. Just my love for Mark matters.

I slide my hands over his tight arms, his bare chest, and up his neck before landing them in his hair. A deep groan escapes his throat, and he tightens his grip around me.

His mouth moves to my jaw, down my neck, leaving me breathless.

Then his lips find their way hungrily back to mine.

Oh, how I wish these moments didn't have to end. How I wish he could hold me forever, that I could ceaselessly touch and kiss him.

But he *can't* hold me forever, and I know we need to stop. I promised him I would help us stop.

So I reluctantly slow my kisses, rein in my touch.

Mark does too. Eventually he rests his forehead on mine and fights to catch his breath.

"I guess I should officially ask you if you'll be mine. Maybe we can get married someday?" he says.

I smile. "Mark, I always have been yours, since the moment I got this vine."

He brings his lips back to mine. "And I've always been yours," he murmurs into my mouth, triggering another cluster of unbridled kisses.

Okay, we should really stop.

After letting myself savor his lips one last time, I let my arms drop and reluctantly pull away.

"We should get back. The others will be up soon," I say.

I should also move my butt. It's officially numb. I roll awkwardly to my knees while Mark finds his shirt and, unfortunately, puts it back on.

When I rise, I pull down the shoulder of my jacket and look at the new mark on my totem. It's about the same length as Sepharine's, starting at my shoulder and weaving down several inches, with three glass teardrops. I finger them gently, replaying in my mind the promise they represent.

"Thank you, Mark." Then I cover it up with my jacket.

"I'll make you some real diamonds when we have more free time. They aren't my specialty yet, but I have some good news." Mark touches his own marker through his shirt. "Glass doesn't conduct electricity, and this sand doesn't contain Peppate, so if you ever do have to withstand

Aitin's powers, these won't be destroyed." Then he smiles at me, taking my chin in his fingers. "But I'll still get you some diamonds."

The corner of my lip lifts. "I don't want diamonds, Mark. I love the glass," I whisper. Then something Mark said pinches at the back of my mind.

Glass doesn't conduct electricity.

My eyes rise to his face, my mind spinning.

"What?" he asks, seeing my thoughtful look.

"Glass doesn't conduct electricity," I say. "Sand doesn't conduct electricity." He shakes his head still confused. I stand, looking around. "Mark, what if Case came here for more reasons than to just escape Peppate? What if he came here to escape Aitin and his powers? To escape the lightning. What better place to do that than in a desert filled with sand."

"You think Case is using the sand to protect himself?" Mark asks. "You think he's ... under the sand?"

I nod.

"Let's go talk to the others," he says, putting his arm around my shoulders.

***

I'm too antsy to eat when we get back to the cabin, but Kapri forces me to scarf down some oatmeal and raisins while we tell everyone what we're thinking.

Flint says that he wondered if Case could be underground but couldn't figure out how he would be able to breathe. There's no sign of any ventilation system. As much as I hate to admit it, he's right, but we have to try.

"So what are we going to do?" Gabbro asks the group once everything is tucked back in our satchels, including the large cabin.

"The water level at both the third and fourth oasis was low," Mark says, piecing a plan together as he goes. "Case could be hiding in between both water sources. I suggest we find a middle point between the two and then command the sand to move. If there's something below, we should be able to see it."

This is when Danny pulls out his full collection of sand buggies. Four of them—one for Mark and me, one for Danny and Kapri, one for Trevor—I'm not sure how well that'll work— and one for Flint.

All together we travel over the sand, following Kapri's guidance. When her buggy stops, we all stop and lay away the vehicles.

"Here. Let's try here."

Everyone gathers into a spread-out circle. I don't know how to command sand, so I stay close to Mark. I try to watch at first, but when the grains of sand start whipping around, it becomes too painful, so I cover my face with my arm. I don't know what's happening other than the sand beneath me is moving. I'm sinking. When the sand ceases to pelt my skin and finally settles, I carefully open my eyes.

I gawk at the structure below.

We're standing on top of a wide slab of concrete with several tan colored pipes poking out of it. Their tops are pointed and open. "I wonder if that's what popped our tire," Mark whispers next to me.

Probably. It looks like the pipes reach all the way to the surface of the sand, but how could they be so disguised? I didn't see a single one. And what are they for? Air?

I look around us. Either we've sunk down into the ground at least twenty feet, or the sand moved has created large walls around us. Probably the latter, but Flint keeps working, moving more sand, exposing more and more concrete.

"We have to find an opening," he says.

More carefully this time, they move the sand up and over the mounds until Kapri squeals in delight.

"I think I found something."

Danny is the first to her side, quickly grabbing at a handle; he lifts a door. With a look of excitement and nervousness, Danny signals to us that he'll drop down first, and then we'll follow.

Flint approaches carefully.

Mark takes my hand, but I plant my feet.

"Wait," I say. "I know you all want to go down there, but Case has gone through great efforts to create a place that is Peppate-free. You all emit Peppate through your totems. He'll be mad enough that we found him, but furious if we make Lilly sick. Do you think Mark and I should go down first?"

This infuriates Flint. "How are we supposed to protect you if we aren't with you?"

I look to Mark for his opinion. He clears his throat. "I think we should all go together."

"Okay," I say, "except for Trevor." I turn to him. "I don't think you'll fit."

Trevor grunts, but even he can see that the opening is much too small for him.

Chapter 10

The hallway is dark and narrow. The air is thin. It makes me uncomfortable, not being able to draw in a satisfying breath.

We shuffle down the hall as quietly as we can, until Danny runs into something.

"I think it's a door," he whispers.

Carefully, he opens it to reveal a wider concrete hallway lit with small candles. Over to the right are three hooks on the wall holding old brown shirts and scarves. Over to the left there's a pile of tools on the floor: shovels, pickaxes, and bellows. Mark shuts the door behind us, but only about ten feet away is another door.

Danny leads us on, into another hallway.

"Is that water?" Mark whispers. I hear it too, the slow trickle of liquid. Sure enough, when the hallway turns a hard right, we find ourselves in a small water room, with a tube extending down from the ceiling dripping sandy water into a large basin. Another tube leads from that basin to another and seems to filter the sand out. I take in a deep breath, something that's easier to do in this room for some reason, and relish the smell that reminds me of Petrichor, of rain.

Then, I admire Case's genius. So he *is* stealing the water from the watering holes, by somehow siphoning the water here. How he's managed to control it so it's not gushing is a mystery to me, not to mention how he's able to filter the sand all out.

I walk past the second basin, past a little privacy wall into another small room with a heating stove littered with pans and a large metal bathing tub.

This must be where they wash up. They take the water from the water basin, heat it on the stove, then dump it in the bathing tub. What a process. It makes me appreciate the simple amenities I've been raised with. I wonder what they do with the water once they're done bathing. Do they recycle it somehow?

Danny doesn't give us much time to study the room.

"Come on," Gabbro says for him.

Soon the concrete beneath us turns to flush carpet, and I almost want to take off my shoes out of respect. The lighting brightens with more candles lit, and the hallway opens up a little wider. We pass what seems to be a bedroom with its door slightly ajar. Its brightly painted walls and clean linens make me wonder if we're still under a large desert of sand, its beauty misplaced.

Just then the low sound of someone murmuring drifts down the hall. Danny brings his finger to his lips, then signals for us to proceed.

We walk quietly, past a beautiful big living room, another room with dripping water, to finally what is probably a large lab. Knowing Case, that's exactly what it is with a table covered in papers, a wall lined with medicinal vials, and microscope after microscope scattered around. On the far end of the room is Case, sitting with his back to us, poring over a table of papers. Next to him sits a beautiful woman in a rocking chair with dark-brown hair and dark-brown eyes. I know immediately who she is. The last time I saw her was when I pulled her from SilverDen.

Lilly.

She sees us first. Her eyes widen and she stifles a gasp, but then her mouth pulls into a smile. "You found us," she whispers. For someone who's been trying to hide, she sure seems happy to see us.

Case's head snaps to her, and then he follows her gaze to our group. "What the hell ..." He's on his feet, a knife in his hand before anyone can blink.

"Don't even bother, Case." Flint steps forward.

Case must know who he is, what he's capable of doing, because his body freezes the moment he sees the red-haired boy.

"Drop the knife." Flint says.

Case reluctantly obeys, then he growls, not bothering to keep his voice down. "How did you get in here?"

Before we can answer, he looks up at the ceiling as if that'll tell him what we did. "Did you move the sand?"

Danny steps forward carefully, maybe trying to defuse his brother's boiling temper, but it doesn't work. Case doesn't seem even remotely happy to see Danny. He's too distracted.

"Did you move the sand?" he shouts again, his voice making me jump.

"Yes, we did," I say, not bothering to hide how irritated his temper is making me.

Case's dark eyes, a storm of anger, meet mine. "Go back up and cover my hideout right now," he demands.

Apparently, nobody moves quickly enough, because he shouts again, making *everyone* jump this time. "*Now!*"

"Okay, okay!" Mark shouts back before pulling out Dacite and instructing him to go tell Trevor to cover up the hideout.

"Trevor's here?" Case shouts.

Goodness, why is he still shouting?

"Yes, Trevor is here," Mark says. It's good he's answering Case instead of me. I wouldn't be nearly as patient or calm.

Case now points a hard finger at Flint, Danny, and Kapri. "You three. Get out of here! I've worked hard to keep your damn Peppate out of this place. Now leave."

I glower at Case. I wanted to give him a chance to redeem himself. I wanted to hope he was really a good person, but I'm already deciding that I still don't like him. For someone who's hurt his brothers so much, he has a lot of apologizing to do, and yet he doesn't seem the least bit eager to make amends.

Danny, Kapri, and Flint obey him, though, quickly leaving the room.

Gabbro stays, humming his way to my shoulder.

Lilly stands now, placing her hand on Case's arm, her smile long gone. She doesn't say anything, but she doesn't have to. Case's anger seems to fizzle out somewhat at her simple touch.

"How did you find me?" He repeats his question from earlier, but this time his voice is hoarse with attempted control.

I'm about to answer, but Lilly steps in.

"They found my note." Lilly looks directly at me when she says this.

Her note? *She's* the one who wrote it?

Case spins. "You left a note?" His tone is rising again, but all it takes is one raised eyebrow from Lilly and he's clenching back his emotions.

"Why would you leave a note?" he grinds out. "What if Aitin found it?"

Again, Lilly looks at me. "He didn't. I'm sure of it." Case pinches the bridge of his nose and turns away. "I'll explain it later, Case, but for now,

I think you need to listen to them. Why don't we go into the sitting room and talk, *calmly*." Lilly overemphasizes the last word.

Without waiting for a response from Case, Lilly takes my hand and guides me through the halls, to the room with the couch. I glance back once to see Mark following right behind me.

When we reach the sitting room, Lilly lets my hand go and allows me to sit on the large sectional couch. I approach it carefully. It's so clean and plush, and I'm covered in sand. I attempt to just sit on the edge of the seat, trying not to get it all dirty, but the moment my body touches it, I sink in. It's so comfortable, so lush and tempting I can't help but scoot back and let it swallow me up.

Mark sits next to me, following the same process, while Lilly sits in a plush chair against the wall.

Case, too restless to sit, speaks first. "What are you guys doing here?"

"We need your help." Gabbro takes on the task of telling Case everything that has transpired since he left the hideout with Lilly. It's odd, hearing things from an outsider's perspective. It makes things seem less personal, less my fault. At least until Gabbro tells him about Tom. Then it becomes very personal. When Gabbro gets to the part about me healing Aitin, Case's eyes finally meet mine. The anger is now gone, replaced with a deep wonder.

"It worked? The dinosaur serum worked?"

Lilly is suddenly standing beside Case, gripping his arm. "She can heal me."

Case doesn't even glance at Lilly when he responds. "Absolutely not. Not until we know more about this."

His words are so final and so discouraging that I expect Lilly to cower away, but she just rolls her eyes in playful annoyance. She was expecting that answer.

I nod, glancing between the two of them, wondering if I should proceed. "Yes, it worked, but I still needed the Peppate-free power. I couldn't have done it without that. Which is why we're here."

Gabbro takes over again, talking about my imprisonment and the battle with the chief. Last, he tells Case about our plan. Hoping to find a way to produce more power so that I can heal the Mixed Bloods for help.

Case looks annoyed at finally learning our reason we've come here.

"You just want to know how to create more power? Alena, you know how to make power by simply morphing."

I shake my head. "We want to make power without needing to kill a Pepp."

I cringe under his terrifyingly demeaning gaze. "You don't need to *kill a Pepp*. Why would you think that?" Then it dawns on him. "Wait. Cody. You think that because she was tied up in the woods, she had to die in order for the power to generate." His gaze twitches slightly when he changes the subject. "By the way, were you able to get her out?"

"Yes, thanks to you, but another Pepp did not get out," I whisper.

"Tom," Gabbro says for me.

Case nods sadly but proceeds. "Alena, the power is generated within your totem anytime *Peppate* is zapped, including Peppate that's in plants, water, or air. Aitin put Cody out there to be killed because we knew that the *more* Peppate that was destroyed, the more power your totem would generate. The Peppate generators within a Pepp are the ultimate power-providing source." As if suddenly feeling the need to clear his conscience, he adds, "I was against it from the beginning. I told Aitin that all we needed for you to do was morph in the woods. It would destroy all the trees but give you some power, but Aitin was determined and tired of waiting. He wanted to get it all over with. To be honest, I was tired of waiting too." Case's eyes wander to Lilly's face.

Quickly, Case's words come together, and I feel a small glimmer of hope take place in my heart. Not wanting to somehow put out that glimmer, but needing it laid out as clearly as possible, I whisper to Case, "Are you saying that if Mark and I morph together in a place without Pepps, or humans, we can *still* generate power?"

Case nods, suddenly looking tired. He finally sits on the couch. "It won't be as much power as you got when the Pepp died, but it will be some."

We can create power. And we can do it without killing a Pepp. Every fiber of my being sags in unanticipated relief. We won't have to kill the chief.

I look at Mark, who places his hands behind his head, closes his eyes and leans back, a smile on his face. The world just got a whole lot brighter. "We're going to need more serum," he says.

Yes, we will.

I turn back to Case. "Will you fight with us?"

"Of course not." Case's answer is immediate, but I don't let him dampen my spirits. That is until he says, "What are you going to do about Aitin?"

Then I'm instantly brought back down. My shoulders slump.

"I don't know. I need to undo what I've done. I need to disabled the serum in all his Peppate generators. But I'm not exactly sure how to get it all out. It took me *hours* to get it all in."

"We could burn him with fire," Mark says, but he doesn't seem too convinced himself that it will work, and I know why.

"That didn't work on you, Mark. It might work for serum on the outside of a body, but fire wasn't able to get rid of all the serum *inside* you. By the time we burn him, he'll be countering the fire with his power. We'd be lucky if we could get that close to him."

"It sounds like you need to practice speaking to the serum with your power," Case says. "See if you can improve the amount of time it takes you."

"I just don't know how I would do it that fast. I would need Aitin to somehow be immobilized first, and I'm not sure that that's possible."

The room is quiet while everyone thinks, but nobody comes up with any answers. Finally, Lilly stands.

"I'm sure you'll figure it out." Then she comes to me and holds out her hands. "I'm guessing you're all famished. Alena, do you want to come to the kitchen with me and help me prepare some food?"

"Lilly ..." Case's voice is full of warning, but Lilly waves him off.

"Case, you don't need to worry about me being with Alena. She doesn't produce Peppate. I'll be safe." This last part she adds softly. I glance between the two until Case reluctantly nods his approval. Lilly smiles big and kisses Case on the cheek.

"You should probably catch up with your brothers," Lilly encourages him. I don't miss the annoyed look that slides across Case's face, before Lilly and I disappear down another hall.

Chapter 11

As soon as we're out of earshot from Case in the small kitchen, Lilly throws her arms around my neck, hugging me tightly. I'm caught off guard but slowly return the hug.

When I pull back, I find her eyes misty. "Thank you, Alena."

I'm confused. *Why is she thanking me?*

"Thank you for saving me from Aitin," she says.

Ah. "Of course, Lilly. I'm glad I found you."

Lilly's face lightens even more. It's hard not to feel happier around her with the energy she is emitting. "And you found my note!" She's practically squealing like a little girl.

"*You* wrote the note? The note in the rat?"

Lilly laughs out loud. "When I was imprisoned in that horrible cave by Aitin, there were rats everywhere. Every time Aitin came to visit me, he made a point of smashing each one with his foot. It was barbaric. He enjoyed it like it was a game. I think it made him feel better. Anyway." Lilly waves her hand, dismissing the memory. "When Case and I were in the lab at his old home packing up to leave, I tried to convince him to let you know where we'd be. You're the answer to everything. But he refused to let anyone know, positive that we needed to be on our own. So I wrote the note."

"And you put the note in a rat," I state in wonder.

"Yes! As soon as I saw that rat running around, I had an idea. I knew Aitin would most likely come looking for Case after he left, and if he saw the rat trapped in the lab room, he would surely smash it. So, using Case's supplies, I cut the rat, slipped the note inside, and then stitched him up. It was sloppy and"—Lilly scrunches up her nose—"disgusting, but I did it. I knew it would eventually decompose and reveal the paper inside for when you visited."

I shake my head. "You just assumed I would see the words scratched into the back of Case's journal and then find the note still almost completely hidden by the fur? By the way, the rat had been eaten by a snake. We're lucky both bodies decomposed enough for me to see it." I continue to shake my head in awe. "It's amazing you thought of it, and even more amazing that it worked."

Lilly shakes her head. "No, Alena. It's a miracle."

I'm touched by her passion. "Why did you want me to find you so badly?"

Lilly's bright face saddens for the first time, and her eyes glance toward the doorway. Lowering her voice, she whispers, "I need your help, Alena. I need you to heal me. Not for my sake but for Case's. He's sacrificed everything to make me better. The totem on your arm, everything he's done, he's done for me. And when it didn't work, he left everything behind and brought me here to keep me safe, away from Peppate."

Lilly drops her head and looks at her stomach. That's when I see it. To anyone it might look like a slightly bloated belly, but by the way she's holding it, I understand.

"Now things are even more complicated," she says.

"You're pregnant," I whisper.

"Case is going through extreme lengths to keep me healthy. He won't go outside, afraid that he'll somehow collect Peppate and bring it back to me. He won't even touch me anymore or hold me because he's afraid that my own Peppate generators will create too much Peppate and hurt us both." Lilly pats her stomach. Then she grabs my hands urgently. "The odds of a Mixed Blood having a live baby are not that great. I think I can survive such a loss, but ... Case ..." Lilly's voice breaks when she says his name. "This will push him over the edge. I think I could lose him forever if this baby doesn't live." She sighs heavily. "I just want to be able to touch Case and love him without him worrying I'll get sick."

Now, everything makes sense. Seeing Lilly, I understand why Case loves her so much, why he's done everything to help her. *How could he not?* But then for it to not work out? To be stuck in a vicious cycle of love versus health. How exhausting and sad.

"You have to find a way, Alena. Please. Go to the Mixed Bloods and work with them, but please promise me you'll come back. I want to set Case free. It's not healthy for any human to forsake Peppate the way he has. He's so unhappy."

I squeeze her hands. "I'll come back, Lilly." Her love and confidence in me has given me new hope, and for the first time in a long time I feel an urgency to do what has to be done, not because everyone else is telling me to but because I want to—for her.

"Thank you." Standing up tall, Lilly brushes back her long dark hair and starts busying herself with food, her brightness returning. "All the food we have is Peppate-free, which isn't as tasty as normal food." Lilly crinkles her nose at this comment. "But it's good enough."

I watch her work in the large, bright kitchen, using the various pots and pans Case has stored for her. Lilly talks about her new home and the ideas she has to make it better. She jabbers on about the new nursery she's working on for the baby and how great a father Case will be.

Before I know it, she's whipped up a vegetable casserole that smells better than it looks. Then she asks me to take it outside.

"I think I saw Case and Mark slip past the kitchen, probably to go out to his brothers like I advised him to do." Lilly winks my way.

"Smart man," I whisper.

This makes her laugh, a gentle sound that could brighten the darkest of rooms. I decide I like Lilly. A lot.

"Just go down the hall to the left," she instructs. "There's a ladder there that'll lead you to an outside hatch door. It doesn't have any sand on it, so you'll be able to open it easily."

Balancing the casserole and plates in my hands, I walk down the hall and find the ladder. Putting the casserole on the floor, I climb the steps to open the hatch. Just like Lilly said, it leads directly outside. Once my eyes adjust, I open it wide, go back down the ladder, grab the casserole, and carry it out. When I shut the hatch door, I find it camouflaged with sand. It's surprisingly hard to see even though I'm standing right next to it.

Shielding my eyes from the sun that's now very hot, I look around.

Across the sand, I see that the others have set up the cabin again. That's probably where they're talking. Shielding the casserole as best as I can from the blowing sand, I make my way to the small building.

When I open the door and enter, I hear Gabbro speaking, telling Case about what happened the night we broke the prisoners out.

I quietly hand out the plates Lilly gave me while listening to the conversations. Mark directs a question at Case.

"Where do you think Aitin will go first when he's fully recovered?"

Case shakes his head and laughs emptily without smiling, "Aitin runs his own schedule. There's no way to know. It sounds like he's promised Jeter help with the GreenLands. If Aitin wants to keep Jeter around, he'll make good on his promise. But if he decides he doesn't need Jeter anymore, then he'll just dispose of him and probably make his way up to Petrichor."

"Is there any way to track him down?" I ask, butting into their conversation.

Case laughs hollowly again. "If Aitin is as powerful as you say, I'm sure he'll leave a trail of destruction wherever he goes. Question is, can you track him down without getting killed? Keep in mind that Aitin not only has the ability to produce lightning, he probably also has power just like you do. Once he learns how to use it, he'll be able to create and destroy, and he won't be afraid to cause death, unlike you've all been taught to do."

The full force of what we're facing slams into me in that moment. Mark and I can track Aitin down without getting killed at least by lightning, but then what? If I disable the serum, will it be up to us to kill him? *How do we do that?* With a simple knife or with power? Am I willing to end another person's life even if it's Aitin? Is that the right thing to do?

And that's all assuming that he doesn't kill us first.

Everyone eats Lilly's food. Trevor loudly grunts his approval over and over again, making me smile. I grab my own plate and make my way over to Mark, who's sitting on a bottom bunk, and squeeze in between him and Trevor. The others talk more, catching up on what's happened, but I slip away into my own mind.

I've guessed at what I might eventually have to do, but hearing it so plainly makes me want to rethink this altogether.

What will the end look like? Will I die? If not, will I be able to live with what happens for the rest of my life?

***

We eat and then rest for the remainder of the day. It's almost sunset when we finally drag ourselves back to the aircraft. Saying good-bye to Lilly is harder than I expected it to be. I'll miss her brightness, but I promise to return. Hopefully, when I do, I'll have more answers for her condition.

Case doesn't say much more to me, at least not until we're getting onto the aircraft.

"Alena," he whispers when I step up to the ramp. I stop and examine his face carefully. He looks so much like Danny, with his brown hair, straight nose, and strong jaw, I have to remind myself whom I'm talking to.

"Keep an eye on Mark," he says, watching Mark, who's out of earshot. "Aitin doesn't care for him at all. Should he somehow capture him again, I don't think he'll make the same mistake of letting him get away." Case shakes his head. "When Aitin was being experimented on by my father, my father would test certain liquids and plants on his skin, trying to figure out what his body was reacting to. This was before we realized it was Peppate. Aitin said it felt like Jose was burning him with fire. He was in so much pain. Since then, he's enjoyed burning other people as a form of torture. It's his way of exacting revenge." Case's eyes move back to mine. "I don't know what Aitin has in mind for Mark or why. All I know is that Mark might not survive it. Keep an eye on him."

I assumed as much. Hearing it from Case, though, terrifies me more, making my stomach sick. *How in the world do I protect Mark?*

Case then speaks louder, so Mark can hear.

"Alena and Mark, there are a couple of things you need to remember about the totem. There's a reason I broke it into two parts. Morphing at the same time creates a forceful lighting that destroys anything with Peppate, which *could* include you two if you have it inside you. The next time you morph, Mark, you should morph first. Your totem is made of the lightning force. It will push the Peppate out of your bodies without zapping either of you. Once it's out, then, Alena, you can morph. Alena, your totem is made of leader strokes that will guide the force and create the lightning."

I stare at Case blankly, recalling the journal we found at Case's old home. It mentioned the leader strokes. It's the reason he split the totem in two, but I'm not sure I understand it.

I look at Mark to see if that made any sense to him, but he looks confused too.

Case picks up on our confusion. Running a hand down his face in irritation, he tries to explain further. "Lightning strikes happen fast, but if you pay close attention, you'll notice that the strike always starts midair, up in the clouds. Then it travels down to the ground, where it can neutralize the pressure. In order for the strike to travel to the ground, though, it needs what's called a leader stroke. It's like a guiding negatively charged element that carves an invisible pathway through the air down to the ground. The rest of the electrical force follows right behind it, like a gush of water pushing through a riverbed."

Sighing deeply, he continues. "Alena, your totem was constructed using generators that had this leader stroke property in them. It was extremely difficult to perfect, but ultimately your morph carves a path for the lightning. Mark's totem was constructed using generators that had the force property in them. He's the gushing water.

"Without the leader stroke, the force just sits there and nothing happens. And without the force, the leader stroke travels on alone and again nothing happens. Hence both totems are needed for a full strike. So, again, before you both morph together, make sure that Mark morphs first. His Doler force will push out all Peppate from your bodies so you don't get hurt. Then Alena, when you morph, your totem will channel that force and create the strike."

I nod slowly.

"Okay, that makes sense," Mark says.

"You were full of Doler the night you came to Aitin's hideout," Case says. "So it probably wasn't a problem then, but if you *are* happy when you morph, it could hurt you. Also, I should probably tell you that the totem doesn't react well to glass."

I narrow my eyes. *Glass?*

"I didn't have a ton of time to experiment with it and figure out all the details, but at one point I kept the totems in a glass case to keep Peppate out. The totems withered inside that glass case. I don't necessarily know what that means, but if you think about it, glass doesn't conduct electricity. I'm wondering if it could potentially cripple your totems. Just be aware."

I glance down at my left arm still covered by my sweater. I recall the small glass jewels Mark attached to my totem only hours ago. Do we need to remove them? Will they hurt the totem?

Just then, Flint turns on the aircraft engine, forcing Case to stop talking and step away.

I watch him, suddenly filled with a weird sense of peace. I officially met the creator of my totem, and just talking to Case, learning more about how my totem was made, has already reduced some of the frustration I've felt since I obtained it. This one simple conversation has instantly changed my perspective. My totem is not a mysterious, terrifying weapon, meant to destroy and hurt, but instead a carefully crafted force with the ability to heal.

I don't want to run from it now. I want to use it, the way it was meant to be used.

Waving good-bye to Case and Lilly, I walk up the ramp with Mark, find a seat, and watch them walk back to the covered hideout.

As soon as I've healed the other Mixed Bloods, I'll come back to heal Lilly.

Flint flies us back to Maracai. I won't say it out loud, but I'm glad he came. He's been more than helpful.

Pulling out some paper, I begin writing a letter to Cody, letting her know what we've found and what we plan on doing. Then I write a note to my family. I'm worried about them, remembering what Cody said about Aitin being able to zap the protective fogs. I'm just now realizing what that means for my family, and I frantically tell them it might be time to find a new place to live. Petrichor is the worst place for anyone to be right now, so I can't even take them there. Instead, I tell them to try to find a place underground to hide until this is all over. Then I send Kapri's Magbaby away the moment we land.

By the time we land, it's morning again, and I'm so tired, even pulling my eyebrows up as high as I can, I can't keep my eyes open. Unfortunately, we still have a lot of explaining to do—to Eli, Mia, and her people. It goes remarkably well, of course, because we can now give them what they want.

By the time Mia leads us to an underground bunker where we can sleep, I practically fall into bed, and for the first time in a while, I sleep.

We have a plan.

Chapter 12

There's no light or noise down in my cave to wake me up or tell me what time of day it is. So, I sleep until I feel the soft brush of lips against my nose.

Those lips, that rustic smell, could only belong to one person. Mark starts to pull away when I stir, but I grip his shirt and pull him back to me. He chuckles in the darkness and finds my lips. I can feel him smiling through the kiss, but then he deepens it, running his fingers down my neck.

"Good evening, sleepyhead."

I freeze, his comment pulling me fully awake. I sit up. "*Evening*? I slept all day?"

"You slept all *two* days."

What? Two days? I must have been tired. I rub my eyes. I do feel more refreshed than I have in months.

Then I reach my hand out, searching for his face in the dark. "Did you sleep?" I ask.

I feel him nod. "I slept better than I have in a long time."

Good.

"I would've let you sleep much longer, Lena," he continues, "but the Mixed Bloods are getting antsy. I promised them I'd wake you after they fell asleep."

"Fell asleep? What time is it?"

"Close to midnight." Mark lights a torch on the cave wall, allowing me to finally see him, the golden flecks in his eyes, the stubble on his face. Man, is he handsome.

I touch his jaw carefully. He's here. Down in the same tunnels that terrified him before, the tunnels effused with the smell of death.

He doesn't seem scared, though, not like he was a few days ago. In fact, the flame he just lit reveals an odd but unmistakable glint in his eye. He seems happy, but why?

"Come on, there's something I want to show you."

Mark steps out of the room for a moment, allowing me to get dressed into a fresh pair of Mixed Blood clothing—a dingy black shirt and black sweatpants. Then he takes my hand and leads me down some narrow tunnels until we reach a big metal door. The door leads into a tiny pass room with a single torch lit. The room is so tiny that when Mark shuts the door, we're pressed close together.

Oh.

These tunnels are hot, and they just got hotter, with his warm hand wrapped around my waist, pressed against my back.

But then Mark leans to the side, the torchlight flickering across his face, and searches for something in his pocket.

He pulls out headphones. Noise-canceling headphones. I question Mark with my eyes, but he doesn't say a word, just smiles big while placing them on my ears. Once they're on tight, he opens the other door in the room and moves outside. I don't hear a thing, not even the scrape of our shoes against the rock, but when we step outside, I see it and instantly know the reason for the muffs.

Just beyond the door is the edge of the lake.

And all across the lake, for as far as I can see, are large bolts of lightning zigzagging through the sky.

Mia and Eli had mentioned that storms plague the lake, but I never could have imagined the surplus of bright strikes I see now. The earmuffs block out most of the noise. Only a low rumble here and there slips through, but not having to cringe at the close sound of each strike allows us to fully appreciate the magnificence of the light. It's magical, how it dances through the sky, across the surface of the water.

I watch how each strike starts in the air, then instantly reaches down to the earth like an arrow searching for a target, exactly as Case described. I'd never noticed it before, but I can almost see it now. There's clearly something that guides the lightning from the air to the earth. I wish I could watch it in slow motion. I'm sure it would be even more evident then.

Man, what a magnificent scene, strike after bright strike lighting the sky. I've never seen a more powerful storm in all my life.

I glance sideways at Mark, whose face is illuminated by the bolts. That mischievous look is still there, and I can't help but feel he has something else up his sleeve. Grabbing my hand, he places an old CD player in it, something that would never be allowed in Petrichor because it has batteries. Mark gestures that I should put the ear buds into my ears. Once I carefully weave them through the muffs, I hear the pulsing sound of a song. It's upbeat, adding more excitement to the scene. After carefully storing the CD player in the side pocket of my sweatpants, Mark takes my hand and pulls me toward the water.

We've only gone a few steps in the sand, when I stop. There's a WaveRunner there, bobbing on the lake.

Does Mark want us to drive *that* on the water in a lightning storm?

Mark is running backward now, egging me on. Then he takes off his shirt and signals for me to follow.

Well, I can't say no to that.

I quickly hush the logical part of my mind and follow him through the sand. Now I do wish I had brought my swimsuit.

Mark gets on first. I take off my shoes and walk through the water toward him. The WaveRunner jounces when I put my weight on the side, but I quickly swing my other leg over to level it out. Once on, I scoot as close to Mark as I can, wrapping my arms around his hot body. I can't hear him breathing, but I can sure feel it, his chest rising and falling beneath my fingertips.

I scoot closer.

The song from the CD player continues to beat loudly, and then a voice joins in, singing. A voice. The Magbabies are great at replicating beat and sound, but I've missed hearing music with an actual voice in it.

Soon Mark is moving us through the water, the WaveRunner at full throttle. Before I know it, we're gliding over the waves, bouncing almost exactly to the beats of the song. I hold on tight, bracing for every crest we catch.

A bolt of lightning strikes the water ahead of us, and even though I can't hear the crack through sky, I can feel the pressure change, the way it inverts the air.

Is this what they call *living on the edge?*

My smile widens, and I try to see through the darkness. The farther we get into the lake, the more the lightning strikes, and soon it becomes a maze of electricity we try to weave through.

I don't know why I do it. Maybe it's the song blaring in my ears making me feel like I'm invincible, or maybe it's the speed of the vehicle making me feel like I'm flying, but I unwrap one hand from Mark, brace myself with my knees against him, and raise my arm in the air, closing my eyes.

It really does feel like I'm flying. With a jolt here and there. And with water splashing in my face. I yell in approval, not even able to hear myself. Then I grab hold of Mark again and open my eyes.

Is it just me, or are the strikes getting closer? How do you avoid hitting lighting when it's so unpredictable? Three strikes extend their arms to the surface of the water all at once. Mark jerks the WaveRunner sideways just in time. We barely miss them but are led right into another. It hits the front of the Runner and sends me flying into the lake.

The cool water feels good in the heat of the night, but it gets up my nose.

Moving my arms and legs to keep myself afloat, I sputter and cough, trying to get the water out. Then I look around for Mark. He's only a couple feet away, the lightning illuminating his still present smile. He comes to me and pulls me flush against his body and kisses me gently. His lips are wet and cold, but his breath is warm and inviting.

I wish I could kiss him back like I want to, but it's frustratingly difficult to swim and kiss, especially with the waves trying to toss us around. When Mark sees how much I'm struggling, he points to the WaveRunner bobbing in the water not too far away.

Soaked, we swim to it and attempt to get on. Mark helps me first. I grunt out loud in frustration. It's much harder to do this from the water than the beach. Mark laughs when I fail to grasp the platform like I'm supposed to and end up falling back in the water several times. Once I finally get it, though, I settle into my seat and help him up.

I cling to him again, a little more nervous to tempt nature.

Then he starts the runner and moves us forward, slower this time, without the CD players that are lost in the water. I look around and decide that the strikes are definitely getting closer.

I don't know how, but Mark moves the WaveRunner at just the right times to avoid getting hit.

Can he sense the strikes?

Maybe it's just luck.

Finally, we reach the other side of the lake. Mark anchors the Runner close to the beach and then helps me off.

Because the lightning is still too close, we don't take off the muffs.

I watch Mark's face during each strike. He must have something else planned if we're this far away from the tunnels. *What's he doing?*

But then Mark's eyes furrow, and he gently fingers my totem. Looking down, I see what he sees.

The sections of my totem under the glass markers he gave me are shriveled. I look closer, using the lightning to help me see better. The brown vine is turning black and looks deflated, dried, almost dead.

Case was right. I forgot to remove the glass pieces after what he told us.

I turn to Mark and examine his chest. Sure enough, the section that's touching the glass looks the same—blackened, shriveled.

Stepping closer to me, Mark pulls the glass from my arm, tossing each piece far out into the lake. Then repeats the process on himself.

I frown. I wanted to keep those, as a reminder of the promise we made to each other. But it's probably for the best. Maybe we can make something else that isn't made of glass.

Mark bends down and writes something in the sand.

I look closely at it, waiting for a strike of lightning to illuminate the word.

Morph?

Suddenly, my good mood fades. That's what this is all about. Morphing. What better place to morph than in a lightning storm. Suddenly I'm back at Aitin's hideout, the fire surrounding me, making me feel like I'm trapped.

Morphing was a mistake then. I silently promised myself that night that I would never do it again. But now here we are, ready to morph for the sake of the Mixed Bloods.

Mark doesn't need to say it for me to know that this is probably the safest place for us to morph. A place where everyone is already prepared for lightning and are safely hidden below. It still terrifies me, though.

Mark takes my hand, reassuring me. I guess it's good we're wearing the Mixed Bloods Peppate-free clothes again. We'll need them tonight.

I rub my hand over the heart of my totem. It's empty since I removed my Peppate power when we reached Maracai, not wanting to make the Mixed Bloods more sick. Hopefully, the space will soon be full.

I look at Mark and nod. I'm ready.

He points to himself, and I know what he's saying. He's going to go first. The lightning strikes are getting closer probably because we're happy—we've absorbed too much Peppate during this little excursion. We need him to emit a load of Doler just to push the Peppate out, like Case said.

I step back to give him some space, then watch him morph. I never got a chance to fully appreciate his eagle form the last time we morphed, but seeing him now in the flashing light, his feathers from head to claw dark brown with a golden shimmer at the tips—he's magnificently beautiful—and ginormous. I step back. When he drops his eyes to mine, I see that they're the same kind brown they always are.

Reaching up, I stroke his head. I want to laugh when his eyes roll back, but I can already feel the diffused Doler filling me up, stealing the happiness from the night.

Man, talk about a mood swing.

Mark nods toward me now. It's my turn. I step back further to give myself more space, then I pound my chest just over my heart. I immediately feel the tingly sensation from head to toes racing down my limbs, into my fingers and toes.

Right away, light branches out from us, brighter and more powerful than the storm we just tempted. The pressure changes in the air repeatedly, offering only small moments of respite, and I fight to breathe. I'm just grateful for the earmuffs. It would be even more overwhelming without them.

The powerful instincts of the bird, or the totem—I don't know which—take over. I know exactly how to move my wings, how to rise, how to turn. Before I know it, I'm in the sky right behind Mark.

How long are we going to stay up here? I try to look down below to observe how much destruction we've already caused, but I can't see past the blinding lights. It probably would have been helpful to discuss this with Mark before the pounding of our lightning forbade any communication. Regardless, we fly across the lake, and a little further, before Mark starts to drop from the sky.

I don't know how long I've been holding my breath, but it all comes out in a burst of air now, anxious to be done with this.

Mark touches down, with me right behind. I try to mirror his graceful landing but fail miserably, thudding to my side. Then I morph back and roll to my knees.

I stay there, breathing heavily, eyes closed. I try to brace myself for the damage we've caused.

It isn't until Mark reaches for my chin and gently pulls my head up that I actually open my eyes. His face is only inches away, and he's smiling, which gives me the strength to look around.

The trees, as far as the eye can see, are of course scorched to dust. A sight I've seen before, one I never wanted to see again. There are some fires in the distance, trees that were too far away to be instantly turned to ashes. Hopefully they'll burn out soon.

Then I look out over the lake. The lightning storm has stopped completely, probably because we stole all the Peppate available to zap, but that isn't what catches my breath. The water level is considerably lower. I take off my earmuffs and instantly hear the sizzle as the lake evaporates into the air.

"The water," I whisper.

"It's okay, Alena. It rains here all the time. It'll quickly fill back up. But look at your heart."

I don't look at my heart, but I look at his. The middle of his totem is black.

I then reach for my own flask.

Despite the crappy Doler feeling consuming me, I want to shout. There's a small black sphere with a small amount of black power in it. It isn't nearly as much as we obtained when morphing at Aitin's silver mine, but it *is* power.

"It worked." Mark stands close, fingering my totem.

It worked.

All of a sudden, my body begins to tremble.

I'm cold.

Probably because I'm still wet. I even note goose bumps on Mark's skin. He mutters something about finding wood for a fire before turning to look around. I walk with him for a while, but there's nothing for miles. We destroyed it all.

Frustrated, Mark morphs, making me promise to stay put. When he comes back with some suitable wood, he goes to work building a very large crackling fire.

Then he sits on the ashy ground and pats the space in front of him. I'm shivering, wet, and so cold. *Does he really want me against his body, his bare chest?* I slip my body down, between his legs, but try to keep space between us.

Mark won't have it.

Placing a hand over my stomach, he pulls me close, his body heat instantly working to calm my shivering.

"I'll be leaving tomorrow to go back to Petrichor." Mark's hands run down my arm, attempting to warm me. I snuggle further into his embrace until I realize what he just said.

"Wait, what?" I turn to face him, but Mark just wraps his arm tight around my waist, forcing me to stare at the fire.

"I need to get you some more serum so you can perform your magic. With Dilo taken by Jeter, I need another dinosaur, one of her brothers to give me serum. Shakir, one of the other Dino trainers, has been trying to extract some, but he hasn't been too successful." Mark grunts, moving my hair, then kissing my neck softly. He's trying to distract me from what he's saying. And it works ... almost.

"I'll go with you," I say. I don't want to be separated from him again. Bad things always happen when we're apart.

Mark sighs and shakes his head.

"They won't let you." His voice is grim. "Sayo is anxious for you to heal his people. There's no way he'll let you leave." I tighten my grip on Mark's arms and sink further into his chest.

"Eli and Mia promised me they'd protect you, and Flint has agreed to come with me and keep me from harm. I'll be back before you know it."

He's kissing my neck again.

Flint. The sound of his name still makes my stomach churn, but at the same time I'm grateful he's going with Mark. I know he'll be a good protector.

"Please be safe," I finally say.

"I will if you will," he says, and I almost laugh. What a joke, this endless cycle of danger.

"I'll try."

Mark chuckles. Then we sit in silence, watching the night sky slowly lighten until the sun appears. Mark fiddles with the ash beside us. "It looks like Case was right about the glass and our totems. I wonder if I can make the marker out of something else." He tries to melt the ash like he did the sand, form it into something, but it's not cooperating the same way. When it gets hot, it just seems to evaporate.

Mark brings his arm back around my stomach. "Fine. I guess I'll just have to get you diamonds."

All too soon, the pull of need rings too loudly to ignore. Reluctantly, we find our way back to the WaveRunner that's sitting in the middle of the beach, too exposed from the evaporated water. Together, we push it forward, then skip across the depleted lake, much slower this time. Eli and Sayo are standing beside the entrance to the Mixed Blood town when we get back, ready to hear how it went. Not that they can't guess based on the destruction of trees.

I get off the Runner and walk up the beach.

"Did it work?" Eli asks when I reach him, his voice full of hope. When I nod, he lets out an exaggerated sigh of relief and wraps me in a big awkward hug.

Sayo, on the other hand, just nods seriously.

"Come on, let's get started," he says, practically dragging me back to the community.

Before I'm ready, Mark is handing me his portion of power, and then he's leaving me, heading to the aircraft with Flint. I stand frozen, holding his power in my hand, watching him leave, willing with every ounce of faith I have for him to be safe.

Chapter 13

Sayo leads Eli and me through the small, empty town. Once again, there are hardly any Mixed Bloods up here, and I'm beginning to wonder if they ever make it up above at all. The only ones I see are a couple of children playing in the courtyard like before. I stop walking when I see Trevor trying to join their simple game of kickball. They seem a little hesitant, having the large bear there. One of them even walks away, but this doesn't faze Trevor. He just steals the ball and kicks it to another young boy. The boy stops it cautiously with his foot and then kicks it back.

That's all I see before disappearing down into the tunnels.

Mia joins us now, asking me the same questions Eli did. She's not just happy with the news; she's ecstatic.

"This changes everything, Alena. Everything."

She swiftly guides us to a door, but before opening it, she turns to me.

"This is the room of the really sick, Alena," she whispers. "It's a dark and sad place for my people. We want the sickest healed first. I've tried to treat them the best I can, but it's never good enough." Mia's words are sad and disappointed.

I nod in understanding. I saw Aitin, but he was probably in fairly good condition compared to some.

"Here is the dino serum Shakir sent us." She holds out a half-filled vial of dinosaur serum. "It isn't much, but hopefully it'll get you somewhere until Mark gets back." I take the syringe.

Then Mia slowly opens the door. The smell reaches me first, and it takes every ounce of willpower not to immediately cover my nose. The smell of vomit mixed with rotting flesh makes me want to throw up myself. But I hold my breath instead. The room is lighter than the tunnel with dozens of torches lit on the walls, but it's still dark, a sad place for one to suffer physically. And there are *many* suffering. I almost gasp when I see the numbers. The cave reaches wide and long, offering an open space for what must be at least a hundred Mixed Bloods crammed together on small cots.

I stop in my tracks. The sounds of coughing, whimpering, and moaning all mix together in a loud cacophony that makes me want to cry. I don't know exactly what type of place I would want to suffer in, but it definitely wouldn't be in a place like this.

"I keep them all together so it's possible for me to take care of them," Mia says. "But I hate that they don't have their own privacy or space." Mia's eyes wander around the cavern as if she's seeing it for the first time through my eyes, talking as if I need an explanation for the disaster before us.

The instincts that are so engrained within me take over instantly, not allowing me to stay idle any longer. "Where do I start?"

Mia is ready. "Over here. This young girl is in the worst condition."

We weave through the plethora of occupied cots—Sayo following closely behind—until we finally reach the cot of a young dark-skinned girl who couldn't be older than seven. Her head is bald, like so many others.

I shake my head in despair. Where two legs once were, there are now two stumps.

"I had to amputate her legs," Mia explains. "She was climbing one of the walls in our town, when she fell. She broke one leg and badly cut the other. I set the bone, but her broken skin must have filled up with Peppate. It never healed properly and turned to infection, which slowly made its way further up her leg. I tried to hold off as long as I could, but, after several months, her condition was not improving. So, I amputated them here. She's doing better, but I fear we could still lose her. The procedure was hard on her little body."

There's a woman sitting next to the cot, who looks like a healthier version of the girl. Dark skin, bald head. I'm guessing she's the girl's mother.

I pull up the fabric covering the girl's stumps and bite my cheek. They're oozing with yellow fluid.

"*You* amputated her legs? How long ago?" I ask Mia.

"Three weeks."

This shocks me. Mia must know what she's doing if the girl has survived this long.

"Are you a doctor?"

"Yes. I did many years of training after I left the Pepps. I was hoping to help the Mixed Bloods."

Eli steps to Mia's side now, putting an arm around her. Mia doesn't shy away from his touch, which surprises me, but I don't have time to wonder about their rekindled relationship. "She uses human medicine," Eli says.

"You help all of them?" I ask, waving to the rest of the sickly people in the room.

Mia nods.

This amazes me. "And you've done this for years, all by yourself? Aren't you tired?"

This triggers tears in Mia. She swallows. "I'm tired of them suffering so much. Which is why I'm glad you're here. How long do you think it will take for you to heal her?"

A bud of respect plants itself inside me for Mia, for her dedication, love, and sacrifice. I can't imagine taking on such a heavy role.

I turn to the young girl. "I don't know exactly how long Aitin's took me, but it was a long time." I hold up the syringe of serum. "I had more serum and power too. Hopefully this'll be enough."

Kneeling, I kindly slide my hand into the young girl's. She's awake, examining me carefully, fear rolling off her body in waves.

"Hello, my name is Alena. What's your name?"

She doesn't answer, just keeps staring at me, sweat collecting on her brow.

"Chima," the girl's mother says. "Her name is Chima." I make eye contact with the mother for a brief moment. I can tell she's trying to trust me but doesn't know if I'm worthy of that just yet. Unfortunately, she doesn't have many other options at this point. She seems to know this too.

I smile my best smile at the girl. "Chima. It's nice to meet you. I'm here to help you if you'll let me."

I still get no verbal response from the girl, so I proceed. "I'm going to put this serum into your heart. This will be the most uncomfortable part of the procedure, but it'll be over quick. Then I'm going to move the serum around your body, until it is in all the right places." I pause, giving her a chance to speak. When she doesn't, I add, "If there's any power left, I'll try to heal your sores and infections so you won't be in so much pain. Is that okay?"

Now, the girl's wide eyes fill with tears, and she opens her mouth. "Anything will be better than this."

Her croaky words weigh heavily on my chest, and I fight to control my emotions. Knowing my voice will betray me, I just nod, indicating the start of the procedure.

With the syringe in my hand, my arm hovers in the air. Jeter had injected the serum into Aitin's heart. Now that it's my responsibility, I pause. What part of the heart do I inject it into? How do I get the needle past her ribs? I close my eyes recalling the anatomy of the chest. The left side of a person's heart is where the blood from the body is returned. The right side of the heart is where the blood is pushed out into the body.

I need to inject it into Chima's right side of the heart, which would be my left. I finger Chima's chest, feeling her ribs. After I inject it, I'll need to repair the puncture hole, keep it from killing her.

Taking in a deep breath, I start.

Chima and her mother flinch simultaneously when I put the needle into her heart, then pull it out. But that's it. She's brave. They're both brave.

The black power is different from Pepp power. It doesn't allow me to hear all the elements of the heart in the same way. I don't have the time to figure out all the heavy muffled sounds, so I speak in my own language.

Close the hole, I say in my mind.

I don't know how I know it closes. Maybe it's the shiver that ripples down my spine or just the cold feeling of the power flowing through my fingers, but I know that Chima's heart no longer has a hole in it from the needle. I know it's healed, which thrills me. *I can use the black power to heal the body.*

I turn my focus to the serum, start moving it around, speaking to it like I did with Aitin. The world fizzles out around me, and my attention tunnels in on the girl. I listen to the Peppate generators like I did the night I healed Aitin.

Cocking my head, I experiment for a moment. Now that I know I can control the body, I wonder if it's possible for me to control the Peppate generator. *Can I disable it without the serum?* I don't really know what to tell my totem to do, but I communicate that I want the generator destroyed.

Nothing.

Okay, can I shrink it? Or tear it apart?

Nothing.

Can I burn it? Maybe I could, if I was good with heat.

I sigh.

The Peppate generators don't respond to the black power, just like the Dilo serum doesn't respond to normal Pepp power.

I guess with this black power I can only control things with Doler. Which means I can control most of this girl's elements. Just not her Peppate generators.

I go back to moving the serum in.

Chima falls asleep at some point during the procedure, and her mother slides over to the wall where Sayo has also taken up residence, probably to keep a constant eye on me. I can't be positive, but I think the girl has fewer Peppate generators than Aitin did. Perhaps because she's younger ... and doesn't have any legs. The smaller amount of serum and power is almost perfect. By the time I reach the last of the generators in her nubbed legs, my back and knees are aching from sitting wrong.

I need to figure out a more comfortable way to do this.

With a small amount of power left, I turn my attention to the infection in her stumps, doing the same thing to them that I did with her heart.

Move the white blood cells, repair the muscles.

It works. A yellow substance oozes out onto the bandages, soaking them until they're dripping.

With new hope, I move to command her skin to bind better, and then try to relieve some of her pain. I can sense many other things in her body that need healing, but they'll have to wait. My power is gone, fizzled out like a whisp of cold air.

I look at the girl's face now. She's sleeping. Good.

Satisfied with my efforts, I look for Mia, finding her sitting against the wall with Eli, Sayo, and the girl's mother.

"It's done?" the mother asks when I walk to them.

I nod, suddenly feeling very tired.

"What now?" Mia asks.

"We wait. I just barely had enough power to heal her infection. I tried to relieve some of her pain too. We'll see how she feels when she wakes up. You can go sit with her now if you'd like," I tell her mother.

Chima's mother slips away from us, and Mia guides me out of the room, through the same door we entered. "I think you should rest," she says.

I *am* exhausted, but how can I possibly rest with an entire room filled with so many sick people?

"How long did that take me?" I whisper.

"Four hours."

Four hours!

This discourages me. Chima was a child, which probably cut my time. It's going to take me months to get to all the people in here. Not to mention the power. I can't create any more power without Mark here. *Are we going to have to morph every night?*

Mia starts to guide me through the tunnels, when someone yanks on my arm.

"Where are you going?" Sayo asks angrily.

I try to form words to tell him I'm unable to do more than this today, but my mouth is frozen. He reminds me so much of Aitin, with his gray bloodshot eyes, scarred skin, and yellow teeth. I take a step back.

Thankfully, Mia steps in and answers for me. "Her power is gone, and so is the serum. There's nothing more she can do until Mark gets back."

"She healed one little girl!" Spittle flies from his mouth in exasperation, and I feel a pang of despair.

I would heal them all right now if I could!

Mia peels his hand off my arm and pushes me through the tunnel again, leaving him behind. She leads me to my same small room with the cot inside.

"Sleep here for now. I'll tell Mark to come get you when he arrives with more serum."

When she leaves, closing the door behind her, I collapse onto the cot and sleep.

Chapter 14

I wake to Mark's gentle touch again and immediately wrap my arms around his neck.

He came back. He's safe.

I don't let him go for a long time. When he finally peels me off, he helps me up, then takes me through the tunnels, leading me outside into another dark night.

I gasp when I see it.

The entire area we destroyed the night before has somehow been fully restored. Water, trees, bushes—are everywhere.

"Mia came up here yesterday afternoon," Mark says as we step into the sand. "When she saw how much life we'd burned to ashes, she wondered how we were going to collect more Peppate here. Rusty said he can't send any totems from the totem tree to be destroyed by us. I guess the tree hasn't been producing as many totems as it used to. Probably because of everything that's going on with the climate up there. That's when Mia thought of another idea." Mark looks around, waving his hand in the air. "She asked for a team of Pepps to come down and restore the place. They regrew the trees and organized some more water. Then they morphed and spread as much Peppate as they could—in turn getting more power."

I look around at the area. What a brilliant woman.

"Now we have more stuff to zap," Mark says, a grin tugging at his lips. He seems to be enjoying this lightning stuff. "This of course means that the Mixed Bloods will have to stay indoors until you can heal them. But that seems to be a sacrifice they're more than willing to pay, considering how well that little girl is doing." Mark takes my hand. "We better beat the lightning storm so we can kill as much Peppate as possible."

Mark and I repeat the process of the night before. Except this time without the WaveRunner—and the fun. We need to gather as much power as we can, so we fly. For a long time. There are no lightning storms tonight, other than what we create.

When the night sky turns gray with morning light, Mark drops down, far from the tunnels and the lake. I follow him, morphing back into human form, wondering if he'll make another campfire.

He doesn't.

"You ready?" he asks.

I stand there confused. "Ready for what?"

He steps closer, taking my hand in his. "Back in Petrichor, you were trying to learn how to sense power so you can deflect it, like Jeter did."

Oh, yeah.

"I'd like to help you."

I sigh. "There's a small problem, Mark. I don't have any Pepp power on me, do you?"

Mark lets go of my hand and rubs the back of his neck. "Well, I've actually been thinking that Jeter's Pepp power isn't the real threat."

I'm confused.

Mark drops his hand. "If you think about it, all we have to do to defeat Jeter is morph. You and me. We'd kill him right away."

"As long as we're together," I say, not bothering to reminding him that Aitin and Jeter have a way of pulling us apart.

"Yes, as long as we're together. Anyway, I think that Aitin is the real threat, not Jeter. We're going to have a harder time defeating him. So maybe we should practice deflecting *his* power—or, in other words, *our* black power."

He's probably right, but I'm tired, a little cold, and I still believe Jeter is the one we should be worried about. He's been listening to the elements much longer than Aitin. For all we know, Aitin might not even know what the elements sound like.

This gives us a place to start, though. Maybe learning how to sense the black power will somehow help me learn how to sense Pepp power as well.

"Okay." I surrender. "What do we do? By the way, I think Sayo is going to be furious if he finds out we used this for anything other than healing." I tap my chest.

A sly smile slips across Mark's face. "We won't tell him." Then he starts to pace in the ashes. "As far as the power goes, I don't really know what to do. I can try to push my power toward you, let it sit in the air?"

Mark's voice is confused, unsure, and I know why. We never use our power to just sit in the air. It's created to connect with the elements around us, control them. Without the instruction to control, the power doesn't really respond. At least I don't think it does. We definitely can't see it, so we don't know if it's hovering in the air or not. And it doesn't make any sounds. How do you know if something is there if you can't see it or hear it?

You try to feel it?

"Okay," I say. "Push it toward me. Maybe pretend like you're trying to poke or touch me with it. I'll see if I can feel it."

I close my eyes and concentrate, focus on my skin, try to sense the whispers of power. There's not much wind tonight to give me false sensations. There are no bugs either since we morphed and probably killed them all. I shiver, though, from the cold.

What does the power feel like?

After a few minutes, I peek through my eyes. "I don't feel anything."

Mark rubs a hand down his face. "I'm not very good at this. Maybe you try."

We switch roles, Mark closing his eyes, me using a tiny bit of my new black power to push toward the skin of Mark's left arm. I watch his face for any sign of change.

"You feel that?" I ask after a few moments.

"No."

I step closer, pushing the power up to his neck and face.

"Anything?"

"No."

I sigh and drop my hands before closing the distance between us and planting my face in his chest. "Do you feel that?"

Mark chuckles and wraps his arms around me. I didn't realize how chilly I was until his warmth embraces me.

Wait. My body straightens. I'm cold.

We're in the south where the heat threatens to melt you every day and night. Last night when we morphed we got soaking wet, which explains why I was shivering then, but now? I shouldn't be cold, should I?

The chilly feeling is so subtle that I almost dismiss it, then shake my head. I have to be sure.

I grip the back of Mark's shirt. "Close your eyes again, Mark."

Mark smiles against my hair. "Yes, dear."

I pull my left hand toward me until it's hovering over Mark's arm. Could it be that the power makes us feel a little cold? I recall a distinct shiver when I was healing Chima. Could it be that simple?

I imagine the power falling from my fingers like pixie dust. I speak to it in my own language, instead of the Pepp totem language.

Just dust him, settle onto his arms, let him feel.

Then I watch, in the early morning light. His skin doesn't react, but I don't give up.

Come on.

Then I see it, an area of goose bumps rising over his forearm. My face splits into a smile, and I look up at Mark. His eyes are no longer closed but shining golden brown in the morning light.

"It feels cold," he whispers.

"Can you resist it?" I ask. "Pretend it's like dust on your skin that you need to push off?"

Mark's eyes are no longer looking at me. They're no longer smiling but staring intently at my lips. "Hmm?" he asks, obviously not listening. "Resist what?" Without warning, he leans down and bites my jaw, pulling my body flush with his.

Oh.

"Mark," I whisper. As much as I would love to spend the entire day out here with him and never go back to Maracai, the clock is ticking. Sayo is probably already pissed we aren't back yet.

"I know, we need to get back," he says but makes no attempt to stop the trail of kisses he leaves down my neck. I weave my fingers into his hair not willing to fight it. When his lips finally reach mine, heat rises up my spine, into my shoulders. Its sharp contrast to the cold has me melting further into Mark's arms, until I realize that something is actually really hot.

I flinch and turn to look behind me, but Mark just pulls me closer, bites my neck again. "Resist my flame, Lena."

He's pushing his power toward me—with fire—and wants me to stop it.

I hiss when the flame gets too close, singes the skin on my back, but Mark doesn't surrender. He just keeps distracting me with that hand, tight around my waist, with his lips so soft and warm.

"Come on, Lena."

His lips are on mine again, working in distracting patterns. I close my eyes, gritting my teeth against him.

Focus. I imagine the power in front of me, like a shield, cold and strong.

I remember the winters back home in the high mountains. I remember some unique days during the harshest of seasons when I would witness ice forming over our living room window. It would start in the corner and spread, its icy fingers aching to cover the glass.

That's how I imagine my power. Icy, cold, spreading in front of me, around me. I feel it the moment my power touches Mark's, combines with it, allowing me to touch him in a new and unique way.

His kisses intensify, and my power spreads until it fully encompasses me, leaving only a small puncture in the spot where Mark's fire continues to burn my back. It hurts, isolated and biting, yet spreading around to my stomach.

I fight the pain, imagine that puncture in my shield closing, imagine pushing that flame away.

Soon the heat against my skin cools, and I sigh in relief.

"Come on, try harder," I murmur into Mark's mouth.

Mark smiles now against my lips and pulls away. "Look, Lena."

I open my eyes. Flickering light bounces off his face, and I turn around. My hand rises to my mouth. The flame in his left hand burns at least three feet high and three feet wide, wild and angrily trying to lick my skin. Mark's free hand wraps around my stomach while I attempt to keep my power shield up.

I poke at it, prod it. It's warm, but not as hot as it should be, being this close. When I push my power toward it, the flame moves away from me.

"How are you doing that?" Mark asks in awe.

I shrug against his chest. "I don't know. I guess I just pictured myself covered in icy protective power. The power did the rest."

I melt against him, dropping my hands. He lets his flame die, then drapes his other arm across my chest, tucking me close to his body.

"We should probably get back," he whispers into my ear.

"Probably," I say. "But next time we come out here, I get to practice on you, see if you can resist me."

Mark leans down one last time to kiss my temple. "I don't think I'll ever be able to resist you."

Chapter 15

By the time we get back to Maracai, the sun is all the way up and the day is hot. Sure enough, Sayo is furious we're late, immediately dragging me down to the underground hospital.

This time, though, we have a little more power in each of our vials.

Then I heal. Because the power is so difficult to obtain, I decide to keep it only for distributing the serum and not for healing the wounds or ailments— as long as the patient will live.

It hurts, though. Leaving so much pain unattended. It's like being forbidden to scratch an itch that really needs to be scratched. I wish I could give them more.

I bounce from ill to ill, day after day, constantly lost in the world of healing until weeks have quickly passed.

Sayo, like a shadow, always makes sure I'm doing everything I can. I hate everything about that annoying man, except for the fact that he hasn't insisted I heal *him* yet. He's allowing those that are sickest to go first. I guess I have to give him some credit for that.

Nobody's heard anything about Aitin, nor have any of the other Mixed Bloods turned up dead. There's a ticking clock that tocks constantly in my head. Every day Aitin doesn't do anything is a day that has me more and more concerned about what is to come.

Slowly, the number of ill in the big cavern dwindles down as they're taken to another cave to heal on their own. So far, it sounds like the treatment is working. The sores are healing, the voices a little less croaky, and the digestive systems a little more stable. At least that's what Mia tells me. I haven't had time to personally go examine them.

Perhaps someday I'll figure out a way to heal their allergy all together, but, for now, this is one small step in the right direction. I sure hope they can heal enough to help the Pepps fight Aitin. Soon.

When I feel the kiss of Mark waking me up for another long night, I can't help but cry. I'm getting a small taste of what Case must feel like. Being underground, in the dark dreariness. Trying to forsake Peppate in order to heal these people is taking its toll on me.

It's taking a toll on Mark too, who's been working day and night underground with Pho, Dilo's brother he now extracts serum from. Now we're Doler filled, and it doesn't feel very good.

"Do you want to go swimming with me in the lake today, after you're done healing?" Mark asks, kissing my chin.

Tears leak out of my eyes.

"There's still too much to be done," I whisper. The weight of my task finds it familiar spot in my aching shoulders, sitting heavy like it does every moment of every day now. "Plus, I don't have a swimsuit." It's such a small problem, but it makes more tears leak out.

"You need to take care of yourself too, you know," Mark whispers, "or else you won't have any energy left to heal."

It feels wrong. Me going for a swim while they continue to suffer, yet a small part of me knows Mark is right, which is why I agree to join him later.

We leave the cave, we morph, and we fly for the umpteenth time. Then at sunrise I force myself back into the dark caves, saying good-bye to Mark and taking his vial of precious power before he goes to Pho.

I make my way to the sick cavern now, still wanting to plug my nose when I walk in, although the smell is a little less potent with fewer patients in here. Then I go to work on the next patient Mia has suggested. An older man, maybe in his sixties, with no hair, dry skin, and lots of sores. His face and eyes are pale, but today he's clenching his stomach, and I know exactly why. He's the eighth patient I've seen with this digestive allergic reaction. The intestines have swollen so much that it's causing a painful blockage, making him vomit. If I don't heal him, there's a good chance his intestines will start to rot, if they haven't already. He could die if the swelling and infection don't go down.

I go to work, using my fresh vial, shaking my head again and again at the horrible condition the man is in. I inject him with the serum, then instruct it to move. My times are getting better. This man only takes me three hours. I stabilize his intestines and then stand, feeling exhausted. I still have enough power to heal at least one or two more.

I look around the room for Mia. She knows which patient is next, but when my eyes scan the cavern all I see is patient after patient. No Mia. She rarely leaves this place, and when she does it's only for a few minutes, so I sit on the floor and wait.

Finally, she walks into the cavern.

I stand and approach her, ready to ask which patient is next, but then my steps slow.

Her face is brighter than I've ever seen it. She looks happy.

When she reaches me, she doesn't give me a chance to speak. Instead, she grips my arm and says, "Alena, please come with me."

I look around the never-ending room of patients, wanting to get my work over with, but Mia insists.

"We won't be gone long."

I follow her down the dark tunnels. *How far do these tunnels go?* I find myself wondering for the first time. It seems like a never-ending labyrinth.

Along the way, Mark meets up with us, answering Mia's mysterious request to meet her. He looks as confused as I am, but we just follow Mia in silence. After walking for a long time, she finally stops in front of a dark door.

Turning to us, she smiles, then grips the handle.

The door leads to a large bright candle-lit room with colorful walls, tiny beds, and plush carpet. Papers with carefully drawn pictures litter the far wall, and tiny glowing stars cling to the ceiling.

It looks like a nursery for children, happy and bright.

It's not just the light that makes the room bright, though. There's something else.

Laughter.

Laughter from little children reaches my ears, a sound I haven't heard for too long. My eyes are drawn to the middle of the room where a large bear on all fours is carrying three children on his back. Trevor. A ball sits on the carpet in front of him, and he kicks it with his paw to another little girl who's standing beside a small bed. She squeals in delight when given the task of catching the ball. Two other children start chasing after her to steal it away, and she frantically sends it back to Trevor. He falls over in an exaggerated manner when the ball contacts him, spilling the kids on his back to the floor, drawing out more squeals of delight.

I can't help but notice the sounds of their voices. They're clear.

"Alena. Mark." Mia whispers for our attention, watching the scene in front of us with misty eyes. "I've never heard these children laugh."

I swallow, her words seeping in. I look at the scene again, now as if through her eyes, and feel a bump grow in my throat. These children were lying on cots, dying, only weeks ago, but now they're here, standing, smiling ... playing. My eyes travel from face to face, recalling each one of their conditions, their severe allergic reactions. I remember their cries.

Those cries are now gone.

A mother, rocking a young girl in the corner chair, smiles at the scene. Trevor pulls himself away from the other children and reaches out for the girl. The room goes quiet.

Chima.

I attempt to swallow again. The young girl will never walk again—her condition stole that from her—but yet she's here, smiling with new hope.

Trevor delicately takes the tiny girl into his huge arms, then turns to the other kids and roars loudly, starting a new game of *run away from the bear*. Chima clings to Trevor's fur with the biggest little-girl smile on her face.

"Thank you, Mark and Alena," Mia says.

I clearly remember when I first met Mia—the skepticism in her expression, the disgust in her voice. She wasn't fond of me then, and she wasn't afraid to show it. Here she is now, though, totally changed. Where there was once disgust and anger, there is now heartfelt appreciation. "Thank you for helping them," she finishes.

I nod and try to smile, but then it hits me.

This.

This is my place.

The place I'm needed.

My mind suddenly starts playing through the painful times of my past. The moments that have had me wondering what the point of life was. What the point of *my* life was. I had decided many times that even if there *was something* good out there for me, some reward at the end of my trials, there's no way it would ever be worth the pain I was going through.

But this.

This moment softens all those difficult times in my mind, caresses them into a new understanding. They weren't designed to be hopeless moments but instead designed to redirect me, guide me, to where I was truly needed.

Here.

I kept wanting to create my own path that would lead me to a normal Pepp life, but that path was never the right path for me. This one is. It always has been, and now I can feel it deep in my bones. I'm meant to be here.

I slide my arm around Mark, clinging to him.

We're abnormal Pepps who will never be like everyone else, and that's okay. If we were like everyone else, we couldn't have done this.

Our Doler abilities have given us the chance to find answers these Mixed Bloods so desperately needed—Mark's Doler ability to work with the dinosaurs led him to the serum, and my ability to command that serum led us to healing. Together we found an unexpected solution, using the odd totems woven through our skin.

I glance down at my totem now.

For the *first* time ... I'm grateful for it.

It was the key to healing these people, and because it's on my arm, I get to be part of this miraculous process.

Thank you. I whisper to it, as I finally recognize it as the gift it is, attached to my body.

Thank you.

Someone clears their throat in the room, and I pull my misty eyes away from the kids to find Danny and Kapri standing beside us now. I haven't seen them much lately since I've been so busy healing, but I heard Danny was working on some sort of suit to allow the Mixed Bloods to go outside without getting sick. Danny has that suit on now, and I snort out a laugh through my tears. It looks silly.

Danny rolls his eyes but then he holds out his arms for a hug. I accept it, clinging for a moment to the boy who first gave me purpose in Petrichor. Gave me friendship.

"Nice suit," I say.

Kapri laughs next to him. "Danny's woven a bunch of Doler into it. We're hoping it'll help repel Peppate." She looks at him admiringly while gripping his suited arm.

"Good job, you guys."

Just then, I hear another familiar voice behind me, but this voice is not happy like those in the room. I turn just in time to be fiercely hugged by Cody.

Cody?

While wrapping my arms around her in confusion, I look over her shoulder at Rusty, who is standing in the doorway next to Eli. The happy feeling coursing through my veins quickly evaporates away at the sight of him. He's changed somehow. Lost weight. There's a new heaviness in his eyes. I guess that's what happens when the survival of an entire species is placed in your hands.

I pull back from Cody, looking at her face. Her blue eyes are swollen and red, as if she's been crying.

"What's going on? What are you doing here?"

Rusty steps up to Cody's side. "We need to talk."

Chapter 16

We follow Eli silently through the halls until we reach the council room, the room I was brought into when we first arrived here. Mia, Sayo, and a couple of other Mixed Bloods are already here. Several chairs have been placed in a circle in the middle of the room, but nobody sits. It's as if everyone senses this discussion will be too tense for the comfort of chairs. Trevor, Danny, Kapri, Mark, and I wait anxiously to hear what Rusty has to say.

The light from the torches moves across his face as he pulls one of the chairs to the middle of our standing circle.

"We have some bad news," he says. Then he pulls out a glass cylinder, revealing a small bug inside. *A memory bug.* "I've had a team evaluating things between Verdure and the GreenLands. Sef returned to Petrichor early this morning, with this. You're welcome to see for yourself what's been done." Rusty holds out the memory bug.

Nobody responds. I'm torn between wanting to see what happened and not wanting that bug inside my head.

Eventually, I clear my throat. "Will you just tell us what it shows?"

Rusty drops his hand to his side. "Fires and ash. They said Verdure has burned, and it burned fast. All of it, leaving very few survivors."

I gawk at him. *All of it?* I've never been to Verdure, but I've seen pictures on the news when I lived at home. The country was monstrous with huge building after huge glass building that stretched on for hundreds of miles. *For it to burn in its entirety?* I swallow down the sickening bile starting to collect in my throat.

"Aitin," I whisper. He's finally morphed.

Rusty now pulls out a map and points to part of Verdure. "Based on the ashes and extinguished fires, they think Verdure burned about a week ago. But more recently, probably within a day or so, a path of destruction has extended further, right up the middle of the country. The fires on the outskirts are still burning." Rusty's finger makes a line up the middle of the country, but it stops at the border of the GreenLands. Any composure he'd been holding, falters now, and his shoulders slump.

"Jeter wanted Aitin to stop the war. He wanted to end Verdure or keep them from progressing through their land, but it looks like Aitin had plans of his own."

I rock unsteadily, waiting for the bad news.

"Aitin never stopped at the border. In fact, he never stopped until he reached the far side of the GreenLands." Rusty looks up now, his voice cracking.

Cody speaks now, resting her hand on Rusty's arm. "The GreenLands are gone."

A dense wave of despair crashes over me. *The GreenLands? That beautiful green country? Gone?*

Sweat collects on my brow, as if my body itself is fighting the news, denying the fact that a human being could be so ... *heartlessly cruel.*

Nobody has ever known Aitin's intentions. I've guessed at them, hoping I was wrong. This news though, confirms the one thing I've feared most. Aitin is set on destroying *everything.* And he's already begun.

Rusty runs his hand through his sandy-colored hair. "His line stopped at the border on the far side of the GreenLands."

I look at the invisible pathway Rusty has created on the map. If Aitin had continued to go north, he would have run into Petrichor. He could have destroyed it already.

"Why did he stop?" I ask.

Rusty shakes his head. "He stopped after Verdure too. It's probably exhausting for him to morph, just like it is for us. I'm hoping he'll need time to recover, which is why we're here." Rusty stands to his full height, speaking mainly to Eli and Mia. "We need help now. We need to quickly train the Mixed Bloods and take them back to Petrichor."

"Not until everyone is healed," Sayo interjects, spittle flying from his mouth again when he speaks. "Nobody leaves until *everyone* is healed."

"How much longer do you need to heal everyone, Alena?" Mia asks me, ignoring Sayo.

My shoulders sag. We've come so far, but there's still more to be done. "It'll probably take me another month or so."

"We don't have that time," Rusty says.

"Can you train other Mixed Bloods?" Mark asks. "To heal now that they can morph and collect power on their own? Aitin did it, so they can too, right?"

I hadn't thought of that. "Yeah, I guess I could. We could ask around and see who might be interested. They can morph ... Wait, how would Mixed Bloods morph? They don't have a totem to pound like the rest of us."

"It's probably similar to how the Pure Bloods morph back home," Rusty says. "It's a natural instinct, but they might need a little coaxing. I'll have Flint show them how it's done."

Flint. Why does the simple mention of Flint's name still make me cringe? It's not like he's been mean to me lately. Maybe I'm jealous of him, the fact that we can't seem to do anything without his skills.

"I'll be sending down a team to help you train the Mixed Bloods. Danny, Kapri, Mark, and Alena, I'd like you to stay here and help. Work with them tomorrow. Teach them anything, especially ways to hurt Aitin."

I break in here. "Rusty, I also need to practice extracting the serum from Aitin. We won't defeat him if he still has power, and he'll always have power unless I can get that serum out. I need to practice. I need to get faster."

Sayo immediately starts shaking his scarred, bald head. "Absolutely not. You haven't even finished healing my people. There's no way I'll let you start extracting *just for practice*."

My shoulders sag. I should've waited and talked to Rusty alone about this.

Rusty clears his throat. "Alena's right. We need that serum out of Aitin. She can practice at the end of each day with a small amount of power." Rusty's voice holds the air of authority, and even though Sayo physically fights to keep his anger in, he lets the topic fall ... for now.

Rusty pulls out another piece of paper and lays out what looks like a drawn map. "All of the Pepps are now hidden in the underground bunker, to protect them from Aitin and his lightning. Hopefully, Aitin will just think the Pepps left and won't know they're hiding below. The dinosaurs have now been set free. We've tried to create some barriers to keep them from leaving Petrichor altogether, but, in all honesty, they could figure out a way." There's a sound of hopelessness in his voice. "That's why we need the Mixed Bloods. If they can somehow slow down Aitin enough for Alena to extract the serum, we might stand a chance. The Pepps will keep their totems on just in case they need power, but they know if they're to leave that underground bunker with Aitin around, they'll most likely die if he morphs."

Eli looks to Mia, silently asking if she agrees with the plan. She doesn't hesitate. "We're ready to start. My people are willing to help, especially after being healed."

Sayo runs an impatient hand down his face and paces the cave. But he doesn't say anything.

"Two days," Rusty says. "That's all the time we have to spare before we need to get everyone to Petrichor. If there are still unhealed Mixed Bloods, bring them with you. Alena will finish healing them when *I* allow her to."

Trevor, who normally remains quiet, starts talking in bear. We're all grateful Gabbro is there to interpret.

"Trevor wants to bring the Pepp children here. He thinks they'll be safer away from Petrichor."

Of course Trevor would be concerned about the children.

"I can agree with that if you can?" Rusty pointedly asks Mia.

"We can keep them in the eastern tunnels," she says. "They're further away from our people and will reduce the risk of Peppate spread to the Mixed Bloods."

"Good, I'll send a message and have a team bring them down tomorrow."

Packing up his things, Rusty says good-bye to the others, then grabs my arm and leads me down the hallway close to the room where I sleep. Mark follows behind.

When we're finally far away from the others, Rusty lets go and releases a big sigh.

"That guy is killing me."

I almost smile. At least I'm not the only one who hates Sayo.

Rubbing his face, Rusty clears his throat. "Alena, there's something else I need to tell you. Your family. I've been worried about them. In fact, I've been worried about all of the human race. With how easy as it was for Aitin to destroy two enormous countries, nobody is safe anymore. Everything is just utter chaos in the non-Pepp world. Leaders are trying to explain away the destruction, but the truth is they have no idea what's going on. Everyone is absolutely terrified. I've created a hideout for your family, deep in the mountains close to where you live. They're no longer at the rendezvous point. I've encouraged them to collect as many people as they can and have them hide there until we tell them things are safe. They have food and water to last them a couple of months."

I shake my head. *A couple of months?* My poor family.

"Thank you, Rusty."

"They've actually been quite helpful in convincing others to hide, especially Caleb with his very convincing tongue. He's done a great job. I just hope they'll be safe until we can get to them again."

It shouldn't surprise me to hear how involved my family is with the Pepps, but it does. They would all make great Pepps if that was ever possible.

"Thank you, Rusty. For watching out for them."

Rusty's tired face saddens me. He's doing a great job as leader of the Pepps, but the burden he carries is snuffing out his normal light. It's too much.

Perhaps it's too much for all of us. *But what choice do we have?*

Chapter 17

I hold the syringe in my hand and gently press the serum into the heart of an older teenager with chestnut skin and thick bones. Behind the symptoms of his allergies, he reminds me a lot of Leinani. He must be from the Islands.

I move my head from side to side, trying to relieve the tightened muscles in my shoulders before I begin. Then I lean over the teenager, starting with his torso.

I'm thankful this boy isn't in critical condition like many of the others were. Still, I try to focus hard. Unfortunately, my weary mind is distracted by the conversation with Rusty and Cody earlier today. I'm also distracted by a small pair of dark eyes watching me.

Chima.

I've seen her sneak into this terrible room a couple of times to watch me work, but she usually doesn't stay too long. Today, however, after several hours, she's still here.

She's sitting in a metal contraption Mark made for her, something that closely resembles a wheelchair. It allows her to move around on her own, even on the difficult rocky floors.

I turn back to the boy in front of me. With his torso done, I move on to his legs.

Chima moves closer.

I eye her again. She uses this as an invitation to state what she wants. "Teach me."

I look around for Mia, or her mother, or even Sayo to simply intervene, but none of them are in the room.

I bite my cheek. "Do you have power yet?" I don't know if Flint has already taught them how to morph.

She shakes her head. I really shouldn't indulge her. Sayo might get mad, but I signal with my head to have her come closer. The least I can do is talk her through it. Maybe it'll come in handy somehow.

I explain my process to her, try to describe the sounds I hear like Mitch used to do for me. Maybe it'll help her listen and identify them when she gets her power. I try to explain the different vessels and parts of the generator, emphasizing the importance of only paralyzing the Peppate part of it and not the whole thing. Chima listens carefully, asking smart questions that catch me off guard.

It takes me longer to heal the boy, who Chima has identified as Folou for me, but when I'm done, Chima grins wide, exposing her almost toothless mouth. She's enjoying this.

Could she eventually apply everything I just told her?

I move on to the next patient, and Chima rolls behind me. I'm just starting to explain everything again, when Chima places her hand on my arm. She looks around the room secretly—rebelliously—as if hoping it'll be absent of someone in particular. Then, leaning in, she whispers very carefully to me.

"I want to help you learn how to extract the serum."

How does she know about that?

I furrow my eyebrows and check around the room myself, looking in particular for Sayo. He's not here.

"I overheard you talking with your friends," she continues. "You said you need to practice extracting it in order to defeat Aitin."

Before I can tell her that I'm not allowed to do that yet, she rushes on. "You need practice, and I want you to practice on me."

I stare at her dumbfounded. "Why?"

Chima's black eyes look down at what's left of her legs and shrugs. "You healed me. I've never felt so healthy in my life. The least I can do is help you out in this way."

What a brave little girl. But I shake my head. "Chima, it might make you sick again. I don't want to do that to you. I'll find someone else."

Chima adamantly shakes her head. "No, it needs to be me, and even if it does make me sick again, I don't think I'll ever be as sick as I was before. Plus, you can heal me." She smiles and shrugs a second time.

She's probably right. I don't see this putting her that close to death again.

I sigh and turn back to my other patient. "Even if I wanted to, Sayo won't let me use the power for that right now. He'll find out."

Chima smiles. "Let's just use a tiny bit each day." Chima pinches her little fingers together showing me how much the word *tiny* means to her. I smile and look around again.

"Okay." I whisper very softly so even the patient I'm working on can't hear if she's listening. "Come in here tomorrow morning. I'll teach you more about healing the patients, and when nobody is looking, I'll practice extracting some serum."

Chima sits up tall and proud, grinning from ear to ear. "It's a deal."

Chapter 18

I stretch out my back, letting the sun warm my cold face. My power is gone for the day, and instead of going to bed like I probably should, I head outside. I heard that the Pepps have started training the Mixed Bloods on the beach. This is something I want to watch.

Gingerly, I climb over the rocks.

Chima assisted me again today. I guess Flint showed several Pepps how to morph last night, including her. She came to me this morning, beaming, telling me how much she loved it. She jabbered on and on about how she doesn't *need* legs anymore. She has something better. Wings.

Her optimism reminds me of Lilly.

Because Chima morphed, she had a tiny bit of power, so this morning I was able to help her identify several elements in the body, including the serum. She's a quick learner, and I have no doubt she'll be able to assist me soon.

She also allowed me to extract the serum in her arm.

I wasn't sure which approach to take at first. With Mark, the serum was in the tissue and isolated in certain parts of his body, but with the Mixed Bloods the serum is all over, in every vessel.

I wondered if I should take the serum out the same way I put it in—through the vessels.

I tried this with Chima.

It was simple, getting the serum from the generator into the vessel, but then I was competing with the pumping heart. I couldn't collect it fast enough and ended up chasing it around and around. Some particles got lodged in different places, making my head ache.

So I decided to try doing what I did with Mark and just pushed the serum through the tissues and out through the skin.

It worked. It was easy and required little power, leaving a thick white film over her arm.

I can't help but smile. Now that I know which approach to take, I just need to get faster at it.

I jump across a large gray rock in front of me. Moving my way down the hill, I finally see the group training on the beach. Waves of water crash onto the sand behind them.

The odd gray Doler suits immediately set the seven Mixed Bloods apart from the two Pepps, and I stifle a laugh. Those suits need *a lot* of work.

Kapri and Danny are the two Pepps, with Gabbro of course, trying to teach the Mixed Bloods the sounds of elements.

I can already tell it's not going so well.

"How are we supposed to teach you the sounds of the elements," Gabbro says, "when the elements sound totally different to you?"

He's right. The elemental sounds are going to be different for the Mixed Bloods. I've already struggled with that myself. They need someone who can identify them better; unfortunately, I'm still not much good at it. I can identify the serum, blood vessels, body tissues, and Peppate generators, but other than that I'm worthless.

Mark runs up behind Danny now, acknowledging me with a wave.

My heart stutters, and I wave back.

His hair is wet and handsomely ruffled, his black clothes fresh. I wonder if he went for another swim in the lake today.

My body warms. He and I went for a swim the other day, like I promised him I would. Things started out simple, just a race to a strategically placed buoy in the lake. But when Mark got to the buoy first and doubled back to me ...

Why does he have to swim with his shirt off? Why can't he swim fully clothed, like me? I couldn't resist the urge to touch him, run my fingers over his skin. When I did, I of course got the response I wanted. He kissed me deeply after that, somehow keeping us both from drowning in the waves.

Now all I want to do is go for another swim.

I bite my lip. Unfortunately, he obviously decided to go without me today. It's probably for the best.

I walk closer, shaking away the memory.

I bet he'll be better at teaching the Mixed Bloods about the sounds.

I sit in the sand, listening to Mark describe each of the elements. He is better. I don't know how he's figured out each one in Doler language, but I apply his words and listen for the sounds myself. I guess that's the good thing about being an enviro. These things come easier for him.

"Hey, Alena." Cody drops down in the sand next to me. She has on some tight black shorts and a loose pink shirt that enhances the color in her cheeks. I don't know how she convinced Mia to let her wear anything other than the dingy black clothes the rest of us are stuck with. Maybe Cody didn't bother asking.

"Are you here to help them train?" I ask. Cody nods, her blonde ponytail falling over her shoulder. "Rusty should be here soon too. He's just helping Trevor get the Pepp children settled in the eastern tunnels."

They got them out? That means that the children are safe, *and* that Aitin hasn't reached Petrichor yet.

"I was here earlier," Cody continues, "just went to get something to eat." She scrunches up her nose and leans in to whisper into my ear. "I have to say, the food here is just awful. I don't know how they've survived eating *that* stuff for so long."

I can't help but laugh. I know exactly what she's saying. Even the potatoes, which are the most normal food here, are tough and bland. Lilly somehow figured out how to at least spice things up a bit. Her food was much better.

"It doesn't help their strength much either." Cody points to the group. "They're so weak. Perhaps it's from being so sick, or the food, but whatever it is, I don't think there's any way for us to get them stronger in the time we have. Let's hope they can at least figure out how to use their power."

I look back at the group. She's right. Even if they were to get proper nutrition, it would take weeks for them to be even remotely strong.

I watch Mark run his hand through his hair, then furrow my eyebrows. Is he frustrated? I tunnel in to hear what they're saying.

"We can teach them to listen for the sounds of the elements," Mark says to Danny. "But we can't teach them how to *speak* to them like we've learned how to do. Our language is for the totems. They don't have totems."

I consider speaking up, telling them to just speak to the power with their minds, their own language, until Gabbro speaks up. "Maybe Flint will be able to give us some insight."

Flint.

My mood instantly shifts. Trying to contain the anger suddenly boiling inside me, I grab a handful of rocks from the sandy beach and throw them one by one. I watch them plop helplessly into the sand.

It's stupid to still be angry with him, especially after all the good he's done.

But after Mia showed us the group of little children who were healed … after feeling like I finally belong somewhere, with the Mixed Bloods, I'm selfishly wishing Flint didn't have to be here too. He already belongs in Petrichor. Why does he have to invade the one place I can finally call mine? Why can't he just let me have one place of refuge?

"Are you okay?" Cody asks, sensing my sudden mood change.

"I'm fine." I grind out the words.

She doesn't buy it, just continues staring at me.

Soon I run out of rocks, and instead of collecting more, I simply expel my breath in a sigh.

"Flint," I finally whisper. "All I have to do is hear his name, and I cringe. I hate him, Cody. But I shouldn't. He's actually been really helpful lately. I'm trying to forgive him for what he did to me when I first arrived in Petrichor, but no matter how hard I try, I just don't want to be his friend. I'm worried I never will."

Cody's ponytail moves in the breeze, her blue eyes studying me thoughtfully.

"I don't think forgiving someone means you'll be best friends."

I recall the time the chief told me I needed to let go of my anger and forgive Mark *to mend our friendship*. He was right. Once I was able to let go, I was able to lessen that icky barrier between us, and it made me feel so much better.

Which is why I don't understand Cody's comment at first. Shouldn't we always try to become friends?

"Alena, there were a lot of things Aitin did to me and my friend when he kept us imprisoned," Cody says, her voice barely a whisper.

I stare at her. She rarely talks about what happened to her. Suddenly, I'm anxious to hear what she has to say.

"When I came back, feeling so ... broken, Sepharine told me that part of the healing process was forgiveness." Cody scoffs. "*Forgiveness*? How the hell was I supposed to forgive that man? Her advice made me so angry, that I promised myself I would *never* forgive him, and instead I would seek revenge."

Cody picks up a handful of her own rocks and moves them around in her palm.

"But the pain I've been carrying is so unbearable," Cody whispers. "I want to live a better life." Looking at me with misty eyes, she says, "I need to forgive Aitin for what he did to me and Abby, but that doesn't mean I'll ever run back to him. I'll never be his friend, and if the time comes, I *will* take his life, because he's too dangerous to be left alive.

"Alena, forgiveness is not about trying to be friends with those who hurt us, although sometimes that's what happens. Instead, I think forgiveness is the intentional decision to not let the choice or action of someone else ruin your life. I can tell you that it's much easier to blame my unhappiness on Aitin for what he did than to go out and seek happiness by letting go of what was unfairly done to me." Cody's voice catches. "But I deserve better. So I've chosen to try. It may take the rest of my life to do it, but I *will* try to forgive Aitin."

I stare at Cody's face, baffled by her words, her strength.

I'm so caught off guard by the conversation that I almost miss the tiny mischievous look that crosses her brow.

"Just so you know, Flint is a real blockhead. Don't worry about becoming friends or being nice to him right now. Just work on forgiving him for your own sake." Patting my leg, she adds, "You deserve to be happy too."

Then she stands and runs out to join the others.

Now that she's said it, I know she's right. I don't know why I feel such a need to be Flint's friend. Maybe it's because I can't stand the thought that there's someone out there who hates me. Or maybe it's the fact that he's so talented and appreciated by others that I think *I need* to be accepted by him in order to be accepted by others. Whatever the reason, though, Cody is right. Perhaps I should focus less on him liking me and more on me trying to forgive him.

My butt and legs are starting to go numb from sitting in the sand. I should probably go back inside and try to get some sleep. Danny and Kapri have organized a little something for the Mixed Bloods tonight, an outing where they can test out their new suits. They asked me to come along, which is why I should get some rest beforehand. Once I wake up for the party, I won't be going back to sleep for the rest of the night.

I roll over, ready to stand, when someone comes running across the beach.

Flint. With his bright red hair and smug tan face.

He slows his jog to a walk and enters the group of Mixed Bloods. Mark explains to him the troubles they're having with teaching the Mixed Bloods to speak to the elements. Flint rolls his eyes as if the solution was so obviously simple.

Instead of standing and leaving, like I probably should, I stand and walk closer, eager to hear what Flint has to say. He gets right down to business.

"Okay, I'm going to teach you all how to use your powers." He rubs his hands together, emphasizing the word *I'm*, as if he's the only one in the world who can pull off such a task.

"Your powers are a little different from mine, but I'm thinking the concept is the same."

I can already tell he's a good teacher. He's calm and collected and even smiles kindly at the Mixed Bloods. Something he's never done to me. I take in a deep breath, trying to calm myself.

"Normal Pepps have a totem that speaks to the elements around them. The totem has been trained in a certain language to communicate with its host. The power is collected in a small glass flask that sits in the middle of the heart." Flint pauses. "But neither you nor I have a totem to do this. Instead, the generators of your power have been inside you all your life. They've listened, they've learned, and they've adjusted without you even realizing it. At least I hope they have. Instead of having to learn a language, all you have to do is listen to yourself. You think about what it is you want your power to do, and it will do it. This of course requires you to have a basic knowledge of what the elements are and what they are capable of. I'm guessing Mark has been teaching you this?"

I can tell Mark resists the urge to roll his eyes. "Yes," he says.

Flint then looks around his group, just before his eyes wander over to me. A sly smile spreads across his face. "Good. To start out, I'm going to teach you all how to do *one* thing with your power. How to create one of the more dangerous weapons with elements that are almost always available."

Flint's smile gets bigger.

"I'm going to teach you how to make acid."

Flint's words slice through me. His gaze breaks away from mine now, returning to his more important group of students, but he's done his damage, and he knows it. My mind is instantly taken back to the first day I met Flint. When he told me I was not appreciated on his team. The day he burned my neck with acid. The skin around my collarbone throbs in response to the memory.

Pff. And I thought our relationship was improving, at least a little.

Choking down the hurt, I glance briefly at Mark. He was burned with acid, but the comment doesn't seem to have rattled him the same way it has me.

When I walk away, Flint's words and hateful gaze follow me like an annoying swarm of gnats I wish I could swat away.

Then I step through the bushes, leaving him behind.

Under my breath, I grind out the words I really don't want to speak.

I forgive Flint.

Chapter 19

Lake Maracai has slowly come to life. The tunnels below are no longer empty but buzzing with activity as Mixed Bloods healthily go here and there.

It's especially livelier with the little outing scheduled for tonight. Even with the worries of our future hanging over our heads, Danny is determined to get the Mixed Bloods out of the caves.

I stand in front of a mirror in Mia's small living space, the only mirror in all of Maracai.

The rest of us who are not Mixed Bloods agreed to wear the suits tonight too, so we all look the same: ridiculous.

I curse.

Then I reluctantly put my hair into a bun at the back of my head before pulling the mask over my face.

At least the clear plastic covering is thin and breathable.

Then I scratch my arm. *Man, what is this suit made out of?*

I grit my teeth and resist the urge to claw off my itchy skin before looking in the mirror again.

I've been slightly worried about how much Peppate we're repressing from the Mixed Bloods with these suits. The Mixed Bloods do need a little bit of Peppate, in order to live happy, healthy lives. I don't want them turning into people like Case—angry and sad. I suppose we'll just have to experiment. See how Peppate affects them in small doses, and try to establish how much Peppate they need in order to feel happy.

I pull at the blue material over my stomach, hating how the bulky stuff sticks to my skin in the humidity, but then I give up.

There's no hope.

I turn and walk out into the early evening air. I relish every breath of fresh air these days. It's one of those things I didn't realize I needed until I was forced to live down in the stifling caves day after day. I breathe in deeply now, past the confines of my Doler suit.

We were told to meet in the town square tonight, the open empty place I saw the two boys playing ball the first time I came here. Of course, everyone was worried about a lightning storm attacking in the open air. So Mark and I morphed an hour ago with everyone underground. Turned everything to dust for miles. I don't think there will be any lightning tonight.

The dirt crunches beneath my shoes, and my suit crackles with each step, while the steady beat of music pulses through the air, along with the happy chatter of voices. I roll my eyes. Of course Danny would include music in the simplest of outings.

The music attempts to liven my tired body, shaking out some of the drag weighing me down.

I round the corner to the square, and then stop, staring at the scene before me.

What's going on?

The gathering area has been totally transformed from a lifeless collection of dirt and rock to a thriving, buoyant garden that gleams in the dusk light. Bright green vines, heavy with large leaves, are the capital of the garden. Their color, impossibly intensified by the setting sun, reminds me of the vibrancy found in the GreenLands. The vines climb up the walls and across the ground, spreading their beauty as far as they can.

Dozens of pots overflowing with bright flowers are thrown here and there and emit smells that have me wanting to breathe in more and more.

The floor of the square has been changed too, from dirt to a brilliant red brick, with a rich colored moss filling the cracks.

Large bonfires and Tiki torches lining the square stand ready to light as soon as the sun goes down.

The only thing this place is missing is good food. I guess we can't get around that hiccup yet. But even without the food, this closely resembles the courtyard above GreenGrotto. It makes me realize that even though Petrichor hasn't always been a place I fit in, it is another type of home for me, and I feel myself yearning for it. Just a little.

So much for morphing to get rid of the Peppate. The plants in this place are loaded with it.

I stand on the border of the square, taking in the scene of the Mixed Blood community with their smiling faces and happy laughter. It's a scene that's been absent from this place since it began.

I feel a soft touch at my elbow. Even the Doler-made suit can't repel the happiness I feel at that touch. I turn to find Mark staring down at me, but I can't hold back my laugh when I see him in his suit.

"Wow, you look especially handsome tonight, Mark," I say.

"You have no place to judge, Lena," he whispers close.

Then he leans back, cups his hands over his mouth, and shouts, "What's going on, Danny? I thought we were just going for a quick walk."

The conversations around us quiet, and I look around, trying to locate Danny. I find him on the other side of the square with Kapri, close to the musical Magbabies. Unlike everyone else here, though, they're not drowning in Doler suits. Instead, they're dressed in attractively loose white T-shirts and tight black pants.

Not fair.

With a pink headband in her long blonde curly hair, Kapri stands out among the crowd. She's beautiful.

Danny pulses his dark eyebrows up and down when Mark calls out his name, and the beating Magbabies pause. The square goes silent, waiting for Danny to explain himself. Danny doesn't say anything, though. He doesn't need to. Instead, he takes Kapri's hand and leads her to the center of the new brick courtyard.

Everyone backs away, giving them room.

Once they've found their spots in the middle of the square, side by side, the Magbabies begin playing a new song with the smooth rhythmic sound of a soft log drum.

Kapri and Danny begin to dance, their upper torsos moving gently to the beat, then they step out perfectly synchronized.

I stare at their feet, the way they move at the same time, so fast, so sure. It's amazing how quickly yet steadily they dance, advancing into unpredictable patterns. And it's not just their feet. Every part of their bodies moves in some way, tugged here and there by the rhythm in the air.

I knew Kapri was a dancer, but I didn't imagine this. Her body is so effortlessly graceful, her steps so unique, that she makes the moves seem so easy. Even the way her hair bounces plays a part in the image. And Danny is just the same, towering handsomely above Kapri's tiny frame.

They don't touch during the choreographed dance, though I occasionally wonder if they'll crash into each other, since they're so close, but they don't.

The crowd starts to shout when their moves get more complex and faster, and before long everyone is bobbing their heads to the fun Island beat.

Then Danny and Kapri, each with a smile on their face, reach out to the Mixed Bloods on the sideline, pulling them into the middle. The Mixed Bloods are hesitant and embarrassed, but Kapri and Danny show them simple dance moves, encouraging them to just *feel* the music. Before long, the entire square is full of swaying people.

Pff. Danny and Kapri didn't plan an outing. They planned a dance, and the music enhances worries within me. We need to get going. We need to get the Mixed Bloods up to Petrichor. We need to come up with a plan to defeat Aitin.

But looking at the Mixed Bloods now, I swallow those worries back. Perhaps they need a little fun first. They're happy. How, I don't really know. They don't produce Peppate anymore, and they shouldn't be getting any inside their suits. Perhaps just the act of dispelling the Doler that's so long filled their bodies is helping. Or perhaps just being absent of physical pain is enough to make any human happy, Peppate or not.

They deserve one night of freedom before we head out.

I spot Eli next to Mia on the sideline. They aren't dancing, but Eli is standing close to the woman. I do hope they can work things out.

I feel a tug on my hand, and turn to find Mark pulling me in, the rough sound of the stiff suits adding their own special touch to the song.

"Can I have another dance?" he asks.

"Yes." I laugh.

Mark and I dance our own simple dance around the others. We aren't out there for long, though, when Mark accidentally bumps into someone else. Turning around, he finds Chima in the arms of her mother, who is clearly straining under the weight of her daughter.

Mark doesn't need to say it for me to know what he's thinking. He wants to help her.

I smile, taking a step back, while Mark carefully takes Chima into his arms and starts swirling her around. I take a few more steps back and end up right at the edge of the square, pressed against the vine-smothered wall.

Then I look around. There's a little boy not too far away watching everyone else dance. I walked over to him and offer my hand and ask if he'll dance with me. His little blue eyes get wide behind his suit mask before he carefully takes my fingers and lets me pull him onto the floor. It's awkward, dancing with someone so small, but the song is upbeat. *We can just jump up and down together, right?*

It works. Halfway through the song he releases the energy he must have been holding inside and takes both my hands into his, to swing me around in circles.

I try my best to avoid running into other people. When we do, the little boy just winces apologetically and then laughs.

I glance over at Mark a couple of times. He's passed Chima on to Danny and is now holding on to another little Mixed Blood girl, her pale skin radiating at the attention.

The sun eventually sets, the tiki torches light, and without any pause the night carries on. My little boy continues to grip my hands from song to song, his smile wide and his bright blue eyes twinkling in the firelight.

We're halfway through a slower song, the little boy resting in my arms, tired, when my gaze catches on something just outside the crowd of people, at the edge of the square. Two eyes glowing in the dark, staring at me. The hair rises on the back of my neck until I realize who it is.

Breccia?

The black form of a rock with white eyes hovers in the air. Is it really her?

I quickly find a chair for the little boy and place him in it, glad he doesn't protest.

Then I practically run to the outer edge of the square, searching for her. I find her, hidden in the shadows.

"Breccia!" I gasp.

I'm more than happy to see her. I want to pull her in, give her a hug, tell her how much I've missed her, but the moment I see her eyes, I stop. I've seen that hollow look too often. I don't like it.

"Breccia, what's wrong. Are you okay?" I remove my Doler head mask now, not caring about the rule.

Breccia slinks back further into the shadows, leading me down the quiet pathway for privacy. When she finally stops, out of sight of the others, I hold out my hands, hoping she'll drop into them. But she doesn't.

Something has happened to her.

My stomach churns. I've been so worried about her since she disappeared, but I always found comfort in knowing she's a rock. I didn't think she could be hurt. Obviously, I was wrong.

"Breccia, what happened?"

When she doesn't accept my invitation to come closer, I drop my hands and wait. If rocks could cry, I think she'd be doing that right now.

Finally, after an agonizingly long silence, she closes her eyes.

"I've betrayed you, Alena."

I shake my head, knowing exactly what she's feeling. Jeter, or Aitin, got to her, got her to do something she didn't want to do, and now she's feeling guilty.

"You betrayed nobody, Breccia. Did Aitin hurt you? Are you okay?"

Breccia opens her eyes. Her look breaks my heart. No, she's not okay.

"Breccia, you've done nothing wrong. You've seen what Aitin has forced me to do. I know exactly what you're feeling. If you tell me what happened, I won't judge you. I'll just try to help. Okay?"

Breccia closes her eyes, taking in a shuddering breath. "Alena, I told him where to find you, after you captured Jax. He shot Sef down because *I* told him where you were."

I nod my head. She must have been following us. "That's not a big deal, Breccia. It's okay."

She continues. "He told me if I didn't cooperate, he would blow me up, eventually find you anyway, and then kill you. I was hoping by staying with him I'd be able to gather helpful information, but he never let me go to get that information to you." Breccia's eyes open now, but she stares at the ground, refusing to meet my gaze.

"He's had me spying on you for the past few months," she continues. "I think he's been waiting for you to heal his people before he headed into Petrichor."

"Headed to Petrichor?" I jump at the loud voice right behind me.

Eli and Mia are here. They must have seen me leave the party and followed.

"Has Aitin reached Petrichor?" Eli asks, his gray hair darkened by the night.

When I turn back to Breccia, her body is trembling.

"It's okay, Breccia," I whisper, trying to calm her. It's startling, seeing her reacting this way.

"Yes," she says.

"So, he kept you captive for so long, but then just decided to let you go?" Eli's blue eyes narrow accusingly.

I glare at the man. *Eli! You're not helping!*

Breccia's tiny body continues to shake. "Aitin didn't let me go. Jeter did." She sighs, then proceeds to explain. "Aitin promised Jeter that he would help save his people in the GreenLands but ended up destroying them all instead. Jeter was heartbroken. He refused to help Aitin after that and attempted to leave. Before he could, though, Aitin removed his totem and left him to die in what's left of his homeland."

Clasping her tiny hands as if trying to get better control of the shaking, Breccia brings her black eyes to mine.

"Somewhere in the midst of their fighting, Jeter let me out of the bag Aitin was keeping me in. I got away before Aitin realized what happened."

"And now he's on his way to Petrichor?" I whisper.

Mark comes running down the path now, his shoes scuffing against the dirt, the material in his suit loud with the movement. When he sees Breccia, his steps slow, and he approaches carefully.

Then Sayo comes.

Ugh.

"Listen, Sayo," Eli turns and says, "we need to get your people to Petrichor, now."

Sayo immediately protests, which launches the two of them into a loud argument.

I'm trying to listen to their debate, knowing Eli has to win this one, when Breccia taps my hand as if she has something more to say.

"Alena, there's something else I informed Aitin of while I was watching you." Her lip trembles in guilt. I encourage her to go on.

"I told Aitin where you found Case."

My heart drops.

Oh.

"As far as I know, he hasn't done anything to hurt Case." Breccia rushes on in a whisper. "But I'm worried about them."

I find the strength to nod to Breccia while gulping down my fears.

"When did you tell him?"

"A couple of weeks ago."

I nod again. I would send Breccia back with a note of warning to Case and Lilly, but I have a feeling it's too late for that.

I glance at Sayo, Mia, and Eli. I don't want to break my promise to them, my promise to heal the Mixed Bloods before I leave.

I also can't sit here and wait, wondering if Case and Lilly are okay.

No, I need to go.

I need to go now.

Chapter 20

I don't tell Mia, Eli, or Sayo what Breccia revealed. I just wait through their arguing, taking the opportunity to tear off the rest of my uncomfortable suit. I can't stand it any longer.

Fortunately, the three of them eventually walk their quarrel toward Mia's office.

And I stay put.

When everyone is gone, I turn to Mark while sliding Breccia into my pocket.

"Mark, Aitin knows where Case and Lilly are."

"Case and Lilly?" he whispers, taking off his own suit. "How?"

I squint at him in the dark, trying to silently relay the message that Breccia informed Aitin. Breccia feels bad enough. Saying it out loud might make her feel worse. Thankfully, Mark understands.

With his suit now tossed to the side, he whispers, "You think they're in trouble?"

"Yes, I think we need to go help them."

I say the words, but deep inside I'm fighting them. I don't *want* to go. I'm terrified of what we might find. Terrified of how hard it might be to get there.

"Sayo won't let us leave." Mark steps close.

"Then we'll have to leave without him knowing," I murmur, looking around. "We could take one of the aircrafts Rusty came here on."

"We could, but I don't know how to fly them. Do you?"

"No, but doesn't Danny know how?"

I recall how Danny used his stolen aircraft to follow me when I left Petrichor to go to the silver mine. Not that I want to bring him into this. It would be safer for him to stay here in case we run into Aitin, but he's the only one I trust, the only one who'd be willing to let us go.

"Yes. He does. Let's go change, make sure there's an extra aircraft still here, and then we'll send a message to Danny."

Mark's words solidify our plan. My plan. I should be grateful he accepted it so easily, *but what if it's a bad idea*? I'm really good at those. Mark would know, wouldn't he? He would stop us from doing something stupid.

I hate it, going on our own, without telling Eli or the others. This feels a lot like the time Gabbro trained me in secret, preparing me for an isolated attempt at freeing the prisoners. *This won't be a repeat of that, will it?*

Mark takes my hand and pulls me down the path. I look back one last time in the direction of Town Square.

Will we ever get to enjoy a real community dance together?

We run quietly through the tunnels.

I go to my room, and Mark goes to his just down the hall.

I open the door and light a single candle. When the light illuminates my small sleeping cave, I can't help but wonder if this will be the last time

I see it. With its single cot, plate of candles, and black dirt walls. I won't miss its darkness or small scope. I'm thankful that I never had to spend too much time in here. It was only meant for sleeping.

Not bothering to change out of my Doler clothes, I grab my satchel resting on the floor beside my bed. My throwing knives and electric belt are there in the dirt too— my only real weapons. I strap the knives carefully around my legs but leave the electric belt. If we do run into Aitin it'll be worthless against him.

Then I pull out my Magbaby harness and carefully put Breccia in. Her compunctious expression breaks my heart.

Oh, Breccia ...

Mark knocks on my open door.

"I'm almost done," I say, quietly inviting him in, then wrap my satchel around my waist. "I wish I had some black power. I used the last of it earlier today. If I'd known we were going to see Lilly, I would have saved some. I need to heal her."

I finish buckling the strap around my waist. When I look up, Mark is standing there, a vial of black power in his hand. It isn't full, but it's enough for me to heal Lilly.

"Where did you get that?" I whisper, stepping closer.

He takes advantage of our closeness in the small space and winds his arm around my waist.

Shivers race up my spine.

"I secretly saved a little after each of our morphs. I knew Sayo wouldn't let you keep any to yourself. But he doesn't watch me as closely as he does you. I thought it might come in handy."

I take the glass flask in my fingers before looking up at his face in the dark room. The candle sheds a little light on his face. His tired eyes are not fixed on mine but on my lips, his expression solemn.

"I'm guessing you have extra serum too?" My whisper cracks.

"Of course," he says but doesn't bother pulling it out. Instead, he just pulls me closer.

I swallow and let my nose graze his chin.

Suddenly, the heaviness of our new plan hits me. We're going to Case and Lilly, a place where Aitin could potentially be. My chest squeezes in response, and I bite my lip in an attempt to harness the worry building up inside. As much as I want Mark's help, I know Aitin won't hesitate to destroy him.

I can't lose Mark. I can't even stand the thought of him getting hurt. Even though I would give my life to protect his, I don't know that that would be enough. Aitin is too powerful, too willing to destroy.

"Mark, why don't you stay here?"

I don't look him in the eye, just stare at the vessel pulsing in his neck.

"Stay here?" he asks low. "And what—let you go by yourself? Not a chance, Lena."

Placing his free hand on the wall behind me, Mark traps me, bringing that pulsing vessel even closer.

"And if you even think of injecting me with that serum to paralyze me so I *do* stay here, you need to know I've been practicing controlling it too. I'll get it out of my body faster than you can say 'boo,' and I'll follow you anyway."

I sigh. Gripping his shirt, I pull him to me.

"Injecting you with that serum was a mistake I'm still struggling to forgive myself for," I whisper against his skin. "I'll never do it again. But I do wish there was a way to keep Aitin from you. I wish I was stronger, better—"

Suddenly, I'm pushed into the cave wall, Mark gripping my face, his warm lips on mine.

My hands don't think twice, knotting themselves in his hair, taking the power with them. I pull him eagerly to me, relishing the taste of his mouth, the feel of his warm chest pressed against mine.

A low growl escapes his throat, and he releases my face to pull my waist away from the wall just enough to wrap his arms tightly around me, then I'm being crushed more, every inch of his body flush with mine.

His fingers dig into my skin. I can't breathe, but I don't want to. Not without him. My heart pounds frantically against his. He pulls me impossibly closer.

Somewhere in the crushing kiss, I taste tears. I'm crying. Of course I'm crying.

"I can't lose you, Mark," I whisper into his mouth.

He gently moves his lips to my trembling chin.

"I'm not going anywhere." His voice is low but desperate. Then he bites my jaw, softly grazing my skin with his teeth.

My grip weakens at his words, a sense of hopelessness threatening to smother this precious moment.

We don't know that. We don't know what's going to happen. This could very well be our last quiet moment together.

"I love you, Mark," I whisper abruptly, needing him to hear the words.

Those words slow him down, bring him back. His kisses stop, and he rests his nose against mine.

"I love you too, Alena Carlston." His heaving breath brushes my lips. "We'll get through this. There's no way Aitin is going to keep me from my future with you. There are too many things I ..." He swallows, not able to finish.

Wrapping my arms around his neck, I tenderly embrace him one last time. I brush my lips against the soft space in front of his ear, noting every soft detail. I let my fingers run over his face, feel his skin. I breathe him in, memorizing his musky smell.

And then, as if the Universe has decided the moment must end, my energy fizzles out like a released dam, telling me—telling us—it's time.

I drop my arms.

Sensing my resignation, Mark reluctantly drops his too and pushes away from the wall. Away from me. My body grieves the loss of contact, the loss of the moment. I want to pull him back, but I can't. We need to go.

I wipe my nose, put the serum into my satchel, pop the power into my totem, and then slip my hand into Mark's.

I let him pull me through the maze of tunnels, through Maracai, past the happy courtyard and into the ashes. It's not hard slipping by everyone. Nobody suspects us.

We walk to the three visible Pepp aircrafts sitting out in the open, completely exposed after we zapped every tree around.

Perfect. They're still here.

But then my hopes fall. Outside each aircraft are two Pepps standing guard.

"I can freeze them," Mark says casually.

He has power. Good. "Okay. Go ahead."

He works quickly without making a sound. They didn't even suspect Mark. I try not to feel bad. *This is for a good cause, right?*

Once everyone is quietly chilled, we walk to the nearest aircraft. Mark steps inside, grabs an old map from the cockpit, and opens it on the dash.

"Case's hideout was right in between the last two watering holes we visited. Here." Mark points at the small lakes of water shown on the desert map. "We could be back before sunrise ... if everything goes well."

If everything goes well.

Mark is writing a message to send to Danny, to get him to come help us, when I hear footsteps behind me.

"Alena?"

I spin around, pulling a knife out of my sleeve.

"Whoa, Alena. It's just me." It takes a second for my brain to work, to recognize the boy in front of me, but then I remember him from the dropdown Rusty took me on. The one who was flying the aircraft, the one I recognized. A Pepp prisoner I freed.

"Luis?"

"Are you guys trying to get somewhere?"

His hair is thick and golden, his face slender, his voice sure. He's recovered well.

But can we trust him? Could he help us instead of Danny? It would save us time not having to pull Danny away from the party.

I look at Mark, hoping he'll know the right thing to do. Unfortunately, he isn't looking at me. He's standing ready to freeze the boy.

I sigh and place my hand on his arm.

"He can fly, Mark," I whisper. "What if he can help us?"

"Help you with what?" Luis asks.

When Mark doesn't respond, I decide to take a chance, hoping I won't regret this. "Luis, we believe Case and his girl, Lilly, are being sought after by Aitin. We believe they're in danger, and we want to go help them."

"Does Rusty know?" Luis asks.

Rusty. Where is Rusty? He wasn't at the dance. Neither was Cody, or Flint ... or Trevor.

I sigh again. "No. Nobody knows. The Mixed Bloods have refused to let Mark and me leave. They want me to finish healing the rest of their people, but I'm afraid that if I wait, it'll be too late."

Luis steps up to the map Mark has displayed on the dash. "This is where they are?"

"Yes."

Luis slides his body into the pilot seat and starts pulling on some levers. When he places his hands on the yoke, the aircraft hums to life.

I stare at him. "What are you doing?"

He doesn't bother looking at me when he responds. "I'm taking you there."

I sit in the seat next to him.

"Luis. It'll be dangerous. We could run into Aitin. There could be ..."

"Alena." Luis grips my wrist, pulling me from my doubts. "You saved me. Now let *me* help you save someone else."

I search his eyes. He's already been through so much. Could I put him through more?

But when I search for reasons to deny him, I only come up with understanding. He's going out there for the same reason Mark and I are. Because, at some point, we've all been saved by someone else when we needed saving. *How can we sit here and do anything less than that*? It's the right thing to do, and I can't say no.

"Okay," I whisper.

"Buckle up." Luis signals with his head. "We gotta go." He doesn't wait for us to buckle up, which I'm grateful for. With the engine roaring loudly, the Pepps are bound to hear the aircraft and come searching. We need to leave.

***

Mark and I sit side by side in the other large cockpit seat, next to Luis.

We fly in silence. Fortunately, the desert lands come into view after a few hours.

Luis waits in the flyer after Mark and I exit. It takes us longer than I wish to find the secret door Lilly showed me. The orange glow blanketing the sands from the rising sun makes it hard to see the small difference in color of the hidden hatch. I guess that's a good thing. If it's still hidden then maybe Aitin hasn't been here yet.

Mark and I open the hatch and drop down the ladder into the tunnels below. It's dark and quiet just like before. Mark lights an available candle and holds it out for me to take. We pass one of the water rooms, the dripping sounds echoing through the tunnels. I push down the eerie feeling inside me.

It's just *dark.* Everything's going to be fine.

But the further we venture into the tunnels, past the living room, without seeing or hearing Lilly or Case, that eerie feeling grows.

"Do you think they're asleep?" Mark whispers behind me.

I shrug. I guess they could be. Living without any natural light would make it easier to sleep longer. I move to a closed door. If I remember right, this door led to a bedroom.

The moment I open it, a familiar metallic smell reaches my nostrils. Blood.

I fling it open wide and wave the light around the room. "Lilly!" I shout, but nobody responds. Without needing to be asked, Mark uses his power to flood the room with more light.

And then I quickly find it. There, next to a mess of a bed, soaked into the carpet, is blood. Lots of it.

"Lilly!" I shout again, a sinking feeling growing in my gut. Did Aitin get to her?

I run around the side of the bed and gasp in horror when I see Lilly there, collapsed on the floor.

I groan, then immediately go to work listening for her elements, grateful Mark was wise enough to save some black power. It only takes me a couple of seconds to realize what's really wrong. My mind is expecting wounds from an attack, but the sounds tell a different story. She wasn't attacked. Her injuries, the blood—they're not from wounds, but instead from her pregnancy.

She lost her baby. And now she's hemorrhaging.

I go to work, stopping the bleeding and replacing her blood count. She's alive but just barely.

It doesn't take me very long to get her looking pinker and healthier, but she remains unconscious. I turn to Mark, who is kneeling patiently behind me, waiting for me to finish.

"Do you think it was Aitin?" he asks, keeping his voice soft.

I shake my head. "No, she was pregnant. She lost the baby and was hemorrhaging." As if my answer snaps me awake, I start looking around the floor. There's blood everywhere, but she was starting to show. There's a good chance the baby ...

I pick up my candle again and look closer at the now red carpet.

It isn't too far from her.

The sight of it brings immediate tears to my eyes ... and makes me want to gag at the same time. Lilly had already put it on a small plate. My gut twists and I look closer, hoping that what I'm seeing isn't real, but it is.

The bloodied and swollen body of a tiny lifeless baby.

Even though its entire figure could easily fit in the palm of my hand, it's formed. It has eyes, a nose, and a mouth, and four little limbs. It was perfect.

Placing my nose in the crook of my elbow, I try to find some fresh air. Seeing the dead body of the baby has suddenly made me terribly nauseated. I hear Mark gasping for breath as well. He must have seen it.

I want to leave the room, I want to get out of this place, but Lilly starts to stir, so I force down the bile in my throat and move to her side.

"Lilly?" I whisper carefully, taking her hand. Her eyelids flutter for a moment before opening and finding mine.

"Lilly, are you okay?"

"Alena?" Lilly's lip quivers before she groans and turns to her side. Her body dry heaves, either from the blood loss or pain, but there's nothing in her stomach. When her body finally relaxes, her head falls to the floor.

"I'm so sorry, Lilly." My words are stupid. They make me angry. But I don't know what else to say.

Lilly swallows, a dry, painful sound.

"This is a lot harder than I thought it would be," she says. "I don't know what happened. I was so happy we made it to sixteen weeks. Everything was going so well. His skin even looks perfect, no sores."

Lilly raises her head, and she moves to sit up. I'm not sure if that's a good idea, but I let her anyway. She looks around the room, at all the blood, then wipes her tears, her demeanor changing completely.

"Alena, can you help me find Case?"

I furrow my eyebrows. "Where is Case?"

Lilly shakes her head, trying to hold back more tears. "He left right after the baby came out. He was so angry the baby died. I think he's gone looking for Aitin, to join him. He's determined to eliminate Peppate."

"Gone *looking* for Aitin? So Aitin hasn't been here?" Relief floods my body, now acknowledging that Lilly is alive. Unfortunately, she lost her baby, but she's alive. It's more than I could have hoped for. And, apparently, Aitin hasn't been here.

"Been here? No. Why?" Concern spreads its way across her face.

"Lilly, Aitin knows where your hideout is." I give her the details Breccia shared with me.

I watch the blood drain from Lilly's already pale face.

"If Aitin knows where our hideout is, do you think he's already collected Case?"

"I don't know." I look to Mark for help.

"Did he leave today?" he asks.

"Yes, maybe a few hours ago."

"Do you know where Case would have headed?"

Lilly tries to stand with shaking legs. "Case thinks Aitin's eventually going to destroy Petrichor. If he's headed anywhere, it's probably there to wait for Aitin."

Petrichor. My plan was to save Lilly and Case, and then return to Maracai after we found them. There's still so much to plan out with the Mixed Bloods and Rusty. But if Case and Aitin are already headed that way, will we have time to go back?

I search Mark's face. He seems to be thinking the same thing I am. "We have to go to Petrichor. We need to find Case and Aitin and stop them from destroying the Pepps."

Icy fear shoots through my veins. Fear for Mark moving closer to Aitin.

"We can't stop him on our own. We need help." I remind him of the whole reason we recruited the Mixed Bloods.

Mark moves to Lilly's side to help her up.

"Once we're in Petrichor, we'll send Luis to get the Mixed Bloods. We'll get help, but maybe we can slow Aitin down until that happens."

I move to Lilly's other side and help Mark lift her to the edge of her bed. I wanted to heal Lilly with the serum, but after pulling down the collar of my shirt, I see that I don't have enough power. Not after stopping her hemorrhaging.

"I was hoping to heal you, Lilly. I brought serum and power, but I don't think I'll have enough."

Light shimmers in her eyes. "Did it work?"

I nod.

"How long does it take you?"

"Two and a half hours, on a good day."

Lilly pats my knee. "Even if you did have power, we don't have time, Alena, but I look forward to when you *can* heal me."

I sigh. Well, I might not have enough power or time to heal her Peppate condition, but I can continue to heal her body from the trauma it just underwent. Paying special attention to every strained tissue and muscle, I give her more blood, more strength, until my power fizzles out. It's gone.

Then a sudden flare of anger rises in my chest when realization hits.

"Lilly, you were hemorrhaging when we found you. Just another hour or two and you would have been dead. Did Case really leave you here like this?"

My words pierce the woman. She closes her dark eyes, tears leaking onto her long black eyelashes. I expect her to make up some lame excuse for Case, but she doesn't. Instead, she pulls herself to standing.

"We need to find him."

I put a hand on her shoulder and gently push her back down.

"No, Lilly, you need to rest. We'll search for Case."

"No, Alena." She shakes her head. "Case won't listen to anyone but me. There's no way you're going to get him to change his mind. *I* need to be with you."

I recall our last meeting with Case, how bitter and lost he was. And that was when things were going well. Lilly is right. We don't stand a chance, but I still shake my head.

"Lilly, without fixing your Peppate generators, you're at risk of being killed by Aitin. All he would have to do is morph and you'd be gone. I'm not willing to risk that."

But Lilly shakes her head adamantly, trying to stand.

"We could hide her," Mark says. "If we take her to the Post and get her underground there, she'd be protected, wouldn't she?"

No, no, no! *What if something happens to her?* I would never forgive myself. No, I can't have her with me. Either of them. Is there a way I could trap them both here in this hideout? Keep them both from coming along?

"When we find Case," Mark continues, "we can figure out a way to get her to him."

Even as the words come out of his mouth, I feel the hopelessness. We have no idea where Case and Aitin are hiding out. It's such a weak plan.

But then I look back and forth between them. They're right. We're going to need her. And I'm going to need him.

I bite my lip hard, worried if I don't, my unsteady emotions will explode.

"Okay."

I reluctantly help Lilly get cleaned up. When Mark and I are collecting food and water, she retrieves some extra things from a room down the hall.

When we're ready, we help her climb the ladder and walk slowly through the sand toward the aircraft. Luis doesn't ask questions when we get on but takes directions from Mark before rising into the sky. I lay Lilly down on some of the seats with a pillow at her head, then gently wrap the belts around her to keep her from falling off during the flight. When I'm satisfied with my work, I leave her to rest and go up to sit with Mark. We travel in silence, looking out over the blurry sands without really seeing them.

***

It's hypnotizing, the passing dunes, the hum of the aircraft, the hot sun beaming in the sky. Even though my eyes are open, my mind feels like concrete, unresponsive, as if in a frozen trance.

Then I see it.

I lean forward and suck in my breath.

The lands below us are still smooth like the deserts, but instead of the beautiful orange color, they're black for as far as I can see, barren of any life. The dark clouds in the sky hover dismally, as if wanting to hide the terrifying earthly damage.

Only the occasional burned tree stump testifies that there used to be more here.

It's an endless sea of destruction—created by what can only be one terrifying thing.

Aitin.

Luis slows, which makes the aircraft bounce more. I grip the dashboard to stabilize myself.

"Aren't we close to Verdure?" Mark asks, looking back and forth between his map, his compass, and the land.

"We're almost directly over where the center of the city used to be," Luis says solemnly.

What? I search the horizon myself, expecting to see the same large Verdure buildings I've seen on TV, but my eyes meet nothing but dark sky and black land.

It's all gone.

I move my eyes from the horizon to directly below us. Then squint and look closer. There's something else down there mixed in with the ash. Even in the darkness it shimmers, as if trying to tell its story.

"What is that?" I ask Mark, pointing to the ground.

"It looks like glass." He leans forward to get a better look.

That's what I thought. Glass, glittering in the darkness, broken into trillions of pieces for miles and miles. The only thing that survived.

"Verdure," Mark whispers.

Luis takes us quickly over the land.

It stretches on and on, deepening the sinking feeling in my stomach. I know firsthand how quickly life disappears from a single morph. It wouldn't have taken much time for Aitin to cover so much ground.

"I wonder if he made it all the way to Petrichor," Mark says, still looking at his map.

I don't know how long we travel like this, the darkness blurring into one endless void. Eventually the glass thins out, and the dead trees appear more frequently. Occasionally we see a fire or two that haven't gone out yet. I sit and gaze at it all. I want to look away but I can't. My eyes stare at one tree stump until is passes underneath us, then they grab hold of another one. I'm not sure what I'm looking for. More glass. Any sign of survival. Any sign that what I'm seeing is actually a big nightmare I'll wake up from.

But I don't wake up, and it only gets worse.

I see it first. A spot that looks like a tree trunk but blue. I stand, narrowing my eyes.

"What is it?" Mark asks.

I point to the spot. "That, right there. What is that?"

Luis redirects the aircraft, and my heart rate quickens.

"It's a person." I almost shout when the image clears. It looks like a man, lying on his back. *Who is he? How did he get out here in the middle of nowhere? Is he still alive?*

Landing the aircraft takes way too long. I bolt from the back the moment the door opens, but the second my running feet touch the ashes, I slip.

I choke back a scream. *Who knows what this ash used to be!*

Trying to ignore my blackened hands, I frantically pull myself up and stumble toward the man, then kneel next to him.

I immediately bring my fingers to his neck, searching for a pulse.

"He's still alive," I shout. Mark is quickly beside me.

I grab the man's face, ready to slap him awake, when my hand freezes.

"Jeter?" Mark whispers next to me.

His body's in bad shape. A gash on his arm has to be the culprit for how pale and deflated he looks. His face that was always so clean shaven is now covered in golden hair, making it difficult to know for sure if it is truly Jeter. But then his eyes slowly open.

They're the same hazel eyes of the man that used to be the most knowledgeable medic in Petrichor.

It takes him a moment to recognize us, his expression so blank that I can't help but wonder if he'll be able to come to, then his shaky hand finds its way to my arm.

"Jeter, what happened?" I ask.

"The w-w-ater." His voice is croaky.

"You need water?" I whisper. Of course. Who knows how long he's been lying out here without water, not to mention the blood he's lost.

Mark jumps up and runs back to the aircraft to retrieve some water.

But Jeter shakes his head as fiercely as his weak body will allow. He gulps loudly and smacks his chapped lips. "No, the b-b-aby."

I narrow my eyes. "What baby?"

Jeter's body shudders, and he tries to take in a deep breath. His eyes close, and his body stills for a moment. I grab his shirt and shake him. That's when I see his bare arm—the arm his totem used to occupy.

"He took your totem," I say, but he's unconscious again.

"Jeter," I shout, still shaking him.

Dammit! I wish I had power!

"Here," Mark says, sliding next to me with a bottle of water. I open the lid and dip my finger in before gently rubbing it on his dry, chapped lips. I look around. Even if Mark and I morphed here, there's no Peppate within hundreds of miles to fuel our power. Except what might still reside in Jeter ... or Luis and Lilly.

"Jeter, wake up. What about the baby?"

Jeter's eyes open halfway, his face scrunching. I've never seen Jeter cry. He wouldn't be able to cry now even if he wanted to. He's too dehydrated, but I can feel the sorrow seeping from him just the same.

"S-s-orry, Alena." His words slur together in a cracked whisper.

I pour more water in his mouth. "Shh. Here, just take some water."

Jeter gulps impatiently, too fast, and coughs, sputtering. I move him onto his side to let the water slip out. When he can breathe again, Jeter squeezes my arm gently. "S-s-top him."

"Who? Aitin?"

He coughs more, then his eyes close, the delirium taking over. I shake him, trying to pull him back, but he doesn't respond. I feel for a pulse again, but this time his vessels are lifeless.

I sit back on my heels, jaw dropped.

This man betrayed me. He betrayed all the Pepps. I should hate him in this moment as much as I did when he captured me for Aitin. But here in the middle of an ash land, his spirit gone, my throat tightens. He was a man. Trying to do his best for a country he loved.

Why couldn't he have made better choices? Why couldn't he have been stronger?

But then tears stream down my face. I know how hard it is to be strong, to know which choice is the right one. The internal fight for right is never easy or clear. Aren't we all wandering, in our own ways?

Now, not only has Jeter lost his battle with Aitin, he's lost his life.

A deep sadness envelops me.

It's almost as if he died for nothing.

"Let's get him into the aircraft," Mark says.

I grab his arms, and Mark lifts his legs.

Aitin just left him out here to die. With so much blood loss, he's light and easy to carry. That's not right.

We shuffle through the ash, then climb the ramp into the aircraft and place him on the seats across from Lilly, then strap him in.

"Jeter?" Lilly asks, trying to sit up.

I nod silently. I don't know how Lilly knows Jeter. But I don't really want to ask about that right now. My mind is too distracted by the words Jeter spoke, about a baby.

Was he talking about Lilly's baby? I want to shake that thought clear out of this universe, conclude that the baby died simply because it was a Mixed Blood. But Lilly's baby died only hours ago. It's too big of a coincidence to ignore. *What was he trying to tell me?*

Luis flies the aircraft into the air again. I graze my eyes over the dead land searching for more life, but find nothing else. Everything that once was here is gone.

Chapter 21

The wastelands don't stop. They stretch on and on and on.

Our journey to Petrichor gets colder, and the clouds get darker. Soon the sinister black lands turn to a snow-covered terrain, the area finally returned to its natural climate.

Its bleakness makes me shiver.

We eventually reach the border of Petrichor, where the protective fogs used to be, where the *warm* weather used to start, but all we see now is more snow and ice.

"Do you think he's already here?" Luis asks.

Mark doesn't have an answer and neither do I, until Luis guides the aircraft further inland and Magnetic Mountain comes into view.

"Oh no. Breccia," I whisper when we see it. My Magbaby crawls out of her harness and follows my gaze. Her eyes immediately widen. Magnetic Mountain is nothing more than a pile of dark ash now.

It's the first sign that, yes, Aitin is here.

I'm reminded of how much danger even little Breccia is in just by being here. I place her on the dash of the aircraft, allowing her to see what we see.

Luis redirects the aircraft to the left, heading around the mountains on the west side of Petrichor, the way I first entered the Pepp world near the aircraft landing. He flies us straight up the cliff until we reach the top. Then all of Petrichor comes into view.

The air in the flyer is silent. Even the shuddering metal seems to still, and my hand covers my mouth.

The once beautiful, warm, green, and inviting Petrichor is now covered in cold, dirty yellow snow. The bunker hole that was dug to create a shelter is covered up with no sign of Pepps. *Did they get underground in time?*

In the distance I see GreenGrotto—or what's left of it. The trees that used to flourish through the mountain are gone, and without their support the mountain has collapsed, leaving in its place a large pile of rubble.

"Even MossyHollow has been destroyed," Mark whispers. Sure enough, the large tree-store that sat in the middle of Petrichor is gone, replaced by more snow.

My eyes move to the right. The Burrows that used to be sheltered by luscious thick trees are now just an exposed collection of hilly bumps in the terrain.

Man, it's only been, what—two, three days since Rusty was here getting the Pepp children out? Within that time, Aitin has arrived and destroyed everything?

Well, almost everything.

Many creatures wander around, stomping and roaring. From up here, they look small and satiated, but I know they're not. The dinosaurs, as always, are probably irritable and hungry. Their screeching and thrashing sounds reach us inside the plane now, making the hairs on the back of my neck rise.

I'm not sure what I expected things to look like, but I definitely wasn't expecting this. With the official scene of a lost Petrichor before me, I feel fear creep into my bones.

Aitin is here, and he's morphed.

"Do dinosaurs like cold?" Luis asks Mark.

"Some do, but some don't," Mark says.

Maybe they already found Aitin and ate him like they were supposed to do.

Or maybe not.

With a solemn face Luis quickly lands the plane.

"Thanks for bringing us here," I whisper, speaking past my shock. "Once we get off, please take the aircraft back to Maracai and warn the others. Tell Rusty and Cody what you've seen. We'll need help from the Mixed Bloods as soon as possible."

Luis nods and pulls out a coat from his satchel.

I stoop closer to Breccia, who's still sitting on the dash. "Go with him. Help spread the word, and then find somewhere safe to stay."

Breccia floats to my neck, a grave expression on her black face. I feel her tiny hands tighten around my skin.

"I'm sorry," she says.

I shake my head. "Don't be. You got away and helped me save Lilly. Thank you. Now go. I'll see you soon." I rub her tiny face with my nose before setting her back down.

"Alena." Mark pulls at my attention. He's looking anxiously out the window. "We need to go. Get dressed in your warmest clothes, quickly."

He emphasizes the word *quickly*, and he's right. We practically blew a trumpet announcing our arrival coming in this aircraft. Aitin probably already knows we're here. I pull out my satchel and remove my warm snow clothes. I'm reminded of the last time I wore them, the time I went to the prison to visit Eli.

The prison. *Did Aitin's morph affect the prison?*

Once I'm fully dressed and warm, I pull out my spare clothes for Lilly, who's now shivering.

"Here, you can use these." I move toward her but then stop. "Wait. These are made from Peppate. I ... wasn't thinking. Do we have anything else?" I turn to Mark.

He shakes his head. Of course we don't.

"Thank you, Alena." She quickly unstraps herself from the seat and takes the clothes. I watch her strain, pushing her feet into the puffy pants. *What's worse for her—to have a severe allergic reaction to the Peppate in the clothing or freeze from the bitter cold?* She's going to get really sick no matter what.

Deciding it's probably best for her to stay warm, I step to her side and help her pull the pants up.

"Let's hope everyone got below in time." Mark voices my concern from a couple of minutes ago. "I would go check on them, but if Aitin is still here, that's probably a bad idea. We can't let them out until we know they'll be safe."

"Which means we need to find Aitin," Lilly says. "If Case is here, Aitin is surely with him, making him do whatever he wants him to do. Case will insist on having a lab. A dark room. Is there a place like that here?"

I zip up her coat. "There are a lot of dark places here. There's Green-Grotto—although that looks a little destroyed. The school is dark. So is the hospital in some places. And the Post." I rub my face in irritation. "We also need power, Mark, but by the looks of things here, there's no Peppate to destroy, so morphing won't do us any good. If we don't have power, how will we remove the serum from Aitin?"

"We'll find a way," Mark says, brushing my cheek with the back of his fingers.

Just then, Luis opens the hatch, and a cold gust of air blasts through the cabin of the aircraft, stealing my breath away. *Man, it's cold!*

Both Mark and I step to either side of Lilly and help her out. Our boots crunch when we reach the deep snow, and my lips quiver regardless of our clothing. I pull my coat tighter.

As soon as we're off the aircraft and clear, Luis draws up the hatch and rises into the air. Then he's gone, leaving behind a heavy, hushed silence.

"The Post is closest to us," Mark whispers. "Why don't we head there first? Get Lilly inside."

I nod in agreement, not wanting to make any unnecessary noise.

We look around. Yes, the Post is close, but with all the snow, it's difficult to see it. We wander a few paces away from the landing field until Mark stops and lets go of Lilly.

"It has to be here somewhere."

"They must have covered the opening," I say, recalling someone mentioning that a long time ago as part of the hideout plans. "We might have to dig around."

While Mark pulls out some shovel capsules from his bag, I help Lilly sit in the snow. She's shivering violently, the clothes I gave her not enough. But just as I'm reaching into my satchel for something more that might help, my eyes freeze on her face.

Fresh raised red splotches are starting to appear where the scarf is touching her neck.

I curse. She doesn't need more Peppate clothing, she needs us to hurry.

I grab a shovel from Mark and start digging. The snow is heavy, wet, and deep. White flurries from the dark sky swirl around us, dropping snow on my hair and my hands, soaking my coat, but Mark and I keep shoveling.

"I think I found it," Mark finally whispers. I tread the few steps to his side. "It looks like the opening has been covered with a metal door. I hope this was put here by the Pepps and not by Aitin."

I help him remove the rest of the snow until we've exposed it all.

Then Mark wraps his gloved hand around the handle and pulls it open.

I stare. It's dark inside. No torches lit, no life visible from where we stand. It's eerie and cold.

"Mark ... Aitin could be down there," I say.

But he shakes his head, and kneels on one knee to see better. "The door was covered by undisturbed snow. Unless Aitin knew exactly where to look and has the ability to create fresh snow, he hasn't opened this door. Also, look, there are dead vines hanging from the ceiling. He at least hasn't morphed in here or else the vines would have been turned to dust."

I bite my lip, still unsure.

"Let's get Lilly down. We'll leave her here and close the door for her protection. Then we'll go look at the school for Aitin and Case."

I hate it ... Lilly protests too, not wanting to be left behind, but then she coughs, and I clench my teeth.

She's getting sick. She's already weaker than she was before.

But we don't have any other options. We can't take Lilly with us everywhere; she's slowing us down. And Mark is right. If Aitin isn't down in these tunnels, this is the safest place for her.

I go to Lilly, help her up, and guide her feeble body down the ladder.

"Be careful. Watch your step," Mark coaxes from the bottom.

Once we're all down the ladder, Mark shuts the door behind us and lights a match. With that single strike the darkness is quickly illuminated.

Lifting a torch from the wall, Mark expands the light further.

"Let's move quickly."

"Where are we going to leave her?" I ask. The Post is an area of Petrichor I've never been too familiar with, but Mark seems to know his way.

"There's a filing room just up here on the left. It's where the council members and the chief keep all their important messages. I'm going to put you in there, Lilly. It doesn't have windows and has a lot of cabinets you could hide behind just in case."

Despair rises sharp and swift at the image Mark just produced, Lilly having to hide from Aitin all alone, in the cold. But I shove the image away. We'll get her out.

Sure enough, only a few yards down the tunnel from the ladder, on the left, is a door to a room. It opens into a darkness that smells like dirt and mold. Mark is right. It's huge with rows and rows of tall carefully labeled cabinets, and no windows.

Mark quickly finds a chair and sets it by the first row of cabinets. I still want to pull Lilly's scarf tighter, give her an extra coat to calm her shivering, but I can't. Not when I see those sores.

"Stay here, Lilly," Mark says. "When we find Case, we'll come get you. Here are some matches in case the torch goes out." Mark places the matchbox in Lilly's trembling hand, and his voice drops low. "Please, stay quiet. I don't think Aitin is here, but we can't be sure."

When Lilly nods in agreement, Mark turns to leave.

I can't move, though. My feet are heavy, frozen. *How can I leave her here like this?*

Lilly must sense my internal turmoil. She forces a smile. "Go, Alena. Find Case. But please, try not to hurt him."

I just stare at her. Her voice is disturbingly croaky. Her eyes are red.

"We'll try," Mark responds for me. Then he grips my arm and drags me from the room.

My shoulders tighten. I wish we had a better plan. I wish we had more help.

Mark pushes me to the ladder and encourages me to climb up after him. I grip the metal steps and pull my body up. Once we're back outside in the cold air, Mark shuts the door and starts throwing a little bit of snow back on it to make it yellowish-white again.

I pull my scarf tighter and look around, taking in every detail I can.

The dinosaurs are everywhere, big and small, and without the trees to hide them, they look about as uncomfortable as fish out of water would be. They're all mixed up too, long necks in the distance are being pestered by some of the meat-eaters. Stupid dinosaurs. Will they even have the mental capacity to attack Aitin if they see him, or will they be so distracted by each other that they'll miss him entirely?

Did that training at the Dino Games even do anything?

Mark's boots crunch in the snow behind me. "What are we going to do?" I ask. Making our way to the school would be easy—if the dinosaurs weren't here.

The cock of a gun sounds through the silence, and I turn to Mark. He's loading a small black handgun. I've seen him with that gun once before. I feel just as unnerved seeing him with it now as I did then.

But then I see his trembling hands.

I stare at him, surprised by the sudden change in his demeanor. He's shaking. His whole body is shaking but not from the cold. Mark tries to still his hands by keeping them busy readying his gun, but I catch the tremor.

Aitin is close, and Mark's afraid.

Stepping toward him, I wrap my arms around his neck. *What in the world can I do to help him?* I can't promise safety from Aitin. The same fear pulsing through Mark's veins for his life pulses through mine. No, the best thing I can do is allow him to put an end to this.

"It'll be okay, Mark."

I don't know if that's true, but I hope it. With every cell in my body, I hope everything will be okay.

Mark is still for a moment, then he slowly embraces me, accepting my hug with the gun still in hand. He buries his face in my neck and sighs deeply. "Thanks, Lena."

Then, pulling away, his anxious attention turns to the land before us.

I quietly finger the knives tucked in my sleeves, promising myself to do whatever it takes to keep Mark safe, while looking out over Petrichor. *How in the world are we going to reach the school without getting eaten?*

Mark reaches into his satchel and pulls out a glass cylinder. It's a shrunken dinosaur.

I lean closer. "Who is that?"

"It's Pho, Dilo's brother. The one I worked with in Maracai to extract more serum."

I hadn't realized he brought the dino with him.

Opening the capsule, Mark releases Pho. The dinosaur immediately thrashes around, angry and disoriented, forcing us both to take a step back.

"I know it's cold." Mark speaks to the dinosaur as if he's an old friend. "But we really need your help."

Pho settles down the moment Mark touches his face.

When I first came here, I thought there was no way dinosaurs could understand humans, but the way Mark handles them makes me think otherwise. Pho will not only be able to get us around Petrichor faster, he'll protect us from the other dinosaurs.

I hope.

Mark turns to me.

"Let's go to the school first. If Aitin's not there, we can check out the hospital, and then the Post if we need to. We're exposed out here, so try to keep a lookout. Aitin could very well attack us from up in the mountains."

I look at the tall snow-covered mountain that used to be the school. And then Training Mountain next to it. He's right. We're like sitting ducks out here, giving Aitin a perfect opportunity to attack.

Mark gets onto the back of Pho, then holds out his hand to help me up. It's a terribly uncomfortable fit. The dinosaurs back slants downward too much, and I feel like I'm going to slip off the end of his tail. Maybe Mark could create some sort of saddle one day for these animals. Make them easier to ride.

Pho takes off, bouncing me into the air. I crash up and down on his scaly back, frantically trying to maintain my grip on Mark.

We run by other dinosaurs. Some are huge, towering above us and Pho. All it would take is one whip of a tail or a snap of some jaws and we'd be dead. Oddly enough, though, nobody attacks. I recall the first run-in I had with one of those dinosaurs at GreenGrotto during the Dino Games. It was terrifying feeling its saliva on my skin, hearing it breathe, but the dinosaur didn't kill me like I thought it would. Either because Bud, my baby dinosaur friend, was there chortling at it or because of the Doler it smelled on me.

Either way, I was grateful it didn't eat me. I'm just hoping we have some of that same luck today.

Pho's speed picks up, and I bounce even more like a pebble on concrete during an earthquake. No amount of strength can keep me harnessed to the dinosaur at this point.

After falling off for the third time, I'm beginning to wonder if this is a help or a hinderance. I land in the icy snow again, this time on my shoulder.

Mark hops off to help me. "Sorry, Lena. I'll try to go slower."

It's then—when Mark pulls me to my feet, and a dinosaur twenty feet away walks forward—that someone comes into view. Icy prickles shoot through my veins.

"What is it?" Mark asks, following my eyes.

There, in the field, is a bald man with a disgusting grin on his face.

All the gravity of the world presses down on my body in that moment, crushing me like a jewel. I can't breathe. I can't blink. I just stare.

It's Aitin.

Chapter 22

"Well, well, well." Aitin's voice is loud and clear, no longer the painful croak I remember.

Mark immediately steps in front of me, his hand snapping to his hip where his gun rests. I barely have time to shut my gawking mouth when something explodes in front of us, sending Mark's body into mine.

I land on my back, my ears ringing, my head hundreds of pounds heavier than it was only moments ago.

Breathe, just breathe. I carefully sense my injuries. As far as I can tell, I'm just cold and have a pounding headache. Nothing worse. I gingerly roll onto my stomach and squint, trying to see through the intense ringing. No, I'm fine except for my head. Blasted Jeter. He must have taught Aitin how to create those stupid explosions.

Squeezing my eyes shut, hoping to clear them, I move my hands around.

"Mark?"

I don't feel him, so I fling my eyes open.

Mark! He's lying in the snow several feet from me. I scramble to his side.

"No, no!" I whisper. His skin is peppered with open wounds. The ones on his face are bleeding, but not as bad as the one on his chest. I take off my coat, then press it over his heart, trying to slow the flow. He took the brunt of the hit.

What was in that explosion?

As soon as the wound is covered and compressed, I bring my fingers to his neck. He's still alive, but he needs help. Dammit, I can't help him!

When the snow crunches behind me, I spin around. Aitin's still here.

I expect him to send out another blast, finish us off, but he doesn't. Instead, he cocks his bald head to the side and stares at me curiously with those creepy gray eyes.

"You don't have power," he says in awe.

I curse under my breath. I wish he didn't know that. Now I'm even more vulnerable. My eyes find the gun on Mark's hip. I need to be quick. Grab it and shoot, maybe in a moment when Aitin is distracted. I need to distract him.

"You'll be out of power soon yourself," I say, still pressing down on Mark's chest. "You've destroyed all the Peppate within thousands of miles. You'll probably run out of power even before you can kill the Pepps."

An eerie smile spreads on Aitin's pale face, exposing brittle yellow teeth, sending icy shivers down my spine. "Oh, Alena. I hear there's a totem tree that's always growing new totems. I have a feeling I haven't destroyed it yet. Jax always said it was *specially* protected. Once I find that, I'll have an endless supply of Peppate to retrieve power from. Also, I don't need power in order to kill all the Pepps off."

Just one look at his smug face reminds me how weak I am against him. He's smart, powerful, and full of hate.

I'm shaky and stupid and don't even have power.

Holding up his hand, Aitin reveals a tiny glass flask. Oh, how I wish I had power so I could hear it.

"You know Jeter had a special appreciation for bacteria, viruses, and bugs that are so microscopic you can't even see them. It seemed a little odd to me at first until I saw what he could do with them. There's something so satisfying about seeing the physical pain caused by something so tiny and unanticipated. Even though I think I'm a little fonder of *burning* my prisoners, tell me, Alena, can you identify all the times I've used some sort of mite or virus to get your attention?"

He's talking to me. *That's good, right?* I force my brain to work. Whittle up a plan to distract him. But it's sluggish. Of course, it betrays me in this moment. Why couldn't it have been me that got knocked unconscious instead of Mark? He's so much better with these things.

I slouch. The only thing I can do for now is play along. So I do.

"The flesh-eating bug you used on the prisoners." That's the first time I was ever exposed to Jeter's stupid little mites. The putrid smell of burning flesh from that night stings my nose now. That's a night I'll never forget.

Aitin calmly nods. He's still not attacking me, and I still don't have any ideas. So I turn my body to see him better. Then continue.

"The stomach bug you gave me in the cave?"

"Yes," he says, but then raises his hairless eyebrow, as if there's more.

I shake my head, not understanding. "Those are the only ones I remember."

"The baby?" Aitin coaxes.

My forehead furrows in confusion. The baby? Lilly's baby? He used a virus on her? But I didn't hear anything abnormal when I was examining her. She wasn't sick. Is there a bacterium that would hurt the baby but not the mother?

Then I know, and my body goes weak. I learned about this in one of the books from the library.

"Listeria," I whisper. The water. That's what Jeter was trying to tell me. He wasn't asking for water; he was warning me about what Aitin had done. Infected them with a virus that wouldn't affect the adults but would surely kill the unborn child.

My horrified expression pleases Aitin. "You really are brilliant. I loaded up their wonderful water source with listeria. I knew I would need Case's help here, and the only way I could get it was by proving to him that as long as Peppate exists, he'll never be happy."

"So you killed his baby?" I grit my teeth, ready to attack now. I've seen the things Aitin has done. I've felt his torture in a small way myself. I've even at one point allowed my mind to understand *why* he would do such things. *But this?* This is beyond my understanding. How could a person be so unfeeling, so cruel, as to intentionally kill an unborn child for their own gain? The image of the perfect baby flashes through my mind, then anger courses through my entire body. I grab at the gun harnessed at Mark's hip and rise to my feet.

This makes Aitin laugh out loud. The fact that he doesn't even flinch irritates me more, and, even worse, makes me second-guess my ability. I can't shoot, and he seems to know that.

Ignoring me completely, he lowers the glass flask in his hand to the ground.

I'm determined to prove him wrong. Taking this chance, I shoot at him.

I miss.

I'm walking closer, cocking the gun, when I see it, the thing he's reaching down to. A pipe poking out of the ground. One similar to those Case used in his hideout. The Pepps' air pipe.

He's pouring the blasted contents of the flask into the pipe.

I shoot at him again. "Dammit!" I recock the gun, then plant my feet into the ground like I've seen Mark do, and try to take better aim. I shoot and miss. Aitin doesn't even turn around. Instead, he pulls out a bellows and pumps the contents of the flask further down the pipe.

I can't hit him with the gun, so I start running toward him as fast as I can. *If I can at least tackle him ...*

I don't get two steps before he sends me flying through the air with some invisible force. I land on my back and gasp for breath, my lungs feeling like they've collapsed.

Man, for someone who's new to power, he's sure good at using it. Better than me.

Rolling to my side, I wheeze, watching him finish pumping the flask's contents down the pipe, then he closes it off.

With the gun still in my hand, I force myself to sit up and take aim. This time he looks at me.

"There. That's dose number three in the first day. I'm guessing most of them have caught it by now. The Ebola virus is terribly lethal, but it's best to be sure."

Ebola.

Horror curls under my ribs. I read about that virus too—also known as hemorrhagic fever. The brutal virus causes internal bleeding all over the body, which in turn causes the organs to fail. In my non-Pepp world there's no known cure, and those who get it almost always die.

I shake my head, tears blurring my eyes. "They're Pepps, Aitin. They'll be hearing it and healing it before it can do any damage."

Aitin's smug smile widens. "The normal Ebola virus, sure. But this ... this is why I needed Case. He's been able to modify the little buggers. He's carefully surrounded them in that precious serum you discovered without paralyzing them. With them encased in that, the Pepps won't be able to heal anything. They can't control the serum."

Any lung function I had left is instantly crushed. Aitin discovered the air pipes that lead right to where the Pepps are hiding. Pumping the virus down them, he's trapped them.

I need to get the Pepps out!

My mind starts spinning. *How do I get them out? Where did Rusty say the entrance was? Somewhere in the Post?* Stars above, I don't know those tunnels!

I'm just barely starting to move again, get on my feet, when another explosion rings out.

Everything goes black.

Chapter 23

I hate being cold. Even in the darkest of sleeps, it bleeds in, mocking me, reminding me that there's something important I need to do.

What was that?

I slowly open my stiff eyes. *Why are they stiff?* Why is my *whole body* stiff? I pull my head up and look down at my legs. My limbs, torso, and feet are all exposed to the cold elements. Based on the ashes surrounding my body, I'm guessing Aitin morphed, burning my winter Peppate clothes to a crisp. My satchel is gone too. Thankfully, the clothes I had on underneath were from Maracai, Peppate-free, but they don't protect me from the cold.

I sit up, my numb hands bracing my body in the snow. I'm beyond shivering and want to lie back down.

I just want to sleep.

But then I see bright-red blood staining the yellow snow in front of me.

Mark! He's gone.

I force myself to my knees, frantically crawling to the spot where I last saw him. "Mark!" I try to scream, but even my vocal cords are frozen, making it more of a hushed whisper. I scrape at the snow where he was lying as if doing so will recover him, but he's not here.

"No, no, no!"

I rest my frozen curled hands on my knees in despair and look around. I need help. But there's nothing here, and my body is starting to freeze.

"What do I do?" I whisper to myself. "What would Mark do?"

My eyes rise to the snow around me. I see dinosaur prints, probably Pho's. They lead to the school, but I don't see any prints from a man, from Aitin. That's probably because he morphed. *He flew.*

Could Aitin be at the school? Did Pho follow him?

I lean forward, ready to head in that direction, but then stop. Even if I do find Mark again, there's nothing I can do for him without power. And then there are the Pepps, dying beneath me. *Do I go try to get them out?* I see the gun lying in the snow and curse under my breath. I couldn't even hit Aitin with a single bullet.

"I need power." I repeat this several times, trying to get my sluggish mind to work. "I need power."

Then what Aitin said hits me.

The totem tree. His power hadn't reached into the Post. Perhaps the totem tree is still alive. If I can remove a single totem, get it to Mark, help him morph with me, then we'll at least have power.

I look behind me in the direction of the Post. If I can just get back there, I can get to the totem tree.

I place my bare foot in front of me. With my boots gone, it's going numb, which is painful and makes walking difficult, but I force myself to standing. I tuck my hands into my armpits to protect them somewhat, take a couple of steps, wincing in pain before falling to my knees. It's so cold.

I repeat the process, though. Over and over again. The movement is warming my body just enough to start shivering. My strained breath comes out in large clouds in front of me, and before I know it my feet are completely numb, which makes them heavy but helps a little with the pain. I find my pace slowly picking up.

I don't know how long it takes me to reach the Post. I'm half delirious by the time I get there, and the sky seems a bit darker. I locate our dug-out square and use my red, stiff, swollen arms to scoot the snow back off the door. I reach for the handle and force my frozen fingers to bend around it.

Then I scream in frustration. *I can't lift the door*! I move around, trying to find better leverage, but the door doesn't budge.

Lilly.

I pound on the metal, screaming out her name, but even pounding my hands isn't working. I can't get enough power behind my frozen contact to make much of a sound. And it hurts!

Trying to control my breathing, I stand again and pull hard on the handle, grunting loudly. I almost lose my balance when the door starts to open.

"Alena?"

I fall back on my butt and look up to the sky in relief. *Thank goodness.*

Lilly steps outside to help me. I roll my body over to the hole and practically tumble all the way down the ladder.

"Alena, are you alright?" I hear the worry in her voice, but responding takes too much energy. Instead, I roll onto my stomach and come back to my knees. Lilly sees my reddened, swollen fingers and takes them in her grasp. Breathing out hot air, she encourages them to warm, sending stabs of pain through the tips.

"What happened?" she asks. "Where's Mark?"

"Aitin took him." I pull my hands away from her. I can't sit here getting warm while Mark's life is hanging in the balance, or while the Pepps are dying. "Lilly, I need to get to the totem tree," I say. There's more I need to tell her. About what Aitin did to her baby. But I don't have the energy. I stand and stumble down the hallway. "I need to find the totem tree."

Fortunately, Lilly doesn't ask questions, just tries to support me, carrying the lit torch in her hand. I kick myself silently. I shouldn't be leaning so much on her. Her skin is well blistered now, and she's so weak, but I don't have much of a choice. We'll both die if I don't get to the totem tree. Actually, everyone will die.

Man, my feet hurt! Even the tiniest of pebbles sends shooting pain through the heavy numbness.

"Here." Lilly stops me. "Let me put this on your feet." She unwraps the scarf from around her neck. I brace myself against the wall, gritting my teeth, while she covers the reddened skin of my left foot. It helps a lot, but it only covers one foot. Lilly pulls the beanie off her head to cover the other.

"Thank you," I whisper.

Then we drag each other further. I curse myself for not learning my way around these tunnels. *Why didn't I pay closer attention to things?*

Then I see the chief's office. Okay, I think I can find it from here. We stagger down more halls until we finally see the door to the totem tree observatory. I laugh out loud, earning myself a worried glance from Lilly.

"Are you okay?" she asks.

Of course I'm not okay! Aitin has Mark! But I don't say that, just open the door and step inside.

The room is dark, unlike last time I came here—when the entire wall on the other side was open to the sky. They must have covered it with something to hide it from Aitin. I take the torch from Lilly and try to get a better view of the tree. The small torch doesn't shed nearly enough light in the vast room, but its flickering illumination does help me see that the tree is still there. Aitin hasn't scorched it yet.

That doesn't mean he can't be in here, though.

Just now, I realize there's one very large hiccup in my plan. I can't touch the tree—not without dying. And I know nothing about removing totems from it. *Is it too much to hope that they have one just lying around in there, ready to go?* Question is, how do we get in there? Bapoto never told me where the entrance is.

I yell in frustration, banging on the thick glass separating us from the tree, scaring Lilly. I turn around, ready to go find the entrance, or find a rock to break the glass, when Lilly grabs my arm.

"Wait, someone's down there."

I turn back around, following her pointing finger. It's difficult to see him, his dark skin blending in with the black room, but he's there. "Bapoto?" He steps into the little bit of flickering light we're casting, followed by three other Pepps. When recognition hits him, he smiles his big white smile and takes off running to a door below us.

"Do you know him?" Lilly asks.

I nod and smile deliriously through my frozen lips. "Yes. He can help us." Then I fall to my knees.

I've never felt so out of control. Aitin's actions have disrupted the entire world, and I feel like I'm holding the lives of so many within my powerless hands. But here is one human being who could be the difference between life and death. Bapoto can tip the odds. Never in my life have I been more grateful for the help of another able human being. Or I should say Pepp. I bury my face in my frozen hands.

When Bapoto comes into the observatory and kneels next to me, he has to shake me out of my hysteria.

"Alena, what are you doing here? What's going on up there?"

I slowly look up, blinking tears from my eyes. Two other Pepps are standing behind him.

"Bapoto, I need a totem. I don't have time to explain, but I need you to give me a totem, and then I need you to stay down here and continue protecting the tree. If I don't succeed, you'll need to destroy Aitin. He intends to use the tree for himself. You can't let him do that. If you see him, you kill him on the spot. Do not hesitate."

As I say this, hopelessness blankets me. I don't know *how* Bapoto could even attempt to destroy Aitin. Aitin is too powerful. Perhaps he can find a way, though.

Bapoto searches my face and then nods. "Okay. Chaz, go get her a totem."

"But we only have five left," the boy whispers behind him, his golden hair pulled back into a ponytail.

"Just go get it." Bapoto's voice is sure and authoritative, making the boy respond.

I eye Bapoto carefully. "What does he mean you only have five left?"

Bapoto unwraps a scarf from around his neck and puts it on me. "It's been too cold here. We've tried to keep this room warm, but we've run out of wood. When the tree gets cold, it pulls its branches in. Including the vines. We don't have access to them. The totems we have were harvested before the cold set in." I remember Rusty refusing to let us use totems to fuel our power down in Maracai. I guess this is why.

Bapoto removes his gloves and carefully puts them on my hands. "Don't worry, Alena. It'll all return to normal soon." Bapoto then replaces the scarf and beanie on my feet with his boots, puts his hat on my head, his coat around my shoulders. His kind gesture makes me cry. I reach up to his cheek.

He's not giving me warmth, he's giving me hope.

"Thank you, Bapoto."

Chaz runs back into the room, heaving from the fast sprint. He has something in his hands, carefully wrapped in a cloth.

"Here you go."

I take it, noting how it's covered. In all the chaos, I can't forget to be careful with it, keep it from touching my bare skin. The last thing I need is for it to attach itself to me.

After placing it in my coat pocket, Bapoto helps me stand.

Once I'm stable, he turns his attention to Lilly.

"Who is she?"

I'm grateful she came with me. Perhaps Bapoto can keep an eye on her, keep her safe until we find Case.

"Bapoto, this is Lilly. She's a Mixed Blood and a very good friend of mine. Would you mind keeping an eye on her? She's getting sick from the Peppate, but could you try to make her as comfortable as possible?"

"Of course," he says.

I hope someday I can repay him, show him how truly grateful I am for his help.

But, for now, I turn to the door. I need to go.

With one last good-bye, I step out of the room.

Then I run.

Chapter 24

I'm just barely out of the Post when I hear my name.

"Alena!" I turn around to find a group of Mixed Bloods coming off an aircraft in the distance. Based on how the aircraft has landed sideways in the snow with smoke coming from the metal, I can guess that the Mixed Bloods flew the thing here themselves.

They came!

I want to run up to each of them and kiss their beautiful scarved cheeks!

"Alena, what do you need us to do?" Breccia floats at the front of the group, presenting the most helpful question possible.

What do I need them to do?

I stare at each of their faces, the creaky wheels in my head finally coming alive. They're dressed in thick snow gear, gray beanies on their heads, scarfs around their necks, gloves on their hands. They stand healthy and ready. I'm sure they have a million questions like me, but I'm grateful they don't ask them. I don't have time to answer.

"I need you all to get the Pepps out," I say urgently, waving my hand over all of Petrichor. "Aitin has sent a deadly virus through their air pipes, and they're most likely dying right now. There's a tunnel that leads to them through the Post, but I don't know exactly where that is. I suggest you dig out the ground."

As I'm giving the instructions, though, an impending sense of despair creeps up inside me again. Ebola spreads so quickly. There's a big chance everyone will end up sick.

Also, I realize what I'm asking them to do would be so easy for the Pepps, but with these untrained Mixed Bloods, it feels as if I'm telling them to do something impossible. Sighing in frustration, I backpedal.

"I guess I should first ask what you're capable of doing. I know Flint taught you how to make acid, but did he teach you anything else?"

Those in the group look at one another in confusion. "Acid? I guess that would be helpful, but Flint didn't just teach us how to make acid."

I'm working through my confusion when another speaks up. "We can do almost anything the Pepps do. We can move any element—rocks, water, etc. We can create fire. Some of us are even good with the elements of the body. Healing is one thing Kaconcha has learned." The boy points to a girl whose dark eyebrows have grown in. They are stunningly well-arched, standing out against her hazel eyes.

"You can heal?" My own eyebrows rise in surprise.

She nods slowly. "Yes, a little."

I gape at them in awe. I recall my last encounter with Flint and his words about the acid. He had said that only to get under my skin. And it had worked. I shake my head. As much as I hate him, though, I couldn't be more grateful for him in this moment. He trained these Mixed Bloods. They'll be more helpful than I ever imagined.

"Okay. Can you move away the earth and get the Pepps out?"

"Yes," a voice says. "Where do we take the Pepps when we find them?"

I'm about to tell them to take the Pepps back to Maracai—that's where they would be safest. But then I realize they can't carry the Pepps while flying—morphed. They'll kill them. And based on the looks of the aircraft now, it's not an option either.

"Just carry them back here to the Post and get them underground. Please remember, from this point on, nobody can morph, for many reasons." I pat my coat pocket where the new totem is. "When I make it back, I'll do my best to heal the Pepps. I'm hoping they're still alive."

Ready to carry out my orders, the team turns, ready to dig out Petrichor.

Just then, Lilly steps out of the Post behind me. "Alena."

I hold back a frustrated groan. "Lilly, what are you doing? You need to stay below."

"I'm coming with you," she says. "It was a mistake for me to stay behind last time. Neither Aitin nor Case will kill you with me around. Plus, you need a companion to help you, now that Mark has been taken."

I want to yell at her, force her back down that hole, but deep down inside I know she's right.

I need her help.

"Okay," I say through gritted teeth.

I turn to lead us to the school, but stop, goose bumps rising on my arms. Things with the dinosaurs are escalating. Fast. What seemed like a field of wandering dangerous animals only moments before has now become a bloody battlefield of *hungry*, dangerous animals. Which makes sense. Aitin destroyed everything that could have been food for them.

So they're eating one another.

How in the world did I make it back alive in my frozen, delirious state?

There's a long neck in the distance, lying on its side, groaning loudly while getting picked apart by an overwhelmingly large group of meat-eaters. The long neck whips its head and tail back and forth, trying to fight the others off, but it's too weak.

The same thing is happening to a triceratops not too far from where MossyHollow used to stand. Flying dinosaurs join in the torture by diving down from the sky, yanking off chunks of meat, then retreating upward.

It's horrible.

How am I supposed to get to the school without getting torn apart? Especially without Mark?

"Hey, wait," I call the Mixed Bloods back. "Do any of you know how to create meat?"

***

The fast-approaching dusk darkens the heavy sky.

Which intensifies my worries for Mark.

I thought working in daylight was impossible, but working in the dark ...?

Lilly and I run as fast as our cold and weak bodies will carry us, staying far away from the dinosaurs. When one gets too close, either on land or overhead, we take out a chunk of meat from the heavy bag I'm lugging over my shoulder and toss in its direction. *I can't believe that Mixed Blood girl could make meat so easily.*

It takes us way too long to reach the school. By the time we're standing outside the entrance my nerves are in knots, and the dark night is crushing. The thick cloud cover doesn't even offer a smidgeon of light from the moon.

I'm more than excited to get out of the open air, away from the dinosaurs.

But then a roar echoes off the tunnel walls of the school we just stepped into.

"Alena, what was that?" Lilly's voice cracks as she scoots close to me and grips my arm.

"The dinosaurs?" I whisper, gulping down the nauseating feeling rising within me. "Please don't tell me they're inside the school."

As if to answer my question, another loud roar bellows out of the dark tunnels in front of us.

My mouth goes dry.

It's dark, I'm cold, and I don't even know where I'm going. I don't know these tunnels, not like everyone else in Petrichor does. The school was probably the part of Petrichor I visited the least, other than the Burrows. And now there are dinosaurs wandering the halls. Oh, how I wish someone else was with us.

Mark could be in there, though. I have to find him.

Gulping down my worries, I step forward. I try to recall what Mark told me a long time ago about the dinosaurs. That they bow to him because of the Doler. Now's a good time to test that theory. See if they bow to me.

But then I remember the first time I met Dilo. She didn't bow to me right away. There must be more to what Mark does.

I straighten my shoulders like I've seen Mark do and hold out my hands in front of me. I'm not sure why. It just seems like the smart thing to do.

Lilly grabs hold of my coat from behind and follows closely. My eyes frantically try to adjust to the darkness of the tunnel. Unable to see the slight incline of the rock, my feet scuff on the floor. *Shoot.* The sound bounces loudly off the walls and I stop, sending Lilly stumbling into me.

I want to groan. There has to be a quieter, more efficient way of doing this.

I close my eyes, picturing what I know of the school. From what I remember, the tunnel splits up ahead. Going left leads you to the skills room, where the Pepps are tested in front of the council. Opening my eyes again, I wave my outstretched hands to the left, searching for the wall. As I do so, my mind pictures a quiet dinosaur waiting there to eat me, so when my hands brush against the rock, I flinch drastically and jump back into Lilly.

"What?" she whispers behind me.

"Nothing," I say, swallowing my heart. I reach forward again and use the wall for guidance. Walking down the tunnel, I feel it veer to the left.

"Is it just me, or is the tunnel getting lighter?" Lilly whispers close to my ear.

She's right. I can see now, so there must be a light up ahead. I slow our steps, trying to be extra quiet. The tunnel takes an abrupt turn, and I have a feeling that stepping a little further will expose us to the lit room.

I turn around and place my finger against my lips, signaling to Lilly that she needs to be quiet. Then I try to tell her to stay put. Thankfully, she obeys.

I press my body against the rock, my heart pounding much too loudly, and slowly slide my head to the side until I can see into the tunnel. I brace myself for jumping dinosaurs or an angry Aitin, but when my eyes spot only a flickering torch perched in the wall, I want to sigh in relief. I look around further. The tunnel does indeed lead to the skills room, which I can see in the distance. The room is also lit with more torches, but, overall, it seems quiet.

If I can reach that torch, we can use it to light our way through the halls. I wish we didn't need light, but with how little I know this place, I won't be able to get around without it.

I'm just about to step into the hall, when the ground rumbles beneath my feet, making me freeze. I slowly turn back to Lilly. Her brown eyes are wide in horror.

What was that? she mouths.

I don't know! I shrug tightly. It was probably a dinosaur, but I don't know which direction it was coming from. *From the skills room or the tunnel to the right?* I open my mouth, trying to quiet my loud, strained breathing.

Slowly looking around the corner again, I find it still empty.

"There's a torch there," I whisper. "I'm gonna try to get it. Just down the tunnel is the skills room. It's a large open cavern with some off-shooting rooms. We could look through them for Case, but I feel like we'll be too exposed."

Lilly nods in agreement. "Case doesn't like being in large rooms, or where a lot of people could potentially be. I suggest we look for a small, quiet room in a hidden place."

Wherever that might be. I chew on my cheek.

"Okay, wait here while I get the torch."

I round the corner, shaking my head. This is such a stupid idea.

I quickly make my way across the tunnel to the other side where the torch is. I press my back against the wall and stop. Looking both ways, I try to sense anything dangerous, but the halls are quiet. So I shuffle sideways toward the torch. When I finally reach it, I wrap my right hand around the thick stick and yank as hard as I can.

It's pretty stuck. Stupid.

I hold in a loud sigh and place my other hand on it. Planting my feet in the ground, I pull hard. This time I'm able to get it to budge, but it drops some pebbles to the ground. That sound, under different circumstances, would have gone completely unnoticed but now, each pebble sounds like an explosion.

The ground beneath me begins to rumble again. *I'm pretty sure it's coming from the skills room.* Not caring about the sounds of the pebbles anymore, I yank the torch from the wall and run back to Lilly.

Her dark eyes are practically bulging from her face.

"Come on," I whisper loudly, running straight down the tunnel that split to the right. There have to be some rooms down here, right?

Lilly follows, and I repeatedly look back to make sure she's still there. I don't see the dinosaur yet, but it sure feels like it's following us. The tremors in the ground are getting stronger.

A roar ripples through the air behind us. Lilly squeals and jumps forward, nipping my heels.

I curse the torch in my hand. Nothing like lighting yourself up when you want to hide. *But I need to see the tunnel!*

Just find a room!

The tunnel turns up ahead. I'm not sure how this makes me feel. It will hide us a little from whatever is coming behind, but it blocks my view from what's around the corner. *What if there's another dinosaur up there?*

Fortunately, right at the turn I locate a door. I don't bother looking around the corner or behind us. Instead, I reach out for the knob and pull the heavy door open.

After yanking Lilly inside, I slam the door shut.

With our backs against the wall, we breathe heavily, trying to catch our breath.

The rumbling gets closer, and I clasp my hands over my mouth. I need to be quiet. I debate whether or not I should put the torch out. *Can the dinosaur see the light beneath the door?*

The rumbling sound stops, and we hear the dino sniffing around through the cracks. *Is it going to break the door?*

Lilly grasps at my arm.

Then the ground trembles again but softer this time, like it's fading. *Is it walking away?*

"You can breathe now," Lilly whispers to me when the ground becomes perfectly still.

I suck in a deep breath, realizing I have been holding it. *It didn't break down the door.*

I quickly look around the small room. *Where are we?* It appears to be a classroom, with desks carefully lining the middle of the floor, and a chalkboard attached to the wall on the right. Foreign icicles pierce the air above us, and the small window on the far wall lets in a terrible draft, the cold, bitter air pestering the flame on the torch.

I pull my coat tighter.

"Well, Case isn't here," Lilly says. "Should we keep looking?"

I nod, gripping the torch in my sweaty palm. Stepping back to the door, I grasp the cold handle again and turn it slowly, pushing the door out into the tunnel. I peek to the left. It's empty. Then leaning out further, I weave my head around the door to the right.

I scream and jump back, panic flooding my body. There, in front of me, with terrifying eyes staring right at my face, is a very large dinosaur. My mind can't decipher which kind it is or even how it's possible for such a large dinosaur to fit in this tiny tunnel. All I can seem to establish is that its huge teeth aren't the kind that belong to a plant eater.

I shove myself back into Lilly, forcing us into the room as fast as I can, but it's too late. It's seen where I've gone. Suddenly the whole place is moving. The dinosaur tries to squeeze his large body through the tiny door and causes the whole place to shake. I feel as though I'm an ant in a box being rattled ferociously by a child. I grab Lilly and try to send us further into the room, when rocks in the ceiling start falling.

No!

I push Lilly under one of the small desks. They're measly little things that offer little protection, but they're the best we've got. I slide my body under another one and cover my head with my hands, closing my eyes tightly. What is probably only a minute or so of intense shaking feels like an eternity. Once the ground actually stops moving and rocks stop falling, I find myself wondering when it will start again. It takes Lilly practically dragging me out from underneath the desk for me to realize the dinosaur has stopped.

I cough and look around. Fortunately, the torch has held strong amid the dust. And, fortunately, there's no dinosaur. Unfortunately, there's no door either. I stand. Where the exit once was lies a large pile of boulders. I turn around, looking in desperation at the room. The window, as large as it is in letting the cold air enter, is in no way large enough for us to exit.

We're trapped.

Chapter 25

It's cold. Lilly slumps against the wall, her lungs making terrible wheezing sounds now. I need to find a way out of here. At first I work on the pile of rocks where the door used to be, but they're so heavy, I can't move a single one. So I turn my attention to the window. I grab a small, jagged rock and desperately hit it against the frozen edges of the small opening, hoping to expand it enough to fit my body through. A couple of pebbles fall to the ground but not much else. Still, I pound. Over and over again, until my hands are frozen and bloodied from the rock gouging my skin.

"Alena, come sit for a minute." Lilly calls to me through her coughs.

I ignore her words and grip the rock tighter. My stomach won't stop burning with worry for Mark. I need to get out. I need to get out!

I keep hitting the wall.

Then, over the sounds of my pounding, Lilly begins to hum. Her voice is raspy, but she exerts it anyway, bringing a song into our somber trap.

I sigh, deeply annoyed. "Why are you singing?" I'm glad my words sound like a simple inquisition, lacking the exasperation I feel.

"It helps," she croaks.

I shake my head and hit the wall again, harder. "It helps? You know, I can almost understand Aitin. Even though his actions will never be acceptable, I can at least understand his motives. But you? You're nothing like Aitin. How can you be so ..." I pause, unable to think of a word to describe Lilly.

"So what?"

I grit my teeth when the word finally comes to my mind. "So at *peace. All the time!*" I don't know why that word aggravates me. Maybe because it seems like something so unobtainable, and yet Lilly seems to have mastered it.

Lilly laughs out loud at this, sending her into another coughing fit. I instantly feel bad. *I shouldn't have said that.* Even though Lilly always seems so at peace, it's unfair for me to assume that I know what goes on inside her head.

I shift restlessly on my feet until she's finally able to regain control of herself. When she settles back against the wall, an awkward silence spreads through the room. I fiddle with the rock in my hand for a moment, wondering what I should do, but then I slump forward and find my way to her side, sliding to my knees next to her.

"I'm sorry, Lilly."

"If you could see what goes on inside my head, you would know that I'm not at peace even most of the time." She tries to clear her throat in vain.

"How do you do it, then?" I ask, nicer this time. "How are you so happy? You've been stuck in the desert, underground with Case for months. The day I saw you in the sand bunker, you seemed to be in such a good mood. If I'd been stuck there that long, I would have turned into a monster." I tap my rock on the floor.

Lilly frowns. "Of course I was in a good mood that day. Seeing a new face after so much isolation would make anyone happy." Lilly fiddles with the scarf around her neck. "But I'm not happy all the time, Alena. Even as hard as I try, it's hard to be happy when you're not feeling well."

Clearly frustrated with the material hurting her neck, Lilly yanks the scarf off.

In the short amount of time I've spent with her, I would call her nothing less than strong. I haven't even thought about how much physical pain she's been in during our interactions. I stand and make my way back to the window, digging my rock into the edge, softer this time.

"Does it hurt a lot?" I ask. "I mean, I know you probably hurt now, but what about when you were isolated?"

Lilly smiles a little, but it doesn't reach her eyes. "Yes, it hurts. The skin sores are the worst. They scare me because of what they can turn into. I hate how long they take to heal. When they get really bad, they make even the smallest of movements painful. All I want to do is lie down and never move, but then lying on them hurts like heck too. You can't win with the skin sores. And if they get in the wrong places ..." Lilly allows her eyebrows to say what her words don't. "Then even something as simple as going to the bathroom becomes excruciatingly painful. Or when they get on the feet?" Lilly shakes her head to emphasize the pain.

"And then there's the food. Luckily, because of Case, I haven't had as many problems with my stomach. He keeps a tight watch on what I consume. But before I met him, I never wanted to eat. Either I would throw everything up, or the food would just sit in my belly for days and bloat. I remember one time I was so bloated I looked like I was nine months pregnant. My mom's boyfriend beat me that week, calling me nasty names."

My hand freezes, and I watch her face in shock. *He beat her? For being bloated?* Suddenly I feel like a selfish brat assuming her life was as blessed as my own.

"How do you do it then? How do you deal with the pain?" I twist the rock into the window edge.

Now Lilly gives me a true smile. "You know, as a young girl, dealing with my condition was not only painful but terrifying. I would wake up in the middle of the night unable to breathe, so close to passing out, but I never knew why. It was scary. When I met Case, though, he taught me exactly what was causing my pain and what I have to do to avoid the reactions. That in and of itself helped. After so much suffering, I finally understood my body, which meant I finally felt like I had some control. Remembering what life was like before helps me remember how lucky I am now." Lilly's smile fades.

"There's also people," she whispers. "If there's anything that takes my mind off the pain, it's being around other people. When I was a prisoner of Aitin's, he kept me isolated, away from all the other Pepp prisoners. But after begging him for weeks, he finally let me slip out of my little cave to go feed the others—or give them a sponge bath. I had to keep something over my face so they didn't see me, but helping them ... helped me." Lilly looks at me and frowns. "It stinks, though, that the thing that distracts me the most from my pain is also what causes it. People. I produce the most Peppate inside myself when I'm around others. That's why Case keeps me isolated, and sometimes I hate him for it. What's worse, Alena? Being in pain? Or being alone?" Lilly stares at the ground fiddling with small rocks.

I don't know.

"I also enjoy being outside," she continues when I don't say anything. "The desert didn't have much to offer in terms of beauty during the day, but at night ..." Another smile tugs at her lips. "Don't tell Case, but sometimes I would sneak out while he was sleeping, and I would look at the stars. Oh, how beautiful they are. I would stare at them for hours. The sky was so big, and even though it made me feel so small, it also made me feel part of something extraordinary." Lilly looks at me. "*Me*, part of something extraordinary." Her eyes drift back to the ground. "Sometimes I feel like each one of those stars has been purposefully placed there for *me* to enjoy."

I stare at her, silently thinking about her words, thinking about the pain she's endured, and about what helps her get through it all. *What would I choose if I had to choose between isolation from Mark or freedom from pain?* I won't ever truly know the gravity of that burden. How unfair that Lilly's had to make that choice daily for her entire life.

"It is possible, you know," Lilly whispers, "to survive life without Peppate. But after watching Case, I've realized that even though you can survive that way, that type of life is not really living. I have a hard time believing we're here to just endure. Shouldn't we all be able to thrive? Sometimes it feels like we're no more than toys tossed around in an ocean, being thrown here and there with no regard for what we want. You ask me how I do it? I fight, Alena. I fight to make one simple choice every day. Not a choice to be *happy* but a choice to *try*. To try to do those things that will open the doors for happiness."

Lilly shifts on her butt and places her blistered hands in her lap. I hit the window edge again.

"Case has made the choice to heal me in exchange for his happiness. And he's given everything to do that. But sometimes I wish he would try for happiness instead. He deserves it. He used to be so ... different, you know. So fun. Now, even if I hit him upside the head with a stick, he doesn't respond. Sometimes it feels like he's so lost, so far away. And now it's only going to get worse. Now that he's lost a baby."

Aitin's words come to me in this moment, and I realize Lilly doesn't know what he's done. I contemplate whether or not I should tell her, especially since I don't want to cause her more pain. But keeping the truth a secret doesn't seem right. She deserves to know.

"Lilly, there's something I need to tell you," I say, walking toward her, sinking to my knees again.

Her dark bloodshot eyes meet mine.

"Aitin said something to me earlier before he took Mark." I bite my lip and take in an uneasy breath. *What if it's not true?* I shake my head at my own thought. No, it makes too much sense in my mind.

"Lilly, he said your baby didn't die because of Peppate."

Lilly's red eyes start to water. I'm not sure if it's because they hurt or because I mentioned her baby.

I wring my hands. "There's a bacteria called listeria. It's deadly for an unborn fetus—however, tricky to know about because it doesn't always affect the mother. Aitin said he loaded up your water source in the desert with listeria in an attempt to get Case. He thought if your baby died in the womb, Case would blame the Peppate and would come running to him, ready to eradicate the Pepps altogether. Aitin needed Case's help."

Lilly's mouth drops open.

No, the water in her eyes isn't from Peppate. Tears spill onto her cheeks now.

"Aitin killed my baby—to get to Case?"

I nod.

"And it worked." Lilly covers her trembling lips with her hand. How horrible. To know that your baby was intentionally killed for a terrible reason. Lilly buries her face in her hands, crying quietly.

I shouldn't have told her. We need to get moving. We don't have time to deal with this now. But then I look around the cave and restrain a groan. It's not like we're going anywhere soon. I pat her arm.

After a little while, though, I begin to worry about her breathing. It was strained before, but now she's gasping for breath. I rub her back gently and try to get her to calm down.

"It's okay, Lilly."

When the cave is finally quiet again, Lilly breaks the silence. "I have to stop him, Alena. I have to stop Case. This has gone too far. I've always justified his actions by saying that he's only doing it because he loves me, but this is no longer about love. It's about his lack of control, and I have to be the one to stop him." Standing, Lilly looks around the room. "How do we get out of here?"

I gingerly stand beside her, my body stiff from the cold.

"Lilly, you sit down and rest. I'll start moving the rocks at the top of the pile." *If I can.* At least it'll give me something to do. Lilly doesn't sit, though. She follows me as I climb. I push at the boulders, searching for one that will at least budge, hoping I don't cause further cave-in. Four, five, six rocks. None of them move. I'm just turning to a large one wedged close to what used to be the ceiling, when Lilly lets out a squeal. Actually, it's more like a croak.

"What's wrong?"

I follow her wide eyes to the top of the pile where the rocks are … moving. I step back. No, they're not moving, they're melting. Soon an opening appears and two white ears poke up, followed by a head.

It's a white fox, holding another lit torch twice its size. Its fur is long but thin, and instead of standing strong like I would imagine a fox doing, it slumps over, feeble. Something's wrong with it.

I move closer. There's something familiar about those eyes.

The fox shuffles weakly through the opening toward us but only gets a couple of inches before losing its balance.

I launch forward, trying to catch it, but I'm too far away. It thumps nastily down the rocks before landing in a fury heap on the floor, the torch clattering along with it until it's extinguished.

"Is it dead?" Lilly whispers.

I'm stumbling down the pile, slipping on the occasional icicle, when the fox changes into human form.

"Sef," I whisper, battling between terror for his condition and unmatched gratitude. He's the morpher that saved me and Mark from Aitin's caves in Dakdete. Lilly grabs the torch we perched into the pile of rubble while I descend. I'm almost to him, when he turns on his side and vomits, the red bloody fluid seeping down into rocks.

Suddenly my body freezes. "You're sick," I whisper, recalling the Ebola Virus Aitin flushed down the pipes. Based on Sef's sickly white skin and thin body, he's not just sick; he's dying. But I can't say that out loud.

"What are you doing here?" I drop down next to him, ignoring the fact that I could very well catch the virus too.

Sef shakily moves his body into a sitting position, wiping the vomit off his face. "I thought you might need help."

I shake my head. "Sef, you're sick. Plus, Aitin would kill you with just one morph. You need to get out of here."

Sef's eyes turn sad, a foreign look on the usually cheerful boy's face. "Alena, if you don't accomplish what you're here to accomplish, we'll all be dead anyway. Tell me what you need."

I open my mouth to rebuff his demand, but then an odd sound reaches my ears. The sound of quiet pattering feet. An attempted smile spreads across Sef's tired face.

"I guess I should say, tell *us* what you need."

I follow his eyes up to the opening he created. Three more foxes appear in the hole. Three more morphers. But they don't look sickly like Sef.

"They're your precious Mixed Bloods, Alena. They got us out of that horrible hiding place."

Mixed Bloods. I look at them in awe. *They know how to morph into foxes? They were able to successfully get the Pepps out*? I look back at Sef. The fact that he's still alive is a miracle, but he's obviously very sick. He might not survive much longer. *How many Pepps didn't make it?*

"What do you need us to do?" Sef repeats his question, bringing my mind back.

I plop down on a rock in despair.

"I need too much, Sef. I need to find Mark, I need to morph, and then I need to get close to Aitin to remove the serum from his body. But I don't know where Aitin is, and even if I do find him, there's nothing holding him back from killing me." I shake my head and look at Lilly, who's now standing beside me. "I wish Rusty was here. He's so much better at coming up with plans of attack than I am."

"We need to find Case." Lilly says, stepping forward with a more helpful instruction. "He can get you close to Aitin."

"If he doesn't kill me first," I say. It seems too much to hope that Case will actually work with me.

Lilly turns to Sef, ignoring my comment. "Can you help us find Case? Bring us to him? We think he's here, in this mountain."

A faint and very tired smile rises on Sef's face. "Absolutely."

Changing back into the white arctic fox, he leads the way for the other foxes, disappearing from sight.

In their absence, Lilly and I work hard to come up with a plan.

***

My body is very frozen by the time the foxes come back. But they found Case. This makes me both happy and terrified at the same time.

Climbing through the small melted hole in the rock, we follow the foxes through the halls.

I want to run, get to Case quickly so I can get to Mark, but Sef's body is shutting down. I almost reach down to carry him the rest of the way when he throws up.

"Alena, don't touch him," Lilly says. "The last thing we need right now is for you to get sick."

As much as I hate seeing him suffer, I know Lilly is right. The best way for me to help him is by getting power so I can heal him.

The cold tunnels stretch on. Occasionally a roar rumbles through the halls, but we never see another animal. Sef and his friends must know where they are, know how to avoid them.

I'm staring at the fluttering shadows ahead of us, trying to calm the nervous pounding in my chest, when I realize I'm not shivering anymore. The tunnel is getting warmer. Does that mean we're getting closer to someone?

Soon an open door appears in the darkness down the hall. Breathing heavily, Sef points to it.

"He's in there."

I swallow.

"Okay. Thank you, Sef. Now, I need you to get out of here. Head back to the Post, get underground. You'll be safe there. I'll be back as soon as I can."

Sef turns to leave, but then I stop him. "Hey, Sef." He turns back around. "Drink lots of water, please, and try to rest."

A red drop of blood squeezes out of his eye, trailing down his white fur. My stomach churns. *Will he even make it back to the Post?* I point to one of the other foxes.

"Will you go with him? Make sure he gets back safely?"

It nods its head immediately and follows after my friend.

Thank you.

I look at the remaining two foxes, grateful for their help.

"Will one of you go get more help? If your people have finished getting the Pepps out, send them over here to this mountain and tell them to quietly try to find us or Aitin. Also warn them about the dinosaurs."

One of them nods, then leaves, running in the same direction Sef went.

That leaves one more fox.

"Will you stay with me?"

It gestures affirmatively with its head.

I take a long breath and turn toward Lilly. We rehearsed the plan together. She goes in first.

Straightening her shoulders, she takes the first step down the hall. She's supposed to talk to Case, convince him to help us.

I sure hope it works.

I walk quietly after her, making sure not to scuff my feet on the dirt floor. When we reach the door, we both peek inside. A wave of warmth hits my face. It takes every ounce of restraint for me to keep my body from crawling further into the warm room.

Case is there, standing against a countertop like the one I saw in his old home. He's wrapped in coats and scarves, a red beanie on his head, regardless of the stove burning to the right.

"Shit," he says, and I jump, worried he might have already seen us. But then I realize he's just mad at the water dripping from the icicles on the ceiling. He wipes off the microscopic glass in his hand.

I almost gasp when I see Dilo chained against the far wall, her orange frills fully expanded in attack mode. Unfortunately, she's too far away from Case to do any real damage, even too far away to spit her serum. Mark will be glad to know she's okay.

With one last breath, Lilly takes a step inside and walks quietly to the center of the room. I wait for her to speak, to get Case's attention, but instead of talking she pulls something out from underneath her shirt. *Wait, what is that?*

Before I can call her back, she extends her arms and takes aim at Case's back with a bright pink handgun. I gulp.

What is she doing? We didn't talk about this. Where did she get that gun?

At the sound of the gun cocking, Case spins around. He's got a knife in his hand ready to attack. My body stiffens. *How did he get that in his hand so fast?*

"Lilly?" His face relaxes but only slightly. "What are you doing here?"

He tries to take a step forward, but Lilly's croaky voice cuts the air. "Don't move, Case."

"Are you ... what ... what's going on?" Case asks in bewilderment.

"Case, you've got to stop this."

"Lilly, please put that down ... You're sick." Case's eyebrows harden over his eyes when he sees the condition she's in. He tries to take another step forward, but Lilly doesn't waver.

"I mean it, Case. Stop or I'll shoot you." Lilly tries to keep her voice as strong as she can.

They stand still for a long time, silently measuring each other, until Case's voice breaks the heaviness in the air.

"Lilly, I have to do this. The baby ..."

The deep pain etching his words softens the tension. Even I feel for him. Sitting down in a chair, he buries his face in his hands. "We'll never be happy unless Peppate is gone."

Lilly's arms relax around the gun, and she brings them down. I don't know Case very well. *Could he be acting to weaken Lilly's stance?* I sure hope Lilly knows him better than I do, because if it were me, I'd keep that gun fully aimed on him.

After what seems like an eternity, Lilly finally speaks as softly as her voice will allow. "Case, the baby didn't die from Peppate exposure."

Case's head slowly lifts, his forehead thickly creased in confusion.

"Aitin killed the baby by putting something in our water source. He wanted you to think that the baby died because of Peppate. He knew you'd be more likely to join his cause."

"How do you know that?"

Lilly sighs. *Here comes the tricky part.*

"Aitin told Alena, when he tried to kill her."

"Alena?" Case's voice booms, instantly flooded with anger.

I cringe. I knew he wouldn't be happy about my involvement.

"And you believe her? Where is she?"

"Yes, I believe her," Lilly yells back. "And I want *you* to help her."

I draw back, surprised at Lilly's tone. I didn't think it was possible for her to respond to Case like that.

Without taking her eyes off Case, Lilly calls out my name. "Alena?"

I tiptoe through the door, careful not to disturb the fragile ground I'm walking on.

Lilly raises the gun to Case's head again. "Case, you *will* help Alena."

Chapter 26

It takes way too long to convince Case to help me. At first, he lashes out at me for bringing Lilly to this forsaken place where she can so easily be killed. If Lilly wasn't here, I'm pretty sure Case would've strangled me to death. But Lilly keeps the gun steadily aimed at him ... and talks. Talks about how I found her bleeding to death in their hideout. Talks about how I saved her life. She isn't as patient and soft-spoken as she was in the desert. Instead, she's commanding and determined, something Case apparently isn't used to because he keeps gawking at her.

Case forces me to repeat my encounter with Aitin several times, word for word. He doesn't want to accept the truth, but after what seems like an eternity, it finally seeps in. He sits in a chair and pulls off his beanie, defeated.

Lilly gingerly gives me the gun before carefully approaching Case. I raise my arms and take aim, ready to shoot if he continues to slow us down. Not that that will do any good. I'm obviously a very bad shot.

Placing her hand on Case's back, Lilly bends down beside him. And then she begins to hum. A melody, soft and beautiful. Even I can tell the song holds a deep meaningful place in both their hearts.

Since the moment I met Lilly and Case, I admired their relationship—mostly because of how much they seemed to love each other regardless of their trials. I've never been blind to the hardships they've had to face, but here, in this moment, it's as if I can see every heartache they've experienced. Every moment they've had to choose love over physical touch. Case has done his best for Lilly but probably feels like it will never be enough. And yet, Lilly has chosen Case over physical health.

Always.

But now she must choose something more. She must do what is right for everyone even if that means hurting the man she loves. And he must do the same.

Case melts into Lilly's arms, crying harder than I've ever seen a grown man cry. I drop the gun and reluctantly back out of the room, trying to offer them some privacy.

When Lilly finally calls me back in, Case is standing calmly, his arm wrapped tightly around Lilly. "Okay. What do you need me to do?"

***

I take off my other boot, silently grieving the cold again. Not wanting Aitin to suspect that I've had help here in Petrichor from my fellow Pepps, I remove the warm clothes Bapoto gave me, revealing the Doler attire underneath—the clothes that survived Aitin's morph when he left me out in the cold to die. Then I carefully place the wrapped totem in my pants pocket.

Case looks down at the pink gun in his hand, a concerned look etching his expression.

"You want me to shoot you?"

I nod, standing now, the cold from the rock like icicles on my bare feet. "Not fatally, just in the arm or leg, or shoulder."

I tell him my plan, that ultimately I need to get close to Mark and make him morph so that I can get power. Once I have power, I can use it to draw out the serum in Aitin.

Then I stop, my mind running into a conundrum. "You can't be there when we morph. Will you be able to get out quickly?"

"You don't need to worry about me. I'll run. I know a couple of hiding spots where I'll be protected from your lighting."

"Okay," I say. Then I wave my hand toward the gun, indicating it's time.

But he doesn't shoot me. Instead, he starts to pace, thinking.

When he stops, he looks at me and says, "I have another idea."

It takes us another fifteen minutes to iron out all the wrinkles in our plan until the three of us are confident it's good. When we're ready, I stand in front of Case. He wants to stab me instead of shoot me so Aitin doesn't hear.

He pulls out an old shirt, then stuffs it in my mouth to silence my scream.

Then he holds out one of my knives. From this perspective, it's long and scary, flashing mockingly in the candlelight. Suddenly, the memory of getting stabbed in the back during initiation pops into my mind, and my body breaks out into a sweat. *What am I doing?*

Case moves so quickly that I don't have time to get out of the way even if I wanted to. I don't feel the pain at first, probably a trick of the mind, but then it hits hard, and I can't hold back my scream. I feel the pain of each muscle, each nerve ending getting sliced. Him pulling the knife out hurts even more, and I bite down hard on the shirt. My leg goes limp, and blood quickly wets my Doler pants. Then a deep shaky ache sets in, and I try not to move. It's a good thing everything is up to Case now, because my mind can't really think in the moment.

Case waits for me to stop silently sobbing into the T-shirt before removing it, then he pulls on my arm.

"Good luck, Alena." I hear Lilly say before Case drags me out of the room and down the hall. Even Dilo seems to say good-bye, slicking her frills back and belting out a chuff. Case promised me he'd get her out safely.

Lilly will stay in the room where Case promised me she'd be safe. The fox is supposed to follow us but stay hidden. As we made our plans, the fox, who is an old man, piped up and told us some of the things Flint taught him. I'm surprised at the insight Flint had. This fox just might come in very handy.

Is it behind us? I can't seem to focus.

I'm supposed to pretend that I'm in distress. I don't think that'll be too hard.

Case drags me down the hall, which seems to stretch on forever. His holstered gun taps against my side occasionally. It's terribly difficult to walk down a hall with such a distracting wound. I want to ask Case how much further, but I bite my tongue. I need to pretend he's really captured me. Tears sting my eyes when Case's jerks become more ruthless. We must be getting closer to Aitin.

Then I hear it. The painful cry of a man. Mark. I sag in despair against Case's dragging. I'm not sure I'm emotionally prepared to see Mark in pain.

When we round the corner, a large cavern comes into view. My foggy brain doesn't capture too many of its details. It doesn't internalize how many people are in here or what they look like. It doesn't apprehend the degree of light or where it's coming from. There's only one thing I see.

Mark.

Chained against the far wall, his head hanging down feebly, his chest exposed. My breath catches in my throat. *Is he dead?*

It looks worse than last time. Dozens of circular burns litter his torso, the skin either sloughing and black or completely missing. I want to cry out when I see the burns on his arms so dangerously deep, the skin so utterly incinerated that the bones are exposed.

Aitin stands there with the culprit of the burns in his hand. A long metal stick, glowing red hot at the tip, heated by the large smoking stove on the far-right wall. The image, mixed with the smell of burnt flesh, makes me gag, but I don't allow myself to throw up. If Mark can endure that kind of pain, I'll endure anything right now.

"Aitin," Case shouts to Mark's torturer before throwing me to the ground in front of the terrible man. "I found Alena sneaking through the tunnels. I was about to kill her but then thought that maybe you'd want to do that."

Case is a good liar.

I want to see Aitin's reaction, but with my face against the rock floor, it's difficult for me to raise my head. I struggle to bring myself up. I've almost risen to my good knee, when a hand grabs my hair and rips my head back. I scream, startled by the pain that tears through my scalp.

"I'm starting to get a little irritated by you, you know." Spit shoots from Aitin's disgusting mouth, his pale face only inches from mine. "You should have just let yourself die out there."

Case steps forward now, interrupting. "I'm surprised you haven't killed *him* yet."

Case's words are important, I feel it, but my brain can't remember why. *Is he trying to determine if Mark is still alive? Or is he trying to distract Aitin so I can do what I need to do?*

Aitin releases my hair and stands up.

"Of course I haven't killed him yet. I have many plans for Mark," he says.

I don't want to hear any more. I need to get to Mark. I force myself to think past the pain in my leg.

Morph. I need to morph.

I don't know who initially constructed the totems, but whoever it was was incredibly smart, making them so a Pepp can morph without needing a sphere of power in the heart. It really comes in handy now because I don't have any power.

Raising my right fist to my heart, I pound it as hard as I can. My body changes quickly, the tingling sensation racing down my arms, enhancing the hot injury in my leg. Biting through the pain, I flap my wings to get into the air. I silently thank Case for thinking this through. I was going to have him stab me in the shoulder so I could walk easier, but then I wouldn't have been able to fly.

Suddenly the cavern comes alive. I didn't realize there were so many other people in here. Mixed Bloods? The ones Jeter healed? I don't have time to count them. Flapping my wings, I fly right over Aitin, my feathery tips brushing against the stone walls on the left. *Focus*. I can't afford to fly into the wall right now.

When I successfully arch over the bewildered man and land beside Mark, I grunt, and morph back as quickly as I can.

"Get her!" Aitin's shout echoes off the walls.

I quickly look back in the direction I last saw Case. According to our plan, he should be gone from the room by now.

Good. He's not there.

Then my eyes slide over to Aitin, to verify the next part of our plan. Aitin is staring at his arms, a look of horror on his face.

"What the ...?"

Sure enough, coating his skin is a light white substance. The serum. Aitin looks at me, infuriated. I almost smile. *Perfect.* He thinks I'm doing it.

"You little b—" I ignore his words and turn to pound Mark's heart, hoping that *the fox* can get all Aitin's serum out before Aitin realizes it isn't me. My hand almost reaches Mark's chest, when something sinks into my upper back. I smell the burnt flesh first, and then I feel it. A scream rises from the deepest parts of my lungs. It takes over my body, my mind ... letting the world know in the only way it can that there's something very, very wrong. I've never experienced such pain.

I fall to my hands.

The poker is in my back. My arms shake, and I slowly bring my body to the ground, the unbelievable heat sucking away my energy.

Mark. I need to pound his chest. I'm so close. But I can't move. *Oh, how I wish I could move!*

Then I see it ... with my cheek pressed against the cold ground, a rope lands only a few feet away from me, followed by a pair of shoes. No, not just one pair. Many. Many people are coming down on ropes. At least a dozen of them.

No, wait, not just people. Without lifting my head, I squint further and try to see their faces. My eyes jump from beanies, to eyes, to noses, to mouths, looking for any familiar features. Then I see the girl with the perfect eyebrows and almost laugh in relief. They're Mixed Bloods. *My Mixed Bloods.* Just thinking the phrase brings tears to my eyes.

My Mixed Bloods.

I lie there on my stomach, looking sideways. My awareness is fading, but I don't need to be totally with it to know that they're here to fight Aitin. I close my eyes. They couldn't have come at a better time.

Thank you.

That's when I feel it. An emotional support, an emotional strength extending from the Mixed Bloods, down to me and back. I can even feel it coming from those outside the room: Bapoto, Lilly, and Sef. I feel their aid, I recognize the sacrifices they've made to get us here, and I feel their pulsing encouragements with every move.

Suddenly, all of Danny's words make sense. Everything he tried to get me to do. The emphasis he made on getting out and building relationships. It was for this. Did he somehow know that eventually I'd reach a place where I'd need the support of others? Or perhaps he just assumed that every being needs a heavy support system in their lives, so I may as well start building it sooner rather than later?

Whatever the reason is, Danny was right to push me this way.

Lilly, Case, the Mixed Bloods, Bapoto ... even Flint. I've needed each one of them.

"You." That voice. I know that voice. Even in my delirious state I can place it, but it's a voice I wasn't expecting to hear. Not in this place. Any movement in my body sends searing pain to every nerve ending. So I just move my eyes as best as I can to find Jax standing in front of me. He doesn't look well. I almost don't recognize him. His slimmed body and bloodshot eyes tell me that the prison didn't treat him very well.

Wait, no, it's more than that. He wipes his nose with his hand, smearing blood across his face and fingers. He's sick. He must have been hiding with the Pepps. He has Ebola. *But what's he doing here?*

Bending down to his knees, he braces his shaky body on the ground so he can look me in the eye.

"I saw them," he says weakly. "The Mixed Bloods. You healed them." It's not a question but a statement of awe.

Jax gets closer to me still, the scar running from the corner of his mouth to his ear coming into full view. "Will you heal her? Will you heal my daughter?"

Gosh this is a bad time.

"Please, Alena."

"Yes." It's all I can get out of my weakened body.

Satisfied, Jax's bloodshot eyes rise to look past me, fuming with anger.

"When the Pepps were moving us down below to prepare for Aitin, I slipped away. Things were in such chaos that it was easy." Jax seems to be talking to me, but at the same time he's speaking loudly enough as if he wants everyone in the room to hear. I can't tell for sure, but I think the others pause to listen.

"If Aitin was healed, that meant he could heal my daughter. So I stayed above waiting for him. But when he finally arrived and I begged him to heal her, he refused." Jax rises to his feet. As painful as it is, I turn my head the other way so I can see Aitin.

I expect to see Aitin's body covered in the released serum, possibly weak, defeated, but he looks normal. I blink my eyes. It's not my vision. The serum is gone, and now there's a dangerous heat in his eyes aimed directly at Jax. It's a look I haven't seen on Aitin's face. So different from the smug expression he always wears when dealing with me. I must be nothing more to him than an annoying bug he thinks he can easily squash.

But when Aitin glares at the older man, there's no annoyance—just a look of pure hatred.

"You're lucky I was weak when you found me." Aitin grinds out. "Or else I would have killed you. Why would I help you after what you've done to me? You always said you'd be there to help me. That you wanted to figure out a way to make *me* better. I never could understand what was in it for you. But then you took Danny, trying to lure Alena out. And what's the next thing I hear? Instead of bringing the power to me, you were going to *use* the power? On your daughter? You didn't care about me! You used me, my torture, acting as a friend only to get closer to a solution for your little bitch!"

Jax reacts so quickly, I don't have time to understand what's going on until I feel something slice through my shoulder again. I scream, my face cutting against the rock ground. The pain in my shoulder sends lightning spasms through my body, from my back all the way to my toes. But I force my eyes open to see what's going on.

Aitin is lying on his back, the metal poker, that was just in me ... now in *his* chest.

Shouts break out everywhere, and the ground echoes with running feet. I can't keep track of it all. My head is getting too fuzzy. All I know is that somehow Jax has fallen to the ground next to me and is bleeding. I drag my beaten body over the sharp rocks that dig into my leg wound. I grit my teeth, trying to hold back my tears.

"Jax," I whisper, gripping his clothing, forcing myself up onto shaky elbows. *He shouldn't be here. I need to morph!* Making a quick analysis of his wounds I find blood coming from his chest, shoulders, and neck. It's as if he's been stabbed in several places.

What in the world happened?

I slide one of my hands to his chest wound. So much for not getting the Ebola virus. Touching his blood, I'm sure to get it now. He must have gone back to the Pepps when Aitin refused to help him.

I know it's a wasted effort, to try to stop the bleeding. Based on how deflated his body already was from Ebola, he doesn't have much more blood to lose. And I don't have power. I still need to morph. But I'll kill Jax if I do that.

Jax grabs my wrist.

"Please, heal her."

"I will," I promise.

Those two words comfort him enough. He smiles, sighs, looks overhead at the ceiling, then lets out his last breath.

I know the moment he's gone. The feeling of death looming overhead so closely to its next victim is something I've become too acquainted with lately. I don't even need to check for his pulse. It's as if my spirit recognizes the absence of his, feels the loss so perfectly.

Unfortunately, I don't have time to grieve him. My arm is shaking so badly. At first I think it's from exertion and pain, but then I realize that the ground is actually shaking. I lie on my stomach and turn back to find Aitin being carried out of the room by two of his people. He's alive, shouting something. That poker didn't kill him.

I lay my face down. I need to morph. And then I need to heal Mark. His pain tugs at me.

With Jax already dead and Case out of the room, I should be free to morph now.

Mustering up a last few ounces of strength, I crawl over to Mark, reach for his chest, and pound it as hard as I can. He moans in pain, his large bird body changing even in the metal chains.

Bringing my hand to *my* own heart now feels impossible, but I clench my jaw, willing the tiny amount of energy I have left to flow through my limb. The pain sends flashes of white through my vision. I rest my head back on the ground and just lie there, trying to breathe while my body changes. I know the moment I'm fully morphed because a loud crack breaks through the air, zapping the totem tucked in my pocket. Unlike every other time we've morphed, though, the lightning doesn't last. Not much Peppate to zap around here.

When the air is quiet, I pound my chest twice to morph back.

Once I'm back in my human form, the elements around me come to life. I can already tell that this morph has given me more power than all the morphs at Lake Maracai combined, thanks to the totem. It surges through my veins, feeling like a lightness, like I'm floating full of cold, comfortable air. I shiver.

The serum in the room weighs heavily in stark contrast to the floating sensation, allowing me to immediately locate it in the Mixed Bloods surrounding me. I don't remember feeling this way the last time I morphed and got a full sphere of black power. But, then, perhaps I was too weighed down by Tom's death to appreciate it.

I go to work, first on myself, calming the scorching injury in my back and then the ache in my leg. I've lost a lot of blood, but I'll work on that later.

Then I pull myself to Mark and pound his featherless chest twice.

It's agonizingly painful just looking at him when he's morphed back, seeing the patches of missing skin. I can hear the elements of his heart fighting to push the remaining strength he has throughout his body, but I touch his neck anyway, needing more validation that he's still alive.

How has he survived?

I bite my cheek. Aitin didn't even bother removing his pants before burning him with the poker. Now the material is disturbingly melted into his skin, at least in the spots he still has skin left.

I recall the nights of terrible dreams Mark suffered through. Recall the look of fear I occasionally caught in his expression. He was afraid of being hurt by Aitin again, and now here he is, on the brink of death. It *all* came true.

I still don't know how to command metal, so I can't release him from the metal chains. He'll have to do that. Instead, I go to work calming his pain. I still resist the urge to plug my nose, trying not to let the terrible smell distract me. There are still screams coming from behind me, but I focus only on Mark. Slowly his body relaxes, his flesh expands, the wounds close, and the burns mend. I'm so focused on healing him, so relieved to see his skin healing so fast, that I jump when his hand reaches my face. Only when he touches it do I realize it's covered in tears.

I collect him in my arms. "I'm so sorry, Mark." I cry into his shoulder.

I feel him weakly wrap his arms around me, released from his chains.

"Are you okay?" I ask through my sobs. *What a stupid question. Of course he's not okay!* I change my question. "Where do you hurt?" Surely there are more wounds I need to heal.

"I'm okay, Lena."

I don't believe it. How can a human being survive something like that ... and be okay?

Mark pushes me away enough to look at my face. "Are you okay?" *Of course he'd be concerned about me in a moment like this.*

"Yes," I say, wanting to pull him back into my arms. I want to hold him forever, never let him go, but all the shouting in the room pulls at Mark's attention. His gaze is no longer on me but on the scene behind me. There's a tenseness in the air that I can feel even without seeing what's going on. I wipe my nose and turn around.

With my body now free from pain, I can finally comprehend what's going on.

Aitin is gone, replaced by a group of *his* Mixed Bloods—the men and women Aitin recruited before we got to Maracai. I can see them better now. They have the same familiar sores, bald heads, and pale skin as all the Mixed Bloods tend to have. But these people aren't nearly as healthy as the ones I healed. Jeter had to use normal Peppate power on them. It looks like they're still recovering from that.

That isn't stopping them from attacking us, though. They have power. I watch a woman focus her attention on one of my Mixed Blood men, hate oozing from her eyes like a deadly tar.

"Emma, please don't do this," the man addresses the girl. The way he says her name so gently ... *Did they use to be friends?*

Of course they did. There's a heavy sadness in the air. These people aren't enemies. Not really. Aitin is just forcing them to fight against one another, friends against friends.

He's tearing them apart, when they care about one another. But they also care about their cause. Now their minds are anxiously seeking for a way to satisfy one side of the battle without compromising the other, but it's too complicated. So they just stand there, hands at the ready, hoping the other will be the first to destroy.

"I can't believe you're helping them, Folou," Emma murmurs. She probably meant for her words to sound more angry, more threatening, but, instead, they come out as a croaky plea. "After all they've done to us, you're helping them?"

Folou. I remember that name. I turn my gaze back to the man. He's the one Chima watched me heal from her little wheelchair. With his darker skin and strong-boned frame, he looks like he's from the same islands as Leinani.

"Alena has found a way to heal without causing us pain, Emma. Trust me—we need to help her, not Aitin."

I don't hear Emma's response. I'm too distracted now by the fox still in the shadows beyond Folou. It hasn't left yet. I follow its focused eyes across the room to one of the other Mixed Bloods. It's drawing out their serum. At least the serum in three of the Mixed Bloods that I can see.

Of course. We need to draw out the serum, and now that I have power, I can join in. I focus on Emma. With her skin so pale, it's hard to see the serum coming out, so I anxiously yank at it, not bothering to look for it on her skin. Unfortunately, I'm not too far before she realizes what's happening.

"They're taking our serum!" she shrieks, looking at her arms. Then she redirects her hands from Folou to the floor. *What's she doing?* Her hands shake, and a vein bulges out of her temple only seconds before the ground begins to tremor, and several cracks splinter through the floor.

No!

The cracks and shaking destabilize the ceiling, sending several boulders crashing to the floor. I barely see Aitin's Mixed Bloods making their way to the only tunnel leading out of this room before dirt drops from the ceiling, sending a cloud of dust that blocks my vision. I cough and swipe at my eyes. "We need to follow them!" I shout.

Blindly standing on wobbly legs, I fight to find my balance on the unstable ground and listen to the body elements around me. I hear many bodies, but I can't tell if they're from Mixed Bloods on my side or not.

Behind me, Mark struggles to get up. Reaching out a hand, I blindly find him, wrap my fingers around his arm, and help him up in the chaos.

When the shaking finally stops and the dust partially clears, I force my stinging eyes to observe my surroundings. There are only about ten Mixed Bloods left in here, and based on the fact that they aren't trying to kill Mark or me, I'm guessing that they're on my side.

I turn my attention to the tunnel, ready to follow the others, but stop and rub my face in frustration. Where the opening once stood, now a monstrous pile of boulders blocks the path. They got away.

Folou climbs the pile now, picking up the heavy rocks and moving them effortlessly.

How are these Mixed Bloods so good at using the power already?

Folou reaches for another rock, but I stop him.

"Hey, let's, um ... Let's try to come up with a plan," I say, my arm still supporting Mark.

Folou straightens and tosses the heavy rock to the ground. "Okay, what do you want us to do?"

I feel odd. Being the one to lead. I'm not good at this at all. I look to Mark, selfishly wanting him to take over, but he just shakes his head.

"You know what we need, Alena. Just tell them."

I swallow.

There are twelve of us here, including Mark and me and the morphed fox. I try to memorize the faces of those who are on our side, but it's hard to do when they all look so similar. Folou stands out a little bit because of his darkened skin. But the others' skin is all the same lighter shade. One of the boys is really short, but they're all wearing black Doler clothes and gray beanies, which doesn't help. *What were Aitin's helpers wearing? Did they have beanies? I wasn't paying attention.*

"First." I rub my temple. "I need a way to differentiate you from Aitin's helpers. I can't afford to accidentally attack one of you. I wish I had a spare cloth, or paint, or ..."

I stare at the dusty ground. Bending on one knee I press my fingers into a pile of dirt at my feet.

Dirt. It isn't a drastic color, but it could be enough. I'm about to spit on it and spread it over my skin, when Mark reaches out his hand and changes the color of the dirt to a dark blue.

Okay, that will be better. I scoop it up with my fingers, wet it, and spread it on my arm. *Perfect.*

"Can I mark you guys?"

One by one they come to me, allowing me to draw three vertical blue lines down the sides of their faces. It's creepy-looking, but it helps me a lot.

Then after wiping my hands on my pants, I pace the room.

"Okay. We need to get the serum out of Aitin's body. My hope is that by removing the serum, we'll reactivate the Peppate generators that will eat away at their power sac. Ultimately, I'm hoping it will take away their power," I say. Then remembering the fox, how he was supposed to have pulled the serum out already, I turn to the small animal.

"Why weren't you able to remove it?" I try not to sound too frustrated.

The fox morphs back into his human form to talk. He's the older man, my height, with a sharp but wrinkly jaw and a big nose.

"He figured out what was happening and pulled it all back in," he says, his raspy voice barely above a whisper. His light-blue eyes tighten in confusion. "I think he knows how to command the serum. I kept trying, but he had such a strong grip on it."

"He pulled it back in?" I ask. *Well, that complicates things.* And if he can do *that*, he can probably heal himself from the poker wound.

"Maybe we need to get rid of his helpers first," Mark chimes in, his arm tightening around my shoulders. "Then it'll just be Aitin. If we all attack his serum at the same time, I bet we could get it out."

I look at everyone's faces for their reaction to this plan.

"You want us to kill them?" Folou whispers, pained by the first part of Mark's suggestion. *Getting rid of Aitin's helpers.*

Mark sighs. "I don't know how we stop them completely without killing them."

I recall the time I disabled Jeter at Dakdete. "You can interrupt the brain signals," I say. "If they can't think, they can't perform."

Kaconcha, the girl I met earlier with the perfect eyebrows and hazel eyes, the one who is good with the body, nods her head in understanding.

But she's the only one. The others seem confused. *Okay, maybe that's not something they can all do.*

"Or we could keep trying to withdraw their serum," the short morpher says. "Once the serum is out, we can easily disable them. I think I was able to get it all out of one of them. Aitin knows how to draw the serum back in, but I don't think his helpers have learned how to."

I carefully look at each Mixed Blood in our group. "How many of you know how to command the serum?"

They all raise their hands, including Mark.

I gawk. *All of them?*

"Who taught you?" I whisper, but I think I already know the answer.

"Flint," Folou says.

I'll figure out how I feel about this later. For now, we need to get going.

"Okay. Draw the serum out, then destroy it with fire. Let's try to get rid of the rest of Aitin's men and women and then go after Aitin."

I turn to Folou. "By the way, were you guys able to get the other Pepps out?" The fact that I saw Sef and Jax in person means that they did. I still want to hear it from him, though.

"Yes," he says, but then a sad look shadows his face. He opens his mouth as if about to say more, but then decides against it. "Yes," he repeats more quietly.

They must not be in great condition. We need to hurry.

Chapter 27

The group works quickly to dislodge the rocks, using power only when we need to.

When the rocks are finally removed enough, we all stare at the dark, empty tunnel ahead. A wave of cold air breaks through the cavern, chilling the air.

Mark grabs a torch off the cavern wall and signals with his head that we should follow him. I hate that he's out front but also grateful. He knows this mountain better than anyone here.

When he steps silently into the tunnel, I follow behind, taking special care not to kick his heels from being so close. The others trail after.

We move quietly, not speaking, not scuffing the ground. The only sound I hear is the crackle of the torch and the soft breath of those behind me. The tunnels are silent for a long time, making me wonder if the dinosaurs mysteriously found their way back outside. *Is that too much to hope for?*

But then a roar vibrates through the rock, and I try to swallow.

At least we have Mark with us.

After walking in silence for what seems like an eternity, I peek around Mark's torso.

Where is everybody? The fact that we haven't run into a single person—or dinosaur—makes the hairs on the back of my neck rise. What are they planning?

Up ahead, the tunnel branches into two, one right and the other left.

"I say we split up," Mark whispers, stopping at the fork. When he turns to us, I see his breath coming out in cold white puffs against the torchlight.

"Okay," I say, trying to keep my teeth from chattering in the cold.

Pointing to Folou and two other Mixed bloods I don't know, Mark says, "You go down the tunnel on the right. See if you find anything. There will be doors to classrooms down there. Look in each one for Aitin. The tunnel itself will eventually lead you to the skills room. We'll all convene back there if we don't find anything. If you need help ..." Mark pauses. "Is there some sort of signal we could send?"

We all silently think. Of course there are signals we could send, but will we have enough time to send them? Will they be heard? I think about the mass chaos back in the cavern. Things just happen too fast.

When nobody else in the group responds, I wonder if they're thinking the same thing.

Finally, Mark breaks the grim pressure hanging in the air. "I guess we'll just all do our best to meet back in the skills room."

Folou nods somberly and leads the way for his small group. Grabbing a torch of their own from the wall, they disappear down the tunnel.

The rest of us continue on the left until we reach another split. Mark does the same thing again. He sends the morpher, Kaconcha, and two other Mixed Bloods to scout out the tunnel on the right.

One more split takes the remaining three Mixed bloods, leaving Mark and me alone.

The fire from Mark's torch bounces eerily off the walls. I rub my arms, taming down my goose bumps, longing for the clothes Bapoto lent me. Then I stare at the skin on Mark's back. He doesn't have a shirt on, but I don't see a single goose bump on him.

Suddenly Mark stops and I run into him, not paying attention.

I'm about to ask him what's wrong, when I realize the air is densely quiet. The silence is different, heavy, not caused by the absence of sound but the pulsing grip of potential danger. Slowly Mark turns around. I feel the tension in his body, see the uneasy look in his eye. I turn slowly too.

At the end of our tunnel, at the fringe of our flickering light, I make out the unmistakable form of a dinosaur, its head cocking sideways. It's one of the smaller ones, but even I can interpret the look in its eye.

We're toast.

"Shi—" My curse is drowned out by an intense roar.

Run! My legs bolt forward, launching me into Mark, who's trying to go the opposite way ... toward the dinosaur.

"Run, Alena!" Placing his hand on my back he pushes me away. *Why is he running* toward *the dinosaur?*

Because he's a dinosaur trainer, of course. The best thing I can do is get us out of here. I lead the way, forcing my legs to move as fast as they can in the dark. With the torch still tight in Mark's grip, I have to rely on the light extended from him. We pass several closed classroom doors, but I don't even think about going inside one. I don't want to get trapped again.

I peek back at Mark, needing to make sure he's still okay.

He's running backward, facing the dinosaur, sending out blasts of ice to freeze it while making the tunnel walls cave in. It's working somewhat; the dinosaur is getting sloppy in its steps. Mark draws down more rocks from the ceiling, trying to trap it. I almost smile when the dinosaur finally disappears behind a wall of rock, but then it breaks through, and I curse.

Move faster!

We round a corner, and suddenly the tunnel opens up into a large cavern. The skills room. It's huge, with high ceilings and dozens of lit torches. Just like Mark said, the tunnel has conveniently led us right to the middle of the skills room arena.

The dinosaur chasing us stops at the door, still growling, wanting to attack, but something must be holding it back because it doesn't take another step.

"Alena," someone whispers behind me.

I turn. The Mixed Bloods we sent down the other tunnels are here too, gathered around the border of the arena, but they're pointing at something, their expressions twisted in horror.

"Holy shit," Folou mutters across the room, then I see what he sees.

The rows of bleachers, tiering high up the sides ... are packed full of dinosaurs. Dozens and dozens of them of all different breeds and sizes. They stand there, huffing silently, leaning forward as if the only thing that's keeping them from attacking us is a tiny thread that's ready to snap.

Mark's back presses against mine, his fingertips brushing my hand. "Stay close, Alena." Our Mixed Bloods take a step closer to us as well.

My eyes circle the arena. I've never seen the dinosaurs stand so still, maintain such order. Are they being controlled? *Where is Aitin?* My gaze rises. I see his Mixed Bloods standing at the very top of the arena, barely visible past the dinosaurs. *But where is Aitin?*

My attention snags on something in the crowd of tense dinos, and I narrow my eyes to get a better look.

Bud? My little dinosaur friend that saved me from Chauly? I shake my head. It can't be. He was so small the last time I saw him, his head only reaching up to my knee. This dinosaur, though, reaches up to my chin. But then my eyes drop to the tail, and, sure enough, it's missing.

Bud!

He sees me, those same black eyes rimmed with red. He sees my face and flinches forward as if he wants to run to me ... but can't. Then my eyes drop. There around his torso is a heavy piece of metal, wrapped tight. Beneath the metal are trails of blood that run down his scaley skin all the way to the floor. I catch a small glimpse of a chain behind.

He's been chained to the floor, and based on the trails of blood, there must be pokers inside that metal piece that pierce him if he moves against the chain.

Oh, Bud.

He's not the only one like this either. Several other dinosaurs are being tortured in the same way.

A loud screech echoes off the far wall, breaking the heavy silence, and I turn my body very slowly.

There, on the other side of our arena, clawing at the ground and gnashing its teeth, is another terrifying dinosaur. Its rough skin is bleach white, and its eyes are wild and hungry.

I gulp.

I know that dinosaur. I saw it during the festival at the end of the Dino Games. *What was its name? White Eye?* It was the one dinosaur the trainers couldn't seem to control.

Oddly enough, this dinosaur isn't being held back with chains, but it still doesn't attack us like it seems to want to do. At least not yet.

"There you are." A grim voice echoes from above. I turn and look up.

There on the mezzanine above us is Aitin, resting his arms on the metal railing. The poker wound is healed, but he does not look happy. The muscles in his jaw are tight, visible even from where I'm standing.

"You will not win this, Alena and Mark. So I will give you one last chance to join my cause. Help me free the world of Peppate." A dark fuzz has started growing in over his bald head, above his ears, and his voice is clearer than I remember it being. The scars on his skin still pucker, though, and his teeth are chipped. He wears an old button-up shirt that looks like it'll never be free from the dirt lodged in its threads. His pants are old and brown too, looking like they might have been tan at one point.

"No." Mark's answer is loud and clear. "No, we will not join your cause."

Aitin straightens and takes in a deep breath. "Very well."

Without another word, Aitin snaps his fingers, and whatever power was holding the dinosaurs back is now released. Chains break open, and the animals attack with force and precision, hungry for our blood.

My jaw drops, horror curling under my ribs. We need to run, but there's nowhere to go! We're trapped!

The flying dinosaurs reach us first. I cower behind my arms, but they don't protect me at all. One dinosaur easily tears multiple chunks of muscle and skin off me with its huge teethy beak. I scream. *What do we do?*

White Eye charges for us next, drooling and manic.

Before he can reach us, though, Mark crouches, dragging me with him, and creates a dome of fire that immediately surrounds us and all our Mixed Bloods.

I cradle my bleeding arm, coughing through the blazing red, yellow, and blue heat.

Folou crouches to my left. I can't see the others, though, through the sweltering temperature.

Pained screeches reach my ears through the crackle of flames, and the smell of burning dinosaur wings reaches my nose. Beaks poke through the fire dome, pecking, trying to reach us, but they don't get far.

White Eye's face appears only once. Mark grabs at the dinosaur with his power and holds the animal in the flame, melting it to the bone. I cover my ears to block the loud pained animal screams. Then Mark lets the animal go, and the pecking stops.

Mark drops the flames.

I wipe my stinging eyes and sweaty face with trembling hands. The flying dinosaurs are now frantically escaping into the night through a broken hole in the wall behind us, their burned wings still simmering with heat. White Eye goes with them, limping and whimpering, his skin sloughing off in a disturbing way.

"You okay?" Mark asks, searching my skin, hissing when he sees the chunks in my arms missing.

I nod and look around, despair pitting in my stomach. I should heal my arms, but there's too much going on. The flyers might be gone, but the meat-eating dinosaurs are still here. Including the dinosaur that chased Mark and me through the tunnel, and Bud ... He's still chained up too. *Why wasn't he released like the others?*

"Mark, can you take the chains off Bud with your power?"

I barely whisper the words, when an explosion erupts off to my right. The force of it rolls my body several feet and makes my ears ring.

I can't even get up before there's another explosion off to my left. Rocks whistle through the air and lodge themselves into my back. Several of my Mixed Bloods scream. We won't survive too many more of these attacks.

"Reach out for their serum!" I shout right before another explosion launches me onto my bleeding back. I don't bother getting up, ignoring the stabbing pain from the rocks, I focus all my energy on listening for the serum in one of the girls in the bleachers above me. I remember my practice with Chima, controlling the serum. I grab it, yank at it, gritting my teeth, resisting the spots I'm now seeing in my vision. I choke on the smoky air, but yank more and more. The serum gives way, spilling through the skin.

I jump when something nudges at my leg and open my eyes.

There's a dinosaur there. I almost kick at it but then freeze.

Wait.

It's Dilo! Case must have let her go!

She goes to Mark, whose vessels are bulging out of his neck, straining to get the serum out of another Mixed Blood. Then she bounds up the bleachers and attacks a man at the top.

The explosions keep sucking the air from the room. A dislodged rock slices at my throat, and blood pours out.

Dammit! *I'm so close to getting the serum out!*

My head feels woozy, and my focus snaps. I need to heal myself before I bleed out. Refocusing my attention, I heal my neck, then sit up and angrily tear the last little bits of serum out of the woman's body.

Only seconds later do the explosions stop, and I notice Aitin's Mixed Bloods screaming from pain of their own. Cradling my ripped-apart arm, I squint to look closer. Shards of rock are gruesomely lodged in their necks and chests, and Mark is panting heavily next to me. He must have pulled them from the ceiling and stabbed them. But they aren't dead.

Even now, they're getting back on their feet, ready to go for another round.

I look at my Mixed Bloods, who are tired and bloody. I don't know how much longer we'll last.

I stand, there in the middle of the arena, panting, time frozen as I take everything in. I see every dinosaur desperately trying to get out of their chains. I see Aitin, whose jaw is tightening more and more in frustration up at the top. I see every danger, every person, every wound.

I feel the pressure of life hanging in the balance in this single moment, and my body straightens with resolve.

We cannot lose.

My arms sting, my legs are trembling, my back still has rocks lodged in it, and my body is beyond tired, but somehow my mind can see past the physical pain. I know what we have to do.

I had thought the best way to defeat Aitin and his Mixed Bloods was to remove the serum from their bodies. It looks like we've gotten the serum out of some of them but not all. And now, looking around the room, I realize there's another way. A more efficient way to disable them, without killing them.

My eyes find Dilo, who is running up and down the seats, desperately trying to find a way to get close to the enemy.

I clearly remember the first time I met Dilo, the time she attacked me when I walked into the dino covert. She had vomited her serum all over my leg, making it immediately go numb.

I step close to Mark, my back against his. "Mark, can Dilo produce serum here?" I whisper.

"Of course."

"We need to cover Aitin's Mixed Bloods with it," I say under my breath, hoping Aitin can't hear me.

Mark is quiet for a split second, probably contemplating the dilemma I'm thinking about too. *How do we get the serum up to the Mixed Bloods quickly enough?* Fortunately, I know the answer.

"Use the power," I whisper.

I know that Mark understands what I'm saying when he squeezes my left pinky.

With a quick whistle, he has Dilo's attention. She runs back to us.

"On three," he says. I feel his chest expand with a deep breath. "One, two, three."

I turn my body in the same moment that Mark shouts something at Dilo. Before I can blink, a white substance is shooting from her mouth, her orange frills open and shaking. Midair, my power grabs at the white serum, controls it, so perfectly I don't even have to think about it, and flings it up to the bleachers on the right, covering three Mixed Bloods there from head to toe. I force it up their noses into their brain so they can't even think well enough to use their power.

Mark does the same thing to the four Mixed Bloods on the left side of the arena, his muscles tightening, his hands outstretched.

Without pausing, Dilo is already vomiting another batch for us to use. I grab at it. Within seconds every enemy Mixed Blood has fallen to the floor, their injuries still bleeding through the serum, completely disabled.

It worked.

And now we need to get Aitin.

With my power still suspending the serum in the air, I swing it around to look for Aitin. My heart leaps clear out of my throat when I find him standing only feet behind me, his eyes blazing, his hands clenched.

I don't even have time to swing the serum in his direction, when pain erupts through my body. Every muscle tenses; every nerve pings. Mark's screams join mine.

What is Aitin doing?

Pain tears through my chest, my heart, and my brain, and tears leak from my eyes.

"It's about time I take this totem from you." Aitin grits his teeth.

My totem? He's removing my totem! My back arches, my body shakes, and my vision gives way to a terrifying blackness. He's going to kill me. Kill us.

There was once a time when I wanted my totem to be removed like this. A time when I thought ending the emotional pain would be worth death.

Through my shaking body, I raise my right hand to finger my strained totem.

It's amazing how things have changed. *I can't lose my totem. I can't lose my life.* It means too much to me.

My fingers reach my vine, and though they're absent, I still picture the jewels Mark gave me. The promise I made.

To fight. *I didn't think my battle would look like this.* But I'd still made a promise.

I fall to the ground, my body trembling violently, the bones in my back cracking as my muscles tighten relentlessly.

Vomit rises in my throat and spills out, choking me by being sucked down the wrong tube. The pain continues to spread, searing my arms and legs, curling my fingers and toes. *How am I supposed to fight against this kind of power? How do I stop it?*

Then Jeter's face comes to my mind, and I remember how he protected himself in Dakdete. Mark and I practiced for this, practiced deflecting the power.

In this moment, though, with my nerves burning at every tip, I can't focus! It was easy practicing in Mark's safe arms. But trying to push Aitin's power away, now when I'm on the verge of death? I don't even feel the *cold* of his power. I just feel searing fire everywhere!

Clenching my teeth, I force myself to listen, past the pain, past the sounds of my own torture. *Can I deflect him before he kills me?* More tears leak out of my eyes as pressure builds in my head. My organs are bleeding!

I focus, listen for sounds within the space between Aitin and me. I scream to the totem in my mind, *Find his power! Push it away.*

The dinosaurs roar loudly around us, chains screeching, claws ripping at the rock.

Then slowly, very slowly, a pressure builds in my body, starting at my heart, and expanding to my shoulders and my head. I'm wondering if this is it, if I'm actually dying ... when the pain starts to ease, and the pressure pushes outward.

Energized, I push harder with my power, forcing it to cover my whole body like a shield to my legs and arms. My totem is swollen and bulging in my skin now, I can feel it—as if the trauma has hurt it too, but it quivers, fighting in its own way. I lie on my back, coughing through the vomit, and force my shield to encompass Mark too.

"What the hell?" I hear Aitin's tight voice.

My hands, my shoulders, my legs all shake. Not from pain anymore but from the strain of holding Aitin back. It's like those arm wrestles I used to have with Caleb. I'm fighting against a strength greater than mine. The only difference here is my life depends on not giving up. Unfortunately, I don't know how much longer I can keep Aitin away.

I scream when the pressure retreats back in my direction, crushing me like a boulder.

Please!

The ground shakes beneath me, more rocks fall around us, and the cavern erupts into more roars.

And then, like the sweetest of reliefs, the pressure disappears and that crushing weight lifts.

Aitin's power is no longer there.

What happened? Where is he?

My arms fall limp at my sides, and I sob uncontrollably. I need to get up—he could try again any second. But I can't move.

Someone screams my name, but my ears are ringing, and my body feels heavy.

"Alena, are you alright?" I think that's Kakoncha's voice. I still can't see. Nor can I stop crying. The pressure may have disappeared, but there's pain everywhere in my body, burning me from the inside out. "Mark," I whisper.

"He's alive, Alena. Here," she says.

I don't know what she's offering until the agony gently subsides, giving me a precious respite from pain. She's healing me. She clears my airway, allowing me to breathe fully, and then clears my vision, allowing me to see.

"Mark?" I whisper again when my brain clears enough. I search the floor around me with my hands, finding him lying next to me on my right doing his best to control his shaking limbs.

"Kakoncha, will you heal him please?" I whisper.

Kakoncha is there, healing him the same way she healed me, restoring his sight, reducing the swelling, but the shaking doesn't stop.

The other Mixed Bloods encircle us.

"What happened?" I ask weakly still staring at Mark. "Where's Aitin?"

The older man with blue eyes points to the mezzanine. "We unchained the dinosaurs and set them free. They chased Aitin up there. Folou and Luca followed him. We should probably get up there to help."

I follow his finger and spot the dinosaurs swarming the mezzanine, attacking one door in particular. Bud is up there, pounding his head into the wood, leading the way for his friends.

Thank you, Bud.

"You guys go up," I tell Kakoncha. "We'll be right behind." I need to help Mark.

They run to the stairs against the wall while I rise to my knees and hover over Mark.

"Lena," he whispers my name when the Mixed Bloods are halfway up the stairs. His shaking hands brush against my arm. I swallow and reach my fingers out to the sagging totem on his chest, but then freeze. My hands, my fingers. They're swollen to twice their size and they're blue. So are my feet.

Kakoncha only healed the worst of the injuries.

"Mark." I whisper when I see his condition. Not only are his hands and feet blue and swollen like mine, but his nose and ears are bleeding.

Is *my* nose bleeding?

I wipe it to find blood smeared across my hand.

We can't go on like this. I glance up the stairs quickly before looking back at Mark. A body can only take so much, and Mark has already been tortured enough today.

Placing my hand over his heart, I flood his body with my power, search for every injured muscle and tissue, every strangled organ. I restore his blood supply and even mend his still-quaking totem.

He's exhausted, I can tell. Physical pain seems to take away something I can't restore but when I pull my hand away, he's at least stopped shaking, and he's staring intently at my face.

"Thank you." After straining to sit up, he grabs my swollen hand. "Now heal yourself."

I reach out for my elements, healing only the necessary injuries this time, force the blood out of my swollen hands and feet so I can at least walk, I clear my brain, and heal my shredded heart. So many distal blood vessels are barely functioning, and I'm pretty sure my head needs some work, but I think I'll survive for now.

We need to go.

"You okay enough for now?" I ask Mark.

He nods and stands, reaching out his hand. "With Aitin's Mixed Bloods immobilized, this is our chance."

I wipe at the steady flow of blood still coming through my nose and stumble with Mark toward the stairs against the wall on the left. We climb, reaching the room everyone disappeared inside. Bud is outside the door, pacing anxiously, his hips too large to get into the room.

I rub his neck and kiss his jaw. "Thanks, Bud."

"Stay out here," Mark whispers to him, then goes inside. I follow, then stand there, letting my eyes adjust to the darkness.

This is the magnifying cave, the room where large glass magnifiers help the Pepps see the tiniest of elements. Folou grabs a torch from the walls of the skills room and brings it in, shedding light on the area.

I recall the times I came here with Mark and Danny, when the room was brightened by the sun shining through openings in the top of each case. It was the light that revealed the distinct qualities of each element.

But now the cases stand dark, the openings in the ceiling blocked.

A loud bang ripples through the air, and I cover my ears, looking for the source.

It's the morpher, hitting the thick glass of one of the large magnifiers.

"Aitin slithered into this glass case through the small opening in the side. I tried to extract his serum through the glass, but it sucked away all my power! Help me break the glass."

I walk closer to the case, bracing my aching head with one hand.

The glass case is black inside. Even in the strained lighting, I can tell it's unusual.

I think of the times I stood in front of these glass cases with Danny. I remember how the elements in little glass vials were sucked into the case through the three-inch hole on the side and how those tiny elements were magnified to such a degree that we could see them with our naked eye. If anything larger than an orange got into the case, all you would see is orange.

Aitin is inside. My mouth goes dry. *He morphed into an animal to slip through that three-inch hole on the side?*

Folou takes the lead, blasting a huge flame in the direction of the glass, but the moment the flame hits the box, it fizzles out. Folou tries again and again, but nothing happens.

"My power's gone," he whispers, looking at his hands.

Another girl steps up to try, but I hold out my arm to stop her.

"Why would Aitin hide inside the magnifying glass? Why wouldn't he just escape?" I ask.

"Glass," Mark whispers. "Case told us our totems don't like glass."

I stare at him. "*Our* totems don't like glass, but the Mixed Bloods don't have totems. Why can't they use *their* power on it?"

Mark sits down, tired. "Because their power is made up of the same thing our totems are made of. Mixed Blood generators. Maybe it's the generators themselves that can't handle glass."

"So what does that mean?" Kakoncha asks. "That we can't touch it?"

Mark shakes his head. "No, it means we can't touch glass *with our power.* Otherwise, that power gets sucked away."

I stare at the case Aitin is hiding in. "Aitin knew this. So he decided to hide away in the only spot we couldn't touch."

Mark holds his head in his hands.

"Lena, you remember the one thing that was left behind in Verdure?"

I nod again, recalling the scorched ash land with nothing left behind ... except glass.

"Cody and Rusty had said that Aitin needed breaks after destroying Verdure and the GreenLands. They thought it was because he needed rest, but what if that's not the case. What if he was weakened? What if touching the glass buildings with his power depleted his strength?"

He's right. Now I sit, crushed by the intensity of this new problem. *How do we get to him if we can't get through the glass?* Aitin morphed to get in there. Should we have someone else morph and go in after him?

Unfortunately, our morpher has lost his power and can't go in there, but even if he could, it seems too risky. Aitin is too powerful.

Perhaps we can bring Bud in here and have him break the glass using his body. Aitin is so slippery, though. Will he find a way to escape us again? Somehow kill us before we can get to him? Is there a way we can surprise him?

I feel a tap on my arm and turn to Mark, who is carefully looking up at the ceiling. I follow his gaze but don't see anything.

I don't understand.

"It's a magnifying glass," he whispers into my ear.

Suddenly my mind goes back to a day long ago when I was about seven years old. Caleb had just gotten a new magnifying glass and had spent the entire day burning ants. I remember him dragging me from the house just to show me. He was so excited.

I watched him find a tiny harmless ant on the driveway, then place his magnifying glass over it just right so that the glass magnified the sunlight. The ant frantically tried to get away, but it didn't stand a chance. Within seconds the poor thing had shriveled up to nothing more than a little speck of dust on the driveway. Dead.

I hated Caleb that day. Hated that he enjoyed doing something so heartless, so appalling. I contemplated stealing his magnifying glass and breaking it just to keep him from hurting more little creatures. But Mom got to him first and forced him to stop.

Now, right here in front of us is one of the most powerful magnifiers in the world. If Aitin is inside, we could kill him—fast. The sooner we kill him, the sooner I can go help the Pepps!

But then I look at the ceiling and frown. "There's no sun."

Mark looks around. "I think there will be soon. And, fortunately for us, we still have some power left."

Mark pulls Folou, Kaconcha, me, and three other Mixed Bloods out the door and away from Aitin's listening ears.

"The glass box Aitin is hiding in is a strong magnifying glass," he explains. "If we can get the sun to hit it just right, Aitin will either die or have no choice but to come out."

"But it's dark outside," someone says. "It'll take hours before the sun will reach a point where it could hit the glass directly."

Mark silently points to the large hole in the damaged wall where the dark night is visibly gone.

He's right. The dark sky is now light orangish-gray with morning only minutes away. *How long have we been in here?*

"The sun will be dawning within the hour. If we make a low hole in the far wall, the sun will hit the glass as soon as it clears the horizon. I've run this mountain hundreds of times at dawn. We couldn't be luckier. The sun rises on this side. It'll hit the side of that magnifier pretty quick."

"What about the clouds?" Folou asks. "They were thick when we got here. How do we know they won't still be there?"

"Moving some clouds out of the way will be easy," Mark says, almost smiling.

Pff, easy for him.

I stare at each of the Mixed Blood's faces, watching them process the plan. Their almost grown-in eyebrows rise in agreement.

"Sounds good to me," Kaconcha finally says.

"Good. I'll take you three." Mark points to the Mixed Bloods whose names I still don't know. "Alena, Folou, and Kaconcha, you stay here and make sure Aitin stays *inside* that magnifying glass."

I try to nod. It's a good plan, but it's not solid, and I worry about Mark. He's seriously tired. We almost died down there.

But what other choice do we have? "Please be careful, Mark," I whisper.

He grabs my chin and pulls my face close. "You too."

My gaze lowers to his bare chest. His totem is still loose and limp. "Maybe you could put on a shirt while you're out there."

Even amid the heaviness of death weighing over us, waiting to steal us at any opportunity, his lips tug upward. "Aren't you the one who's always trying to get my shirt *off*?"

Folou actually laughs behind Mark, and my cheeks heat, thinking of the times I actually *have* removed his shirt.

"I'll be back," he says, letting go of my chin. Then, without another word, he turns, morphs into his beautiful brown eagle form, and flies through one of the holes in the ceiling, leaving me cold and despairing.

The others disappear with him.

Kaconcha, Folou, and I slink back into the room.

I pick up a black jagged rock with my semi-swollen hand, and distract myself by hitting the glass. As long as Aitin thinks our plan consists only of trying to break the glass, he might just stay in there.

I hit the glass as hard as I can. The movement sends a powerful vibration into my shoulder but does nothing to the glass. I hit it again.

***

Banging the thick case takes a toll on my body and my head. My nose has stopped bleeding, but the sound of the banging is giving me a headache. It's also aggravating the aching pain still etched in my chest. I switch the rock from arm to arm, trying to give each a rest, but after a while I decide to stop. Aitin isn't going anywhere, and if he does somehow slip out, Kaconcha, the two other Mixed Bloods, and I still have power. I've given them instructions to immediately remove the serum should Aitin attempt to escape through that three-inch hole on the side. I've also explained in detail how to stop his heart.

More and more light breaks through the cracks and holes in the walls, allowing us to better see our frozen cave. Since we've stopped moving, the cold air has seeped back into my body all the way down to my bones.

I don't know how long it's been since Mark left, but my cold body is starting to shut down. The adrenaline is wearing off, and I'm getting tired. Which scares me. Letting out a huff of cold air, I force myself to stare at the glass case opening.

I hope Mark hurries.

Suddenly a vine bursts through the hole in the side of the case, moving so quickly that I don't have time to warn the others. It wraps itself tightly around my neck, immediately cutting off my air supply. Then it pulls me so fiercely, that I land face-first on the rock floor. My nose snaps, and more blood gushes everywhere.

My skin tears as the vine pulls me, the jagged rocks cutting into my face and hands. I try to flip my body over, try to release the pressure around my neck, but don't succeed. When my head reaches the glass case, it hits it so hard that I see bright lights behind my eyes. Even if I could scream for help, it would be a vain effort. I can hear the others struggling as well, their shrieking muffled, their lungs suffocating.

How is he using power? By not touching the glass? Can I force my power through the small opening in some way to get him? *I wish I knew how to create vines!*

The vine gouges my skin so tightly, it feels like my neck will disconnect.

We were so close!

Suddenly, a bright light floods the room.

Within seconds the vine around my neck goes limp, and my body instantly responds by taking in the deepest breath of my life. When my lungs tell me that they can't possibly inhale anymore, I breathe out, a cough interrupting my progress. It takes several moments before the spasms in my lungs stop, but when my mind clears enough to recognize my surroundings, I scramble to my feet, moving far away from the vine, pulling Kakoncha and Folou with me.

My eyes follow the light, now seeing a large opening in the side of the wall. Mark is there in the sky, his brown feathers golden in the sunlight, expanding the hole in the wall he just made to ensure we get all the light possible.

Is it working?

I turn my aching body toward the magnifying case. It's lit up so brightly as if it was the sun itself, emitting a strong heat that warms the shivers on my arms.

I step forward, staring at the small circular opening, where five vines now hang limp and parched, starting to steam. I clench my fists.

Is he dead? How will we know?

I jump when a small black snake slithers from the glass, morphing into what looks like a dead, fried man. Ignoring the blood still pouring from my nose and the gashes stinging my face, I crawl over to him.

"Get his serum." My words are barely a wheeze, but the others hear. I can tell that they're already grabbing hold of the serum inside his body and yanking it out when I join in. Quickly, a thick white substance seeps through his skin. Aitin isn't even fighting anymore. He doesn't have the strength.

Mark quietly slides to my side, morphed back into his human form. He sees the serum and immediately burns it with fire, the flames licking Aitin's skin urgently.

The smell of charred flesh reaches my nose, and I gulp down vomit. I hope after this I never have to smell that again.

Ever.

Aitin screams, the sound searing its way into my brain, joining the many other memories that haunt my dreams. I look away, but it doesn't stop. It only increases to manic despair, with no pause for breath.

When the air finally quiets, I look back and stare at Aitin's chest.

Is he dead?

No. It's barely noticeable, but I see his chest rise. Searching his body internally, from head to toe, I listen for the serum, making sure it's gone.

When I'm sure I can't hear a single drop, I let my hands fall into my lap. They're shaking. In fact, my whole body is shaking. Mark puts an arm around me.

"Please." Aitin pleads, his voice muffled, unrecognizable. "Please, don't heal me. Just let me die."

I look at Mark. His jaw twitches, and he grinds his teeth but doesn't speak.

I turn back to the brutal man and rub my neck that still aches profusely from getting strangled.

"I can find another way," I whisper. "I can find a way to heal you without using the serum. A way to get rid of your reaction to Peppate altogether. I just need more time."

Aitin shakes his head, sending waves of tightening pain through his body. He arches his back, gasping frantically.

"I'm tired," he heaves through gritted teeth. "Please, just end it." Another wave of pain racks his body, sending it into tremors. "Please!"

I stare at him. The idea of killing another human being goes against everything I believe. But knowing everything he's done, it doesn't seem right to let him live. Nor does it seem right to make him suffer.

I look at Mark again.

The sun lights his face, reflecting off the golden color in his brown eyes. If there's anyone who deserves to kill Aitin, it's Mark. But as I watch him, I see the twitches in his jaw ease. I watch the hate in his expression change to something else. Exhaustion. He's tired too.

"What was her name?" Mark eventually asks through Aitin's moaning. The question catches me off guard. I don't understand it, but apparently Aitin does.

"Bretalia." The name flows reverently from Aitin's tight lips. "My mother's name was Bretalia."

They stare at each other for a long time. Two half-brothers. Same father. Completely different lives. There's probably so much Mark wants to know. So much that Aitin could tell him. But as I study his face, I see that he's accepted it. Accepted that he doesn't have all the answers, and that's okay. Accepted that it's time to stop fighting. Time to end Aitin's pain.

"I'm sorry, Aitin ... for everything," Mark says.

There's a warmth that fills my cold body, hearing Mark's words. A warmth only possible because of a tender forgiveness. He's forgiving this man. The man that disrupted his life, killed his father, and tortured him in inhumane ways.

He's choosing to move on.

I admire him and appreciate his choice more than my tired spirit can ever explain.

Aitin almost smiles through his crisped cheeks. Laughing. I don't really know why, but it doesn't last long. Aitin's body tenses and shakes violently one last time and then ... he's gone.

Chapter 28

I don't know what I expected. Maybe for things to magically right themselves the moment Aitin breathed his last breath. That this heavy burden I've carried for so long would finally disappear the moment he passed away.

But that isn't what's happens. If anything, my heart feels heavier.

My eyes grow heavy. I'm so tired, but there's something else we need to do. Something very important.

The Pepps.

I muster up all the strength I have left and rise to my feet. As much as I want to use the remaining power I have to heal my broken nose and close the bleeding gashes in my face, I refrain. I need it for the Pepps. Unfortunately, there's not much power left.

Holding each other up, we fly out of the school toward the Post. My body is still shaking, and it's not from the cold air. Exhaustion and stress consume me. I fight in vain to regain control of my trembling. When we reach the Post, I'm fighting back a swarm of tears. There's still so much to be done.

Bending down, Mark pulls the hatch open and we go inside. It doesn't take long for the stench of death and bloody vomit to reach my nose. Shaking uncontrollably, I lean to the side and throw up onto the tunnel floor. Unfortunately, it doesn't really help, especially with the exhaustion. When I stand up, I find Mark and the others doing the same thing.

How in the world can we keep going on like this?

I start to think of all the things we'll be faced with.

"We'll need more power if we're going to help them," I say in despair, trying to help Mark up. "We can morph with another totem from the tree, and then we can heal."

But it's too much. I fall to my knees next to Mark. It's too many steps, too many painful breaths. Too much to do, and I don't have the energy.

Then, like a warm light, Kaconcha is there. Within her capable hands, she creates a large loaf of bread.

I breathe in deeply. I've never smelled anything so wonderfully hopeful.

"Eat," she says, joining us on the cold floor.

I don't know how a piece of bread could move the despair I feel, spin it around, and send it away. But it does. I break off a warm piece and press it to my lips.

How did she make it warm?

I push the piece in further and let it rest on my tongue. My eyes close in awe. It tastes so good I cry. It isn't until I swallow the piece that I'm reminded of the pain in my throat, reminded of where I am. But I take another piece, chewing it this time, enjoying every second the bread is in my mouth. More tears leak from my eyes. I don't bother stopping them. I shouldn't waste so much time enjoying the bread when there's so much pain down these tunnels, but I keep eating, feeling the pieces drop into my empty stomach.

We go through four large loaves of fresh warm bread, Folou and the others taking as much as they can swallow as well.

"Do you feel better?" Kakoncha asks.

I look down. I'm still shaking. In fact, it's even worse now that I have more energy, but I don't feel as utterly hopeless, and my tears have stopped.

"Yes," I say.

Then I look at Mark. He's sitting against the wall, leaning his head back, his eyes closed. He needs rest. We all need rest. I need him to come with me, though, to help me get more power.

"Mark." I crawl toward him, placing my hand on his jaw. His eyes open. "You okay?"

"Yeah," he says, then twists to the side and rolls onto his knees. "Let's go."

I help his fatigued body stand as best as I can.

Folou knows where the Pepps have been taken, but he doesn't know the way to the totem tree, so I force my mind to think again. Remember the tunnels we need to go down.

I stop, frozen in place when we reach the first room loaded with sick Pepps. They're all crammed in there, practically lying on top of each other, coughing, spitting up blood. I spot only one Mixed Blood in there helping them.

Is he able to get the serumed virus out?

Folou tugs on my arm. He's right—we have to hurry. With new energy, we make for the totem tree as fast as we can, ignoring room after room full of Pepps bleeding from the inside out. Ignoring the cries.

I recall the times these tunnels were busy with Pepps. It's odd to see them now busy with Mixed Bloods running back and forth, trying to help as best they can. Many yell out my name when they see me, but I keep moving forward, Mark at my side.

When we reach the totem tree observatory, I burst through the door. The totem tree room is now lit up, with torches everywhere. This room has also been packed full of sick Pepps taking refuge.

"Bapoto!" I yell blindly into the crowd below.

I'm glad it doesn't take long for me to spot him or for him to respond.

"I need one more totem," I yell through the observatory glass, gesturing with my hands. He understands and spins on his heels to get me one. I go out the door, ready to meet him from wherever he emerges from.

Once I have the wrapped totem in my hands, Mark and I run back through the tunnels, to the entrance. We climb the ladder, go outside, shut the hatch, quickly morph, and then come back in.

Then I run to the first room. I scan it, wondering where to begin, when I spot a Pepp girl with a red-wrapped totem lying on the ground.

A medic. I go to her first.

"Do you have power?" I ask. Her eyes are bleeding, and her skin is deathly white. I almost wonder if she's already gone, but then she nods.

It's amazing they still have power and can't even use it against this virus.

"I'm going to remove the serum from the virus infecting your body. Once I've removed it, you'll be able to speak to the virus and eradicate it."

Without waiting for her to respond, I quickly connect to the serum. There isn't much in her body, but it's moving with the bugs. I chase it around, tugging on each heavy piece I sense. As soon as it surfaces on her skin, Mark steps up behind me and burns it carefully with fire.

"I need you to find the virus now. Get rid of it and then heal your body."

My tired spirit comes alive in this room full of illness. It's as if it's awakening from a deep sleep, eager to play a part in this healing.

If healing could be a sort of living spirit within a person, it's definitely alive within me.

I find a boy, lying right next to the girl. I begin working on him while keeping a close eye on the girl. I need as much power as possible to remove the serum from the others. If she can help me by healing herself, my power will go much farther.

Slowly the color comes back to her skin. Her depleted body begins to inflate, and I feel a small light of hope bud within me. By the time I remove the serum from the boy, she's sitting up.

"Will you help me now, please?" I ask her, moving to the next boy. "I'll remove the serum, but if you'll come behind me and remove the virus, then heal the body, that would help me so much."

She doesn't need me to ask again. She goes to work on the boy. Then we move to the next man and woman. We work through that first room quickly.

I'm almost ready to believe that we got here just in time, until I emerge from the room to go to the next. I see a pair of Mixed Bloods carrying a body down the tunnel.

"Here, let me heal him." I try to stop them, but they keep going.

"He's dead," they say.

Dead?

Where are they taking him?

I don't ask. Instead, I find myself wandering along with them, leaving Mark behind to continue extracting serum. When the room comes into view, my hand rises to my mouth, stifling my gasp. Body on top of body is piled in the room, the stacks reaching almost to the ceiling. I gag at the smell of death, at the blood everywhere.

So many bodies! The shaking in my hands worsens, and I almost fall to my knees. If it wasn't for the medic girl I had just healed, I probably wouldn't have been able to leave that room. She practically drags me out, leading me to another one with Pepps still alive.

I work harder, refusing to add more patients to that pile of dead bodies. I extract, extract, and then extract some more. I call for Mark to burn, until I find another Pepp who can help me do that. This allows Mark to continue working on his own, doubling our progress.

I extract the serum from the virus in a woman, then move on to the next patient, not stopping until the woman grabs my arm.

"Alena."

I pause to look at her. It takes me forever to recognize her, but when I do, my heart falls.

"Pam," I whisper. The woman I still haven't talked to since I killed her husband, Tom. Cody's Pepp mother.

I've always run away from her, not wanting to face the harsh truth that I killed her husband.

But I don't do that now. Instead, I ask, "Are you okay?"

It's brief, but it's a smile, twitching at the corners of her lips. The world seems to pause for just a moment.

"Yes, I'm okay," she says. "Thank you." Then she stands and begins helping in the chaos.

I could let her go. There's too much to do.

But, instead, I reach for her arm. Her body stills, and she searches my face.

I swallow past the sudden lump in my throat. I've needed to say something to her since that horrible night at SilverDen but have always been too afraid.

"I'm sorry," I say. My lip trembles. "I'm sorry about what happened to Tom."

I can't see her face through my blurry eyes, but she grasps my hands in hers. "It's okay, Alena. It's okay."

I nod. Knowing I need to accept her forgiveness and keep healing, I blink away the tears.

"Thank you."

She smiles and then she's gone. Off to help.

Someone is tugging at my arm, one of the medics, pulling me back to the disaster before us. Taking in a deep breath, I turn my attention back to those in front of me.

The Mixed Bloods are there, working right alongside me, some removing the serum, some burning it, some healing the bodies.

Then the healed Pepp medics join in healing, and the Pepp enviros join in burning. Scance and Leinani are among the medics I heal. I'm more than relieved to see they're okay. Carlos is okay too.

I recognize another man, the one who worked with Jax. Chauly. It seems he survived. A couple of Pepps take him away as soon as he wakes up confused. Good. I hope they lock him up tight.

It seems the more we heal, the faster the work goes. Soon the whole room is rising and moving on to help somewhere else.

Somewhere in the disarray, Breccia buzzes to my side. I don't have the energy or time to express how grateful I am to see her alive. Nor do I have the time to explain everything that's happened, but she asks what she can do. I consider for a moment and then request that she go back to Maracai and tell Eli that Aitin is dead. That they need to come back and help us.

After she leaves, I wonder briefly about Rusty, Cody, Danny, Kapri, Sef, Leinani, Carlos, even Flint.

Are they okay?

After healing the last Pepp in a particular room, I turn to the girl who has so diligently followed me this whole time. "Where do we go next?"

She musters up as much of a smile as the circumstances will allow and says, "We're done."

Those words. They open the floodgates of exhaustion that have been waiting to take over. My knees instantly cry out from kneeling on the hard rock for the past ... *How long have we been at this*? My nose screams in pain, and my face burns when my tears touch my wounds.

"Here," the girl says. Gently holding my face in her hands, I feel her heal my body, my many wounds. Her power extends from my head, through my skin, down to my aching feet. I want to cry when it feels like her power goes even deeper, healing my spirit. *Is that even possible?*

When she's done, I slowly stand and move toward the door. The halls that were barren and cold when Mark and I first got here have now come to life. Large heating stoves radiate comforting warmth into each of the rooms. Pepps walk with purpose, re-creating order.

I find Mark.

He's in a room just down the hall from me. I watch him help a man rise to a sitting position. He's still shirtless, dirty, and tired. But so handsome.

His mournful eyes meet mine from across the room, and he stands. Unable to be apart from him any longer, I walk to him.

When I'm standing directly in front of him, I wrap my arms around his waist and rest my cheek on his warm chest.

The medic girl interrupts us. "You guys need to get some sleep. Why don't you follow me? There's a room down the hall we've put a bed in. You can get some rest there."

I look around the room. Everyone is doing better. Even if they do find another Pepp who needs healing, the Mixed Bloods and Pepps are more than capable of handling it. Maybe it's time we can actually rest.

The girl leads us out of the cavern and down the hall. Unfortunately, there's a room we have to walk past in order to get to the bed.

The room of the dead. An opening has been carved out of the ceiling, leading to the now night sky.

It's night again?

They're removing the dead from the room. The sound of wailing reaches my ears, and I realize many Pepps are holding onto their loved ones, refusing to let them be taken out.

The girl pulls on my arm, but my feet don't move. My eyes scan the bodies for familiar faces, friends.

I don't recognize anyone I know personally. That is until my eyes land on a man. My knees buckle beneath me.

Sef. My morpher friend.

His body is pushed up against the wall on the left, so depleted I almost don't recognize him, but it's him. I want to walk to him, but my body won't move.

"Alena, let's go." Mark is pulling on me even through his weakness.

"I need to see everyone who died," I whisper.

"Alena, don't torture yourself like that," he says. "Let's go, please. We'll find out eventually."

The medic girl stands on the other side of me. "We aren't burying them yet. We're just getting them out of this tight space. You'll be able to see them all later, but, for now, I think you two need some rest."

Rest. The word sounded so wonderful only moments ago, but now it sounds terrible. *How could I possibly rest?*

"Come on." The girl pulls on my arm, then pushes me from behind. I try to swallow, to wash the terror from my dry mouth, letting the girl lead Mark and me down the tunnel.

She pauses at a door before opening it. Somehow this room, lit by only one candle, has remained clean, untouched by vomit and blood. At least I think it's clean. My mind is really foggy now. My eyes fall to a huge plump mattress that takes up most of the room. Without needing to be asked again, I walk to it and fall in. Mark drops down beside me.

I want to think about the bodies of my friends. I want to grieve them. But I can't even cry. Before I fully pull the blanket over myself, I'm sound asleep.

Chapter 29

My mind slowly wakes up. I'm so warm and comfortable that I don't want to open my eyes. But when I hear that loud gurgling sound again, the one that must have pulled me from my sleep, my eyes reluctantly slide open. There's only a sliver of flickering light still in the room, probably from that same candle. I shift slightly, only to realize that I'm snuggled closely against Mark's chest. I breathe in his scent and let my eyes drift up to his face. He's still asleep. Good.

Something gurgles behind me again. *What is that against my back?* I stretch my neck around to find a large furry animal there, snoring.

Trevor.

I smile and sit up, then stifle a laugh when I see the bed loaded with the rest of my friends. Danny and Kapri are sleeping on the other side of Trevor, along with Lilly and Case. *Did somebody bring them here?*

The three brothers. I never thought I'd see them all back together like this.

I burrow myself back in between Mark and the bear and try to go back to sleep, but I can't. Instead, I stare at Mark's relaxed face. Not wanting to wake him up, I resist the urge to touch his jaw.

A sense of sadness floods over me at the thought of his burned body. I almost lost him again.

Because of Aitin. Aitin almost killed him.

I shouldn't be filled with anything less than hate and anger toward that man, but I have to admit, right now looking at Mark, I'm mostly just sad.

So many lives have been lost. Good lives.

And those still alive are scarred with nightmares.

And all for what? Aitin claimed that he was fighting to find a cure for his ailment so he could live a better life. I'll always agree that he deserved better. Nobody should live a life filled with pain. But, in the end, even when he'd found a *cure* he wasn't living a better life. He was seeking power.

He was seeking revenge.

I recall Cody's words about forgiveness. How it's the intentional decision to not let the choice or action of someone else ruin your life. How it's much easier to blame our unhappiness on someone else for what they did than to go out and seek happiness by letting go of what was unfairly done to us.

Aitin couldn't let go. He couldn't forgive the wrongdoings done to him, and now look at the damage done.

I still can't blame him, though.

I reach up and gently brush my fingers against Mark's jaw. He shifts slightly in his sleep.

Aitin didn't have the proper support. He was never shown how beautiful relationships can be. Even Lilly, compared to Aitin, received more love than Aitin could have even imagined. Which is probably why two people with the same terrible condition turned out so differently.

From the time Aitin was young, everyone was out to hurt him, and by the time I came along with the desire to help him, he was much harder to reach. I still believe he could have turned his life around, chosen to let go of the things that happened to him and instead allow himself to move on. But it's unfair for me to say that that's what he should have done, when I was never faced with anything remotely as difficult as his challenges. I don't truly understand what he went through.

For the first time in my life, I realize how damaging hate can be.

"You didn't sneak a kiss, did you?"

Mark's voice breaks through my thoughts. I realize that my touch probably woke him up.

"I'm sorry, I didn't mean to wake you."

Mark smiles, the curl of his lips making my heart leap. "It's okay as long as you didn't steal any kisses without me being conscious."

Now I smile. "Oh, I've been kissing you for the past hour."

Mark grins wide.

"How are you feeling?" I ask. Mark tightens his grip around my waist, pulling me closer to him.

"I feel good."

I bury my face in his bare chest and take in another deep breath. "Me too."

Trevor's large arm swings around and pounds us in the side.

"Shut up," Gabbro says for him.

Never have I been so happy to hear Gabbro's voice.

I close my eyes.

There's so much to do. So much more to face, but for this small moment, surrounded by my friends, I feel safe.

I feel at peace.

***

We stand in the dark night air, in the area that used to be called the Burrows. The last few days have been full of moving bodies to the new cemetery—or *memorial*, as Eli is calling it—located just south of the Post. The chief is among those who died. He got Ebola like everyone else, and in his already deteriorated state couldn't hold on.

I pull my sweater closer around my torso. Along with getting the dead bodies settled, the Pepps have been trying to regulate the temperature here again. We aren't quite there yet, but at least it's not snowing anymore and we can see the ground. It'll take a lot of time to get everything in the world back to normal, along with rebuilding Petrichor. A couple of teams have even gone below to start planting growth again in the GreenLands.

I'm just glad we can start moving forward.

I look around at our group. The Pepps. According to Cody, we used to have over fourteen thousand Pepps. Now we're down to just over seven thousand. We lost almost half our people. I see Flint standing at the side of our gathered group with his mother and a man I've only seen in a picture on the prison cabin wall. His uncle. With everything that's happened, I'm glad Eli let his uncle go. And I'm glad his mother is okay.

Mark wraps his arm around my shoulders, pulling me into his side, kissing my temple. Considering all those who've lost their loved ones, I'm extremely lucky that I still have Mark. I wrap my arms around his torso.

Next to Mark is Dilo. Case kept his promise and got her out, which saved us in the skills room.

Behind me is Bud, my favorite dinosaur.

I'm lucky my family is also okay. Caleb stands next to me with his arm around Jess. Eli agreed to bring them to Petrichor to live with us. I'm grateful that Aitin never reached their territory, where there were so many people in hiding. Now they've joined our cause. We need all the help we can get anyway, and Caleb was more than happy to become something that'll give him power. Mom and Dad have also received totems and will gradually be trained along the way. Even Dr. Brown, his wife, and loud Rick are here.

My eyes graze the outskirts of our large crowd. Lilly and Case are out there somewhere. I expected them to leave Petrichor right after I healed Lilly a couple of days ago, but they wanted to stay and pay their respects with everyone else.

I lift the paper lantern in my hand. With the sun now set and the night sky dark, it's almost time. I look down at my lantern. The names of those I'm grieving tonight are listed on the paper. I don't think I could squeeze one more name on it even if I tried, but I have many lives to grieve tonight. I read through them now, their pictures evoked in my mind.

Mark's father. I didn't know him, but he was the beginning of my journey.

Each of the Pepp prisoners—who died from the flesh-eating bug. Gabbro helped me compile all their names.

Mitch.

Tom.

Jeter.

Lilly's Baby.

Jax.

Sef.

The chief.

And every Pepp I could fit who died from Ebola.

Each of these people have left their imprint on me forever. The world is a darker place without their light, but tonight we'll see it one last time. We wouldn't be standing here without their efforts and sacrifice.

"Go ahead and light your lanterns," Eli says, standing at the front of the group. I guess I should say *chief* now, as he's finally accepted his role as leader. Rusty is somberly standing behind him, his arm draped around Cody.

The dark night lights up immediately. Flickers of light roll over the hills all around us as the thousands gathered here light their lamps. Mark lights mine with his fire and then his own. I feel the pull of the lamp. It's wanting to fly away immediately as if the spirits of those named are anxiously waiting to move on. But I hold on to them a little longer. I breathe them in one last time.

Eli doesn't speak but gently releases his lantern as a signal that we're all free to let ours go too.

I release mine.

My lip trembles as it soars out of my hands along with the thousands of other lamps going up into the sky. The air is silent as we all watch the lights rise. I grip Mark tightly.

His father is named on his lamp too, and Mark's eyes glisten as he officially releases his spirit.

I watch the sky for a long time, the beauty of the flickering lights filling my saddened heart with hope. Slowly, my eyes rise to the other flickering lights above us. The stars.

I remember what Lilly said. How we're part of something bigger and more beautiful than we can comprehend. As vast as it all is, we are part of it. And those whose spirits we're releasing ... it feels as if they're still part of it too, somehow.

Slowly people start talking again, and the area comes back to life. When I bring my attention down from the sky, they fall on a boy not too far from me.

In order to keep history from repeating itself, there's something I need to do.

Breaking away from Mark for a moment, I walk over to Flint. He's still looking into the sky.

"Hey." I tap his arm softly to get his attention.

When he sees me standing there, his somber expression is immediately swallowed by a scowl.

I try to keep my voice low and sincere. "I'm sorry, Flint." I let the words come out slowly. But as scared as I am to say them, they sound as genuine as they feel.

Flint spins on his heels ready to walk away. I roll my eyes, trying not to get frustrated, but knowing I need to get my words out, at least for my sake, I gently grab his arm and make him face me.

"I'm sorry that you didn't get to participate in initiation because of me."

My words catch him by surprise, something even his angry face can't hide. I proceed, "I'm also sorry for those you might have lost."

Flint keeps his face hard, unreadable. I know he won't continue to listen to me for much longer, so I finish. "I also need to thank you for everything you did to train the Mixed Bloods. We never would have beat Aitin without their help ... without you."

Flint doesn't say a word. Then, when I fall silent, he raises his eyebrows. "You done?"

I nod. Flint spins around again and walks away. I don't know what I was expecting, but, knowing Flint, I shouldn't have expected too much.

I turn to go back to Mark, but behind me I hear Flint's reply, "You're welcome."

Then he's gone.

I can't hold back the smile that creeps across my face.

Chapter 30

Pine trees.

Walking up Training Mountain, I breathe in deeply. Someone planted a lot of pine trees up here, and they've started exuding their scent. I can't seem to inhale the smell deeply enough. It reminds me so much of home.

While my legs climb, enjoying the strain of purposeful movement, my eyes leisurely wander over the shady scene before me. Every single tree has been amazingly restored to maturity, with tall trunks covered in rough brown bark and full branches with needles that reach for the sun. And then there's that stunning green hue. Just that color alone allows me to breathe deeper, see things purer.

If I could create things like an enviro, I would make the whole world this color. Bright green. It's just beautiful.

As good as the Pepps have been at returning things to the way they were, though, there's still a lot to be done.

The climbing wall I passed a while ago is still a crumbled pile of loose rubble and mud, as is GreenGrotto. I'm hoping that what I'm coming up here to see is still intact, but there's a good chance it's gone.

My new tennis shoes, made by the Pepps, lazily move me forward, one slow step after the other, as if enjoying the stroll themselves.

I think I'm getting closer. I don't know how I know that, considering I was never familiar with this place. I just do.

It's when my feet round another bend in the dusty trail that my body comes to a stop. I smile.

It's still here.

Danny's rock.

Bright sun rays reach through the trees, casting a luminous glow that pulls me forward. How it survived the chaos, I'll never know, but I'm sure grateful it did.

Quieting Breccia's music for a moment, I walk to the warm stone and sit.

It's been a long time since I've been up here. A long and trying time.

Several yellow wildflowers speckle the dirt at my feet. Bending down, I pluck one off, rolling the stem between my fingers.

This is where Danny first taught me about Peppate.

My eyes slide to the spot where Danny sat then.

I've been thinking about that day a lot lately. About the things he said to me. I can't stop wondering if Aitin's life would have been different if he'd been taught the things I was taught— about happiness.

While staring at the yellow flower, my mind goes back to the months just before I came to Petrichor, before I met Danny. I'm immediately bombarded by the way I felt then. Lost. Empty. Worthless.

My body sags now under the weight of those emotions. Worthless. That's what living without Peppate does to me. It illudes my sense of purpose.

And, oh, how that scares me. I hated wondering if I'd ever feel like myself again.

I chew on the inside of my cheek.

Did Aitin know himself? Did he ever have a Danny in his life, to teach him who he truly was?

Maybe the angry and hurtful man I knew was the real Aitin.

But I kind of doubt it.

Thankfully, I had a Danny in *my* life. He helped me see why I felt so lost. He taught me about truth, how I couldn't see it anymore because the Doler was snuffing it out.

He was blatantly honest with me, told me that happiness was still possible, but that it would require effort on my part.

And then he taught me about the WIGGEMS. I laugh into the quiet air around me. What a silly acronym that surprisingly works at getting rid of the Doler so that Peppate can step in and help us see the important truths we need to see.

Work, Interaction, Grace, Gratitude, Exercise, Music, Scenery.

Fortunately, my learning didn't end with Danny.

I think about the chief, how he taught me that *all* emotions are important. At the same time, though, he warned me of the dangers that come from holding on to anger too long. He encouraged me to forgive.

I think about Mark, how he taught me that sometimes there's nothing we can do but just push through the darkness—move forward even though we don't know which way forward is. That sometimes we just have to fight, fight and fight some more.

I think about Lilly, who taught me that each one of us has a place in some grander picture, and even though we may not know what that place is, *we're* the only one who can fill it.

I think about Breccia, who carefully held on to precious moments of light in my own life, allowing me to recall them during difficult times. She helped me remember the good.

I think about Sepharine, who showed me that it's not only okay to ask for help, it's important.

I think about their words, their lessons, their encouragements, how they sustained me through so much.

But then my spirits fall.

What about those who don't have amazing friends like I do?

I think about the war, how so many lives were tragically lost. I think about how much was taken from those in the GreenLands. The nightmarish destruction.

I think about others who are trapped, abused, and broken in the worst ways possible. I think about those who suffer with lifelong illnesses.

Where is happiness then? How do they achieve it when so much has been unfairly ripped from their lives?

I stare at the flower still holding strong in my hands and recall Sef, his story of hope.

Hope didn't necessarily restore his mother's life, but it allowed him to believe that no matter what happened, someday, somehow, everything would be made right. That maybe the one thing more powerful than *achieving* happiness is *believing* in happiness.

I have to believe that—that everything *will* be made right. That the chains of life will be released. That fairness and balance will be restored no matter what, that our pains will be taken away. That our courage will be rewarded, and that we'll all eventually see and feel truth.

The truth that we have incredible worth.

I stare at the beautiful greenery below, the newly developing Petrichor, stretching on for miles and miles.

Each one of my friends has taught me something different about the emotion I've so desperately wanted to command. Their words float around in my mind, slowly coming together, forming a new picture, a new idea of what *I* believe happiness is.

What is happiness to me?

Suddenly my mind is taken back to a time when I was younger. My dad had taken us on this trip to tour a labyrinth of caves that sat at the base of our mountain. I remember being excited, especially to see the bats Dad had talked about so much.

But when we finally reached the cave, I saw how dark it was inside. It was so terrifying that I didn't want to go in.

Fortunately, the tour guide was there. I remember the old man assuring me that there would be lanterns on the inside to guide our way.

I took the first few steps inside. The darkness swallowed us up, and my chest tightened with each progressive stride. It was so dark.

But just when all the light seemed to disappear, a tiny little lantern arose ahead. It was small compared to the daylight, but it was enough. It pulled me forward, giving me just what I needed, not only to maneuver through the rock but to see the beauty of the stalactites. They were amazing, unlike anything I'd ever seen.

We continued on. Some rooms were lit up more than others, allowing us to see the hanging bats and shiny rocks. Other times the lights were so dim and far apart that I truly did feel like I was lost in total blackness.

That's when the tour guide took my hand and helped me keep moving. He knew the way. I just had to trust him.

I remember anxiously searching through that pure darkness, waiting for something to appear. I remember the relief, the joy I felt when I finally saw the tiny speck of light.

I quickly learned that in those caves there was always a light ahead. Always. I just had to find it.

A warm gentle breeze brushes against my skin.

That's what happiness is to me. Small moments of light, there to guide me through my journey.

I recall the moments of happiness I've experienced this past year. Moments with Danny, with Mark, with my family. Moments healing as a medic. Sometimes they were such profound experiences that they made my heart almost burst with happiness. Other times the light was softer, like a gentle stream, calm and steady. But, either way, they were rich moments that sustained me, pulled me forward with purpose. They were always moments when I saw the truth Danny taught me about. Moments when I felt my worth.

I look down at the flower now resting in my lap.

I guess a part of me has wished all along that I could somehow make happiness a permanent piece of my life, never wavering. I'm my best self when I'm happy.

But I've learned that that's not how it works. Happiness isn't like a long-lasting bright light that never goes out. At least not for me. Instead, it's a sporadic guide of carefully placed lanterns. Lanterns that I have to find ... and then remember.

My mind floats back to the moment in Maracai when Mia took me to see Trevor playing with the Mixed children. That was a moment when my heart did burst. The light I felt then was as bright as the sun itself. Even now I feel that experience physically pushing me forward, giving me a sense of purpose in this life.

But that experience didn't just *happen*. In a way, I created it. Every step, every painful decision I made after coming to Petrichor, paved a way, brick by brick, and lit that lantern in my future. It guided me there so I could eventually feel that light.

It's odd to say, but it's as if the things, or the *wiggems*, we do today light our lanterns of tomorrow.

The people I made connections with—Lilly, Bapoto, the Mixed Bloods—they all saved my life. I needed them.

I glance down at my totem wrapped with a simple red ribbon, remembering the glass jewels that were once there.

I promised Mark not too long ago that I would continue to fight, fight to see my worth. Fight to try, but today I want to make myself a promise.

That no matter what happens in life, no matter what other people say, or how many mistakes I make—I promise I'll fight ... to live.

To live my very best life.

Today, I choose. Not to be happy. But to make small daily decisions that will light my future lanterns.

Chapter 31

Mark grasps my hand, pulling me through the brush, the four-wheeler capsules tucked safely in his pocket.

It didn't feel right riding them through here. Not yet.

Mark's hand tightens around mine when the old cabin comes into view ahead.

This is the first time he's been back since his father died. I'm grateful I get to come with him.

The leaves beneath our feet crunch loudly until we step onto the creaky wooden porch. It's just as it was when I came looking through here with Rusty. The day I found the picture of Mark with his father.

I asked Mark if he would ever want to fix it up, maybe live in it one day.

He just shrugged and said, "We'll see."

With his abilities with power, it wouldn't be hard at all for him to restore it.

I watch Mark now, walking from room to room. His face is solemn but not too sad. As if he's simply here to officially say good-bye.

It only takes him a few minutes to lament over each room. Before I know it, he's leading me back outside into the bright afternoon light.

"You ready to go for a swim?" he asks, looking over the outside of the cabin one last time.

My heart stutters. Mark was nervous to come see the cabin again, but I was nervous to come to the hot spring. I still have dreams about vines trying to drown me.

"It'll be okay," he whispers, winding his warm fingers through mine.

I walk with Mark up the trail in silence. Occasionally, the sun catches the new jewels on my arm just right, sending little glittering lights over the leaves of the trees. Mark made me some new jewels out of diamonds. They're beautiful.

Much too quickly we reach the bubbling hot spring. *Well, I guess it's still here*. The hot, steaming water travels down the crevice until it reaches the pool.

Jess and Caleb are on their way up with Cody, Rusty, Danny, and Kapri. They'll be here soon, but we wanted to have some time alone before that. Having changed into our swimming suits before coming up here, we're almost ready to get in.

Mark pulls his shirt over his head.

Pff. I scoff, trying to ignore his bare chest while pulling off my own shirt to reveal my light-blue tank top and black shorts.

Then Mark slowly gets in.

I know nothing is going to hurt me. I know the worst has already happened, but I'm still hesitant. I stall by lazily putting my hair into a messy bun.

Unfortunately, I can't delay forever.

I put my toes into the water first.

It's hot.

Then my calves. I sit on the side of the pool for a second. I'd probably stay here forever if it wasn't for Mark, standing there, looking so handsome with his shirt off. My fingertips just ache to touch him.

Taking in a deep breath, I push off the edge and send my body into the water. Ah. I *have* missed this place—the heat, the smell of pine, the cool air.

When I look at Mark, I find him watching me with those captivating eyes. I'm swimming toward him, when my toes brush against the mud below. I instantly recoil, gritting my teeth.

I swim very awkwardly the rest of the way, trying not to touch the bottom. His strong arms reach me before mine reach him, and he pulls me in close.

"I'm not sure about the bottom yet," I mutter, wrapping my legs around his torso.

"I guess you never know. There could be a live vine down there ready to ruin your life."

I laugh at his joke but still anxiously cling to him.

There really could be!

When I finally feel calm enough to take my eyes off the guilty-looking murky water, I look at Mark, who is remarkably close.

Unwinding one arm from around my waist, he brings his fingers to my jaw.

"I'm sorry for everything that's happened to you since the day you came here, Lena," he whispers, his eyes searching my face, landing on my lips. His voice lowers. "But I'll always be selfishly grateful you found that vine. If you hadn't, I never would have met you."

I observe his face, his terribly attractive scruff, his thick eyebrows, his burning expression.

I touch the scruff now, letting my fingers glide over it.

"I guess I'm grateful I found the vine too," I tease.

Now my eyes drift to *his* lips. Those lips. Everything is worth it as long as I can kiss those lips.

Tightening my legs around him, I pull myself closer, brushing my mouth against his ever so softly.

No, nothing bad will ever happen in this place again.

Mark doesn't need any more encouragement. Suddenly, one of his hands is tangled in my bunned hair, sending shivers down my neck—and his other hand is gripping my thigh.

Spinning me around, he presses me against the muddy wall of the hot spring, working through my mouth hungrily.

Of course, with his shirt off, I can't help but touch his bare skin, gripping the muscles in his chest, shoulders, back, arms ... neck. My hands wind through his hair, and I lean back, bringing him with me. He responds by crushing me further into the mud, his kisses growing terribly intense.

"Hey." A voice cracks through the air, ripping the moment. Mark groans deeply at the interruption but doesn't turn. Instead, he moves his lips down my neck.

I peek around Mark's head. It's Caleb, with Jess, pumping his eyebrows up and down.

Now I groan.

"Anybody want some birthday s'mores?" Caleb holds up a bag to show us the goods he brought for our birthday.

No. I don't want s'mores right now!

But I loosen my grip on Mark's arms, and his mouth stops moving. With a heavy, defeated sigh, he bites my neck one last time before reluctantly moving his body off mine and settling into the water next to me.

Without Mark there holding me afloat, my feet fall to the bottom of the spring.

It's soft and gooey. When I feel some twigs, I close my eyes, expecting them to move. But they don't. It's just a normal muddy bottom.

I let my aching lungs finally release their stressed air and pull myself to Mark's side.

His jaw is twitching in frustration.

I nuzzle his neck. "Don't worry. I still owe you many dances accompanied by many kisses," I whisper, letting my fingers wander over his tight stomach under the water.

Wrapping his arm around my shoulders, he pulls me in.

"*Many* kisses." The tiniest of smirks plays at his lips.

Oh, how I love this man.

Danny and Kapri both show up just as Caleb and Jess get in the water.

And then Trevor shows up. With so many people in the hot spring, things are getting crowded, but Trevor doesn't care. With his big bear body, he squishes in, forcing us to scoot closer together. Mark pulls me in front of him and wraps his arms around my stomach. I lean my head back on his chest and look up.

Breathing in my favorite scent of pine, in the arms of my favorite man and accompanied by my favorite people, this might just become one of my favorite life moments.

And there above us, high in the sky are white lines crisscrossing back and forth.

The Pepps are here. They've been busy and now they're having fun, air skiing behind the aircrafts, leaving their mark.

Life is good.

In loving memory of Talyn Giersdorf.
You left this world too soon,
but you sure made a mark on my heart.
Fly high beautiful girl!

Acknowledgements

'It always seems impossible until it's done'

It's been almost nine years since I started plotting The Vine series. Every single day of those nine years I wondered if I would ever finish the impossible. The fact that I've reached this point is nothing short of a miracle.

I again want to thank my family for all their help and emotional support. To my husband and boys. Thank you! Thank you for enduring my struggles with me, for letting me do this, and for always cheering me on! I love you!

Thank you to my parents, my two sisters, and my brother. Thank you for teaching me, loving me, and helping me grow over the years! I sure love you all.

To those who first read the entire series, Abbie Conley, and Kymbree Mitchell. You were the first to see my world! Thanks for your help!

Thank you to those who support me at my book signings: Desiree Chappell, Samantha Johnson, Zoey Bown, Laura Sulser, Tess DiPiero, Brenna Berry and more! You make something that is very awkward for me ... less awkward.

And thank you, my dear readers!! I love this trilogy, and whenever you tell me you love it as well, it makes my heart VERY happy! Thanks for giving the books a chance and letting my world become a part of yours!

This is officially the end of the trilogy, but before I close it, I want to tell you all something very important.

In book #2, when Alena is on the dropdown in the Greenlands sitting on the side of the cliff, Sef tells her an important story about hope. As Alena contemplates his words, she concludes in her mind that hope doesn't promise that things will return to the way they were. Instead, it's the belief that somehow, someday, everything will be made right.

I don't name that *somehow* in the book, but I would like to name Him here.

Jesus Christ is that *somehow.*

Over the years, through my own challenging experiences, my testimony of Christ's power has grown. He is the one who takes away my pains. He's the one who comforts me when I feel alone. The one who rewards me for my courage and who balances out all the unfairness in life.

And through His sacrifice, He is my ultimate source of hope.

The wiggems and other techniques I talk about in these books have been incredible tools that have helped me through this difficult life. They sustained me while I gained that solid testimony of Christ for myself. But they are only the first step. True happiness has come to me through knowing my Savior. It's come from experiencing His grace and knowing that no matter how much I might fall short, my efforts are enough, *I* am enough for Him.

True happiness comes from knowing that He's aware of our personal losses, our struggles, and it comes from having faith that through His power, someday everything will be made right.

I know that Heavenly Father and Jesus Christ live! I have felt their love! It is such a powerful feeling that could have only come from a superior being! I have felt their forgiveness, and their promise of a heaven made of peace and light.

If I have felt it, I know you can too!!!

Thanks everyone!!

www.ingramcontent.com/pod-product-compliance
Lightning Source LLC
Chambersburg PA
CBHW020601310726
48979CB00008B/1293/J